16/10/17
24/11/20
11/2024

Please return/renew this item by the
last date shown to avoid a charge.
Books may also be renewed by phone
and Internet. May not be renewed if
required by another reader.

www.libraries.barnet.gov.uk

BARNET
LONDON BOROUGH

THE CHRISTMAS PROMISE

Award-winning author Sue Moorcroft writes contemporary women's fiction with occasionally unexpected themes. She's won a Readers' Best Romantic Read Award and has been nominated for others, including a RoNA (Romantic Novel Award). She's a Katie Fforde Bursary Award winner, a past vice chair of the Romantic Novelists' Association and editor of its two anthologies. She also writes short stories, serials, articles, writing 'how to' and is a creative writing tutor.

The daughter of two soldiers, Sue was born in Germany and went on to spend much of her childhood in Malta and Cyprus. She likes reading, Zumba, Pilates, yoga, and watching Formula One.

You can follow Sue on Twitter @SueMoorcroft and find out more by visiting www.suemoorcroft.com.

The Christmas Promise

Sue Moorcroft

avon

AVON

A division of HarperCollins*Publishers*
1 London Bridge Street,
London SE1 9GF

www.harpercollins.co.uk

A Paperback Original 2016

1

First published in Great Britain by
HarperCollins*Publishers* 2016

A catalogue record for this book is
available from the British Library

ISBN-13: 978-0-00-817552-8

Set in Sabon LT Std by Palimpsest Book Production Ltd,
Falkirk, Stirlingshire

Printed and bound in Great Britain by Clays Ltd, St Ives plc

MIX
Paper from
responsible sources
FSC www.fsc.org **FSC C007454**

Acknowledgements

Partly because I'm a research junkie but also because so many lovely people were willing to help me write at my best and most authentic, I have numerous acknowledgements to make.

Abigail Crampton of Abigail Crampton Millinery, on the strength of a chance meeting at BBC Radio Cambridgeshire, allowed me to invite myself to her studio. She advised on what Ava needed to know about couture millinery as a skill and as a business, arranged for me to tag along to an Abigail Crampton hat-making demonstration, answered a plethora of emailed questions, read and commented upon the manuscript and lent her expertise to the material at the end of this book.

Adrienne Vaughan of AVA PR Ltd helped me create Sam's comms agency from the backstory onwards and also a fantastic viral marketing campaign for him to mastermind, then read and commented upon the manuscript. As well as running a PR agency and writing her own books, Adrienne fitted dinner and drinks into her busy schedule whenever I suggested it.

Mark Lacey, independent member of the parole board and retired detective superintendent of police, advised on legal matters and provided insight into being a police officer with a family. If he gets tired of helping me with research, he's too polite to say so.

Leigh Forbes offered her impressive knowledge of phone and server technology and came up with the 'tell-tale' I needed to make my plot work.

Myra Kersner and Pia Fenton, not only offered their usual unstinting friendship, hospitality and writerly chats, but their company on research trips: Myra (Camden and Balham), Pia (comic show).

Andrea Crellin shared her experience of Rotary clubs.

Social media friends and followers were a delight, as always, especially those who knew more about the workings of Facebook than I did.

I'd also like to express grateful thanks to:

My trusted beta readers, Mark West and Dominic White, for reading early drafts of my books and filling the margins with wise comments and wisecracks. I look forward to every word.

The fab members of Team Sue Moorcroft who provide advocacy and support, ie like my books enough to tell everyone else about them. That they do this for me is a source of constant wonder. (Details of the street team on www.suemoorcroft.com for anyone who'd like to know more.)

The fantastic book bloggers who are so interested and so interesting, and who write countless reviews to share around the internet. Their dedication is awesome.

Juliet Pickering of Blake Friedmann who offered to represent me and made a huge difference. To benefit from her quiet good sense and determination is a constant pleasure.

Everyone on the Avon Books UK team who, to my joy, wanted *just* such a Christmas book as this at *just* the time I'd written one! It's a pleasure to work with you all.

Last, but definitely not least, every reader who enjoys my books – especially those who send me lovely messages to say so.

In memory of my mother
Connie Moorcroft
17 January 1934–17 March 2016
My number one fan

Chapter One

Christmas begins in Blaggard's Bar

Saturday 1 December

Battling her way along the crowded pavements of Camden High Street, under the red and green Christmas lights and past the huge boots and aeroplanes displayed on the shop fronts, Ava didn't feel entirely in the mood for going out and having a good time. Today, her first day as a 'casual' stallholder in the West Yard market, had seemed endless. And she was pretty sure there would never be a second.

'Even though I've been home to warm up, my feet are still burning and freezing both at the same time,' she complained to Izz. They'd linked arms to share body heat as sleet danced in the air around them but she wished her dress would magically transform itself into a thick water-proof coat until she reached the warmth of Blaggard's Bar. 'It's only the beginning of December and I've already had enough of Christmas shoppers who browse without buying, try on without buying, and especially, *especially* those who gasp, "*How* much? For one hat?" and drop one of my precious samples. Also without buying.'

Izz's teeth chattered, although she was marginally more

warmly dressed in glittery jeans and a top. 'Sales were a bit thin, were they?'

'To the point of being anorexic, even though I slashed my prices and prayed that none of my bespoke customers would appear and demand to know why they'd previously paid double.'

'Your hats are amazing. You should be charging more, not less.'

Ava gave Izz's arm a squeeze. 'Aw, thank you! But needs must. I do need to eat, even if I can manage without luxuries like restaurants or the gym. I get anxious every time I think how much I spent on tarpaulin, skirting cloth and display stands, all of which look likely to end up on eBay after Christmas. If another casual hadn't offered us a lift home I'd probably have stuffed the lot in a bin. I should have listed my stock on Etsy or Notonthehighstreet and saved myself a lot of freezing disappointment.'

She gave a little skip to keep up with Izz's long stride. 'I hope this drinks party is worth coming out for. It's a bit early for a Christmas do, isn't it?'

'PR and marketing people will be frantic for the rest of the month with clients. Anyway, three of the associates from Jermyn's were already over here today with a new client. Oh, look, there's Tod, going into Blaggard's.'

Ava watched the back of their mutual bestie Tod with envy as he hopped out of a cab and into Blaggard's Bar, safe from the December drizzle. 'Clients on a Saturday?'

'It's not necessarily a Monday-to-Friday industry.' Izz was on a short contract at the communications agency where Tod was an associate. Tod was taking his newish and bossy girlfriend, Louise, to the agency Christmas do, and so Ava had agreed to be Izz's plus one, Izz not currently having a boyfriend or feeling sufficiently brave to go alone.

Izz's next words illuminated why giving the event a miss had not been an option. 'Sam says the agency Christmas bash is a cornerstone of team building, so everyone will probably be here.'

'Ah! If Sam said it then it must be true,' Ava teased, shooting thankfully through a midnight-blue door spangled with stars and into the happy and familiar din of Blaggard's Bar, the rough-hewn wooden pillars incongruously strung with fairy lights and mistletoe tied with red and black ribbon. Typically Camden, Blaggard's was about crowds and diversity; suits mixing happily with gothic black or steampunk satin.

'Tod!' Ava managed to grab Tod's arm as he was about to vanish beneath a cardboard and tinsel archway. 'Give me a hug for coming out on such a horrible night.'

Tod blinked behind his glasses and wrapped her awkwardly in his warmth. 'You could always wear a coat or take a cab.'

'But then I have a coat to hold or a cabbie to pay.'

Tod immediately let the subject drop. They all knew that Ava didn't have the dosh to spend on cabs and would prefer not to freeload in a cab Izz had paid for. He gave Izz a hug, too. 'Sam and the others are here already. It's going to be a great night.'

Ava had to raise her voice to be heard over the Christmas revellers and pulsing music. 'So I get to meet Sam the Big Important Man tonight?'

'He's over there' – Izz was tall enough to see above people's heads – 'with Patrick and Jake. I can see some of the girls, too, over in the corner. Nobody else seems to have brought guests,' she added uneasily, doing the looking-without-looking thing that was more obvious than staring.

3

Ava gave her arm a reassuring pat. 'But you were told you could. And I can always disappear off home if you think I'm in the way.' She paused to check the angle of her black-feathered pillbox hat fixed to the coil of blonde plaits at one side of her head and made sure that the rest of her hair streamed smoothly over her shoulder. No point turning herself into a walking display of her work if she wasn't meticulous with the effect.

'No!' said Izz in alarm, fluffing up her short hair, a pretty brown that, in Ava's opinion, could do with a more exciting cut. 'If you go home early I'll have no one to talk to.'

'What about Tod?'

'He'll talk to the others.' Izz glanced back at the door, as if contemplating baling out before the evening began.

It wouldn't help Izz if Ava were to demand to know how she could be shy with people she'd worked with for weeks, so Ava simply said, 'OK, let's pile in.'

Without the benefit of the height enjoyed by Izz and Tod, Ava was corralled by backs and shoulders as they battled through the melee, and could only gauge that their goal had been reached by a sudden chorus of, 'Hey, Tod! Hello, Izz.'

Izz hung back, allowing Tod to tug Ava forward. 'Ava, meet Patrick and Jake.'

Patrick had dark eyes, crisp curls and the kind of smile that was probably supposed to be a smoulder. Jake was more of a vague beamer.

Ava smiled politely. 'Hello, I'm Ava—'

'And,' Tod barrelled on as if he couldn't wait to get to the important stuff, 'this is Sam, our creative director.'

Ava hadn't intended to be impressed by Sam Jermyn, the golden boy who'd handled PR for a high-profile football player and, at thirty-five, made enough money to invest in his own communications agency. But as Sam turned his gaze on her she couldn't help but be aware of him. He was tall, even taller than Tod or Izz. His tawny hair fell across one eye and was just long enough to tuck behind his ears. In his dark suit and white shirt he looked as well put-together as an expensive car.

With a slow smile, Sam took her hand in his. 'Ava. I've heard a lot about you.'

'Likewise.' She smiled sweetly. She wouldn't embarrass her friends by telling Sam that Tod and Izz sometimes seemed to have no other topic of conversation.

'What are you drinking?'

'Thank you, but I'm not feeling flush enough to get involved in rounds. I might only stay for a couple, anyway.'

'You've been invited for Christmas drinks. No need to reciprocate.' Sam consulted Tod over Ava's head. 'What does Ava drink?'

'Zinfandel rosé.' Tod cheerfully ignored Ava's exasperated stare.

'It's not PC to dismiss a woman's perfectly valid wishes,' Ava half-joked at Sam's departing back as, having swiftly taken orders from Tod and Izz, he made towards the bar.

Sam flashed her a glance over his shoulder. 'Except for wine, surely?'

She had to concede the point. Zinfandel made everything better, even 'I can't earn enough' woes, and 'Christmas is coming' woes, and 'with people I don't know just to please my friends' woes. Or, at least, it made them no worse.

Upon his return, Sam passed her a large glass of rosé. 'So, you're friends with Tod and Izz?'

Ava only got as far as, 'They're my best friends. I share Izz's house and Tod lives not far away, in Kentish Town,'

5

when more agency people arrived in a flurry of greetings and cold air and, enlisting the help of Patrick and Jake, Sam once again turned himself into a drinks waiter, before the new group drifted further into the bar.

Oh well. That was probably her ration of small talk with the head honcho. Ava gladly turned to her friends. 'Thanks for helping me pack up that horrible stall today, Izz. I never dreamed I'd still have almost all my stock. I thought the only good thing about Christmas would be that I could sell a shedload of stuff on the market. I think my mistake was taking proper couture samples. I should have bought shapes and decorated them with readymade flowers and feathers. That way I could sell at what people want to pay.'

'It's not the only good thing about Christmas!' objected Izz, her tongue loosening now there was just the three of them in the conversation. 'What about new films and Christmas DVDs?'

'And the food.' Tod pushed back his floppy fair hair, which, maybe because of his Harry Potter glasses, always seemed to end up looking schoolboyish, no matter which trendy salon created the cut.

'Drink.' Izz brandished her beer approvingly.

'Video games launching in time for Christmas shoppers,' Tod contributed.

Izz grinned at him. 'For Christmas geeks and spoilt kids.'

Tod's eyebrows shot up in mock affront. 'OK, I'll be the Christmas geek if you'll be the spoilt kid – still funded by your parents at twenty-nine.'

'Oi, I work! It's just that Mum likes to give an allowance to my sister, Danielle, and me. It would be rude to refuse.'

Ava smiled at Tod's snort of laughter but her mind was

drawn irresistibly back to her problems. She'd been hopelessly optimistic in thinking market punters would leap at samples made for summer weddings or Ascot, the Ava Bliss Millinery labels removed. Christmas shoppers wanted fun cocktail hats, sexily veiled pillboxes and feathery fascinators. At workaday prices. Hand-embellished readymades – 'dressmakers' hats' – might fall short of her couture ideals but, if it meant she could pay a few bills, she'd resort to them. Black for the goths and brown for the steampunk crowd. In fact, she wished she'd thought to search out a Christmas steampunk convention. She might have made a fortune from mini top hats with corset lacing.

'Anyway, Ava's parents paid her rent for years,' Izz pointed out, breaking into Ava's thoughts.

Ava replied lightly, 'Then they had to fund their retirement to Alsace.' Worry dug its claws into her abdomen. Finances right now were more difficult than when she'd been a student, or even during the period before uni when she, Izz and Tod had had such a fantastic time working around Europe in cafés and bier kellers that one gap year had stretched into two.

Izz stooped to peep into Ava's face, eyes soft with concern. 'They must get an income from their bookshop café?'

'I don't think it can compare with their old salaries. Le Café Littéraire Anglais is in a market town, Muntsheim, not a swanky part of Strasbourg. It's mainly somewhere for Mum and Dad to hang out with ex-pats over pork pies and loose-leaf tea.' Ava manufactured a laugh to counteract a threatening prickle of tears.

'But they must have their pensions—'

'Which are allowing them to enjoy dabbling in the

7

bookshop.' Ava shook her head. 'I'm *thirty*! They're entitled to have me off their hands by now. I'm not going to run to them with my problems when I've already told them that I'll be OK.' *Scraping by* would have been more accurate. 'Hopefully I'll be sorted soon. I would be, if bloody Ceri Mallory had made good on her promises.'

Tod placed a comforting hand on her shoulder. 'It should have been a fantastic opportunity, working in an upmarket milliners. The prices at Ceri's are staggering.'

Ava took a sip of her wine to ease a lump in her throat. 'Because she's spent decades building up a client base and her reputation in the Old Brompton Road. I thought her vague "stick with me, kid, and I'll take you places" would get me more than experience and her name on my CV. But look what happened when I reminded her how many years she'd been dangling the carrot of a junior partnership while I rode the donkey of low salary: a full-on row and the carrot vanishing completely. I should have struck out on my own after six months, then maybe I'd have had time to establish myself before Mum and Dad took off.'

'Well, it's not as if you have a horrible landlady,' Izz reminded her, gently. 'I've already told you that you can take a rent break—'

'My landlady is absolutely the loveliest, but I won't sponge!' Ava gave Izz a grateful hug, though the offer prodded awake one of the monster worries that a good day at the market today might have caged for a while – *what if the time was near when she couldn't afford Camden?* The few years she'd had here weren't nearly enough. She still felt new in this mad, colourful, happy, bohemian place, so much cooler than the Frimley Green side of Farnborough where she, Izz and Tod had grown up. How would she survive being separated from the others? All that was left for her in Farnborough was an aunt and whichever school friends had stayed put. She chugged down the rest of her wine. 'Either of you guys up for a refill? No?' Ava set out alone on the trek to the bar through the claustrophobic press of warm bodies.

In her peripheral vision she noticed Sam Jermyn talking to Patrick and Jake, apparently having left their colleagues to their own devices. Sam's bottle of Cobra was almost empty. She sighed. Sam the Important Man had bought her a drink. It was standard alcohol etiquette that she should now buy him one.

It took her several minutes to get served. She wriggled back through the crush, drinks held high in an effort not to end up wearing them. When she finally reached her target she stretched forward to press the bottle of beer upon Sam with a gracious smile.

But then she caught a laughing comment from Jake. 'You bought her a drink, that means you have the right to hit on her.'

Chapter Two

The trouble with an ex-boyfriend

Ava hesitated. Focused on their own conversation, the three men showed no signs of having noticed her approach.

Jake ploughed on. 'Hitting on women at Christmas is almost obligatory. Take a punt!'

Heat flooding her face, Ava used the Cobra bottle to deliver a hard rap to Sam's elbow. 'Here you go. Now "she" has returned the favour. No "rights" or "obligations" involved.'

With a jump, Sam swung around, looking horrified. 'Look, I hope you don't think—'

Behind him, Ava saw Patrick and Jake go wide-eyed with embarrassment, smiles falling from their faces. 'I don't think anything.' She began to turn away.

But Izz had come up behind her, blocking her escape. 'Louise has arrived and she's talking to Tod so I thought I'd join you guys.' Her voice rose hesitantly at the end of the statement, as if asking Ava whether she was doing the right thing.

Ava stepped aside, ready to say, 'I was just moving on.' But the words died on her lips as she saw the wary way in which Sam was regarding Izz, and that Patrick and Jake were looking ever more uncomfortable.

As if feeling the weight of expectation under all those gazes, Izz stumbled into speech. 'So, Sam, do you get up to Camden for the music? I'm going to see Jeramiah Ferrari at Barfly in January. They've got a new album out.' Self-consciously, she cleared her throat. 'Who are your favourite artists?'

Patrick buried his face in his drink. Jake began to inch away, craning over the heads of the crowd as if searching someone out. But Izz's eyes were on Sam.

Ava's heart sank as she recognised her expression.

Oh, right. Izz had one of her crushes. On Sam.

And Sam and his smoothly dressed cronies were embarrassed. Indignation burned in Ava on her friend's behalf. Izz couldn't help being Izz. She wasn't confident with men, probably because boys had bullied her for her size at school. Hunching apologetically as if to try and hide her height, her flirtation technique was a bit like a needy dog looking for a pat.

Sam, Ava had to admit, at least had grace enough to bear his part in the conversation. 'I've been to Dingwall's a few times.' He sent Ava an encouraging smile, inviting her in. 'Do you and Ava go to gigs together?'

But Patrick asked at the same moment, 'Ava, you live locally, don't you? Camden's pretty cool. Do you work here, too?'

Feeling bad for Izz liking Sam when he was being polite rather than liking her back, Ava answered Patrick. 'I share Izz's flat and have a studio there. I'm a couture milliner.'

Patrick made a performance of looking confused. 'You're going to have to tell me what that is. I'm just a bloke.'

'I make hats. Bespoke hats, by hand.'

His gaze moved upwards. 'So that's why the headgear?'

'Yes. This is a pillbox, but I make all styles.'

'Sounds like an interesting career,' Sam put in, when Izz took a breath in her comparison of Dingwalls and the Roundhouse.

'It's fantastic. So creative.' Patrick raised his drink in a toast.

Ava smiled. Patrick's flirtatiousness was too obvious to be attractive but if Ava responded to him Izz would have a chance to chat to Sam. How would Izz become more at ease with men if they didn't stay in her conversations? 'But aren't you PR types creative, too, Patrick?'

Sam turned politely back to Izz, leaving Ava to listen as Patrick chatted about his place in the communications agency and the mix of commercial creativity, incisive innovation and sales craft that went into writing successful advertising copy. 'We get a bit fed up with people saying that anyone in promo and publicity just plans parties and hands around champagne.'

Ava gave him a smile. 'You mean you have to make the sandwiches, too?'

'No – I order them from the deli.' Patrick laughed.

Ava's attention was taken when Izz, perhaps running out of conversational steam, turned to fight her way to the ladies.

Sam clapped Patrick on the shoulder. 'Your turn to organise a round of drinks, I think. I just want a word with Ava.'

Patrick nodded and began to push his way towards the bar, leaving Sam and Ava together in the crush. She fidgeted, feeling slightly as if she'd been asked to stay behind by a head teacher.

But Sam was looking apologetic again. 'I'm really

sorry. Jake wasn't expecting to be overheard, obviously. I'm not sure what to do but apologise. There seems no good way to say "He wasn't saying things about you behind your back. He was saying things about your best friend."'

Ava gave him the benefit of her best raised-eyebrows stare. 'Not very nice of him.'

'Sorry,' he repeated. He did look sorry, his frank gaze unwavering. 'Jake doesn't mean any harm. The alcohol's washed away a few of his social boundaries, that's all. Izz hasn't been at the agency long and she can pull together the server, network, intranet and database in her sleep, but people are finding her a bit . . . hard going.'

'Not everybody finds it natural to be outgoing and schmoozing. Is it obligatory in a publicity shop?'

'Probably not actually obligatory. But useful.' He looked pained. 'And we generally call Jermyn's a comms agency rather than a publicity shop.'

Ava sipped her wine. 'Noted. And I generally call Izz shy rather than hard going.'

A smile lurked at the corners of his mouth. 'Also noted. And I usually call myself personable rather than schmoozing.'

She widened her eyes. 'Seriously?'

He laughed, but subsided without further comment as Patrick came back, drinks clutched awkwardly. And then Izz returned, too, accepting another bottle of beer.

Patrick brushed Ava's fingers with his as he passed her a glass of rosé. 'So, are you ladies looking forward to Christmas?'

Deliberately, Ava looked at Izz, including her in the conversation.

'We'll eat and drink too much for a couple of days,'

responded Izz, cautiously, when it became obvious that the floor was hers. 'And we'll probably come down to Camden High Street because there's always something to do and it's on our doorstep.'

Ava waited, knowing what would come next. And, sure enough . . . 'But Ava doesn't like Christmas,' Izz added.

Patrick did a theatrical double take. 'Not like Christmas? When everybody has too much to eat and drink and there's loads of partying? I love it all! Then, at New Year, we usually go skiing but it'll just be me and Jake this time. Our mate Elliot doesn't come any more and this year Sam can't make it.'

'Illness in the family,' Sam said, briefly. He glanced curiously at Ava. 'What don't you like about Christmas?'

She shrugged. 'Most things. Except, I agree that the parties can be good.'

A small frown quirked Sam's brow. 'What about when you were a child? Did you at least like it then?'

Ava was assailed with a rush of memories of putting up the Christmas trees at Gran's house, a stately real one in the sitting room and a wonky little silver one in the kitchen. Ava had loved the kitchen tree best, twinkling multi-coloured lights at them as they baked mouth-watering mince pies and gingerbread Santas that smelled of Christmas. Ava's heart clenched to remember Gran's red apron with jolly robins on and her grey curls bobbing energetically as she rolled out pastry, laughing because she always managed to sprinkle flour over every surface in the room.

When it was all cleared up and the baking rested on cooling racks, present wrapping at the big kitchen table in a joyful muddle of paper, foil ribbon and sticky tape would take over, while carols played on Radio 4.

On Christmas morning, after present opening, they'd

make dinner together, lighting a fire in the dining room grate to make it a special occasion.

Sometimes one of her parents made it to Gran's for Christmas dinner, Ava and Gran scheduling the meal to fit in with a shift if necessary. Or else it would be just Ava and Gran pulling crackers and wearing paper hats that were too big, munching succulent turkey and Yorkshire puddings with tiny sausages baked into them.

Ava shook her thoughts back to the present, realising that Sam was waiting for a reply. 'Yes, when I was very young. But Gran was the one who made Christmas happen in my family and she died when I was thirteen.' Gran had smilingly seen to the everyday care of Ava while her parents pursued their careers and her loss had left a gaping hole in Ava's teenaged soul. She avoided Izz's gaze, not wanting to see reflected there the painful knowledge that Gran had died at Christmas, making Ava feel like hurling the gaily lit Christmas trees to the floor and jumping on them.

'That must have been hard.' Sam's gaze was sympathetic. 'Didn't your parents take over?'

'Not exactly.' It was no new thing to be regarded with curiosity for not enjoying what everyone else in the country looked forward to all year and Ava had a well-honed explanation. 'Mum was a doctor, Dad a senior police officer. Mum patched up the drunks in A and E and Dad dealt with the drunks who ended up in the cells. They don't really believe in Christmas and think it's a phoney exercise in commercialism. They always volunteered to work so those who valued the season could have time off.'

Patrick goggled as if Ava had just admitted that she came from a family of aliens. 'If they don't believe in Christmas, what do they believe in?'

She made a face. 'Hard reality, I suppose. My parents

15

are lovely, and we all love each other, but they were career-orientated and so much of their focus was outward.' Not inward, on their family. Family. The word conjured up siblings – not just the one child who had occasionally felt in the way and had grown to realise the best way to please her parents was to be as independent as possible. She remembered their congratulations when she'd begun to make family meals, the proud smiles as they told their friends how good she was at it.

Sam's frown deepened into a cleft between his eyes. 'I've never heard Christmas made to sound less fun.'

'You should come to my party!' Patrick jumped in. 'Next Saturday, in Balham. Loads of nice people, lots of alcohol, a bit of food. Music. A proper party, none of this standing shoulder-to-shoulder stuff, frightened your drink's going to be knocked from your hand. Hasn't Tod mentioned it to you? He'll be in Balham for something, anyway. His girlfriend lives there, doesn't she?'

'She does. It's because he's always over there for BalCom that he met her,' Ava admitted unenthusiastically.

'BalCom?' Sam looked mystified.

'Tod's comic club. We go to their Christmas meeting at the Snooty Fox every year. In fancy dress. The comickers create stunning costumes, everything from Superman to the Joker. It's OK for us more ordinary folk to aim a little lower, though. Last year I was a reindeer with antlers made out of branches stuck in a pair of tights.'

Patrick looked pained. 'Ah, erm, he's invited me, too, but I'll be too busy with the party. But why don't you come on to my place when the pub shuts? I'll make sure we keep some goodies back for you.'

'Thank you,' Izz stuttered. She flicked a glance Sam's way.

Intercepting that fleeting look and reading hopefulness there, Ava felt she had little choice but to smile and accept, too, although she was pretty certain that Tod hadn't mentioned the party because Patrick had only this instant decided to invite them. But Izz was looking at her boss as if he were made of her favourite chocolate and obviously wanted to grab the opportunity of spending more out-of-office time with him. It would take a harder heart than Ava's to deny her.

And, as they'd already arranged to stay at Louise's, she couldn't even claim it would be too difficult to get home to Camden in the early hours. She was still pondering an escape strategy when Izz's expression altered. 'There's Harvey,' she whispered, grabbing Ava's hand.

Ava shrank down. 'Oh no. I don't want to see him.' She could hardly hiss, 'Duck!' at Izz, but she was all too aware that Izz's height made her hard to overlook. If Harvey spotted her, he'd assume Ava to be nearby.

'Boyfriend?' Patrick sounded wary.

'Ex. He just can't seem to get used to it.' Ava took a surreptitious peek, absorbing, between the sea of constantly moving heads and shoulders, Harvey's bloodshot eyes and uncertain movements. 'Damn, he's drunk.'

Izz shifted uneasily. 'Nothing new there, then. He's heading over.'

'Hell.' Ava tried to make herself smaller still.

Sam leaned in, as if to help her hide. 'You don't have to talk to someone if you have concerns about them.' His face had set in forbidding lines.

'I know.' Touched at this unlooked-for support, Ava found herself unexpectedly aware of the brush of warm breath against her cheek. 'He's not a concern. Or not exactly. I ended things and he's proving that he's not a good loser.'

'Ava!' Harvey hailed her when he was still yards away, making no friends as he shoved his way rudely through the crowd, pulling tinsel awry as he brushed past the big wooden pillars. 'I've been hoping to bump into you. Haven't you been out in Camden?'

Resignedly, Ava was obliged to acknowledge him. 'Harvey. How have you been?'

In the heaving bar most men had discarded jackets and ties. Harvey, however, was tailor-shop perfect, his dark curls running smoothly over his head and even his thick eyebrows looking as if they'd been brushed. Only his movements and his sliding gaze were untidy. 'I could have been better,' he proclaimed meaningfully. 'A lot better.' All his attention was on Ava. He treated Izz as if she were invisible.

Ava tried to head him off from yet another dissection of their relationship's demise but Harvey plunged in. He was sorry, he vowed. How many times did he have to apologise? She must understand he'd had a few drinks and hadn't known what he was doing. How could he make her forgive him? They'd been good together, hadn't they?

A couple of times she tried to break in, 'There's no point—', but Harvey just became increasingly hectoring. Ava's compassion for his struggle with rejection warred with her irritation at being harangued, and her feeling of vague surprise that they'd ever been an item. They had had fun, in the early days. It was just that the good memories had been overlaid with bad. Hard to credit though it was, looking at the red-faced loud-voiced embarrassment standing in front of her, when Harvey wasn't drunk he was smart, articulate and interesting.

They'd met just before Ava left Ceri, who had become

a client of the accountants Harvey worked for. His dark eyes had glowed whenever they rested on Ava and the time they'd been together had begun fuelled by lust. Healthy lust, admittedly – but that had fizzled on Ava's side as she became increasingly aware of Harvey's hard drinking taking up more and more of his life. She'd fallen for sober Harvey and fallen out with drunk Harvey. Crunch time had been more about relief than grief for Ava.

Now, as he loudly pleaded his case, Harvey managed to edge out Izz and Patrick by insinuating his way between them and Ava, but Sam proved harder to turn his back on. Quite openly listening in, he shifted, coming to rest with his arm against Ava's.

Harvey focused on Sam and scowled. Then he switched on a big smile for Ava. 'You're under the mistletoe! If you don't kiss anyone you'll get bad luck all year.' To Ava's horror, he made an unsteady but purposeful lunge in her direction.

Before she could decide which way to dodge, an arm around her shoulders swung her neatly out of Harvey's path. Sam brushed a kiss on her temple. 'Just in case you're superstitious.'

Ava blinked, stunned and half-admiring that he'd thwarted Harvey so effectively, even if it had meant taking a bit of a liberty.

Harvey halted foolishly, mouth ajar. Then, frowning like a goblin, he began to back up, barging into people and spilling their drinks, lifting his voice higher the further away he travelled. 'Ava, Ava, I need a private word with you, Ava. Over here.'

Sam looked down into Ava's eyes. 'If you don't want to go with him, you can tell him we're on a date.'

19

Ava debated, twisting her hands in indecision. 'That's a tempting offer.' But people were wincing at Harvey's loud mouth, frowning from him to Ava, making her feel responsible. She squared her shoulders. 'But it's obviously time I put an end to his pestering me. I must be able to find a way to convince him.'

'It's probable that he'll only—'

Disregarding whatever advice Sam was about to dish out, Ava dumped her empty glass and followed in Harvey's wake, fighting through the crowd, attempting, at the same time, to convey apologies to everyone he'd knocked into, remembering how this behaviour had proved the norm amongst his friends. However well-cut their suits and dresses and however shiny their expensive shoes, they'd habitually begun an evening as clever, funny, successful people yet been mortifying embarrassments by the end. Cocktails or ale, it hadn't mattered, just as long as they could get drunk on it. Then they'd play down each other's behaviour by terming it 'getting merry' or 'taking the edge off'.

Eventually Harvey reached back a hand and grabbed her wrist, pulling her out through a door that said 'Staff Only', which led into a dusty corridor with dirty paintwork barren of tinsel and jolly messages, crates of empty bottles stacked at one side, smelling of stale beer.

Harvey came to rest against a wall, clinging on to Ava's hand, his face fixed in lines of woe. 'Don't date other men, Ava. Be with me. Deanna and Ollie, Ali and Jen, they all keep asking where you are.' He dipped his head and tried to plant a wobbly kiss on her lips.

Ava stepped smartly back, yanking her arm free. 'Don't, Harvey! I'm sure your friends don't miss me in the slightest. And I'm not dating anyone. Sam works with Tod, that's all.'

His step forward matched her step back. 'Then let's see if we can't sort this whole thing out.'

She warded him off with raised hands. 'It's been sorted since August, when you got off your face at V Festival and I found you and a woman naked in our tent.'

'But nothing happened!' he protested. 'C'mon, Ava, that's the thing with being that drunk. Nothing, y'know . . . happens.' He pumped his hips suggestively, putting in an inelegant stagger to maintain his balance.

'Something did happen. I got tired of your drinking, and that was the end.'

'But I love you—' He lunged at her.

Ava tried a calm smile and a side step, although her breathing quickened with the first stirrings of alarm. 'Now you're just being dramatic. I don't want to hurt your feelings but I'm leaving now. Bye, Harvey.' She made to step around him.

He remained stubbornly in her way. 'You don't love me?'

'No.' She tried to squeeze through the other way.

'You used to.'

That halted her. 'I did not!'

'You *did*—'

She jammed indignant hands on her hips. 'I did not! We never even talked about it. We went out for a few months, that's all. You're getting things out of proportion. Get over it! We're done.'

His hand clamped once more onto her arm. 'We didn't need to talk about it. It was understood.'

Ava jerked her arm free once more, flushing, hating his hands on her, hating that he thought it was OK to badger her and ride roughshod over her wishes. 'Forget it.' She made another dart for freedom.

21

He simply swayed his drunken body into her path, his smile turning chilly. 'Let me . . . *persuade* you.'

'Don't be a loser.' The door out of the claustrophobic little corridor was but two steps away. The stale smell was beginning to make her feel sick. She began to edge an arm past Harvey.

'Do you remember when I got my new phone?' His words were slow, heavy with meaning.

She paused. Her hand hovered over the door handle.

He fumbled his phone from his pocket and began prodding and swiping at the screen. 'We had fun. Izz had gone off to visit her parents and we had the flat to ourselves. You took me to your studio for a private fashion show.'

Harvey turned his phone over to let her see the screen.

Stomach plummeting, Ava found herself gazing at a picture of herself, champagne glass in hand, a scarlet cocktail hat on the side of her head. And wearing nothing else but a mischievous smile.

With exaggerated showmanship Harvey swiped from one photo to another: Ava in hat after hat. Pose after pose. He squinted at the phone lasciviously. 'Look! You're doing one of my favourite things in this one.'

'But I deleted those images from your phone,' she whispered in horror.

Jerkily, he nodded. 'Yeah, you waited until I was in the bathroom and did it behind my back. But as I was hooked up to your wifi, the photos had already automatically backed up. Lucky, eh?' His laugh was low and unpleasant. 'I could send them to my contacts list, put them on Facebook—'

Her eyes flew to his. 'You wouldn't.' Ava could hardly breathe for the horrifying vision of his self-assured friends laughing at her humiliation, swapping the images like trading cards. Her friends could see the images, too, if he posted publicly.

'Wouldn't I?'

Panicky scenarios flapped through her mind. The police? But she'd been a police officer's daughter long enough to know that the police could only act once Harvey had posted the photos. Threats made where nobody else could hear them weren't something they could investigate.

Shit. Perhaps getting snappy with him had been a tactical error. Calmly, so he wouldn't see how much he'd rattled her, she tried to de-escalate the situation. 'What you're threatening is deliberate humiliation.'

Harvey's eyebrows shot up. 'Who, me? Threatening?' His expression switched jerkily from malice to a dopey smile. 'You're beautiful, Ava. I want us to get back together. If we were back together . . .' He waved his phone in an airy circle. 'All this would just go away.'

And blackmail is such a pretty reason to be in a relationship. Quashing the urge to spit that thought in his face, she tried a conciliatory smile. 'I have to trust the guy I'm with. If I could trust you, you'd delete those images from the cloud.'

'You can trust me. Sweetheart, darling, you can.'

Ava felt rising hope. 'Can you get on the internet here?'

Harvey's gaze lost focus as he processed her words. Finally, he gave a co-operative nod. Then, with a bit of fumbling, he hooked up to the pub's wifi. The connection was grindingly slow, and Ava felt she might burst with the tension, but his cloud sign-in page did eventually appear. Holding the phone at an angle, so that she could watch his actions, he went over the intimate images, deleting each

23

one from his online storage and the phone's memory, while Ava silently gritted her teeth as he lingered lovingly over every explicit one, especially those in which Harvey featured. Ava cringed to think she'd ever . . .

As the last image changed shape and swooshed into the little trash can icon in the corner of the screen, she breathed properly once again.

'Thank you.' She forced herself to speak pleasantly, though hot fury was licking through her at what Harvey had just put her through. Now all she was interested in was getting out of this horrible little corridor that smelled like a drunk in the morning, and away from Harvey. The noisy crowded bar the other side of the door was beginning to feel like an oasis of safety. 'I really appreciate you doing the right thing.'

'So we can begin again?'

For goodness' sake! You've just shown yourself to be lower than a worm's man-parts! She took a step towards the door. 'Sorry, Harvey. What happened at V Festival proved to be the last straw but I wouldn't have stuck around much longer in any case. You're mean when you're drunk and you do things that can't always be undone.'

Silence. His expression darkened. But then he tipped back his head and laughed. Blinking, he focused on her once more. 'I can undo stuff. I can undo plenty. I can undo deleting those pictures.' A few taps and gestures over the screen of his phone and he turned it back to face her. The box next to *Automatically back up images across all devices* was ticked, making a chill run down Ava's spine. 'They're still on my iPad. It's not magic that I was able to get those photos to reappear on my phone, Ava. It's technology.'

'You bastard!' The desire to escape overwhelmed her

and Ava shoved blindly, uncaring that Harvey bounced drunkenly off the wall.

Tears burning the back of her throat, she wrenched open the door and fled.

Chapter Three

Not currently dating

Sam didn't realise he'd been watching the door that had closed behind Ava and her ex-boyfriend until she catapulted back through it.

His breath caught. Her blue eyes, big and doll-like anyway, looked enormous. Her chest was heaving.

What had just happened? Was she furious? Frightened? He even toyed with the possibility that she'd just had sex. Something had to account for her wild look of disorientation.

A quick backward glance, then Ava cast about the room until her gaze fell on Izz, presently talking to Tod and his girlfriend. As she started towards them, Sam detached himself from Patrick and Jake and plotted an intercepting course.

'OK?' he enquired casually, as their paths met.

Ava nodded. The feathers on her hat trembled.

'Another drink?'

This time she accepted without protest. 'Thanks.'

He watched her resume her route towards Izz and Tod before he undertook the tiresome process of carving a way to the bar. He checked on her again while he waited to be served. Unspeaking, she was giving no indication of listening to the others. Her gaze was focused inwards and she looked as if she'd been thrown into the bar from a different planet.

Interesting woman. Tod and Izz had talked about Ava and he supposed he'd expected someone . . . well, someone like them. Not exactly cool kids. But Ava was coolness personified. A profusion of plaits showing beneath her stylish hat, dress like a second skin. Next to Izz's long straight lines, Ava was all curvy neat ones.

When Sam finally got back to the group after waiting what seemed like an hour to be served, Ava muttered her thanks but stared at the drink as if she'd forgotten what to do with it.

He tried to engage her. 'So you've been friends with Todd and Izz since . . . ?'

'Since school.' She glanced at Tod and Izz as if reassuring herself that they were nearby, then glanced back over her shoulder.

He read her uneasiness. 'If you're looking for your ex, he came out a few minutes ago and disappeared into the crowd.'

'Right. Thanks.' Fractionally, her shoulders relaxed.

He waited, giving her an opportunity to take part in the conversation. She didn't take it. He tried again. 'Did you tell him we're on a date?'

She looked down into her wine. 'No.'

He watched her thoughtfully, suspicious about what had turned her into this Stepford version of herself. He lowered his voice. 'He didn't hurt you?'

'No.' But there was no conviction in the word.

'Is he still "ex"?'

'Yes!'

Maybe she needed something to snap her out of whatever spell was on her. He'd been planning to attempt a connection – a plan he suspected Patrick of sharing, judging by his friend's expression whenever he looked at Ava. Sam might as well see if he could steal a march. Patrick had no guy code and would do the same in a heartbeat. 'Would you like to?'

Her breathing had calmed now and she was beginning to look more aware of her surroundings. 'Like to . . . ?'

'Go on a date.'

A tiny frown nipped the skin between her brows. 'With you?'

'I'm not in the habit of pimping for anyone, so yes.' He smiled. He was used to a certain amount of success with that smile. 'I'd like to.'

Intrigue stole across her face. For a second he thought she was going to say yes, she'd love to.

Until Izz chose that moment to join in hesitantly with the conversation. 'Sam, I was just thinking – if you want, that is – shall I tell you next time I'm going to a local gig? If it's a band you like I could get us tickets.'

Frustrated at the interruption, Sam kept his answer short. 'I don't think that anyone I like is playing in Camden any time soon.' Then realising that Ava's nascent smile had switched to a hard stare, tried, belatedly, to soften his response. 'But thanks for the offer. It's really kind of you.'

Izz's face fell. 'Oh. OK.' Blushing furiously, she turned quickly back to Tod.

Ava moved closer. Even above the rest of the crowd, Sam caught a hint of her perfume. 'What's wrong with you?' she hissed. 'She just asked you out. Do you know how hard that was for her?'

He winced. 'Hell. She did, didn't she? I suppose that as I was asking you out at the time I was focusing on that. Look, Izz is great but she's not my type. Maybe I'm intimidated by her obvious intelligence.'

'But I'm a thicko, so I'm OK?'

Though taken aback at her prickliness, he wasn't up for someone putting words into his mouth specifically so that she could feel slighted. 'I didn't say that. Forget I asked.'

For a millisecond he thought she looked contrite, or hurt, or both. But then she assumed a politely bland expression. 'I'm not currently dating, to be honest. I have to concentrate on other aspects of my life.'

'Fine.'

The swirling racket of the bar made it hard for Ava to order her thoughts as she took Izz's arm and gave it a comforting squeeze. Louise was recounting some story but she might as well have been speaking Russian. Tod had asked Ava twice now whether she was OK. Even when Patrick came up wearing mistletoe on his belt buckle, grinning as if he was the first guy to ever think of it, Ava wasn't able to summon a smile.

Why had she ever let Harvey take those photos? It had seemed like a bit of naughty fun at the time. Yet everyone knew that once digital images existed they had the potential to become uncontrollable beasts, shared and replicated with one quick click. Or even no clicks at all if the right boxes were already ticked.

Did she have any rights over images she'd consented to having committed to somebody else's memory card? Ethically, perhaps. But had Harvey and ethics even shaken hands?

She could appeal to his better nature once he was sober but if several months had elapsed and he hadn't permanently deleted the images, then he wasn't going to.

Stomach churning, she acknowledged that the damage was done. Her only option was to wait on tenterhooks to find out whether Harvey would share the pictures on his social networks. Or with strangers. Or sell the images to some scuzzy website. Her bile rose at the idea of being turned into an unwitting porn star.

And what if he'd done it already?

Chapter Four

A bit of a redo

Ava was jolted from her unhappy reverie by a phone being waved drunkenly before her eyes.

An image blazed from the screen – flesh, hat, breasts, legs. *No!* On a wave of panic Ava snatched at the handset but, at the same moment, was shoved hard. Drink shooting from her hand, head whipping back, she crashed into a nearby group.

Through their tuts and squeals she heard Sam snap, 'Hey! Cut that out!'

Then Harvey's familiar laughter ringing in her ears.

By the time Ava had regained her balance she was too late to see more than Harvey's rear view as he cannoned his way out of the bar. She didn't have a hope of catching up with him. Bastard. People around her glared at her as they brushed wine ostentatiously from their clothes.

'Sorry,' she croaked.

Sam's brow was ridged in a black frown. 'It wasn't your fault, that idiot just gave you a hell of a shove. Are you OK? What was all that about?'

Humiliated tears lodged in Ava's throat as she realised

that Sam could easily have caught a flash of what had been on Harvey's phone screen.

But there was no sign of it in his voice. 'He's gone. You're safe.'

Izz broke in. 'Get the police, Ava. Get him locked up.' She looked white and upset. Izz had a thin skin so far as hostility was concerned.

Sam's focus remained on Ava. 'You're safe,' he repeated. 'But there are plenty of witnesses here who saw you were assaulted. Izz's right, you could call the police.'

Tod patted Ava's arm, worriedly. 'Are you hurt? Your feather's, um, a bit . . .' He made a crooked shape with his finger.

Ava unpinned her hat. The tallest glossy black feather was comically crushed. She rubbed her neck, which ached from the whiplash effect of being flung through the air, and swallowed down her tears. 'I don't want to call the police. I'll go home.'

Izz looked anxious. 'Don't you want to go for the Indian meal that's arranged? The booking's in twenty minutes.'

'Maybe Ava's not hungry?' Sam suggested.

Ava glanced at him gratefully. 'I just want to go home.' If she didn't, she might bawl like a child.

Tod slung a protective arm around her, his very awkwardness comforting. 'I think we ought to go with you. We can cancel the Indian.'

Ava gave him a grateful hug. 'I'm all right, Tod. It's been a long day and a bad day and I want to be on my own. You guys go and enjoy the meal.' She fought to keep her voice steady. 'See you, everybody. Nice to meet those I hadn't met before.' Turning away quickly, she cut out the opportunity for further protest.

Outside, the cold air snatched her breath. Dismayed to discover that she was trembling, Ava hugged herself against the chill as she turned down Camden High Street, still clutching her hat. The sleet had thickened whilst she'd been in Blaggard's. Hurrying as much as her heels would allow, she crossed the canal and turned right past blocks of flats and railway bridges, children's play areas and graffiti. People thought Camden must be so cool but once you got away from the High Street, the markets and the venues, it wasn't that different to anywhere else. Anywhere else with a canal and goths and punks, anyway.

The streets grew quieter once Camden High Street was behind her and in ten minutes she reached the familiarity of School Road. Houses of twenty different colours lined up shoulder-to-shoulder like an anxious family waiting for her to come home. She paused. Then swung around.

Thirty yards away, a man was standing, watching her. Her heart leaped to her throat.

Then she realised that the tall figure was Sam Jermyn.

'What are you doing?' she called, not sure if she should be outraged that she apparently couldn't be trusted to walk a few streets on her own, or appreciative that he'd been concerned enough to desert his co-workers and shadow her.

Slowly, he stepped into a circle of light at the base of a street lamp. 'Sorry if I'm crossing a line; I was concerned that your ex might have still been in the vicinity when you left. As he was drunk . . .' When she didn't respond he jammed his hands into his pockets. 'I'm not usually weird enough to follow girls home.'

It actually hadn't occurred to her to be alarmed when she realised it was him hovering, a guardian angel in a three-piece suit. 'I expect you were being kind.' She tucked her numb hands under her armpits. 'Are you going off to the restaurant?'

'I should. I'm supposed to be putting the bill on my credit card.' The lamp's halo of light suddenly began to shimmer as the sleet turned to snow, floating down to glisten on the pavements. Hunching his shoulders as he glanced around at the falling flakes, he pulled up his collar.

'You're going to get frozen.' Ava's teeth began to chatter. It was as if the two of them were in a snow globe that someone had given a good shake.

He nodded philosophically.

She pushed at the door, unwilling to stay out in the inhospitable winter evening an instant longer. 'You could come in. Call a cab and wait in the warm or have a hot drink and see if the snow passes.'

He was beside her in seconds, snow beading his hair. 'A hot drink sounds fantastic.'

The hall was cramped and she was aware of the fresh coolness of the rain emanating from his clothes. 'The sitting room's through that door.' She flicked the lights on and pointed the way, dumping her abused pillbox hat on the hall table. 'Make yourself at home. I'm frozen and I'm going to change.' She wasn't shivering any less violently now she was indoors.

As he headed up the hall, she ran up both flights of stairs and into her bedroom in the attic, pulling off her clothes, damp from rain and spilled wine, huddling thankfully into jeans, jumper, two pairs of socks and mulberry and cream Peruvian knitted slippers. Warmth over style.

Back downstairs, she found that Sam had hung his damp jacket on the sitting room door and claimed the jewel-green armchair in the corner. He was turning her bedraggled hat over in his hands contemplatively. 'Is this fixable?'

'Yes, it just needs a bit of a redo. I think the whole evening does,' she joked feebly.

He grinned. 'It did look a bit too exciting for comfort.'

After ascertaining that he would prefer coffee to hot chocolate Ava went into the kitchen and switched on the kettle. 'Sorry it's only instant,' she said, as she carried both mugs into the sitting room. She took the other armchair, ruby red, and regarded him from under her lashes.

He smiled apologetically. 'Sorry to impose on you. I've texted Patrick to take care of the bill on the agency's behalf and I'll call a minicab when I've drunk this.'

'It's OK.' It was true that she'd rather have sunk into a hot bath before bed than entertain someone she'd only just met, but she could hardly blame Sam for the rain now clattering at the windows. She tucked her feet up into the squashy cushions and savoured the heat of the coffee. 'It was good of you to worry about Harvey. I didn't really think about him still being outside.'

Her phone beeped the arrival of a text message and she slipped her phone from her pocket to look at the screen. Then froze. The caller ID said *Harvey*.

Her finger hovered over the message icon. Slowly, reluctantly, she opened it. No words. Just an image.

Nausea swept over her in a cold tide. That wasn't a view of herself she could usually see without a mirror.

Sam was watching Ava when she checked her phone. He didn't think he'd ever seen anybody change colour so quickly. It gave him an odd feeling, as if a string ran from her emotions to his guts.

'OK?' he queried, neutrally.

She blinked huge eyes. 'Fine.'

But he could almost see her heart pounding. What the hell was going on? Why had that arse of an ex been so unpleasantly physical?

Sam dropped his gaze to the small round hat and made his voice conversational. 'My mother's involved in a support group for women who have been made to feel unsafe. In terms of situations to be wary of, your ex raises a lot of flags. Alcohol. Anger. Violence. Perhaps unresolved conflict. I was probably being overly cautious in suspecting that he'd hang around outside the bar but I've read the literature her support group puts out and I know bad stuff happens too easily.'

'It was very responsible of you to check I got home.' Her voice was almost entirely without inflexion.

He shrugged, as if being called responsible was a criticism, turning the small hat over, careful of the mashed feather. The hat smelled like new clothes. 'He worried you. He was violent. If that concerns me then possibly it should concern you. It's an option to seek support, either from a group or from the police.'

'Harvey can be an arse and he's risen to new heights. But he's never tried anything like he did tonight.' Absently, she began to uncoil her hair, running her fingers through it until it fell, crinkly from the plaits, nearly to her waist.

Sensing that she was reluctant to dwell on the subject, he offered her an escape route. 'Tell me about making hats.'

Rather than becoming animated and enthusiastic, as he'd envisaged, she rolled her eyes. 'If it was that easy to explain I wouldn't have spent four years at university to learn the craft, let alone worked for peanuts to gain experience.'

'Right.' He took out his phone, ready to ring a cab before the snow could settle and make getting home a chore. The agency Christmas bash wasn't his idea of heaven but he'd taken responsibility for it as part of his role to encourage bonding among the creative talent. Ms Fine-One-Minute-Terse-the-Next here was undoubtedly a creative talent – but not Jermyn's. Not his problem.

But then she sighed. 'Sorry! It's a bit of a sore point with me right now, that's all. But I can show you, if you want. It's easier than trying to explain.'

He paused, his thumb hovering over the name of a taxi company. 'You're going to make me a hat?'

A smile fleeted across her face. It sparkled her eyes and softened the fullness of her lips. 'I was thinking more of showing you my workroom. If you want me to make you a hat it'll cost serious money.'

He finished the last of his coffee and deposited the mug on the wooden floor. 'Sounds interesting. I've never met a hat maker before.'

'Milliner.' She put down her cup and rose to her feet. 'Let's go upstairs.'

Let's go upstairs. Sternly, he told himself not to return an appreciative reply or let his thoughts show on his face. Ava's faint flush told him that she was already all too aware of how it had sounded.

He followed her up two flights. When they reached the top floor, they passed a door on the right and she pulled it shut. *Bedroom.* A none-too-subtle signpost that he wouldn't be getting in there. She switched on the light in another room and he found they were under the eaves. A skylight gazed up at a starless night and snowflakes landed on the glass before slithering slowly down.

'Welcome to my studio. Here's where I take a variety

of materials, add steam and a little enchantment – and out come hats.' She swept a theatrical hand towards the shelves of teetering circular wooden forms, a whole spectrum of thread racked on spools near the window and a scarlet hat perched on a stand. A sink hugged one wall and a full-length mirror gleamed from a corner.

He picked up a fold of bright blue hessian-like fabric from a work surface. 'Do you make the hats out of this stuff?'

'Some of them. It's sinamay, a natural material, woven by hand. It dyes beautifully. But I use all kinds of materials, like felt, crinoline or straw, too.'

Boxes stood in the centre of the floor. Ava flipped the lid from one and lifted out several hats nested inside one another. 'Fancy a fedora in magenta and navy hoops, sir? A black picture hat with loops of twisted sinamay? Or maybe you'd prefer a turquoise headpiece with a back-swept crinoline knot? Perfect for your next cocktail party.'

'Damn. I don't have a cocktail party in my Christmas diary.' He took the turquoise cocktail hat and turned it over in his hands, feeling the fine nap of the felt, the contrasting stiffness of the crinoline. The hat was beautifully made. He looked in vain for a stitch or spot of glue. It balanced on his palm like a humming bird.

The fun faded from Ava's expression. 'These are my samples from the summer and autumn. I hoped to get money out of them in the West Yard Market today but they're not right for it. They're too expensive. I should have tried to get in the Apple Market at Covent Garden. I was being lazy, I suppose, with Camden markets right on my doorstep.'

He returned the cocktail hat and had a look at the no-nonsense lines of the fedora, the ebullience of the broad-

38

brimmed picture hat, its loops of twisted sinamay somehow giving the impression of having been frozen in motion. 'Isn't that how you normally sell?'

She sank down cross-legged on the floorboards, taking up a saucer-like blue-green hat and spinning it on one finger. 'No. It was my first time and I suppose I was hoping for miracles. Bespoke business is slow.' She gave a mirthless laugh. 'Understatement.'

He stooped and carefully picked up a purple wheel-like number, its finely woven straw spiralling up to a domed crown, a froth of net around its brim. 'So, suppose that I was a bespoke customer—'

'Client.'

'Client. What would be your approach?' He folded himself down on the floor across from her.

She propped her elbows on her knees, chin on hands. Her eyes were the blue of the deepest sea on a sunny day. 'You'd contact me and we'd talk. You'd make an appointment. You'd arrive. After offering you a cup of something, I'd invite you to sit on the stool in front of the mirror. You'd probably bring the outfit that the hat's to go with. I'd be pleasant and positive.'

He chuckled. 'You don't look pleasantly positive, tonight. You look pissed at the world.'

A faint smile flitted across her face. 'If you were a paying client I'd be pleasantly positive, don't you worry.'

'OK.' He got up and settled himself on the small wooden stool. 'Pretend.'

Discarding the hat, she rose to stand behind him, running her hands over her hair to tidy it and pasting on a wide smile. 'Well, Mr Important Man, shall we begin with the occasion? Is the hat for a wedding – and, if so, are you of the bride's entourage? Or perhaps it's for a garden party? Or maybe you're interested in something burlesque?'

Burlesque made him think of short shiny skirts, fishnet stockings and low-cut corset tops. 'I want to be outrageous and say go for burlesque but I'm worried you'll have to pretend I'm a woman.'

Through the mirror, he caught her eyes dancing. 'I don't have any men's hats so I will have to pretend that.'

'Then I'm worried you'll think I'll enjoy it.'

This time, she laughed, and her face filled with light.

He watched her as she studied him for several seconds, stepping side-to-side. She looked different without her slinky dress but he'd always been a sucker for well-fitting jeans. Hers fit particularly well, distressed to the degree of softness that allowed the fabric to hug her shape, a hole on the thigh giving him a glimpse of smooth white skin.

Turning to the boxes, she lifted out several more hats. Some she lodged on a nearby surface, one she placed precisely on his head, so light, so silky inside that he could scarcely feel it. However, the phrase 'total buffoon' had been invented for exactly the way he looked.

'I don't think pale orange is me,' he pointed out, drily.

'It's peach. Quite a rich peach, but definitely peach.'

'I don't think peach is me.'

She viewed his reflection critically. 'It's not masculine but the colour brings out the coppery lights in your hair. It's a smart little straw trilby but too small a brim for the size of your head, and the crown isn't big or deep enough. It perches instead of fitting.'

'I look like a seaside donkey in a sun hat.'

She frowned in mock reproof. 'You look like a man in a hat that's too feminine a colour for his tastes and the wrong size. And if you were a donkey, there would be holes for your ears.' Popping the hat on the work surface, she lifted another. 'With quite a large head—'

'That's not very positive.'

'With a strongly sized head,' she amended smoothly, 'a definite shape brings balance. This picture hat's made from elegant velour felt.' She settled on his head a navy blue and white hat with an enormous brim, paying attention to the degree of tilt. 'This hides a lot of your pretty hair—'

He snorted.

She kept a straight face. '—but it balances out your strong jaw without hiding your eyes. It lends itself to a jaunty angle—'

'I think I get the idea.' He removed the hat. The velour felt as soft as a cloud.

Eyes twinkling, she reached for another creation.

'Not pink!' he protested, jumping up. He'd let her gently ridicule him to cheer her up but a man had to have some standards. 'Even donkeys would object to pink. Thank you for the fitting. I'll remember you if my mother or aunt go to a wedding.'

'Please do,' she said, seriously, placing the hat on a stand with a tiny sigh.

'So these are the shapes you make hats on?' He walked to the shelf of wooden forms. 'They must represent quite an investment.'

'Much more of an investment than I'd ever appreciated when I worked for someone else. Unfortunately, there was a dearth of pre-loved equipment around when I bought.' She began taking hats out of one box and stands from another, arranging them on the broad work surface, red, navy, pink, mint, coffee, lemon.

'You make the hats all by hand?'

41

'Yes, I individually design, hand block, hand stitch and embellish.'

'What's blocking?'

She paused in unpacking the boxes to take down a couple of the wooden forms. 'These are blocks. This one's a brim, this is a crown. I put them together, like this.' The crown atop the brim block made a recognisable hat shape. 'Then if I'm making a straw, for example, I take a cone, apply stiffener, steam it, pin it on the blocks, let it dry. Repeat. When it has dried for the second time, I have the basic shape of the hat. I make a lining and a head fitting and I make the decorations.'

'It must demand quite a skill set.' He wished that he did have a relative who was going to a wedding and wanted one of Ava's creations. He'd enjoyed the glimpse of her sense of fun that his 'hat fitting' had generated. He picked up a large yellow sinamay hat with an extravagant and intricately tied bow and turned it over, reading the label. 'Ava Bliss Millinery. Is Bliss your surname?'

She went back to setting out her stock, a whirl of shapes and sizes, a rainbow of colours. 'Blissham. But who isn't attracted to a little bliss?'

Who indeed? He replaced the cartwheel hat thoughtfully. 'How much would it cost to have one of your hats made?'

'About as much as it might cost for two to four people to go to a West End show, depending on the theatre and the showing. And the hat.' She'd finished setting hats out, some on stands, some hooked to a trellis on the wall, a few scattered on the surface in artistic profusion. She stacked the boxes beneath the work surface.

'Could you make one for Christmas? If I brought you a client at the weekend?'

'Bet your arse.' Slowly, her gaze sharpened. 'I mean, yes, if the materials are readily available. There are occasions when clients are so particular or specific that it takes me a while to source something, but not many.'

He tucked his hands into his pockets. 'This person is one of the easiest people in the world to please. She's never had anything as fantastic as a bespoke hat and she probably won't know what to do with it. But . . .' Taking a long deep breath, he looked into Ava Blissham's face. 'It's my mum. She's had ovarian cancer and she's starting chemotherapy after Christmas. She's got this bit of breathing space while her body gets over the hysterectomy.' He swallowed. 'She and my Aunt Vanessa brought me up. They gave me a great Christmas every year and I've probably taken for granted everything they've done for me. So I'm giving them Christmas this year, and if ever there was an occasion for Mum's gift to be expensive, frivolous and blissful, this is it.'

Ava's expression spoke of surprise and shock. 'Wow. I'm so sorry.' She gazed at him for several long moments, colour creeping into her cheeks. She swallowed. 'I don't want to be rude but I can't afford to be polite. I'm incredibly sympathetic about your mum but I can't offer you a special rate.'

'I don't want a special rate. I want a special gift.'

Her eyes shone with a suspicion of tears. 'I can make her one.'

Izz arrived home when Ava was flicking through television channels, wondering whether Tod's or Izz's techie talents stretched to sending a horrible virus to Harvey's phone. Let *that* sync across all his devices!

Izz's hair was no longer spiky, and clung damply

around her head. 'It started snowing and I couldn't get a cab,' she shivered, dropping down into the green chair. Her gaze fell on the two empty cups on the table. 'I saw Sam follow you out of Blaggard's.' Then she nodded at the TV screen. 'Look – Hugo Boss Christmas Man. I think he's hotter than Dolce & Gabbana Christmas Man, this year.'

Ava paused in her channel hopping to let Hugo Boss Christmas Man smoulder from the screen. 'I haven't seen the Dolce & Gabbana ad. I'll have to watch out for it. Sam made sure I got home OK in case Harvey was hanging around. When it started to snow I gave him a cup of coffee while he waited for a cab.'

Izz pulled off her jacket and dragged out a tartan throw from behind the chair to curl up in, using the corner to dry her face. 'Sam likes you.'

Ava's heart gave a squeeze at her friend's wistful tone. 'What makes you think that?'

Izz shrugged. 'I can tell. Men usually do like you.'

Ava tried to make it into a joke. 'Harvey likes me and I don't want to be liked by him. He's a shit.' She groaned. 'He's got some, um . . . bedroom photos of me and he's threatening to let them escape into the wild.' Even telling Izz, her face heated with mortification.

Izz swung away from the TV screen where Hugo Boss Christmas Man was being replaced by an advert for wincingly boring coats, her eyes widening with horrified sympathy. 'Oh Ava. Harvey *is* a shit. What are you going to do?'

'No idea.'

Another advert came on. Izz nodded at the screen. 'Joop! Christmas Man. He'd be OK if it wasn't for the beard. Sam's not a shit. I wanted him to like me. I wanted that a lot.' She wiped at her face with the throw again. She might have been wiping away tears.

Ava felt a pang in the place inside her that she thought of as her 'Izz spot'. She began searching the channels for a *Big Bang Theory* rerun. Izz loved Sheldon Cooper. She probably loved Sheldon Cooper more than Amy Farrah Fowler did. 'Maybe he'll get to like you.'

Izz clambered to her feet. 'I'm frozen, so I'm going to bed. Sam probably thinks I'm as flaky as pastry because I can never think of what to say to him. I get stuttery.'

Ava put out her hand to her as she passed. 'Izz? You're not as flaky as pastry. I love you to bits. I think you're awesome with all the things you know about techie stuff and music. You're the best bestie.'

Izz managed a smile. 'Well, thanks. Even if you're not Sam.'

Chapter Five

Princess Leia Claus

Saturday 8 December

'I hate Tod's geeky comic stuff and I hate fancy dress.' Izz was dressed up as Mr Punch, black lines drawn either side of her mouth and a pointed hat making her tower to new heights. Cropped trousers, a ruff collar and a few brass buttons completed her outfit.

Ava lowered her voice as they trailed Tod and Louise past the 'Impressions of Balham' friezes along Balham Station Road. 'If you hate Tod's geeky comic stuff and fancy dress and I don't like Christmas, maybe we shouldn't have agreed to come to Tod's comic club's fancy dress Christmas thing? I could have stayed home and attended to the depressing business of listing samples on Etsy.'

Izz held onto her hat as a sudden gust of wind threatened to snatch it. 'But then we wouldn't have been invited to Patrick's party.'

Ava refrained from confessing that the idea of Patrick's party wasn't exactly filling her with joy. She knew exactly what – or rather who – attracted Izz to Patrick's Christmas gathering. Sam. 'At least we can dress normally for that.

Anyway, don't I look just as ridiculous as Princess Leia Claus? My hair looks stupid in two doughnuts and everyone will think my robe's a red toga.' Shortage of money rather than time had dictated Ava's costume, made from fabric once bought as a backcloth for a wedding fayre. The white cotton wool trim she'd added was already sticking messily to everything.

But Ava was glad to have something to joke about. Earlier in the evening, she'd found an opportunity to get Tod alone and tell him about Harvey's pictures. The horror on his face as he'd breathed, 'Oh no. Wow. He could do anything with those, Ava,' had made her feel a bit as if she were holding a wasps' nest. It was only a matter of time before the contents stirred, pouring forth to attack her with stinging venom.

'No, you look great,' Izz declared. 'I just wish I'd got a better costume because now Sam says he might drop in to BalCom. He'll see me looking like a dork.'

Ava's head swivelled. 'Since when is Sam dropping in?' She could completely understand that Izz didn't want Sam seeing Izz looking like a dork. Ava had just this second discovered that Ava didn't want Sam seeing Ava looking like a dork, either.

Izz sighed. 'Once Tod knew that you and I had been invited to Patrick's, he jumped in and invited them all to come to the Unwashed Geek's Comic Club of Geekland before heading to the party, and I didn't have enough time to get a better costume.'

'Fantastic,' muttered Ava, tripping over her hem.

'Excuse me.' Tod marched back towards them, fists lodged indignantly on hips. He was looking really cool as Jack Skellington from *The Nightmare Before Christmas*; Louise had forced on one of those bald head things and covered his face and neck with clown white. The black make-up stitches either side of his mouth looked almost real.

But then Louise was into cosplay, which was almost worse than being a comic geek. Especially when she felt the need to explain for the twentieth time that *cosplay* was derived from the words 'costume' and 'play' and how it differed from merely wearing Christmas or Halloween costumes – hardly at all, in Ava's opinion.

'Excuse *me*,' Tod repeated, severely. 'Please don't refer to BalCom as "the Unwashed Geek's Comic Club of Geekland". People will get upset. Our hygiene is more than adequate.'

Izz's face fell. 'I was joking.'

Ava linked her arm through Izz's. 'So's he.'

'Of course I'm joking!' Tod gazed at Izz in the familiar exasperation of one who had had this kind of explaining-I'm-joking conversation before.

Louise, as Sally the Rag Doll to pair with Tod's Jack Skellington, and looking surprisingly sexy in the raggy dress, rolled her eyes. 'Come on, Tod. We'll miss registering for the costume judging.' Louise cast her gaze over Ava's and Izz's half-hearted costumes. 'Are you two entering?'

Ava and Izz shook their heads. Ava wondered whether Louise knew that last year the winner had been covered with squirty cream and Christmas streamers while everybody screamed with laughter.

'Probably best.' Louise turned eagerly for the fire escape that led up to the function room over the Snooty Fox pub, BalCom's usual meeting point.

Behind Louise's back, Tod frowned at Ava and Izz. Ava blew him a silent extravagant kiss in return, which, unfortunately, Louise turned around in time to see.

*

In the bar of the Snooty Fox, Sam and Jake were fortifying themselves for the evening to come.

'Remind me why we're going to this thing?' Jake crossed his eyes to make a bamboozled face.

'Because Tod asked us and Tod's a co-worker so deserves our support. And because once Patrick had invited Izz and Ava it was obvious that if they can attend the comic thing *and* Patrick's party, then, unfortunately, so can we.'

'Not because Izz's got the hots for you and you can't resist seeing her twice in one evening?' Jake winked.

Sam opened his mouth on an arctic retort about Ava being much more his style then remembered how ridiculous it would make him look to be pursuing a woman who wasn't currently dating. Also, that he was temporarily Izz's employer. 'Let's have another beer.'

When they finally got around to following the cardboard 'BalCom' arrows to the foot of an external metal staircase, passing a Superman and what looked like a giant green slug coming the other way, it was to find Tod leaning miserably against the dirty red brick wall, eyes closed in the black skeletal eye sockets of clever make-up. Sam probably would have walked straight past without recognising him if not for Ava in a curious long red robe patting Tod's arm. 'Do you need to throw up?' Izz, standing silently to one side, went scarlet when she saw Sam.

'I'm not *that* drunk,' Tod protested, slightly slurred. 'Maybe it's a food allergy.'

Louise, in a costume as impressive as Tod's, was almost dancing with rage. '*Somebody's* obviously put something in his drink. Eh, Ava? He never gets like this!' Louise all but barged Ava out of her way as she took over the arm patting.

49

Ava arched indignant eyebrows. 'As we've known Tod a lot longer than you, Louise, I can assure you that occasionally he does get a bit tipsy.'

'You would say that. You've obviously got a thing about him.'

Ava's eyes widened to cartoon proportions. 'Tod's one of my best friends – we don't have "things" about one another. And why would I spike the drink of someone if I did have a thing about him? If I ever did anything as stupid and irresponsible, which I don't. Lighten up, Louise. It's Christmas and Tod just did a few Jägerbombs with his mates.'

'And a couple of bottles of Peroni,' Izz added, helpfully.

Tod gave a giant burp. 'I'm not that drunk. I just feel a bit nauseated. I've probably eaten something I shouldn't have.'

Louise promptly put her rage dance into reverse and got out of range.

Ava frowned at her.

'Having fun?' queried Sam, mildly. 'Are you Mrs Claus in her dressing gown?' he hazarded, to give himself an excuse to keep looking at her robe thing, which, though dotted with mangy cotton wool, skimmed and draped her body, somehow defining it at the same time as covering her from neck to toe.

Ava seemed to notice him and Jake for the first time. 'No fancy dress?'

'Too short notice,' put in Sam smoothly. 'Nothing would have pleased me more than wearing Santa's dressing gown, otherwise.'

He thought he caught a glimmer of a smile. 'Actually, I'm glad you're here. We could use your help to get Tod to Louise's.'

Jake groaned.

Sam sighed. 'Is it far?'

Getting Tod to Louise's flat was tiresome, not because they had to stop a couple of times while Tod battled waves of nausea, nor because Sam and Jake had to keep Tod on the pavement as he was inclined to weave. It was because Louise stalked beside them in furious silence and it was left to Ava to direct operations. 'It's around this corner. Up the steps with the green railings.'

Helping Tod up the concrete flight to a yellowing PVC front door, Sam and Jake paused while Louise unlocked it and Tod repeated, 'I'm not *that* drunk.'

Shunting back and forth, they threaded him through the doorway. Louise thrust open a door to a bedroom, and Tod zigzagged over the threshold and flopped unceremoniously onto the quilt. 'I'm *not* that drunk,' he said again.

'Thanks,' Ava said, as, breathing heavily, they stood back to survey Tod, who, despite his declarations of sobriety, looked asleep already.

Louise ushered them out of the bedroom. 'You two will have to bunk up together, Ava and Izz, because I'm not sleeping with him tonight! That's if you still want to stay,' she added, pointedly.

Ava exchanged a look with Izz, whose pencilled-on puppet eyebrows had nearly disappearing into her hair in alarm at the idea. Ava tried to be diplomatic. 'We could stay if you think you might need help with Tod. Otherwise, it might be better if we grab our overnight bags and go.'

'I'm sure I can cope. You go and enjoy your party.' Louise evidently harboured no desires to have Ava and

Izz as guests now that her evening had reached a premature end. In fact, she fetched their bags for them.

Ava found herself backing through the front door. 'We'll be in touch in the morning to see how Tod is.'

Louise gave an eloquent snort and soon Ava and Izz were on the outside of the closed door with Sam and Jake, who hadn't even been thanked for dragging poor Tod around the streets.

Chapter Six

A Christmas kiss for Ava Bliss

'I think we're dumped,' Sam observed.

'Wow,' breathed Jake. 'Scary girlfriend.'

Suddenly realising she was still in her Princess Leia Claus robe, which was looking more like a moth-eaten dressing gown every moment, Ava groaned. 'I wish she'd given us a chance to get changed.'

'You'll be able to use a room at Patrick's.' Sam stood back to allow the two women down the garden path ahead of him. 'It's on Bedford Hill.'

Patrick's place proved to be two floors over a shop, handily situated for Balham and Clapham South tube stations and within sight of the railway bridge, its high-ceilinged rooms currently populated by a significant number of partygoers eating pizza.

'Thought you bastards had been kidnapped by the comickers,' roared Patrick, as they stepped through the open door. Spotting Ava, he switched swiftly to charm mode, taking her hand to kiss theatrically. 'But good things are worth waiting for.'

Sam snorted. 'Cheesy.'

Ava stood back and glanced at Izz, obliging Patrick to kiss Izz's hand, too. Izz went pink.

'Sorry we're dressed so stupidly. Tod's comic book party was fancy dress. Is there a room where we can change, please? We were going to stay at Louise's but Tod had one too many.'

Patrick tucked Ava's hand into the crook of his arm. 'I'll show you to a room you can use. In fact,' he added, 'I have more rooms than I know what to do with. You can stay here tonight.'

Ava regarded him dubiously. 'We can get the bus home.' The idea of paying for a cab gave her a pain in her bank account.

'Aha!' Patrick waved his finger theatrically. '*But* . . . the bus drivers have come out on strike tonight. It's all to do with their pensions and our glorious mayor. The last tube service is just after midnight so it's a good job Saint Patrick's here. Just stay. Other people are staying – Sam for a start. Everyone's very friendly.' He gestured extravagantly in the general direction of the babble coming from the other rooms.

'Well—' began Ava.

But Izz was looking relieved. 'It'll be much easier to get home in the morning, won't it, Ava? If you're sure you don't mind, Patrick?'

'Not in the least. Who are you meant to be, Ava?'

Giving up on getting home that evening, Ava looked down at her ridiculous costume, heat rising in her face. 'Princess Leia Claus.'

'Shame you didn't pick the Princess Leia slave girl outfit.' Patrick began towing her over turquoise carpet to a staircase that looked as if the corners had gone uncleaned for about a decade. Izz and Sam followed.

When they'd climbed the stairs and reached the end of the landing, Patrick threw open a white-painted door. 'Here we are. Best room in the house. Hope you girls don't mind sharing. Not all the rooms have beds.'

Ava stepped inside. It was, she saw with relief, actually an OK room. The twin beds were made up with quilts that didn't match but looked clean; there were curtains.

Izz dropped her bag on a bed and thanked Patrick, who lounged in the doorway.

'You've really saved us,' Ava agreed, wondering whether Patrick thought he was going to continue to lean in the doorway and watch as they changed their clothes.

As if reading her thoughts, Sam put a hand on Patrick's shoulder and eased him back. 'We'll let them sort themselves out, shall we? The bathroom's two doors down, ladies.'

'Thanks.' Ava smiled gratefully as Sam reached in and shut the door. The sound of the men's voices receded down the landing.

'Thank goodness we can change.' Izz divested herself of her puppet costume. 'I'll go wash this stuff off my face and put on some proper make-up.'

Ava sighed as she thankfully dragged off the red robe, examining her surroundings as she did so. The building was obviously old and had been gracious but the room wasn't warm; old-fashioned sliding sash windows allowing in more draughts than the big ugly radiator could counteract. The room's pleasantly fusty smell made her nostalgic for child-hood sleepovers in her grandmother's spare room when both her parents had been on shift. Music and laughter from downstairs filtered up between the floorboards.

She was conscious of a bit of a headache. Hoping it wouldn't develop into a migraine because prescriptions were expensive, she sank down onto the bed and looked in her bag for paracetamol. Her gaze caught on her e-reader, nestled in its pocket, and she was tempted to burrow straight beneath the quilt with it. But that would be unacceptably rude. So she changed into the jeans and top in which she'd arrived at Louise's earlier, unravelled her hair from its doughnuts and twisted it up more comfortably behind her head.

Then Izz returned to bundle her costume back into her bag. 'I wonder if anyone would mind if we grabbed some of that pizza. I'm starving.'

Two hours later, Ava was surprised to find she was actually having a good time. Most of Patrick's guests were dressed casually so she didn't feel excluded by a host of fabulous party dresses. She'd encouraged Izz to introduce her to others from the agency that she'd missed at Blaggard's – Manda Jane and Emily in jeans and boots, and Barb, Jermyn's business centre manager.

Barb looked her up and down with a knowing grin. 'Are you with Sam? He's kept you quiet.'

'I'm not with anybody. And Sam's just a friend of friends.'

Barb added raised eyebrows to her grin. In her late forties, built for comfort more than speed, Barb wore purple-framed glasses and a cheery expression.

Manda Jane raised her voice over the music, sloshing a few drops of wine on Patrick's carpet as she waved her glass. 'Barb's fantastic. She can organise anything. We love you, don't we, Barb?'

Barb accepted an effusive hug. 'You love the chocolate I keep in my top drawer, Manda Jane. Now move over and give Ava somewhere to sit.'

Barb made Ava and Izz part of a group of women who'd staked a claim to a large area of lounge carpet, scorning the corner sofa in favour of sprawling on cushions, drinking wine and polishing off a pile of onion rings and popcorn chicken that Barb had moved from Patrick's freezer to his oven until just the perfect crispiness to dip in ketchup and mayo.

Ava estimated that there must be fifty or so people scattered around the flat. They wafted between rooms, drinking, eating, changing the music on the iPod docked to a big speaker. They danced, shouted jokey insults, roared with laughter and occasionally fell over in the flickering candlelight. Izz wandered off in the direction of the kitchen when she heard news of a fresh pizza delivery.

Sam passed through the lounge a couple of times. Faded jeans clung to his long legs and his T-shirt was emblazoned with the legend *This way up* between two upward arrows. Without a business suit he looked quite unlike Sam the Big Important Man.

He didn't look any less hot.

When he drifted into the room a third time Barb waved him over. 'We'll admit a little testosterone into the group, seeing as it's you.'

Lowering himself down cross-legged, Sam hooked an arm around her. 'You're not too old to have forgotten what testosterone's about?'

Barb planted her hands on her ample hips and thrust out her boobs, peeping at him from under fluttering eyelashes. 'I know exactly what to do with testosterone, don't you worry. Mind your manners or I might give you a demonstration and it'll take you a week to recover.'

Ava giggled at Barb's exaggerated vamping.

As the party gained traction the group members shuffled

around to accommodate newcomers and Ava found herself sharing a leaky beanbag with Sam.

She'd never seen him without a bottle of beer this evening, and his hair was more in his eyes than usual, but she suspected he was making each beer last because his speech was perfectly controlled when he asked, 'Will Louise forgive Tod, do you think?'

Ava occupied herself by picking beanbag stuffing off her jeans. 'He's not the first bloke whose girlfriend got upset with him over drink, is he?'

Sam leaned closer as someone switched the music volume to 'blare'. 'Like Harvey?'

'Not exactly.' Ava ignored the warmth that slithered through her at his shoulder brushing hers. 'With Tod it's just Christmas. He usually controls his drinking. It doesn't control him. Tomorrow he'll be hungover and apologetic and I hope Louise doesn't make too much of it, because he's not confident with girls.'

'I hadn't met Louise until last week.'

'She's fairly new.'

'Do you like her?'

She answered diplomatically. 'All that matters is whether Tod likes her.'

'At the agency Tod's a fully functioning adult, though he has his quirks. He's creative and imaginative and popular with clients. I'm interested in why he accepts Louise being so . . . forceful.'

'Bossy!' said Ava, abandoning diplomacy. 'Sorry, that probably makes me sound horrible. Louise and I don't really appreciate each other. OK, let's go with "forceful". Tod hasn't had many girlfriends to compare her to so I've tried to talk to him about her but he changes the subject.'

'Perhaps as the relationship's quite new she's pushing his boundaries and he hasn't decided where they are yet?'

More people bumbled up to join what had evidently become the epicentre of the party and a game began that involved a lot of violent swaying and raucous shrieking. Sam braced himself with a hand on the wall behind Ava against the worst of the pushing and shoving. The group was growing and Ava could see Patrick trying to find space in the thick of it.

Sam raised his voice. 'Speaking of "pushing boundaries" makes me revisit the subject of Harvey. Had any further issues with him?' Ava had to move her head closer to hear, breathing in a pleasant combination of beer and tea tree shower gel. 'Whatever you argued over, there was no excuse for violence. The guy needs anger management counselling.'

'I think he needs more than that.' It would usually go against her personal code to badmouth an ex-boyfriend but Harvey's recent behaviour had vanquished any loyalty. 'I'm pretty sure he's got a real alcohol problem. He was drinking more and more in the time we were together and behaving badly. Things came to a head so I got out but it hasn't improved his behaviour. Today he tagged me in a photo on Facebook.'

A long pause. 'That bothered you?' Sam frowned, obviously trying to understand the import of Harvey's action.

'Oh, I—' Flustered, Ava sipped her wine, not wanting to explain why her heart had done a double flip before she'd clicked on the link and discovered that the picture was only an old selfie of them kissing at the top of The Shard. 'It didn't feel appropriate because I don't want to interact with him.'

'You could unfriend or block him.'

'True.' But then she wouldn't know if he did post one of *those* photos.

'He still seems to have feelings for you.'

'That's the way it goes, isn't it? Relationships begin by being about chemistry and end up being about compatibility. Sometimes not both of you move from one phase to the other. Sober Harvey knows that Drunk Harvey's behaviour is tragic but both of them seem to think our relationship's not over, whereas I know that it is.'

He studied her. 'That doesn't seem much justification for shoving you around, and you don't have to accept that kind of conduct.'

His kindness made Ava almost want to confide in him about Harvey's frightening threats. But then those playing the game going on around them chanted, 'One, two, three, *four*.' The catcalls and laughter grew louder and a wobbling and flushed Barb came to crouch in front of them.

'Come on, Sam, it's you.'

'What's me?' Sam glanced round at the laughing faces.

Barb thrust a sprig of mistletoe into his hand. 'Patrick rolled a four and you're fourth along. It means you have to give a Christmas kiss to the nearest woman.' She laughed a deep, belly-shaking laugh. 'Looks as if it could be me or Ava. You have to choose.'

It didn't take Sam long to make up his mind. 'Ava. May I?' He held the mistletoe above her head.

The air around them seemed to change, preventing Ava from voicing any of several random and conflicting thoughts. She felt his arms close around her and then his lips were finding hers. Neither hesitant nor intrusive but warm, soft, confident, as if they'd been there before, and often.

Surprise – or something – made her open her mouth to him and suddenly they were involved in a deep, proper kiss. Not a gentle brushing of the lips, not a quick pucker up, but searching tongues.

For several seconds, Ava was physically incapable of pulling away. She was aware of Barb wailing in mock disappointment that Sam hadn't chosen her, of Patrick grumbling that Sam was a lucky gamer. But the din of the party became distant as if she were once again up in her room listening to it through the cracks between the floorboards.

Then it was over. Sam gently removed his arm from around Ava in order to calmly shake the dice onto the floor in front of them. 'Three.'

'One, two, *three*,' everybody shouted. Then the mistletoe moved on to a man Ava didn't know, who planted a big jokey smacker of a kiss on Barb and made her shriek with laughter.

Ava sucked in a couple of breaths, waiting for her heart rate to steady. It was the surprise, she told herself. And you made a fool of yourself by kissing him back so enthusiastically. He's probably not sure whether to feel embarrassed, amused or invited. She tried to make herself look at Sam and laugh it off. But she couldn't. All she could feel was his mouth on hers.

Bloody Christmas. When she was directing all her energy to making a success of her life, or just surviving, Christmas made it not only socially acceptable, but actually required, to kiss a lovely man.

A kiss that accelerated her pulse and snatched her breath. She didn't have room in her life for a distracting man. Men wanted to be the centre of your universe and Ava had too much space debris in her orbit, not least the fact

61

that her Christmas kiss had come from the man her friend was crushing on.

Sam put his mouth close to her ear. 'Hot.'

Chapter Seven

Not dating at Gaz's Caff

Sam knew that he shouldn't have gone for it quite as he had. But, hey, it was Christmas. Ava's entrancing mouth was incredibly alluring. When her lips had parted he'd recklessly followed his inclination.

He definitely shouldn't have commented, even though he'd picked up a flustered vibe from her and that didn't happen when a girl felt nothing for you. But now, avoiding his eyes, she was following the progress of the game with a fixed smile, every line of her body saying 'awkward'. When she saw that the mistletoe was beginning to make its way back in their direction, she glanced at her watch, climbed to her feet and picked a path through the bodies.

As she slipped out of the lounge, Sam felt her disengagement sinking through him like bad news. Had a kiss – even a burning hot kiss – been worth the snapping of that thread of connection between them?

He breathed in slowly.

Connections could be re-established. He couldn't regret that kiss.

*

It was some time before Sam saw Ava again, long after he'd come to the regretful conclusion that she must have hidden away in her room. The party was winding down and people were digging out their coats from the heap in the hall.

In sole possession of the large sofa, Sam was enjoying a contemplative JD Honey he'd liberated from Patrick's stash, thinking, reluctantly, about starting a Christmas shopping list on the Waitrose site. Would Mum and Aunt Van prefer turkey or duck? He liked duck but was cranberry jelly eaten with it? And stuffing? Would they feel cheated if he didn't buy a Christmas pudding? Nobody ever seemed to like eating the damned thing. Maybe he could find an app that would take the painful guesswork out of being the best Christmas host he could be. Help him to make it the most special Christmas his mother had ever known.

Then Ava appeared in the doorway, gaze flitting around the party debris. After a hesitation, she crossed to where he sat.

'Do you know where Patrick's gone? He was chatting with me and Izz in the kitchen but he's vanished.' She was at least managing to meet his eyes again.

'Haven't seen him for ages. What's up?'

She looked away. 'I wanted to ask him something.'

'If you can't find him, he may have already gone to his room on the top floor. Is it something I can help with?' Patrick might not thank them for interrupting him in his bedroom, as he'd consider going to bed alone after the party a colossal failure.

'Izz.' She grimaced.

He tried to read her expression. 'Is she OK?'

'Well . . .' She scratched her nose and looked embarrassed. 'I didn't really want to tell you, you being her boss. She's not as tipsy as Tod was but she claims she can't get upstairs and, at the moment, she's trying to go to sleep with her head on the kitchen table.'

He sucked in a breath to keep from laughing. 'Are all your friends drunks?'

Ava's eyebrows lifted like commas of dismay. 'Izz and Tod aren't *drunks*! It's damned Christmas. Too much alcohol and too much stupidity. Too much *Christmassing*. Too many excuses for behaving as we usually wouldn't.'

If that was a veiled shot at their kiss, he decided not to acknowledge it. 'Don't worry, I do see the difference between a few Christmas drinks and habitual alcohol abuse. What happens at a Christmas party stays at a Christmas party and my memory will be expunged the instant we've seen her to bed.' Reluctantly, he rolled to his feet and tossed back the last of the JD Honey. 'I'll help. But I need to see someone about my hero complex.' At least that got a smile out of Ava as she led him away on their rescue mission.

In the kitchen, they found Izz folded peaceably onto a wooden chair, her cheek pillowed on her arms on the table.

Ava shook her friend's shoulder. 'Come on, Izz. I can't leave you here. Sam's come to help you upstairs.'

Sam positioned himself so that he could hook Izz's arm around his neck and help her to her feet.

'Hello, Sam!' murmured Izz, sounding delighted to find him somehow in her embrace. 'It's a good party.'

Sam caught a stifled snort of laughter from Ava as she positioned herself at her friend's other side.

'It *was* a good party,' Sam agreed. 'But now it's bedtime. You need to go back to the room you're sharing with

Ava,' he added, in case Izz got the idea that she was being invited into Sam's bed. 'Ava wants to go to sleep and she can't leave you down here on the table, can she? Ouch!' He bounced uncomfortably off a doorjamb.

'It's a nice table.' Izz seemed disposed to see the good in everything. 'This is nice stair carpet. Nice flat. Patrick's nice, too, isn't he? When you get to know him. Isn't he, Ava?'

'Oof,' Ava panted, as she banged into the banisters. 'Yes, very nice. Don't lean back!' She let out a small shriek of dismay and Sam had to shoot his arm around her and catch the opposite handrail to have any hope of preventing them all being pulled backwards down the few stairs they'd so far put behind them.

He paused, panting. Nearly six feet of squiffy woman was definitely not an aerodynamic positive.

Izz's arm tightened around his neck. 'Hul*lo*, Sam,' she breathed.

Choking back another laugh, Ava came to his rescue. 'Izz! It's not nice to take advantage of a man when you're drunk. Now lean forward a little bit – yes, like that! Just a few more steps now.'

Finally, panting, they got Izz up the stairs and along the landing to the door of the room Patrick had designated as theirs. Ava slapped at the light switch, then, with a last concerted heave, they let Izz down onto her bed.

'Holy crap.' Ava was breathing hard, her hair slipping from its clasp to curl down beside her face. 'I'm glad she doesn't do this very often.'

Sam could only agree. Relieved of his burden, he waved a tired hand and backed out of the room.

'Goodnight,' he heard Ava call softly, as he closed the door.

Sunday 9 December

Ava awoke slowly, aware of more traffic outside the window than there should be in School Road and an insistent, regular noise. Her memory began trying to supply her with facts. The party at Patrick's. Sleeping over at Patrick's. Izz . . .

She groaned.

The noise was Izz snoring. Like a tractor. A tractor that had had a lot to drink and was now lying on its back, snoring.

'Izz!' she hissed, experimentally. 'Izz, turn over. Shh. *Shhhhhh.*'

Izz just carried on emitting '*Rnnnnnnnnh . . . hnnnnnnnnnh*' at steady intervals.

Ava found her phone and checked the time. Not long after seven. She'd only had about four hours' sleep. She turned over, curling up small against the draughts swirling around the room, wishing she'd brought a glass of water upstairs with her last night as, although she'd not overdone it to the same extent as Tod or Izz, she was conscious of an unhealthy alcohol thirst. Closing her eyes, she tried to ignore both her thirst and the *rrrrrrnnnh . . . hnnnnnnnh* increasing in volume from the opposite bed, and drift back to sleep.

Deep breaths . . . in-two-three-four . . . out-two-three-four . . . don't think of that kiss.

Rnnnnnnnnh . . . hnnnnnnnnnh

In-two-three-four . . . out-two-three-four . . . The kiss would hurt Izz's feelings if she got to hear of it. Lucky that she'd been elsewhere when the kiss had grabbed Ava up out of her worries and shocked her libido into life.

Rnnnnnnnnh . . . hnnnnnnnnnh

Her phone chirruped a loud text message alert. Ava jerked into a sitting position, muttering darkly.

Izz started awake and up on her elbow, gazing down with puzzlement at her jeans and top, visible in the light filtering in from the landing. Then she let her eyelids down again on a groan. 'Your *phone*, Ava. It woke me up.' She sounded so aggrieved as she shifted and stretched on a series of grunts and groans that Ava forgot her irritation and grinned.

'Sorry,' she whispered. 'I hadn't thought to put it on silent.'

Within three seconds, Izz had settled back into a peaceful routine of *rnnnnnnnnh . . . hnnnnnnnnnh.*

Ava looked at her phone screen and sighed. *Harvey.* A message and an image. Stomach sinking in anticipation, she opened it.

A pain began behind her left eye. Now she knew she looked like *that* when she did *that* she'd probably never do it to anybody again.

I thought you were going to delete those? she texted back frantically, wishing she hadn't been right when she'd doubted Harvey's good intentions.

Oops. lol.

Are you drunk this early in the morning?

It's morning? Haven't been to bed. How would you like it if I sent this pic to your dad? Would bigshot Met Commander Graeme like seeing exactly how his little girl has grown up?

Ava licked suddenly dry lips. Her dad had survived thirty years in the Met without a speck of dirt adhering to him. The idea of him being humiliated along with her filled her with dread. This shitty situation wasn't showing any signs of letting up.

Neither were Izz's excruciating snores – *rnnnnnnnnnh . . . hnnnnnnnnnh.*

Dragging her clothes on under the duvet to avoid the

worst of the room's frigid air, Ava slid her feet into her boots, pulled on her coat, and went downstairs in search of a gallon of water.

It took a little investigating of Patrick's dubious kitchen cabinets before she discovered a pint mug that looked clean. She was just emptying it of cold water for the second time when a voice behind her made her jump.

'Are you OK?'

Ava snorted water up her nose. 'Fine.' She wiped inelegantly at her face with the back of her hand and offered Sam a squinty morning smile. He was wearing a different T-shirt – this time the slogan said *I'm not strange, I'm gifted*.

'Why are you up so early?'

'Izz snoring, cold room, thirsty.' Ava was beginning to feel more human now she was rehydrating. 'Why are you?'

He glanced blearily at his watch. 'I need to get home and I need breakfast inside me to get me through the journey. Want to join me?' He began to thrust his arms through the sleeves of his jacket. His hair was only finger-combed and stubble shaded his jaw but otherwise he looked none the worse for a few beers and a night in whatever accommodation Patrick had allotted him. That was men for you. A wash, a pee, and they were ready to face the world.

'Um.' Ava tried to focus on the discarded cans and bottles strewn around the room, along with two non-matching abandoned shoes. A huge caffé latte and maybe a salmon bagel seemed eminently more appealing than hanging around amongst the hangovers. 'OK. I'll have a go at waking Izz to see if she wants to come.' She finished the second pint of water, rinsed the glass and refilled it for Izz, then yawned her way back upstairs.

Nothing had changed in the bedroom, unless it was that Izz's snores had actually increased in volume.

'Izz!' Ava hissed. 'Izz! Izz!' She gave Izz's shoulder a hard shake.

'Wha'?' Izz didn't even open her eyes.

'I'm going to a café to have breakfast with Sam. Want to come?'

'Wha's the time?'

'7.26,' Ava reported, precisely, consulting her phone.

'In the morning?' Izz settled more deeply into her pillows. 'Too early. Not even daylight.'

'OK. I'll be back in an hour or so.' Ava doubted that Izz would be awake in an hour, or even three or four, but she found a couple of paracetamol in her bag and left them, along with a drink of water, beside Izz's slumbering form.

Creeping along to the bathroom in the silent house, Ava washed away the make-up she hadn't quite cleansed away last night, brushed her teeth and clipped up her hair, grabbed her bag, then trod softly downstairs.

Sam was sitting on the kitchen table frowning over his phone when she found him. He slid the handset into his pocket. 'Are you coming back here after breakfast?'

'Yes. Izz isn't exactly a morning person and she'll be out for hours. Also, I need to check that Tod's OK.'

Opening a kitchen drawer, Sam found a key on a green tag and tossed it her way. 'I'm going straight to the tube so you'd better take one of Patrick's spares. Put it back in this drawer before you leave to go home.' He was obviously au fait with Patrick's systems.

Outside, the air was dank and the sky was just beginning to grow light above the street lamps. They strolled down to Gaz's Caff, where other early birds huddled over coffee mugs and bacon rolls, and the air was heavy with the smell of fried food.

Gaz's Caff was neither recently decorated nor trendy. Sam, ignoring the years of neglect and thick paint, hung his coat on a wonky hook and sat down on a scarred bentwood chair at a small window table looking across the street to Sainsbury's car park. He didn't, as Harvey would have, gaze in astounded distaste at the pensioners tucking into a full English breakfast, wipe the chair before sitting his expensively clothed behind on it, or insist on going to Starbucks instead.

He just ran his eye down the menu board screwed to the wall. 'What are you going to have?'

Ava turned to look. No salmon bagels. 'Scrambled egg on toast and about a bucket of coffee, strong.' Before she could push back her chair Sam was up at the counter.

A big man with 'Gaz' written in marker pen on his hat waddled over, scrabbling his order pad out of the top pocket of his white smock. 'What can I getcha?'

'Scrambled egg on toast, twice, please.' Sam turned back to Ava. 'White toast or granary?'

'Only got white,' observed Gaz, pen poised.

'White, then, and two of the largest coffees you have, double-shot.'

'"Double-shot" just means two spoons of Nescaff here, mate, OK?' Gaz scribbled it down. As he moved off he winked at Ava under the white cap that kept what was left of his hair clear of the food. 'Hello, love.'

She returned the greeting sweetly as Gaz flipped the lid off a catering-sized tin of Nescafé, happy to form a friendly connection with the man who held the fate of her coffee in his hands.

She smothered a yawn as Sam carried two steaming mugs back with him. 'Thanks.'

He smiled an acknowledgement but once he'd resumed

his seat, fell to gazing outside at the steely fingers of early light that touched the road.

Ava cast around for a subject with which to start the conversational ball rolling. 'Tod really enjoys working with you. Izz, too. No,' she corrected herself. 'Tod works *with* you but Izz works *for* you, right?'

He shifted his gaze her way. Ava had once had a tiger's eye ring that shone with the same browns and golds as his eyes. 'That's right. Tod's an associate. The associates are freelance, paying rent and occupying space on a fully serviced basis. Tod's a graphic artist, Manda Jane's a media buyer, Patrick's a writer, Jake's a photographer and so on. I offer space at Jermyn's based on area of PR, people skills, can-do attitude and client focus. We have individual areas of expertise but we have the capacity to form teams to work on specific projects.'

'But Izz says she's on a short-term contract, improving the agency network and database?'

Stirring his coffee, he nodded. 'The agency only employs one full-time member of staff, and that's Barb. She runs front of house – greets clients, answers the phone, keeps the printers and photocopier going, makes coffee, that kind of thing.'

'But I've heard Tod say that he thought the agency could use a full time techie.' Ava massaged a point behind her ear that was giving gentle throbs.

He took the first gulp from his mug and then sucked his top lip as if he'd burned it. 'Probably, eventually. The agency's pretty young so it's too early to know. And,' he added, carefully, 'should that day ever come, I'd owe it to the associates to ensure that I hired absolutely the best person for the position, someone who would see what the agency needs and be able to enthuse others and get them on board.'

Ava sighed, hearing what Sam wasn't actually saying. *It wouldn't be Izz.* 'Izz can't help being shy. It makes her a little bit awkward, that's all.' She took several sips of her coffee, choosing her next words. Even though her own business was as slow as a sloth she'd love to see things go well for her friend and, remembering the unguarded comments she'd overheard Jake make about Izz, she couldn't quite let the subject drop without assuring herself that Izz wasn't losing out for the wrong reason. 'It must be hard,' she said, 'to be objective if, say, someone at the agency lets their personal feelings show for someone else at the agency.'

Sam leaned back in the chair that looked small in comparison to his frame. Behind him a lady with a dandelion clock of white hair chatted to Gaz and two young mums with pushchairs giggled over their phones. His gaze sharpened. 'We have a personal relationships policy. I would be disappointed if anyone at Jermyn's showed partiality, or was discriminatory, based on personal feelings.'

Ava slid him a sideways look. 'Even if you suspected someone showed personal feelings for you?'

'*If* that were to happen, I would simply maintain my professional relationship with that person.'

The food arrived and Ava began on Gaz's perfect, creamy scrambled eggs.

It was Sam who broke the silence after munching his way through half of his first huge toast doorstep. 'But, as you've brought the subject up and I would appreciate your perspective, does . . . *anyone you know* often find herself with feelings for someone?'

No longer seeing any point in pretending that they weren't talking about Izz, Ava admitted, reluctantly, 'The last crush was on one of Tod's housemates, Frankie. Until he got interested in drawing for comics, then she went off him. She really is not keen on comickers, even though Tod's into it.'

Beginning on his second raft of toast, Sam steered the conversation back in the arena of polite small talk. 'You and Izz obviously get on well.'

'Definitely. She's a really lovely person, and fun when you make the effort to get to know her. I love living with her. She doesn't intrude on my space, she's always got enough food and her laundry's always up-to-date. Secondary to that, I'm her lodger and she doesn't overcharge me. It's my home and my workplace and I'd never get anywhere else like that.'

'And you said you'd known her since school?'

'That's right. We all lived close to each other in Hampshire. Izz's parents are lovely. They've got a fabulous place with a pool because Izz's dad designed some kind of simulator-type software years ago that earned him buckets of money. He used to be on TV shows about innovators and entrepreneurs as technology was just beginning to boom. We used to hang out at their place a lot. Izz's house was full of eccentricity, Tod's was full of books. Mine was aseptic in comparison. I wish my parents had been as cool then as to run a bookshop café, instead of having deadly serious high-stakes careers.'

She mined a few more memories. 'One day at school Izz was being picked on by this boy from two years above. I tried to come to her defence but the bully started shoving me around. Tod, who we didn't even know then, waded in. So the boy turned on Tod.'

Sam was looking interested so she carried on. 'He got Tod by the shirt and got ready to punch him.' She remembered Tod's look of frozen terror as he waited for the blow to explode in his face. 'So I kicked the bully in the nuts.'

Sam winced.

'The bully's mates took the piss out of him for being beaten up by a girl. He left us alone, we began to hang out with Tod, and Izz wasn't picked on so much. We went travelling together pre-uni, as well.'

'Then I can see why you're all such good friends.' Sam, as if to emphasise his general niceness, caught sight of the dandelion haired woman heading for the door with her walking stick, and got up to open it for her.

When he returned to his seat, Ava turned the conversation to him. 'Tell me more about your role at the agency.'

Stretching out his legs, he leaned back. 'I'm a partner. The junior partner so far as money's concerned. I used to handle media stuff for someone—'

'Chilly, the football star,' Ava put in. 'Tod told me.'

He inclined his head. 'Aidan "Chilly" Chiltern. It was a fantastic experience but I was tiring of all the travelling and had begun planning the agency for when I could finance it. Then Chilly got injured and had to retire anyway, so he put in a lot of money, and brought us an important client who has us on a media management retainer. I brought my plans forward and began putting out feelers for the right people. Open minded, self-starting, self-motivated, able to work under pressure to deadlines, reliable and giving clients what they want.'

'Tod's never been so happy as since he's been at Jermyn's.'

Sam looked at her as if searching that statement for honesty. He must have been happy with what he saw because his expression relaxed. 'Good. That's what I want. Apart from trying to keep everyone happy, my role changes to meet circumstances, but I'm kind of a creative director. Brand image awareness tends to come into everything and that's my background. I often advise on campaigns. I challenge briefs, suggest media and frequency, look at objectives and products and generally see where I can help. In a football team I'd be both coach and manager.'

'And owner.'

'Co-owner. Chilly's the main moneyman. I'm just a workhorse with more to do and more to lose than the other workhorses. I'm also the guy who stresses about turnover and profit.'

'Tod always makes the agency sound awesome,' she confessed. 'I wish I could afford you.'

Sam smiled politely.

Ava flushed. 'That sounded like a big fat hint that you should give me help, heavily discounted.' She pulled a face. 'In fact, you can't discount heavily enough for me to afford you. I'll leave you to the celebs.'

'Tod said he'd helped you with your website.'

'Yes, if you mean "Tod made Ava a website and Ava chose the colours".' She checked the time. 'I'll text Tod after breakfast and see if he's conscious yet, and whether Louise is speaking to him. She can be pretty judgemental.' Which made her realise that she hadn't asked Tod not to tell Louise about Harvey's pictures. If he had, Louise would no doubt give Ava a long lecture and Ava so didn't need that.

Sam interrupted this unhappy thought. 'I'm fetching my mother later today to stay with me for a few days. May I organise her hat fitting?'

The thought that Ava was going to help make Sam's mum happy at Christmas was instantly diverting. 'Of course. I'm glad she's well enough to come up to town.' She was also glad that she'd be able to ask for a deposit.

He propped his chin on his fist. 'I'm not convinced that she is well enough. It's less than four weeks since a quite major op but she's determined and her doctor's given her a cautious go-ahead.' His brows curled down. 'She wants to make the most of this Christmas in case . . . in case the future proves uncertain.'

Shocked, Ava looked into his face and read his soul. Behind the scowl burned the fear that he was going to lose his mother in a way so harsh and protracted that he'd never afterwards be the same. She discovered a desire to reach out to him. 'Then let's make it as fun for her as we can. What would make it special?'

He swallowed. 'Just make a fuss of her. Make it into an occasion.'

'I can do that.' Then, as she saw Sam glance at his watch, 'I'd better let you go, hadn't I?'

Sam went for his pocket.

'Let's split the bill,' she said quickly.

He had his wallet in his hand, now. 'Really, it's my pleasure to get this one.'

But Ava had already pulled out her purse. 'Thank you, but I like to pay my way. I'm sure you understand.'

He stared at her with a hint of irritability. 'Not really, as I've offered and I can afford it. But, fine, split the bill if you feel strongly about it, before you turn it into an opportunity to remind me that we're not dating. I presume we're still not? Christmas kiss notwithstanding?'

'Everybody knows that Christmas kisses aren't taken seriously,' Ava protested, flushing at the memory of his mouth on hers and the way that she'd totally taken it seriously for the duration of the kiss.

77

He stared intently into her face as if trying to read the truth. His voice dropped, so that only she could hear. 'Even a kiss as hot as that?'

The glow in her cheeks increased but she answered lightly. 'You're being unreasonable. I've already explained why I've given up on men for now, so it would be hypocritical of me to let you buy me a meal.'

'Are you going to try women? Let me know if you need tips,' he countered. They rose and made for the till in unison.

She tried not to laugh at his expression of not-quite-joking frustration. 'No, I'm not going to try women. If I did, I wouldn't need tips. I am a woman.'

He opened his wallet. Ava, opening her purse, decided it was time to change tack. 'Anyway, are you suggesting that you paying would make it a date? That's a bit old fashioned. Even if it was a date I wouldn't—'

Sam gave in with an impatient wave of his hand. 'You've won, we're meticulously splitting the bill. There's absolutely no point in getting into date-paying etiquette with someone I'm not dating.'

Bills paid – separately – they said their goodbyes to Gaz and strode out into the December morning. A weak sun was thinking about painting colour onto the streets.

Sam halted her with a hand on her sleeve. 'In case you were wondering, if we were on a date, it wouldn't be here.'

Ava hesitated. She was almost surprised that he still seemed to be thinking about her in terms of dating. She felt a dart of regret that she hadn't simply said yes when she'd had the opportunity and that her unwillingness to let him buy her breakfast had somehow morphed into reinforcing their non-dating status. She'd been thinking about him a lot over the past week.

He was at least a hundred degrees of hot.

He wasn't a shit, like Harvey.

But the truth was . . . 'Unfortunately, if we went somewhere lovely on a date I'd have to let you pay the bill because I've made big fat nothing in the last two weeks. I'm not the kind of woman who likes that.' Also, she was going to have to ask him for a hefty deposit on his mother's hat to be able to count on any income in the next week, which made things awkward.

He paused in pushing his arms into his sleeves. And just looked at her.

Then she realised she must be staring at him as intently as he was staring at her and felt an idiot. In her bag, her phone began to ring.

As if it jolted him out of his reverie, Sam finished putting on his coat. 'Dating or otherwise, I don't see anything wrong with one person paying the bill if the other one's going through a hard financial time. You'd better answer your phone.' He lifted a hand in farewell and turned in the direction of the tube station. Then swung back, tilted Ava's chin, stooped and brushed his lips over hers. 'Thanks. About the hat.' His voice was gruff. Then he turned and strode across the road, leaving Ava alone except for a feeling on her lips as if he'd touched them with a sparkler.

Delving in her handbag, Ava halted, phone in hand, and groaned. The screen said *Harvey*. She hesitated. No! Yes? Her finger hovered.

She stabbed the green button before the call went to voicemail.

'I'm ringing to apologise.' Harvey sounded sheepish and subdued.

Ava watched Sam's shoulders and head progressing above the stream of traffic. A shiver flitted down her neck. 'Have you sobered up already?'

He avoided the question. 'I am really sorry. I shouldn't have sent those texts. I've deleted the images.'

Ava sighed. 'It's hard to know what to say.'

'Say we can try again. I know I've been out of order—'

Ava interrupted. 'It's the drink. You're a monster when you drink. It doesn't really matter what you say now, Harvey, because when you've got a few beers inside you you'll be a completely different man. In Blaggard's last weekend you threatened me and you were violent.'

A pause. 'I – I'll stop drinking,' he promised. 'If that's what it takes to get you back, I'll stop.'

'You should stop for you,' she said, as kindly as she could. 'That's the only logical reason. You're the person you're harming most.'

'I really have deleted all those images now. On my phone and my iPad and my laptop. Even in the cloud.'

'That's fantastic. Thank you.' She tried to feel relief. But relief didn't come. Harvey had become about as reliable as a 99p umbrella.

Those images could turn up anywhere.

As Sam strode towards the station, he glanced back and saw Ava still standing outside Gaz's Caff. Her coat was made of different flowered fabrics on a background of pale grey. She was completely motionless, like a pencil drawing in the weak light.

He felt like a dog that someone had been teasing. Uncertain, irritable, but still wanting to go back for more.

From his pocket, his phone sounded. For an instant he wondered whether it would be Ava. But *Mum* on the screen bounced fear into his chest. 'Are you OK?' he demanded the instant the call connected.

'Oh, yes.' Wendy sounded surprised that she might be

anything else, as if the months of bad news and hospitals hadn't happened. 'I just want to talk about the Christmas shopping trip.'

He had to stop and sit down on a seat in a bus stop as relief washed the strength from his legs. 'Of course – sorry, my mind was on something else. I'm coming to fetch you this afternoon, if you're absolutely certain that the doctor's OK with it.'

Wendy's voice was determinedly calm and bright. 'Yes, darling, we've already been through this. The doctor says I'm to carry on with as normal a life as I feel up to. The oncologist has agreed it will be OK not to start chemo until I've enjoyed Christmas, and that will let me recover a bit more from the op.'

'So how much do you feel up to?' He realised he was gripping the phone quite hard. He tried to unlock his muscles.

'I feel up to me and Vanessa coming to London on the train.' She sounded tentative, as if already hearing his objections.

'But it's already arranged for this afternoon. There's no need to come on the train when I have a perfectly good car.'

'And there's a perfectly good train, darling. There's no need for you to put yourself out. I like the train.' Her voice shifted pitch. 'I need to start doing things for myself.'

His hand gripped up on the phone again. *I want to put myself out. I want to do things for you! You're ill. You might even die. I've let you look after me every Christmas and your cancer's made me horribly aware that I've taken you for granted. I've never invited you to my place for Christmas Day or Christmas shopping before. You ought to have minded. It would have taken hardly any effort on my part.*

The unspoken cry crowded up into his throat and made his voice a suspicious growl. 'Has the doctor specifically OK'd you taking the train?'

'Yes! We'll put everything in a wheelie case and Van will pull it. I'll take lifts and escalators rather than stairs. The doctor said not the bus to the station so Vanessa's new boyfriend, Neale, has volunteered to take us.'

He cleared his throat. 'That's good of him. I'll meet you at Euston.'

'I'll be all right getting a cab with Vanessa—'

'Mum! Have a few days of being spoilt. I've got a nice surprise for you while you're here but I have to finish arranging it.' Because he'd let himself be distracted by arguing about the bill with Ava and then been caught standing gazing at her like a kid at a sweetie shop window, instead of arranging an actual appointment for Mum's hat fitting. Ava had looked at him as if he were acting like a twat. No wonder.

'Oh.' Wendy's voice gave a wobble of pleasure. 'A nice surprise will be lovely. There have been so many nasty ones lately.'

Chapter Eight

A hat, but no kid gloves

Tuesday 11 December
Sam had telephoned late on Sunday and arranged the hat fitting for Tuesday evening.

Cheered by selling a red glittery fascinator on Etsy, Ava made decorations for her studio from ribbon, cheap silver bells from a pound stall and ivy from the wall near the bus stop. The first Christmas cards had arrived so she tucked them in the top of the mirror, then heaved her bedroom chair into the studio for Sam to sit on while Ava worked with his mother.

Ava hadn't been able to shake the memory of Sam's bleak expression when he'd talked about his mum. It had certainly put her woes and worries into perspective. She'd gone home and phoned her own mother, sobered to think what it would feel like not to be able to hear Katherine's warm, no-nonsense voice.

Promptly at seven-thirty Sam arrived not only with his mother, Wendy, but also Wendy's sister, Sam's Aunt Vanessa.

'I'm so looking forward to this!' exclaimed Wendy

breathlessly. She looked as if the evening breeze could blow her away and not as if she could possibly have anything to do with creating someone Sam-sized. Next to him she looked like a child, her glasses too large for her face.

'I hope you don't mind me coming along.' Vanessa shook Ava's hand energetically, very much the bigger, healthier, more vibrant and outgoing sister. Both her short stylish cut and Wendy's shoulder-length bob glinted with the same tawny highlights as were in Sam's hair.

'The more the merrier.' Ava led the way upstairs slowly, reminded by Wendy's careful movements that this woman was recovering from surgery.

Wendy stared around the studio in excitement. 'Ohhhh . . . lovely hats.'

'Have a look around. I'll get another chair.' Leaving Wendy time to get her breath back, Ava turned and ran back down the stairs.

She didn't realise that Sam had followed her down to the kitchen until he reached around to take one of the folding chairs from her.

He'd gone for a monochrome look this evening – black trousers, white silk shirt and a black leather jacket. 'I just want to give you a heads up that she's emotional at the moment.' He looked haunted. 'She burst into tears when I told her why we were coming so . . .'

'So you've chosen exactly the right gift,' Ava finished for him gently. 'I'll give her plenty of time to enjoy the fitting.'

'Thanks,' he said, gruffly.

Back upstairs, Ava sat down with Wendy. 'Are you enjoying staying with Sam?'

Wendy's face lit up. 'It's wonderful,' she breathed. 'But London's a bit overwhelming. So many people. Sam's lived

84

in London since university and Vanessa comes on business, but I usually stay at home and let Sam visit me.'

'Where's home?'

'Middledip. It's a village in Cambridgeshire with stone cottages and a village green.' Wendy giggled, her glasses catching the light. 'I've no idea when I'll wear a posh hat unless someone in the village gets married. My only hat's a woolly one for walking the dogs.' She gazed at Ava's hat display with an expression of awe. 'These look as if they deserve an invitation to a Buckingham Palace garden party at least.'

Ava paused. 'If you want another woolly hat you've come to the wrong person. Don't let Sam push you into this if you hate the idea.'

Behind her, conversation between Sam and Vanessa halted abruptly. Ava kept her gaze pinned on Wendy.

But Wendy's eyes were shining. 'Oh no, I want a lovely hat. I'm just not sure . . . I've never had a dress made for me, much less a gorgeous, frivolous hat. I feel a bit weird about it.'

'Let's see if we can make it fun instead.' Ava set the mirror in front of Wendy, then began to talk about different hat shapes: the elegance of a beret, the dash of a fedora. Taking her time, she displayed various materials, describing them as 'fine' or 'rich' and 'jewel colours' or 'pastels'. She showed her the versatile material that was sinamay, woven from fibre from the abaca palm of the Philippines. 'Sinamay has a bias, so it's flexible and versatile,' she said. 'I use three layers if I block it for a hat, but in smaller quantities for curvy three-dimensional shapes like spirals and bows.'

'You're so clever.' Wendy began to visibly relax as she stroked the fabrics or crumpled them in her hands.

Ava began to place hats on Wendy's head. 'This is a pillbox, a classic and enduring style. It's deceptively simple with its brimless, flat-crown shape, but so versatile, tipped to one side, forward, back or set squarely on your head. Its mood's determined by how plain or decorated it is. Black and stark, like this, or' – a change to a pillbox hat in lemon –'a softer colour like this.' Another change. 'Or maybe a picture hat, if you want something more fun? Lots of people love wide-brimmed hats.' She changed the hat again, this time for a burnt-orange disc with a spiral of stiffened sinamay and a fall of black netting. 'This is a contemporary cocktail hat; very fun and flirty.'

Wendy sighed happily. 'I love them all.'

Ava prepared to move into sensitive territory. Every milliner came across clients facing chemotherapy hair loss and was used to exercising tact about comb fixings and scratchy materials. 'I'm wondering about a nice soft felt. Maybe a cloche? A twenties style would be dashing but would perfectly suit your face.'

Wendy proved in no need of kid gloves, though. 'It's important that it fits me when my hair's fallen out. I'm having chemo soon.'

Ava glanced at Sam. His face had gone very still. 'I can use an elastic head fitting so the hat will fit with or without hair.' She picked up a pretty cloche from her samples and turned it over to show Wendy inside its bell shape. 'This is the head fitting, the band that runs around the inside of the hat. I can use silk for the lining so that it's soft against your scalp.'

'Let me put my hair up so I can get an idea of how it looks without.'

Throat tightening, Ava carefully held Wendy's upswept

hair in place and slipped the hat over, adjusting it delicately until the brim came just above Wendy's eyes.

Wendy tilted her head and studied her reflection. 'Nobody would really know whether I had hair or not, would they?'

'No, and it looks very good without hair showing. In fact, the Eton Crop often went hand-in-hand with the cloche – or head-in-hat,' Ava agreed huskily. 'It's the perfect style for you. Not so large as to overwhelm your face but stylish enough to have presence. If you're sure about the shape, shall we talk about colours?'

After much poring over charts and decorative materials and Ava making sketch after sketch, Wendy settled for elegant jade wool felt with gold ribbon loops and a geometric spray of trimmed peacock feathers.

As Ava measured Wendy's head, just above her eyebrows and ears, Izz came home, appearing in the doorway with her coat unbuttoned and a bottle of wine in each hand. 'Anyone care to join me?' Her gaze flicked to Sam with a mixture of hope and apprehension. Ava hadn't said anything about Sam helping put Izz to bed on Saturday, and Izz appeared to have forgotten. Or had chosen to forget.

'Lovely!' chorused Wendy and Vanessa.

'We've finished, so would you like to go downstairs where you'll be more comfortable?' Ava didn't want wine all over her hats. 'I'll follow you down when I've made a few notes.'

Picking up her pad and pen, she listened to their voices fading down the stairs. Then, feeling the presence of another person, she looked up.

Sam was watching her. 'Thanks,' he murmured.

Ava laid down her pen. 'Your mother's lovely.'

He moved closer. 'She's also a frightened woman trying to be brave. You brought some fun into facing the future and she'll look fantastic in your hat.'

Ava's throat ached with tears. 'We should have talked about the subject of hair loss before I brought it up in front of you all. I didn't think.'

'You handled it beautifully. Whatever your fee, it's worth it. You've made her happy.'

'I wish I could grandly waive the fee—'

'Don't even think about it.' His laugh was shaky. 'I'd have to scour my brain to think of something else to buy her for Christmas and it couldn't be a tenth so good. Can you tell me the cost now or do you need time to do the sums?'

'I can tell you in a few minutes. Wendy didn't ask for anything hard to source.' He sat back down and she returned to her notes, consulting online catalogues for material costs, estimating her hours. It didn't take long to come to the total.

Sam didn't blink at it. 'Would it be helpful if I paid the whole sum up front?'

'It would.' Though appreciating his sensitivity to her precarious finances, honesty compelled her to add, 'But most people usually just pay one-third as a deposit.'

He waved that information aside. 'Give me your bank account details and I'll pay electronically later tonight.'

Ava managed not to jump up and hug him in gratitude. 'Thank you.' She wrote out the necessary strings of numbers just as Izz reappeared at the door.

'I've brought Vanessa back up because she wants to ask Ava something.'

'Thanks again, Ava. I'll go see if there's any wine left.' Sam stood back to allow Izz to precede him from the room. Izz looked flustered.

'Could I buy one of these fascinators?' Vanessa patted at her hair self-consciously. 'I have a Christmas ball shortly and I wouldn't mind impressing my date. There's no time for you to make me one from scratch and my dress is black so you don't have to match to anything.'

Hardly daring to believe her luck at a second sale falling into her lap in one evening, Ava scooted off the stool and beckoned Vanessa to take her place. 'What about embellishments? If the dress has sequins or something it can be fun to echo those.' In twenty minutes she'd sold Vanessa a flirty black and white beaded fascinator with black roses and curled coque feathers, one of the most expensive amongst her samples.

As she wrapped it carefully in tissue paper and boxed it she thanked the Jermyns from the bottom of her bank account.

When Sam, Wendy and Vanessa left, Wendy looked tired but was still able to give Ava an excited hug.

Feeling warmed by the events of the evening, after she'd closed the door behind them, Ava plonked herself down in the sitting room with Izz, laptop at the ready to finalise her list of materials for Wendy's hat.

But Izz wanted to chat. 'Sam talked to me tonight. He said I was doing a good job at Jermyn's.' She smiled uncertainly. 'I don't know if he likes me a bit now. What do you think?'

'I think he wouldn't say something and not mean it.' Ava tried not to feel anything, knowing that if Izz ever did succeed in snaring Sam then Ava would have to try not to feel a whole lot more. Ava had instigated a man embargo for good reasons and wasn't about to bring up her own feelings for Sam. Partly because she didn't know what they were and partly because it was definitely in the best-friends' code that you tried hard not to like a man your best friend liked, even if – or, maybe, especially because? – he was her boss and unlikely to see a workplace relationship as appropriate.

Izz began to flick through the channels for music documentaries. Ava helped herself to wine just as her phone signalled the arrival of a message.

Harvey: *How about dinner on Friday evening? Grovelling apologies for being difficult recently. It's just you're doing my head in. We were good together.*

Ava's answer was brief. *Not dating at the moment. All my attention on business matters.*

Not dating anyone? Or me?

Anyone.

Hard to believe.

Ava restrained herself from returning *Go to hell!*, and turned her phone onto 'do not disturb'. She opened her laptop but instead of running comparisons on the price of peacock feathers and silk lining she typed 'revenge porn' into Google and clicked on the site highest in the rankings.

Revenge porn is the sharing of intimate images of someone without their consent, often by an ex-partner, hence the word 'revenge'.

She skipped down the page. *Disclosing private sexual images to cause distress was made an offence in February 2015. It carries a maximum jail sentence of two years plus a fine. There are both men and women currently serving prison terms thanks to this law.* That was fantastic . . . but didn't help if the images hadn't actually been shared.

She found something that seemed more relevant. *'Sextortion' is a term used when someone, often an ex-partner, threatens to release sexual images as a form of blackmail. Unfortunately, technology can leave the victim open to ridicule while keeping the bully anonymous. Past innocent play becomes a terrible weapon and providing proof that threats have been made can be difficult.* Bingo.

Izz looked away from the television as a tinselly advert came on. 'Are you on Facebook?'

'No. I'm worried about Harvey being a dick with those photos. I'm trying to find out if there's any way of stopping him. He says he's deleted them but it's hard to believe a word he says.'

Izz didn't glance back at the television screen, even though Hugo Boss Christmas Man came on. She looked close to tears. 'I hate how horrible Harvey's being to you. He's making threats. Get the police. Your dad was a senior cop.'

Ava rubbed suddenly sweaty temples. 'That's one of the reasons I'm trying to avoid it. The idea of him somehow finding out makes me squirm. Or can you imagine me telling him? "Dad, Harvey has images of me naked giving him a . . ."' She let the thought trail.

'Oh.'

Ava returned to her reading. *Although revenge porn is sometimes used against men, in ninety-five per cent of cases the victim is female and the revenge porn is intended to bully, humiliate or control. Typically, victims are scared, embarrassed and emotionally devastated. They perceive the threat as real whereas perpetrators frequently see this digital crime as a prank, however juvenile and obnoxious.*

That resonated.

Victims report being told they should never have allowed the photographs to be taken and fear they'll be blamed, or dismissed, under the stereotype that women overreact to problems and are overly sensitive complainers.

Finally came the positives. *A government campaign has been mounted to advise the public of the facts about revenge porn, with its own helpline. The hashtag #NoToRevengePorn has been introduced to encourage awareness in social media.* With a heavy heart, she bookmarked the article in case the day came when Harvey carried out his threats and shared the images on social media.

But then, with growing dismay, she read of sites that made Facebook and Twitter look the soft option, sites that existed purely to exhibit revenge porn – making a handy income out of advertising owing to plentiful traffic on their site. She glared at a headline pointing out that these sites were *not concerned with making friends of women.* Advocacy groups actually existed to protect the rights of the posters to post whatever they wished, however it was obtained, no matter whose life was being ruined. *The proponents of such groups demonstrate an impulse to favour the democratic values of some at the expense of those of others. The right to privacy of the victims is not seen as an issue.*

The internet can be untamed, lawless and with undefined frontiers. It often lacks accountability or clear areas of jurisdiction, so the introduction of the new law is a welcome step in the right direction. We may even see fewer reports such as this from a revenge-porn victim:

'Perhaps it's understandable, but the police pay more attention to exes wielding axes than wielding explicit images.'

By the time she'd read to the end, gloom perched on Ava's shoulder.

Izz's voice swam into her haze of misery. 'Harvey's such a shit.'

Ava blinked away a sudden tear. 'No argument from me.'

Chapter Nine

Seeing, not 'seeing'

Wednesday 12 December
It hadn't been a great day. In view of time constraints, Ava had visited her favourite millinery suppliers in Victoria rather than waiting for the materials for Wendy's hat to be delivered. Frustratingly, they'd proved to be out of stock of peacock feathers. Ava's second-favourite supplier was in Spitalfields, so she'd ridden east on the District Line.

At intervals during her day, texts from Harvey had buzzed into her phone.

I think you're dating that bloke I saw you with in Blaggard's.

I'm giving drinking a rest.

If you're not dating anyone, why not start seeing me again?

Ava finally answered: *Repeat: I'm not dating anyone, INCLUDING you.*

By the time she had her peacock feathers, carefully protected in a cardboard tube, it was past five and she was dying for the loo. Jermyn's was only a couple of streets away and she hurried towards it, texting Izz as she went.

Are you at the agency? Can I come and use the ladies? Bursting.

No reply. She turned into Fashion Street, texting the same message to Tod.

No reply. Left onto Brick Lane, hurrying along the narrow pavements past restaurants, shops and graffiti. Past the glittering edifice of the mosque and within sight of the Old Truman Brewery, she saw the door to the building that housed Jermyn's. With no time to spare for the bell marked *Jermyn's – communications agency* to be answered, she brushed past someone on their way out with a hasty, 'Thanks! I'm meeting Tod and Izz,' and raced up to the first floor. Catapulting into Jermyn's reception area she almost ran into Wendy and Vanessa.

Wendy beamed. 'Ava! Oh.' She halted. Her smile broadened. 'Are you here to meet Sam?'

'Actually—'

At that moment, Sam strode up the corridor. He stopped short when he saw Ava. Before he could speak, Wendy got in, 'We didn't realise you had plans with Ava. We can easily get a cab back and look after ourselves.'

Sam looked uncomfortable. 'Not necessary.'

Ava glanced from one to the other. She wasn't sure why Wendy would think she was lying in wait for Sam but Sam could clear it up while she took care of urgent business. 'Sorry,' she interrupted breathlessly. 'But please may I use your ladies' room? Like *now*?'

'Of course.' Sam turned back the way he'd come with Ava dancing impatiently in his wake. He turned a corner into another corridor. 'Second on the left.'

'Thanks.' She abandoned her purchases at the side of the corridor and sprinted past him, clattering through the doors and into a stall with a 'Hoo-ee!' of relief.

When she had washed her hands and smoothed her hair, she found Sam leaning against the wall of the corridor outside. His suit just the charcoal side of black and shirt crisp white, he reminded her of the Hugo Boss Christmas man. But better. 'You didn't need to wait.' She swooped up her packages. 'Sorry to barge in but I was desperate and neither Izz nor Tod answered my texts.'

'Izz left before five today so she may already be down in the underground. Tod's with a client.' He cleared his throat, shoving his hands into his pockets. 'I sort of need a favour.'

'From me? What?' She peered into the cardboard tube to check that her precious feathers hadn't suffered from being dumped on the floor.

'It's going to sound so lame.'

Intrigued by the strangled doom in his voice, she switched her attention to the colour that had risen up to emphasise his cheekbones. 'What is?'

He inhaled loudly. 'Mum assumed that you were here to meet me.'

'But you can explain that my friends work here and I wanted to use the loo.'

'I could.' His gaze slid away and then returned to her. 'But she's sitting out there in reception, hoping that you'll come home to dinner with us. Expecting me to be persuading you, in fact.'

Ava puzzled over his obvious discomfiture. 'Why?'

'You're not making this easy.'

Putting her bags back down, she folded her arms. 'Tell me what "this" is and I might. Are you embarrassed that they've asked?'

His brown-gold gaze levelled. 'Yes, I'm embarrassed. They've asked because they think we're seeing each other.'

Sam forced himself to keep meeting Ava's gaze, willing her to 'get it'. In vain, it seemed, judging from her wide-eyed bafflement.

'Why would they think that?'

His shirt collar would choke him if his awkwardness index went any higher. 'Because I told Mum we're seeing each other.'

Bemused brows quirked. 'Why?'

Now he had to look away, as he struggled to explain. 'Mum's situation has made her emotional. This morning she was crying and trying to hide it. You appreciate,' he paused and swallowed, 'that there's a chance she won't be here to see another Christmas. A one-in-ten chance, if you want the stat. A three-in-ten chance she won't see Christmas in five years. I appreciate that the odds are on her side but it's still a shitty deal and she has months of chemotherapy coming up.' He stole a glance in Ava's direction. He wished she wouldn't do the wide-eyed thing. For some reason it struck him as incredibly alluring and now was not the time for that feeling. 'I brought up the subject of her Christmas hat as a distraction. I said something about seeing you several times lately. In stereotypically maternal fashion, she seized on the mere whiff of me "seeing" someone, although I didn't initially realise I'd made it sound like "seeing" as in . . .'

'"Seeing",' she supplied helpfully, nodding, as if completely seeing the 'seeing' thing.

He ploughed on. 'It distracted her from her cancer worries. It made her smile and even laugh and joke. That's something I can't buy. So now she and Aunt Van are hoping that you, the woman I'm "seeing", will join us, and I'm hoping you'll be my faux date for this evening. I'll truly be in your debt and as seeing each other is a vague term and we have been in the same place at the same time a couple of times, it really doesn't involve lying. As such. And,' he added, 'I promise that this is not some creepy plan B I've come up with because you turned me down for a proper date.'

He waited.

She regarded him thoughtfully for several seconds. 'OK,' she said.

His stomach gave a somersault of surprise that it had been that easy. 'OK?'

'OK. If you honestly think that something that simple will cheer your mum up and she won't expect us to get married on Christmas Eve or anything.' Then she grinned. 'It's been quite fun watching you squirm.'

He smiled faintly. 'I admire your ability to hit on the positives of the situation.'

'If I'm your faux date, you can carry my bags. And, obviously, be nice to me at all times.' She thrust the bags into his hands and skipped off down the corridor.

He followed, sighing. 'Might be a challenge.' Since Tod had first brought Ava out from behind his back at Blaggard's, Sam's occasional irritation with her had jock-eyed uneasily with his almost constant wish to have sex with her. He wasn't sure that combination came under the heading of 'nice'.

Chapter Ten

Faux dating

In the cab on the way to Stratford, Sam's mother and aunt chattered enthusiastically about their afternoon 'shopping', which had involved admiring the Christmas lights strung across Oxford Street and drinking hot chocolate topped with marshmallows in Selfridges. Wendy looked tired and pale but the smile seldom left her face.

Sitting on one of the jump seats, Sam was able to watch Ava under the guise of politely following the conversation. Her hair was loose today and tumbled by the winter wind. It was the only the second time he'd seen it falling free over her shoulders, and he liked it. It softened her. Made her look more carefree. The more he looked, the more he liked.

When the cab dropped them at the modern elegant block of flats that his days handling PR for Chilly had allowed him to live in, Sam led the way through the security door.

Ava gazed around the lobby approvingly as they waited for the mirrored elevator. 'I love this building. Glass and class. Function and design. Awesome.'

After gliding up twenty floors, he unlocked the door to the flat, saying to Wendy and Vanessa, 'I'll leave you to entertain Ava while I change.' He deposited Ava's bags beside the sofa.

Ava sent him a look that said 'don't be too long' and he smiled a reassuring 'don't worry'. Then he went to his room, worrying. Had he absolutely and completely lost his mind? Why the hell had he entered a relationship charade? It might make a good plot for a chick flick but now he'd put himself in A Situation.

Mostly that situation would mean being around Ava, which, as he'd already discovered, could be a frustrating experience.

Then he thought of his mother's expression that morning when she'd murmured, 'Oh Sam. I didn't realise that you're seeing each other,' and pleasure had replaced the mixture of fear, worry, stoicism and determination that had lurked in her expression since the diagnosis of ovarian cancer.

With nightmarish clarity, his imagination replayed a scene from more than two months ago, when he'd sat beside Wendy in a cream-painted office and Doctor Russell had turned her sympathetic eyes on them and said, 'It's not good news I'm afraid.' Clutching each other's hands, unsure of who was comforting whom, Sam and Wendy had listened to Doctor Russell murmur gently about the trickiness of ovarian cancer, how positive it was that it had been caught so early, at stage I, but that effective treatment would include surgery and chemotherapy – to begin sooner rather than later.

The anatomical diagrams and models scattered around the room had seemed to whirl in reds and blues on the periphery of Sam's vision and Wendy's hands had begun to tremble in a way that almost brought him to tears.

So when he'd seen real happiness in Wendy's smile this morning, his heart had tipped on its side, turning common sense's face to the wall, and all Sam had wanted was to keep that light in her expression by any means possible.

And it didn't seem as if the charade was playing with Ava's emotions, because she appeared to have her heart well under control.

He was beginning to realise that it was his that was in danger.

Ava paced along the floor-to-ceiling glass wall, staring out at Stratford station, the Olympic Stadium and, in the middle distance, the City of London, spread out like a black carpet bejewelled in many colours, awed that this apartment was apparently within Sam's financial reach. It wasn't huge but its uncluttered open plan made it feel spacious. Reluctantly giving the balcony a miss in view of the rain currently hurling itself across the rooftops, she turned back into the room, where Wendy and Vanessa had settled themselves expectantly on the chaise sofa.

Casting around quickly for a conversation that wouldn't involve her supposed relationship with Sam, she smiled brightly. 'I've bought the materials for your hat, Wendy. I'll show you.'

As she emptied the rustling carrier bags, Wendy and Vanessa were satisfactorily impressed with the felt cone that was going to magically be transformed into a gorgeous hat – with just the addition of steam, stiffener, embellishments and Ava.

'Gosh, you're so clever. I wouldn't know where to begin. I just do a bit of sewing and embroidery.' Wendy brushed the peacock feathers across her cheeks.

'I did train for quite a long time. I have to be able to

sew, but there are other skills involved and I love the excitement of working in three dimensions. Do you remember seeing all those wooden blocks at my place? By the time I've wafted the cone around in the steam and stretched it over the correct block, your hat will be in the early stages of creation.'

Wendy returned the peacock feathers reluctantly. 'I suppose that Sam's going to make me wait until Christmas Day to have my hat.'

'I'm going to need most of that time, anyway.' Ava displayed the hat's lining material, tipping it to the light so that it shone with the dull iridescence of an exotic insect. 'I have to block twice, and what with drying time, the lining and the decoration, it takes a while. I'd usually allow myself longer but I'm not madly busy right now.' Understatement.

Wendy sat back and curled her feet underneath herself. She dropped her voice to a conspiratorial whisper. 'I'm so glad Sam's seeing someone again.'

Vanessa twinkled. 'Don't make her blush, Wendy.'

'I'm not blushing.' Ava instantly felt the curse of the fair-skinned scald her cheeks. She stowed the bags between the sofa and a chair so that they couldn't be inadvertently stepped upon, giving herself time to formulate a suitably vague reply. '"Seeing" can mean almost anything, can't it? We haven't known each other long and only met because my friends work at Jermyn's.'

Wendy didn't bother to hide her smiles. 'But I've seen how he looks at you . . . I'm just pleased. I began to think he'd never quite get over Mariah. He was really bowled over by her. They were an item for a while.'

Ava smiled politely. 'Mariah?'

'Wendy,' Vanessa warned. 'Sam probably never gives her

a thought.' She jumped up. 'Let's put the kettle on. Do you know Sam's plans for dinner, Wendy? I could get started.'

Preparing dinner proved a group activity as Sam's sitting room and kitchen were separated only by a black granite dining counter, its shape reminding Ava of a speech bubble in one of Tod's comic books.

Wendy spent most of the time seated on a leather and chrome bar stool on the sitting-room side while Sam and Vanessa created enticing smells with lamb steaks, rosemary and onions. Ava made coffee, laid out the cutlery, and then sat with Wendy.

She was struck by the easy family rapport. Sam and Vanessa didn't trip over each other in the kitchen as the lamb browned. Sam teased Wendy and Vanessa gently. Wendy and Vanessa teased him less gently in return.

Ava had time to return to her study of Sam's home. It was decorated in monochrome colours with occasional accents of muted blue and green. In the kitchen, a black range oven gleamed and the counters were the same black granite as the dining section. It managed to be somehow functional, casual and beautiful. The lounge furniture was eclectic, grouped together like old friends. There were no plants, few ornaments, but the plain carpet was luxuriously thick and a rug in rich ocean shades was even thicker.

Trying not to sigh over how long it would be before she could finance a home of her own, let alone one as fantastic as this, Ava was careful not to ask Sam how long he'd owned the flat, or whether he'd used a designer, in case they might be expected to have already covered that kind of basic getting-to-know-you stuff.

In the event, Wendy and Vanessa made most of the conversation during dinner asking Ava question after question about her business. As it seemed a nice safe topic Ava was perfectly happy to explain how she'd arrived at where she was. 'A designer called Ceri Mallory had seen my work at my degree show and liked it. Her creations were mainly for occasions like weddings and posh parties and so I fitted in well. I interned with her, then she gave me a job as her junior milliner and helped me hone my design skills. It was good experience but I wasn't paid much and she let me believe that one day I'd be taken on as a junior partner, which didn't happen.' She made light of what had been a catastrophe at the time. 'Also, she gave me the jobs she didn't like, like demonstrating millinery techniques at her preview evenings. She preferred to loll around chatting about her current samples to the ladies of Kensington and Chelsea over wine and nibbles, subtly selling all the time. Fair enough, though; she knew her clientele and I quite liked doing demonstrations.'

She halted.

Vanessa was staring at her, fork poised. 'You'd be perfect,' she breathed. 'It's my regional Rotary Christmas Ball on Saturday and the speaker has had to cancel because of illness. Would you do it instead?'

Ava tried not to choke on her wine. 'I'm not sure—'

'It's a £300 fee plus expenses.'

'Oh.' Ava had been about to say that a little demo of blocking in front of a dozen targeted clients was a bit different to talking to a big room full of glammed-up people. But the £300 caught her attention. 'Where's the venue?'

'In Port Manor, just outside of our village, Middledip. Very nice. I'll be there with my boyfriend, Neale, and Wendy. You can stay over with us, if you want. Sam can drive you.'

'But—' Ava glanced at Sam, expecting him to say that he had plans. But she found him looking thoughtful instead.

In fact, he was nodding. 'It could be good for picking up business. Lots of the female guests would be in your target market, Ava. You could take a stack of business cards and some of your samples. A hat display would be OK, Van, wouldn't it?'

Vanessa looked hopeful. 'Perfect. A display, a demonstration, a fashion show – anything you want. People just like to be entertained for about forty minutes after dinner. So can I put you down for it? You'd be doing me a huge favour and if it would be good for business, as Sam says . . .'

Ava felt a small buzz of incredulous excitement that something else good might be happening. She glanced at Sam. 'But it sounds like I'd be trespassing on your good nature.'

He grinned. 'It's as good an excuse as any to have dinner with you.'

'As if you need an excuse!' laughed Wendy. 'It'll be great for me, too, because I'm seeing a lovely lot of Sam at the moment but there's no such thing as too much.'

The conversation missed a beat, as if everyone paused to wonder how much more of anyone Wendy would see in the future. Ava saw pain flit across Sam's features. 'Any time, Mum,' he managed.

Another beat.

Wendy kept up her smile as if it were her shield against the world. 'I'm going to do a charity thing at the ball, raising money for ovarian cancer awareness and my women's support group.'

Ava didn't feel there was much she could say about the

spectre of ovarian cancer but she couldn't help feeling curiosity over sweet little Wendy's involvement with women's support. 'You've got a group?'

Wendy dropped her gaze to her plate. She hadn't eaten much of what was on it. 'I'm no firebrand, but I get angry about women who find themselves in a bad place through no fault of their own. I sort of helped set the No Blame or Shame group up. Now there are proper professional counsellors, a helpline and message boards. Most of the people who come to us are women who've been attacked or threatened, but sometimes it's one of their family members who needs support.'

Ava gazed at Wendy with new respect. It was odd to think the slight and self-effacing woman dealt with such painful reality. 'Good on you. If I get any commissions at the Rotary Ball I'll donate five per cent to your fund.' Commissions were more than she dared hope for but if by any miracle she got one she could spare a small portion of her good fortune for a cause for which she presently felt particular sympathy.

Wendy beamed. 'I hope that you get lots of commissions, then. The Rotarians can be generous.'

'What's the event? Do I need to buy raffle tickets or something?' Ava could just about manage that.

Wendy's gaze dropped to the remains of her meal again. 'Not a raffle. More of a collection on the evening. I'll sort of rally people.' She brightened again. 'If you stay over with us, you can come to our village Christmas Fayre on Sunday afternoon.'

'I'm not sure how that would fit in with my weekend. Or Sam's.' Ava could feel alarm writing itself over her features.

Luckily, Sam came to her rescue. 'Maybe we could decide

that on the night of the ball, Mum? Between then and now Ava may wish to make other plans.'

'OK. But the village is lovely at Christmas, so do come if you can.' Wendy let the subject drop.

An hour later, when she declared herself tired and ready to go to bed to read, Ava took it as her cue to gather up her things.

Sam rose. 'I'll drive you home.'

'You don't need to—'

'Oh let him,' put in Wendy quickly. 'Then we'll all know that you got home safely, won't we?'

In view of the earlier discussion, Ava felt she had no choice but to humour Wendy, who perhaps viewed London as a cauldron of sin in which no woman should be alone after dark. 'I suppose it'll save me quite a tube journey.' It was obviously OK for a date to see you home, even if it was clear across London, so it would look odd for her to argue the point.

Soon she was seated in Sam's red BMW, which lived in a garage beneath his apartment block.

'Why am I even surprised that you drive a BMW?' She admired the all-black interior. 'It's such a yuppy-mobile.'

'"Yuppy" is an outmoded term.' He twisted to check over his shoulder as he backed his status symbol out of its parking bay. 'None of the hipsters are saying it.'

She laughed. 'I guess you publicity types are attuned to what the hipsters say.'

'Live and die by it,' he agreed gravely, exiting the under-ground car park. 'If the hipsters are shaving their beards and eating beetroot crisps this Christmas then nothing else will do for me.'

Ava enjoyed being driven through London at night. The traffic generally flowed better than in the daytime and even a Christmas curmudgeon could appreciate the twinkling lights across every major thoroughfare.

Sam changed gear at a junction and glanced both ways before swinging out. 'Thanks for the faux date.'

'It made me feel better about the help you've given me.'

He raised an eyebrow at her before returning his attention to the road, the wash from coloured lights flickering across his skin. 'Oh-kay. That wasn't what I was expecting. I don't seem to have done much.'

She shrugged. 'Seeing I got home after Harvey turned scary. Helping with Tod and Izz. Commissioning your mum's hat, which led to Vanessa buying a fascinator and, tonight, her offering me the speaker's fee for her Rotary Ball.'

They moved onto the Mile End Road under an impressive display of illuminated snowflakes. 'I'm glad it's made a difference.'

'Anything makes a difference. At the moment I'll count it a success if I avoid debt or hitting up my parents.' She smothered a yawn. Faux dates weren't so bad if you got driven home past all the scurrying pedestrians huddling into their coats. She settled snugly into her seat. If she were ever rich, she was going to employ a chauffeur.

'If I can help—'

'You're not going to offer to lend me money, are you?' She closed her eyes and mentally corrected her earlier thought to employing a chauffeur who didn't speak. 'You probably weren't even thinking of it but just to let you know that my pride will only take so much.'

His laugh was little more than a breath. 'You're right, stupid idea, bearing in mind your outrage at the mere suggestion of me standing you scrambled eggs and a mug of coffee when you're skint and I'm not.'

Opening her eyes, she turned to search his profile. 'Try and understand. I find it more comfortable if I share bills rather than accepting largesse, however kindly meant, because I have a compulsion to reciprocate and then the spend isn't under my control.'

After a moment, he shrugged. 'OK. I'll concede the point, if buying you breakfast was interpreted as beckoning you into debt.'

The traffic got going and he gave it his attention. When they finally turned into School Road, Sam had to drive past 146B before he found a parking space. He removed the key from the ignition. 'I'll walk you to your door.'

Ava gathered her bags. 'No need.'

He glanced around. It was quite dark here in a residential street where street lamps and festive lights were fairly small scale. Instead of arguing, he posed a question. 'Is it OK to talk about the situation regarding your ex?'

With Harvey put in her mind Ava found herself glancing around, too. Then she realised what he'd done. 'That was a bit mean,' she protested, unable now to take her eyes off the shadows.

He sat back. 'You're right. I've no business making you frightened of coming home to your own street. It's just . . .' His face was more than half in shadow. He fell silent for several seconds. Then sighed. 'I'm going to tell you something so you can see where I'm coming from and why I am as I am. I don't usually tell people this.'

He paused. His voice was husky when he spoke again. 'I'm a product of rape.'

Chapter Eleven

No blame or shame

Ava had no idea what to say.

'Not a random violent attack,' he carried on. His voice was even, but strained. 'It was what would now be called date rape. Mum was young and naïve and went to a party. Alcohol was the least of the evils circulating. Some bloke chatted her up, gave her a drink, probably with something in it, and as the party began to wind down she found herself alone in a room with him. She can remember feeling giddy and him laughing a lot. He refused to take "no" for an answer and I was conceived.'

Ava had to make herself breathe as shock shimmered through her. 'Oh no,' she whispered. 'What's wrong with some people?'

His laugh was bitter. 'Lots.'

'Your poor mum. Poor you.'

He shook his head. 'Apart from not having a father – I don't count the shit who forced my mother – I've had it easy. Mum and Aunt Van have given me everything and we've been a family unit, if an unusual one. My grandparents weren't happy when Mum, who has a lot of backbone under her gentle exterior, wouldn't have an abortion, so she left. Aunt Van went with, pursuing her career and supporting Mum and me along with herself.'

'Did you never meet . . . Don't you know who he was?' she ventured.

A single shake of his head. 'It was one of those party things. Nobody seemed to know who he was. I suppose he gatecrashed. But knowing where I came from has made me aware of the damage the less moral of my sex can cause. I hate drugs. I'm moderate so far as alcohol's concerned. Patrick sometimes calls me his "straight-edged friend" but I'm no paragon. I'm just mindful of what I owe my existence to and wish I'd come into the world via love or affection.

'But you can understand Mum being involved in No Blame or Shame. Occasionally she even turns scary and crusades.' He gave a twisted smile. 'On No Blame or Shame's website you'll see common reasons for not reporting attacks or abuse or harassment and Mum ticks every box. Her parents wouldn't be sympathetic to her going to a party full of people she didn't know and getting drunk, so she didn't tell them what had happened until she realised she was pregnant. Then, of course, they thought she was making up a story to excuse what they termed "misbehaviour". They blamed her and they made her ashamed. Society's more enlightened now but the principle of blame and shame causing damage holds good.'

Ava groped for his hand in the darkness of the rapidly cooling interior of the car. 'Your mother and Vanessa obviously adore you.'

'I know, and I don't want you to think that I drag some enormous burden around with me. I don't feel

111

guilty. I don't blame my mother. I'm a pretty balanced person. It's just that my family history gives me a slightly different view of certain situations to most people.' His smile was bleak. 'One reason I'm telling you is to flag up that whatever the scenario is between you and your ex, there are people you can talk to, people who can help with support and information. People who understand.'

Support. Understanding. The exact things she craved. She opened her mouth, words rising up to breach the dam on her desperate anxieties about Harvey.

But Sam hadn't finished. 'And so you understand what makes me do things like check you got home from Blaggard's OK. It's not in me to turn my back if I feel a woman's in a bad situation, like my mother was.'

A horrible thought brought Ava up short and she closed her mouth again without speaking. She wasn't a young girl who'd been pushed further than she wanted to go at a party, or one of those poor women who was attacked as they walked innocently home. Ava had given Harvey a private strip show and giggled as he'd taken photos, giggled harder as those photos became ever more explicit and action-packed.

No blame or shame? She *could* be blamed. She was certainly ashamed, and guiltily aware that Sam probably assumed Harvey was the bad guy.

Slowly, she disengaged her hand from his. 'You're a good man.' She pretended to yawn. 'Time I went in. I've a hat to begin tomorrow.'

Sam climbed out of the car and walked her to the door of the little yellow house. Ava didn't protest that it wasn't necessary.

Maybe it was necessary to Sam.

A psychiatrist would probably say that he was indulging an impossible desire to have been there to protect his mother. He'd certainly overdeveloped his sense of responsibility, but it didn't hurt Ava to let him satisfy his urge to protect. In fact her heart was touched.

Sam hunched into his jacket as she paused on the doorstep to search for her keys. 'To change the subject to less weighty matters, have you realised that you've actually accepted a date with me to the Rotary Ball?' The teasing note she was used to was back in his voice.

Ava followed his lead. 'A faux date,' she corrected.

He laughed, dropping a kiss on her cheek. 'Faux or not, you're going to have to save all the slow dances for me or face the combined wrath of Mum and Aunt Van.' He winked and turned back up the street towards his car. 'Don't feel pressured to stay over for the Middledip Christmas Fayre, by the way, but you might want to consider having your overnight things with you just in case you'd rather stay at Mum's. It'll be about two-and-a-half hours each way.'

'That far? I hadn't realised . . .' But Sam was already pulling up his collar and jogging away so Ava called goodnight and let herself into the house. She refused to feel slighted that he hadn't hung around to see if she'd invite him in for coffee. Faux dates didn't do that. Faux dates went to bed alone.

If she was developing feelings for him, she didn't want them.

She'd remain a faux date even though Sam's vulnerability had made her ache with the knowledge that he was, as she'd told him, a good man. He also had a smile to melt her bones and buns that looked good in everything.

It was no longer a case of needing all her energy for

113

her career. Now she knew just how dear it was to Sam to be the man in a white hat . . . she felt kind of grubby and grey.

Chapter Twelve

The beautiful business of hat making

Thursday 13 December

On Thursday Ava worked on Wendy's hat. She painted stiffener carefully onto the felt cone under the open skylight to allow the nail-varnishy smell to escape, admiring the glowing jade colour in the bright December sunlight, making sure the stiffener sank right into the material.

A small cloche could be made on a single hat block so, after selecting the right size and covering the wooden block with cling film to protect it from the steam, she turned the cone in the steam spouting from the steamer to release the stiffener. The steamer's familiar gurgling sounded friendly and comforting. Then she pulled the cone taut over the block, stretching the fabric and beginning the familiar pull-pin, pull-pin technique that would ensure evenness, carefully placing her pins as if around the face of a clock – twelve then six; nine then three – rotating the block until the brim was secured by a constant run of closely placed pins. She paused often to return the hat to the steam, humming to herself as she worked.

Taking the hat from the block to dry before repeating

the blocking process to make the hat tighter and stronger was essential, but would take about twenty-four hours. She didn't have a drying cupboard but the heating was on and, once she was happy she'd progressed as far as she could for now, she powered up her laptop and located the No Blame or Shame website. She began to read, her mind filled with Wendy and what had made her want to help women having a hard time.

> *You might think that there's no one you can trust.*
> *But there is . . .*
> *No Blame or Shame.*

On the message board women talked matter-of-factly about situations that should never be considered matter of fact; women who'd done nothing to deserve the things that had happened to them. Many, like Ava, had trusted somebody that they knew. Or thought they knew. In many cases there was a troublesome ex who exerted pressure to make the woman return to him. *He thinks he's got a grievance and it's eating at him,* one posted. *He can't leave me alone, he wants me to give him the opportunity to dump me in revenge. He thinks it will somehow reverse the rejection he suffered.* Ava sighed as she closed the window. Not one thread she read mentioned willingly posing for explicit pictures.

Friday 14 December
Ava had just blocked Wendy's hat for the second time and left it once again to dry when she received a text from her mother. *Are you available to Skype?*

Returning, *Yes, give me a minute,* Ava powered up her laptop and clicked on the Skype icon. In a minute she was clicking on *Katherine Blissham calling* and her mother's face appeared on the screen.

Katherine looked relaxed and happy, fair hair in a bouncy short cut. 'Hello, darling! Tell me all your news.'

Ava gazed disbelievingly at the swags of frosty-looking boughs decorated with stars and bells that were visible over her mother's shoulder. 'You've got Christmas decorations!'

Katherine laughed, shrugging. 'It's the book café. *Joyeux Noël* and all that – the customers expect it. It's Christmas that I wanted to talk to you about, actually. Are you sure that you don't want to come out here?'

Ava twisted her hair around her finger. 'I've got plans with Izz. You never "do" Christmas!'

Another shrug. Perhaps Katherine had caught shrugs from the French. 'I suppose we've a bit more time for it this year, and you have to have Christmas events in the shop to get the punters in. I'm finding it quite fun, actually.'

'Even Dad's doing Christmas?' Ava heard the outrage in her voice but she could scarcely credit that Graeme Blissham, late of the Metropolitan Police Service, purveyor of the mantra 'If you saw what I saw on the roads and in the cells every Christmas, you'd wonder why we bother', had shifted his stance, however commercial the reason.

'He's even dressing up as Papa Noël for evening opening. Are you sure you can't come over? Izz could come, too.'

Ava quashed the desire to bellow, 'Papa Noël, for goodness' sake?' and remained mindful of her maxed credit cards and barely there bank account. 'Maybe next year.' *But, seriously? Papa Noël? The same man who wasn't home for Christmas Day for seven years running. Papa Noël?*

Katherine tilted her head. 'That's a pity. Shall I send you some money for your present or would you like something lovely and French?'

Ava was tempted by 'lovely and French' but, welcome though the recent injections of cash into her account had been, they'd been almost immediately swallowed up by bills. 'Money, please.' *Don't ask me what I'm going to spend it on. You may not want to hear that it's going to help me pay my rent and I definitely don't want to have to tell you.*

They chatted for a little longer, then Katherine's phone began to ring. Ava shut Skype down with a sigh. She went onto Cadhoc and paid for her parents to each receive *un chèque-cadeau* on Christmas Day, reflecting bitterly that this was exactly what her father what have previously called a 'pointless Christmas ritual' – them sending her money and her sending them gift certificates.

Their gifts, and those for Izz and Tod, she resolved, were going to form her total Christmas expenditure. She'd send all her cards as e-cards and tell friends, aunts, uncles and cousins that she wasn't doing presents. It would be no hardship to miss out on scratchy scarf and glove sets, and she could live without replenishing her perfume supply. These minor losses would be amply balanced out by having fewer reasons to dip into the meagre contents of her purse.

For the first time, though, she felt a stirring of doubt about her Christmas Day plans. With Tod having Louise to consider this year, it would just be Ava and Izz to open the fizz, stuff themselves stupid on turkey then sprawl in front of the TV eating chocolates. Izz had said nothing to suggest that she was unhappy with this programme but if they'd known Christmas in France might be something

118

special maybe they could have booked tickets sufficiently far in advance that Ava's Christmas gift from her parents would have covered hers? She allowed her mind to fill with visions of happy pre-Christmas chaos at Le Café Littéraire Anglais, English delicacies mingling with French tidbits; friends and customers buying gifts and pausing for a restorative English tea while schoolchildren sang carols in nearby La Place de la Liberté.

Maybe they would have gone to Midnight Mass on Christmas Eve or been invited to a proper French Christmas Day lunch with her parents' friends.

She pictured them walking through the town of Muntsheim when it was bedecked with millions of tiny lights, admiring the huge Christmas tree that she knew was erected in the centre of La Place. There was probably a Christmas market, too, with *glühwein* to warm the marketgoers as they shopped. If not, the border into Germany was so close that it would have been possible to nip across for a taste of Christmas there.

Vaguely depressed at knowing that none of these wistful imaginings would come into being this year she wondered what her mother was saying to her father about their Skype conversation, and whether she realised how different things would have been if they'd decided to enjoy Christmas years ago.

Did they ever feel a twinge that it had been Gran who'd been the main purveyor of Christmas in Ava's childhood, helping Ava with Christmas shopping and present wrapping, getting the tree out so that they could decorate it together? Never letting her touch the lights until they'd been tested 'just in case'. She blinked back the tears. Once Gran had died, it had become obvious how much effort Katherine and Graeme used to put into Christmas.

Not much. Her dad certainly hadn't dressed up as Papa Noël.

That evening, Ava and Izz tramped through rainy streets to Tod's house in Kentish Town, crossing Kentish Town Road near the Abbey Tavern. Tod was an inspired cook with a natural ability to combine ingredients that sang on the palate in the same way that he had an instinctive understanding of colour and layout when it came to graphics.

They trod carefully over the black and white chessboard tiled garden path, a skidpan in wet weather, hung their coats to drip in the hall and settled at Tod's big old kitchen table while he stirred and sprinkled the battered pans on the hob. Dunc and Frankie, Tod's housemates, wafted in to say hello and out again to play Xbox on the big flat-screen TV in the living room. Ava watched Izz. Frankie had once been Izz's big crush but now she didn't even bother to follow his long glossy black hair with her gaze.

'Mulled wine!' announced Tod, sniffing the contents of one of his saucepans and steaming up his glasses.

'Can I have real wine?' Ava asked, hopefully. She hadn't brought a bottle as – in the constant round of Tod visiting Ava and Izz, and Ava and Izz visiting Tod – it was generally considered pointless to bother. She had relied on him having a nice rosé in for her.

Tod lined up three glass cups. 'Not yet. It's the time of year for mulled wine.' He transferred wine from pan to cup, ensuring each received a quarter slice of orange. 'Merry Christmas, ladies.'

'Merry Christmas.' Izz blew across her steaming beverage.

'Likewise.' Ava accepted the inevitable and enjoyed the cinnamon sweetness, watching Tod cook, listening to Izz chat, trying not to feel glad when there was no sign of Louise.

Tod waited to bring up the subject of his absent girlfriend until he'd served three steaming platefuls of chicken in Riesling sauce with baby carrots and perfect miniature roast potatoes. He produced the desired rosé, poured three glasses then raised his to Ava. 'Official sorry for me getting merry and Louise overreacting.'

'You don't have to apologise for Louise.'

'Someone has to.' Tod coloured, so presumably Louise was not going to apologise for herself.

Ava smiled at him across the scarred table, guiltily wishing for an end to Tod's enchantment with Louise. 'Did you, erm, *mention* to Louise that she'd overreacted?'

'Well . . .' Tod picked up his knife and fork.

'You're allowed to,' said Ava, gently. 'She was fairly free with her comments on your behaviour.'

'So I should reciprocate?'

'At least feel you can. We all get sloshed once in a while.' Ava turned the conversation. 'Tell me the news from the agency.'

Izz glanced sidelong at Ava. 'Apparently, you're going out with Sam on Saturday.'

Tod paused mid-chew.

Annoyingly, Ava felt her colour heighten. 'I told you about his aunt inviting me to speak at a dinner.'

'But not that Sam would be going with you.' Izz cut into a roast potato.

Ava automatically arranged the facts in the order that would cause Izz the least pain. 'He's going anyway and is just giving me a lift, really. His mother will be there, for

121

goodness' sake.' Ava searched her conscience. Should she apologise for spending time with the man her friend was crushing on? It wasn't as if she was seeking Sam out or even genuinely dating him but her heart gave an uncomfortable bump. She hadn't thought about the faux dating hurting Izz. She laid down her cutlery. 'Sam's Aunt Vanessa's giving me the chance to do a bit of a show in front of loads of ladies who might give me orders. I couldn't get there without a lift. It's in Cambridgeshire, right out in the country.'

She was trying to unstick the words 'It may even mean an overnight stay' from her throat when Izz gave a gusty sigh. 'I expect you're getting a lift because he likes you. Patrick's been asking about you, too.'

More uncomfortable by the moment, Ava scrabbled around for a reply. 'You couldn't find anything more interesting to talk about?'

'He does like The Pigeon Detectives and Shed Seven, so we talked about music and Camden venues for a bit,' Izz replied, with her usual tendency towards taking things literally.

Tod came to the rescue. 'Ava, did Izz tell you we had some of Sam's celeb footie stars at the agency this week? Chilly and his protégé, Tyrone Glennister, and Tyrone's WAG, Ruby. Patrick, Jake and Emily are going to run an image-boosting campaign for Ruby.'

Thankfully, Ava followed his lead. 'Isn't she the one the press has taken against after she lied about her boob job?'

'The tabloids call her "Booby Glennister" instead of Ruby Glennister.' Izz looked almost as mortified as if it had happened to her. 'I feel sorry for her.'

Tod agreed. 'Her only sin has been to be a bit naïve

and defensive. Tyrone catapulting into the premier league has meant a whole new world for her. She was a model before, of course, but not big time. The press take almost as much interest in her as they do in Tyrone – because she's more accessible, obviously, not being closeted away at training sessions with Liverpool or Man U or whoever Tyrone's signed to. She was invited onto daytime TV chat shows to discuss make-up or clothes and her input was applauded.'

'Then her double D boobs appeared,' Ava put in.

Tod rolled his eyes. 'Right. She probably thought that no one would be crass enough to demand details, but she underestimated the tabloids. At that point, she had two reasonable avenues. She could have simply said, "Yes, do you like them? Tyrone does. I've always wanted this kind of figure and big boobs are the one thing that my work in the gym wouldn't provide." Or she could have turned it into a fun speculation with a bit of flirty joking. "Haven't you heard of WonderBra?" Or "I asked for them in my letter to Santa."' He sighed. 'Instead, she did the worst thing possible – adopted an air of outrage and downright denied that she'd had breast augmentation. It didn't take the red tops two minutes to find her out.'

'Those cringe-making headlines!' breathed Izz. '"Ruby! What boobies!", "Porkies from Booby Glennister", "Goodbye, Ruby's old boobies".'

Ava frowned. 'Poor woman. I suppose if you take on the persona of a "sleb" you have to take the rough with the smooth, but that seems cruel.'

Tod polished the sauce from his plate with his last roast potato. 'It was a gift for social media, people sharing the articles or making up their own captions to her pics.

Carnage when "Booby Glennister" trended on Facebook and Twitter. Ruby's hurt and bewildered so Sam's advising on a campaign to mend her image. He says she's got to be seen to take a joke. A sense of humour goes a long way with the media and Ruby needs to learn to deflect awkward questions with a quip.'

'It must be great having celebrities in.' Ava sighed enviously. She loved working in her studio but the nearest she got to footballers and WAGs was listening to the radio as she worked. 'I think Tyrone and Ruby seem OK, for hipsters.'

Tod laughed. 'Sam's always using that word, usually ironically. Considering he works in frontline PR he's a touch sceptical about the supposed influencers and trend-setters in pop culture. But I'm sure he'd say that Tyrone and Ruby are way too mainstream to be hipsters.'

He turned to Ava with a frown. 'Speaking of Sam, Harvey's texted me, asking if you're seeing him. I haven't answered, but I could tell him to piss off, if you like.'

Slowly, Ava sipped, letting the cold wine dance across her tongue as she followed the advice on No Blame or Shame and kept calm to think the situation through. 'I don't want to aggravate or escalate the situation, so ignore him. Hopefully he'll get bored and fade away.'

She so wished Harvey would fade away. She'd received another coaxing text from him this morning.

Just to let you know, got an app to monitor drinking.

Ava wanted to reply *Who cares?* but mindful that he was at his most unpredictable when upset sent back *Good choice* instead.

I can send you the results so you can see for yourself.

Do this for you, not me. Of what possible value was a report from an app he entered data into himself?

How about going for a drink sometime?
? Joke re drinking? Sorry. Not dating at the moment.
She should take her own advice and ignore him.

Chapter Thirteen

The Christmas ball

Saturday 15 December

Ava had no chance to work on Wendy's hat on Saturday, as she had to prepare for the Rotary Ball. Making Ava feel guiltier than ever, Izz helped her stack hatboxes and hat stands in their narrow hall and, later, to carry them out to Sam's car.

'Thank you.' Ava was left with little to do but pick up her bags and trip across the pavement – for once it wasn't raining – while Sam and Izz scratched their heads over how to get five hexagonal boxes into a car boot.

Sam thanked Izz pleasantly for her help but pulled away with no sign of sparing her another thought, whereas Ava, even having given Izz a grateful hug, felt bad at leaving her standing alone on the pavement watching them leave.

Endless clogging traffic blighted the London end of the journey. Ava gazed out of the windows, trying to remember what streets looked like without Christmas decorations. It was a nice change to get onto the blandness of the motorway.

It was nearly three hours later, half an hour over Sam's original estimate, when they finally drove up the steep drive to the sweep of the gravel before the pink brick Port Manor Hotel. The night was ablaze with the headlights of vehicles queuing to turn in to one of the car parks so Sam pulled up at the foot of some stone steps flanked with enormous urns. Instantly, a man in a black suit appeared to tell him he couldn't park there.

Sam hopped out. 'Help me unload what the guest speaker needs and I'll park wherever you want.' The hapless man, who turned out to be the event manager, found himself hefting a tower of hatboxes while Ava had only her dress and her bags to carry up the steps. She could get used to people fetching and carrying for her.

Wendy and Vanessa met her in the foyer. 'Were the roads very busy? Hope you're not exhausted by the journey. We'll show you where to get changed.' They bore her off to a palatial white and gold powder room where she checked in her coat and exchanged her jeans for a corset-style evening gown with a handkerchief hem, fixing her fascinator to the side of her updo, black to go with her dress. Herds of women would be wearing black but Ava knew it wouldn't clash with any hat she put on or held aloft for the admiration of the audience.

Also, she had only one formal dress. A black one.

Vanessa tweaked her own fascinator fondly. 'People are already asking me about this. Hopefully everyone will want one by the end of the night.'

'That would be wonderful.' Ava tried to sound excited rather than desperate.

'I can't wait to see my hat.' Pensively, Wendy took out her comb.

Heart giving a squeeze, Ava wondered how many more times Wendy would perform the simple task of tidying her hair. 'I'll make it as fabulous as I possibly can.'

Wendy smiled. 'You're a lovely girl. We know it's early days and Sam's given us strict instructions not to crowd you, but he means so much to us that it's lovely to see him happy again. After Mariah.'

This time, Ava couldn't contain her curiosity. 'He hasn't told me much about Mariah . . .' Like nothing.

Sniffing disapprovingly, Wendy took out her lipstick. 'Sam had a girlfriend, Mariah, and a best friend, Elliot – then he had neither, if you get my drift. It happened around Christmas time, too.'

Vanessa tried to frown her sister down. 'Perhaps he would have told Ava if he'd wanted her to know?'

'Don't worry,' said Ava hurriedly, seeing Wendy's face fall. 'I won't mention it.' But poor Sam to run foul of the dreaded double betrayal. No wonder Wendy was fixated on seeing him happy, her current uncertain emotional state supercharging the most sentimental of her maternal needs. Ava gave Wendy's hand a quick squeeze as they headed for the twinkling lights of the ballroom.

There, Vanessa stepped up into hostess mode, installing Wendy in a chair with a, 'We don't want you to tire too early,' and introducing Ava to Vanessa's patiently waiting boyfriend. Neale looked a little older than Vanessa, with his short silver hair, but had captivating dark eyes. Vanessa looked at him as if she'd like him on toast.

Ava found her hatboxes and stands stacked behind the top table at the far end of the room. Sam reappeared and he and Vanessa unpacked hats for Ava to set out. After half an hour Ava was satisfied with her colourful display of stylish shapes graced with arcing plumes and frothing net. Perhaps those hat stands wouldn't be going on eBay after all.

As she stacked business cards elegantly at the front corners of the table, Sam volunteered to transport the hats to her as needed. 'Just make it easy for me to identify the colours. None of this "puce" or "violet" stuff.'

The level of noise climbed as guests flowed into the ballroom and Vanessa introduced Ava and Sam to the important people of Cambridgeshire Rotary Clubs. On the few occasions Ava had attended black tie dinners her seat had been in the body of the hall and it was an enjoyable novelty to find herself a top-table VIP.

Mingling accomplished, Sam grabbed glasses of fizz from a passing waiter and they had time to check out the ballroom, its white-clothed tables glittering with silver. Huge portraits of somebody's ancestors gazed down haughtily, as if objecting to the indignity of their heavy picture frames being adorned with sprigs of holly.

Ava had a moment to check Sam out. Instead of buttons on his sparkling white shirt he had those little onyx stud things that matched his cuff links, and wore a dinner jacket without looking like a waiter. In fact, he looked as comfortable as he had in the *This way up* T-shirt.

Then she realised that he was checking her out, too. 'You look great,' he murmured.

Conscious of her low neckline and how tall her companion was, she fought the urge to glance down and check that she wasn't flashing her headlights. She flushed but managed, 'You too. And your mum.'

Sam followed Ava's gaze. Sadness touched his smile. Wendy had abandoned her armchair and was chattering happily, the soft mulberry of her floaty dress lending colour to her cheeks. 'I hope that she doesn't stand up for too long. Or wear herself out rushing round collecting money for her causes.' He edged closer to Ava as the crush around them got greater.

'If her fundraising is a collection, then others can share the work.'

He nodded. 'Chilly's coming, so I think she's hoping he'll overawe people into digging deep into their pockets.'

Ava glanced up in surprise. 'Your mum's got *Aidan Chiltern* to help?' Her imagination struggled with the vision of a collection plate being shaken under Rotarian noses by a man who had made it into just about every magazine and newspaper in the world.

'Mum met him at the agency this week. I'd told him about her illness and he offered. He's got a cottage between here and King's Lynn so he said he could be in the area.'

Ava felt warmth ooze into her heart. 'Nice to know that celebrities aren't above aiding others.'

'Charity work's good for the image. I don't mean that Chilly's doing this for that reason,' he amended hastily. 'The press aren't even here. It's just something that anyone working in image awareness thinks of automatically.'

Ava was on the point of asking about the Ruby 'Booby' Glennister campaign but resisted, not at all sure Tod and Izz should have been gossiping to her about the agency 'slebs'.

The toastmaster called the guests to their seats and the top table was served first, another nice perk of being guest speaker. Vanessa leaned across Sam and Wendy. 'Ava, you're on after dessert has been cleared and coffee served. I'll introduce you and you'll have a microphone. Then the dancing begins. Wendy's charity appeal will happen about eleven when wallets have been loosened by alcohol.'

'Oh,' said Ava. A whole flight of butterflies launched in

her stomach as she remembered that she wasn't only here to be treated as if she were someone special. She had a job to do and Vanessa was relying upon her not to mess it up.

She didn't drink much at dinner. She toyed with her food, trying to keep her gaze from the scary number of people packed around the tables in the body of the ballroom. The dance floor was now clear and what Ava hadn't really taken in during the mingling was that the long top table was alone on one side of it, looking down at the horde of lesser, circular tables, from the stage.

She was going to feel frozen by the spotlight when she had to stand up with a microphone. She tried desperately to remember how she'd intended to begin. Something about herself and her training. Or should she just talk about hats? The materials? The techniques? How to wear them? Hats and fashion? Her brain solidified. The scent of her own perfume was making her feel sick.

'What's up?' murmured Sam. 'Don't you like the soup?'

She wiped sweat from her top lip with her napkin. 'Ask Vanessa what she said about a microphone. I'll need both hands for the hat show and won't be able to hold it.'

'Don't worry. I expect it will be a clip on job.' He finished his soup and laid his spoon neatly in the bowl

Ava nudged his thigh with hers. 'Please ask Vanessa. I've got the shakes about it. I've never even held a microphone.'

'Got it.' He turned to Vanessa for a whispered consultation.

Ava gave up all pretence of eating. She would have quite liked some more of the iced water from the middle of the table but didn't trust herself to pick it up without letting the jug slide from her damp palms.

Consultation with Vanessa complete, Sam returned her nudge. 'The microphone won't be intrusive. The AV person will clip it to you at the right distance from your face and Van stood in on the sound test before we arrived. You can literally forget it. Don't try and dip your mouth close to it and don't shout as if you think you can't be heard.'

'Right.' Ava tried to absorb Sam's reassuring details.

'If you feel uncomfortable looking directly at the audience, fix your gaze immediately above their heads. Remember that this is a non-hostile situation. These guys want to like you. Let them. Chat as if it's the ten or so people you're used to. Be yourself. They'll love you.'

'Thanks,' she whispered, grateful that he made it sound so doable. A few of the butterflies cruised in to land.

Sam watched Ava still wiping her hands nervously. He changed tack. 'Don't forget about the slow dances. All mine.' As he was driving he was making his glass of wine last but he noticed that Ava had scarcely touched hers, either. 'I take it you tango?'

She turned panicked blue eyes to him. 'What? No! Not unless you count messing about with Tod when we were watching *Strictly*.'

'Oh dear,' he said, gravely. 'Can you rumba? Or do the lambada? The guest speaker's always expected to put on an exhibition of dancing when her spot's over. I've heard that last year it was pole dancing. I'll help you up on the table.'

Her consternation was overlaid by laughter. 'You *idiot*. You had me going for a second.'

He grinned, arrested by her sudden sparkle. 'It's a coping strategy I used with Chilly when he was nervous. Terrify him. Then whatever he felt nervous about would seem easy in comparison.'

With a rueful expression, she nodded. 'It works.'

'I'll introduce you to Chilly later. He'll love you.' Any red-blooded male would. Ava looked fantastic in her black dress with its up-down hem swinging above her ankles and lacings up the back. The square neckline was torture and Sam had had to force his gaze elsewhere all evening.

'I don't think I've ever met a proper celebrity.' Ava looked intrigued. 'Working for Ceri I met plenty of people with money but nobody actually newsworthily famous.'

'Chilly's a great one to begin with. He's a good bloke.'

Sam launched into a stream of anecdotes about what it had been like to be so close to Chilly, to be the one with a cool head no matter what was happening, constantly monitoring the impression Chilly was giving to the media. He continued while the wait staff cleared the table. Then the lighting changed and a woman in a suit appeared.

She reached around Ava to clip a mic on her neckline. 'Hello, I'm doing the AV. Fab dress,' she whispered. 'I'll switch you on when you stand up and tweak the levels if you need it. I'll switch you off as soon as you've finished talking and come back to remove the mic for you.'

Ava looked apprehensive, but nodded.

'Here we go,' hissed Vanessa. 'I'll introduce you.'

'Hats!' Ava squeaked, turning to Sam.

Sam was already on his feet. 'Which?'

'I can't remember!'

'I think I can.' He chose black, pale blue, pale purple, yellow and pale orange. OK, peach. He made two swift journeys, positioning the stands to Ava's left.

Then the toastmaster's voice boomed. 'Ladies and gentlemen! The festival secretary, Vanessa Jermyn.' He passed the roving microphone to Vanessa who rose confidently to do the usual welcome and thanks thing.

Sam leaned over to put his lips against Ava's ear as she sipped hurriedly from her water glass. 'Plan your moves for the pole dancing.'

Her giggle was picked up by the mic. The audience applauded and she rose to her feet still smiling. Her inhalation was audible but she didn't, as he'd feared, dry up. 'I usually do this in front of a smaller group but Vanessa says that you're very nice – so don't let her down.' Her delivery was a little breathless but the audience laughed.

Sam relaxed. Some of Chilly's best TV chat-show appearances had followed truly crippling nerves in the green room.

Ava moistened her lips. 'I'm going to talk to you tonight about couture millinery and ask a few of you beautiful ladies to help me out. Gentlemen, I'm sure you don't mind watching pretty women wafting around.'

Male laughter.

Sam listened as Ava steadily gained confidence, making mass-produced hats pressed out in factories sound all very nice but a bespoke couture hat the height of desirability. He eased his chair slightly to the left and back, giving her room to move her hands as she spoke while keeping himself within arm's reach in case she knocked over a hat stand. He found himself briefly distracted by the resultant close-up view of the curve of her bottom but resolutely returned his gaze to the audience.

All eyes were on Ava as she lifted up a tiny pale blue number. 'This I'd call a cocktail hat. It has a three-dimensional base and I've formed it by steaming it on a block. The feathers are stripped so that only the tips remain, creating movement. Vanessa, would you model this for us?'

She deftly removed Vanessa's fascinator and perched the tiny hat, not much bigger than the lid of a coffee jar, in its place. 'Perhaps Vanessa will walk down onto the dance floor while I tell you a little about how this hat is made, the materials, and when you might wear it.' Vanessa obligingly glided around the table and down the two steps to the dance floor, hamming it up with a wiggle that was greeted with a ripple of amusement.

When the blue cocktail hat had had its moment in the spotlight Vanessa returned and Ava removed the cocktail hat and refixed her fascinator with, it seemed, no more than a flick of her fingers.

Sam found himself watching her hands. Her nails were short but her long tapering fingers moved gracefully as she talked. Pretty hands.

Ava's hat show lasted for forty minutes. Men in the audience seemed as engaged as the women. Whether that was because they liked hearing how things were made or because Ava looked amazing, her long blonde hair caught up in a twist and shining beneath the lights as she occasionally demonstrated how a particular hat should be worn, he wasn't sure.

She wound up. 'If anybody would like to come and look at the samples, try them on or ask me questions, please do. My business cards are here. A percentage of any sales generated tonight will go to the nominated causes, and, as it's nearly Christmas, gift vouchers are available to spend at any time during the year.'

'Tell anyone who wants gift vouchers to come and give me their details and we'll follow it up,' Sam murmured.

Ava repeated the information smoothly and thanked everybody for their attention.

Applause. The microphone made a soft 'thunk' as it

was switched off. Ava dropped down into her seat with a huge sigh.

'Fanbloodytastic.' Sam grinned, still clapping. As she turned to him to reply, he leaned in to plant a soft kiss on her lips.

Chapter Fourteen

Football stars and Booby Ruby

Almost high on relief, Ava found herself kissing Sam back, exchanging heat.

Instantly, his kiss changed, deepening as his hand slid slowly around her waist, travelling upwards until his palm rested on her naked back above her dress. An unhurried, thoughtful kiss, as if he were measuring and enjoying her response.

Then a voice interrupted over Ava's shoulder. 'How much is the mauve one? One of my granddaughters is getting married in spring. Would it go with yellow?'

With a jolt Ava broke away, becoming aware of a silver-haired lady gazing beadily at her and a sea of people crowding behind the top table, talking, exclaiming, examining hats and trying them on. Not just people – potential clients, in fact.

Sam gave Ava a slow smile. 'Business is business, Ava Bliss.'

Blushing, she jumped to her feet, jamming her business head on, and treating the silver-haired lady to a professional smile. 'It's hard to be certain without seeing the yellow of your outfit but it might be safer to go with white, cream or gold. The gold would look lovely with your hair colour and those tall feathers would give you real presence. Shall we try it? Or, as the wedding isn't until spring, if you'd like to bring the outfit to me, I could create something bespoke so we wouldn't be restricted to what I have with me this evening and I could pick up details of your outfit.'

'Sounds expensive,' the woman decreed. 'Let's try the mauve.'

Several other women wondered excitedly about their own hat-worthy occasions on the horizon. Business cards began to fly from the table into evening bags. The lights went down, a DJ jumped up onto a small sound stage in the corner of the room and music began to pour into the air as the scrum around Ava took over the space between the top table and the hat display.

Sam gathered up a pile of cards, gave her a wink and moved off to the fringe of the crowd. She could see him circulating, chatting, smiling easily. When he drifted close enough she caught occasional phrases: *exciting designer . . . always enjoy something creative . . . mother and aunt both bought . . . lucky to have this chance to view her work . . .* Nothing as brash as a sales pitch but somehow creating buzz and positivity. A few men slid their business cards into his hand and she felt her heart lift in excitement that they might be wishing to buy gift vouchers. Tod had designed some for her but she'd so far only sold one.

Then Ava had to stop watching Sam in order to answer a hail of questions.

'How would I wear this? Tilted?'

'How much would the blue one cost?'

'Do you run workshops?'

After one steadying slurp, she took temporary and regretful leave of her glass of wine, depositing it well away from the display while she helped settle hats on heads at fetching angles.

Camera phones appeared from evening purses and people began taking photos of each other so they could check out how fantastic they looked. Ava would bet that some of those photos would find their way onto Facebook and that a few clicks of 'share' and the images might reach those who thought copying designs was OK. Compared with the prospect of Harvey posting certain other photos a few unauthorised snaps of her samples didn't seem to matter, but Ava made a mental note to take a mirror if she was ever invited to another such event.

Finally, the last hats were returned and people drifted off to their tables or to join the now heaving dance floor. Ava retrieved her wine and collapsed into her chair.

Sam, already lounging in his seat, raised his glass. 'You did great.'

'I hope I looked as if I deal with this kind of reaction daily and not as if I was shocked to be mobbed. At least I feel a bit more optimistic about finances – if even a couple of commissions come from tonight it'll help. Four would be great and six would be fantastic.'

With a satisfied smile, he placed a small stack of cards and one torn off piece of menu before her. 'Six people want details of your gift vouchers.'

'Wow,' she breathed, gazing at the booty with awe. 'Thank you! I'm so glad I accepted this gig.' Her fingers actually shook as she transferred her haul to her evening bag. Her mind moved quickly along the twin tracks of business and money. 'I ought to pay you petrol money for driving me here—'

'Don't be so fucking annoying, Ava,' he said, amiably.

She blinked. His tone was so much at variance with his words that she almost failed to absorb his meaning. 'What?'

Sam placed his wine glass very precisely on the tablecloth, which had taken on a myriad of colours from the lights pulsing in time with the music. 'You got Vanessa out of a hole by agreeing to do this event and you've helped me out with the whole faux date thing so don't let me kiss you one moment and nitpick over pennies the next. It's insulting.'

She responded sharply. 'Sorry if it's gauche to offer petrol money to a man with a BMW. You'll have to put it down to my poverty.'

After a moment, his hand slid over hers. Regret had replaced his irritation. 'My turn to apologise. I was enjoying sharing your success and it stung to realise that you can't seem to accept even the tiniest thing from me and your instinctive reaction is to shove me away.'

Ava felt her pulse kick in. His warm skin seemed to tingle against hers. 'I'll try to remember not to do that.'

He went as if to speak again but then interrupted himself. 'Hang on, message,' he said and drew out his phone. 'Ah. Chilly's in the foyer. Let me introduce you.' Spikiness forgotten, he pulled her up out of the chair. Skirting the dance floor, the temperature rose as they moved into the room. Ava wasn't sure if that was because of the press of bodies or Sam looping one arm loosely around her to pull her to the other side of him, shielding her from the flailing elbows of energetic dancers.

It was ironic, she thought, that in the exact moment she'd been preoccupied with the awful business of being poor she was swept along to meet a huge football star, a man she knew from the pages of *Hello!* and *OK!*, a man who'd hit the television news when knee injury had ended his career. Aidan Chiltern's dark curls and faintly acne-scarred skin were sufficiently familiar to people around the world to have secured sponsorship, advertising revenue and appearance money, in addition to his player's salary.

They emerged into the foyer to brighter lights and a cooler, quieter space. Half a dozen Rotarians were gawping at three people leaning against an ornate sideboard that probably wasn't meant for such casual treatment.

Sam swore under his breath. 'The Glennisters are with him.'

Ava almost fell over as she realised who he was talking about. 'Ruby and Tyrone Glennister?'

'Tyrone's a big friend of Chilly's but I didn't know they would be with him tonight.' Sam didn't sound as if he considered the Glennisters a bonus.

'Sam!' Chilly beamed as he strode forward to shake Sam's hand. He turned to Ava before Sam could introduce her. 'I'm Aidan. These guys all call me Chilly.'

'I'm Ava.' Ava wished she didn't sound so squeaky.

Chilly's eyes were deep brown and kind and he looked endearingly ordinary in a pearly grey lounge suit with a red tie. Ava wasn't certain what she expected of celebrities, perhaps that they'd have little sparkly auras or glide around in glistening bubbles to save them from interacting with Joe Public.

Ruby Glennister looked a lot more like Ava's perception of a celeb. Her conker-brown hair was long and shiny, her smoky-eyes perfect, her skin flawlessly tanned. Ava wouldn't attempt to guess how much her snug dress had cost but it accentuated the boob job that had caused her so much trouble with the press.

Ruby smiled, apparently prepared to be as friendly as

Chilly. 'Hello, Ava, good to meet you. Say hello to Ava, Ty.'

Ava was stunned to find herself being kissed on both cheeks – if somewhat sweatily and cursorily – by current footie superstar hero heartthrob Tyrone Glennister. He smelled of beer and he was wearing a suit with no tie, one side of his shirt collar up like a dog cocking its leg.

'All right there?' he mumbled. 'Do we get a drink, Sam?'

'I think we need a meeting first.' Sam was noticeably unsmiling. 'As I was expecting only Chilly I need to be certain that everybody's expectations are being met.' He spoke briefly in what Ava mentally designated PR-speak about concerns and awareness and the importance of selecting the right vehicles for a campaign.

Ruby and Tyrone listened seriously. Chilly grinned and looked as if he were taking Sam a lot less seriously. After a minute, he took one hand out of his pocket to lay it placatingly on Sam's sleeve. 'Look, mate – we don't have any expectations of this evening except to help raise a few quid for your mum's causes. There's no agenda. Ruby's not expecting you to summon up half of Fleet Street and make them magically turn sympathetic. Tyrone and Ruby are staying with me this weekend and so we came here together. OK?'

Sam gave him a long look. Then nodded. 'OK. I'll look after you.'

Tyrone grinned. 'We don't need no one to look after us. Just show us the bar.'

Sam's searching gaze switched to him and the air seemed filled with something not said.

Ava watched, intrigued by Sam's po-face. But then she caught his gaze flicking meaningfully her way and realised that whatever he wanted to say it was plainly her presence that was preventing him from saying it. Oh. Right. If Sam wasn't comfortable with her mixing with such starry people then she wasn't comfortable either, not least because he seemed disappointingly changed in their company, almost vibrating with tension.

'Um, it was lovely to meet you,' she said brightly to the celebrities lined up in front of Sam like naughty kids. 'But I need to get back to the ballroom.'

Sam nodded. 'See you in a minute.' As Ava left she caught his low-voiced opening gambit. 'OK, here's my concern—' Sam had drawn on his Big Important Man persona.

Because she was waylaid several times by people exclaiming over how much they'd enjoyed her show, Ava hadn't made it back to her seat when Sam caught up with her. At least he looked more relaxed than he had a few minutes earlier. 'I said we'd meet them at the bar. Mum and Vanessa are heading in that direction already.'

'Would it be better if I left you to look after your celebrities?'

He shifted his hand to her waist and altered her trajectory from table to bar. 'No, it wouldn't.' He rolled his eyes. 'Thanks for taking the hint and giving me a minute back there. I had to make sure Tyrone won't drink too much this evening. He's a twat when he's drunk and if he stuffs up my mother's appeal and embarrasses my aunt in front of Rotarian bigwigs I'm going to be annoyed. As several of my associates are going to be working with his wife soon, if I get annoyed with him, they're going to get annoyed with me. Also,' he dropped his voice, 'Tyrone's the important client who has us on a media management retainer, which pays much of our monthly overheads. But even if I have to watch over him and Ruby for the agency's sake, I refuse to give up my faux date with Ava Bliss entirely.'

Ava laughed, as she knew he had meant her to, but was instantly empathetic. 'People who can't control their drinking have enormous potential to create embarrassment.' She knew from Sam's emphatic nod that she didn't even have to say, 'Like Harvey.'

Then, seeing that Wendy and Vanessa had already reached the bar, she shut Harvey from her mind. Chilly was making introductions. Wendy and Vanessa were gazing at Ruby in her towering heels and spray-on dress with awed expressions and, as Sam and Ava joined the group, Ava felt as if everybody in the room was trying to watch them without appearing to.

It was fun to be a part of a buzz but if anyone expected 'sleb' behaviour from Chilly or the Glennisters they were disappointed. Tyrone was quieter than she expected and Ruby chatted easily about her father having been a Rotarian who crossed to the dark side – Freemasonry. Wendy laughed, so Ava presumed that a joke had been made.

Far more interesting was the subdued conversation that she could hear between Chilly and Sam.

'Are we cool?' Chilly was frowning uncertainly.

Sam gave a kind of combined nod and shrug. 'I just wasn't prepared for him to be here. You know I'd normally make certain he was looked after one-on-one. And you know why. I like Ruby and I want to help her and I don't want him screwing things up for her . . . or for the agency.'

'Point taken,' murmured Chilly. 'I didn't think it through. When they knew I was coming up the country for a few days they kind of invited themselves and so I suggested they come with me tonight. I'll make certain he behaves.'

Sam clapped Chilly's shoulder in a 'then we're cool' gesture.

Vanessa claimed his attention. 'Sam, we'll do your mum's charity thing in half an hour. The event manager's arranging for the top table to be removed.' She dropped her voice to a whisper. 'People are going to love me for the guest line up tonight. May I bring Neale over to meet Chilly and the Glennisters? He's footie mad. I won't let him do anything gauche like suggest a selfie.'

Sam's shoulders moved as if upon yet another sigh, but he smiled and said, 'OK with you?' to Chilly.

Chilly gave an easygoing smile. 'Of course. Bring him over.'

Chapter Fifteen

Wendy gets a real buzz

Almost midnight. Ava and Sam were still standing at the bar when Vanessa climbed back onto the main stage. She didn't have to try too hard to get attention – with celebrities in the room everyone was waiting for something interesting to happen. As the music tailed away and the lights rose, the roar of conversation subsided to an excited hum.

'So we've come to tonight's appeal, headed by my sister, Wendy,' Vanessa said into the hand-held microphone. 'We're raising money for research into ovarian cancer and for No Blame or Shame, an organisation that supports women who have at some time found themselves in jeopardy.'

Unexpectedly, her voice caught in her throat. 'I've only just found out about a surprise Wendy's concocted for us but I think you'll all understand her choice when you learn that she'll be undergoing chemotherapy shortly after Christmas.' She paused for a wave of sympathetic murmurs. 'I hope that you'll dig deep for the collection for these two worthy causes. Let me introduce Wendy and our honoured guests, Aidan Chiltern and Ruby Glennister.'

'Shit,' Sam muttered, as Ruby and Chilly began to thread their way between dinner jackets and sequinned gowns towards the stage, everyone craning to watch.

Ava glanced up at Sam uncertainly. 'Do you know what's happening?'

He shook his head, the muscles of his jaw bunching, his eyes fixed on the action. 'No. I'd guess I've been carefully kept out of the loop. Which gives me a bad feeling.'

Returning her attention to the stage, Ava watched Wendy, holding hands shyly with Chilly on one side and Ruby on the other, join Vanessa to loud applause. Ruby and Chilly wore professional smiles and Wendy a nervous one.

Chilly took over Vanessa's microphone and raised his hand for quiet. 'We have a very brave lady here tonight and I know that we're going to make a great collection out of admiration for her.' More applause. Vanessa brought out a tall bar stool and set it down centre stage.

Helping Wendy up onto it, Chilly patted her shoulder, returned the microphone to Vanessa and held out his hand towards Ruby.

Then Ruby brought out from behind her back something that appeared at first glance to be another microphone. But, when she flicked a switch, a mosquito-like drone filled the room.

Ava realised, with a jolt of horror, what Ruby held, and her hand flew to her mouth. 'Wendy's going to have her hair buzzed. Ruby's got electric hair clippers.'

'Oh . . . *shit*,' said Sam, hoarsely.

A sudden silence fell as everybody saw what was about to happen. Ava found herself fumbling for Sam's hand and holding it tightly as Chilly asked Wendy kindly, 'Ready?'

Dumbly, Wendy nodded. Her hands were clasped tightly in the lap of her pretty mulberry gown.

'Sure?'

Wendy nodded again. 'Go for it,' she said clearly.

The buzz of the clippers was surprisingly piercing in the hush. Gently, Chilly ran the clippers in a first pass over Wendy's head. As if in slow motion, locks of her shoulder-length hair began dropping to the ground. Her smile wavered but somehow she held it all together.

The audience began to clap, first quietly, then gaining momentum as the clippers left neatly shorn rows. Women shook their heads in admiration and fished tissues from their bags. Vanessa covered her mouth with her fingers.

Ava's heart was thumping and her hand was sweating in Sam's as Chilly finished the right side of Wendy's head and passed the clippers to Ruby, who took care of the left side, methodically and carefully, her lips moving as she kept up a stream of chat.

The naked head being revealed was hard to look at. Ava found herself screwing up her eyes and watching through the slits as Wendy's smile wobbled and broke until she was somehow both laughing and crying.

Sam's lips were pressed together so hard they'd all but disappeared.

'So brave of her,' Ava whispered but her heart ached for the grief she saw on the face of the man beside her. She brought up her other hand and held his in both of hers as if it would somehow take some of his pain away.

By the time the deed was done Vanessa was unabashedly weeping. Wendy rose slowly and dusted the last remains of her once-crowning glory from her shoulders and onto the floor.

Chilly took back the mic. 'Let's hear it for a valiant lady!' The applause rose to new heights, Chilly and Ruby clapping with their hands high in the air.

Then Ava found her hand discarded and the space beside her empty. Rising on tiptoe she followed Sam's progress as he shouldered through the crowd and leaped up onto the stage, his arms open to sweep his mother into his embrace.

The two clung together like survivors from a shipwreck.

Chapter Sixteen

Mixed messages

Sunday 16 December (early hours)

The Rotary Ball was due to end at one. It was twelve-thirty and Sam hadn't achieved what had been his goal for the evening – to get Ava up against him for the slow dances. He scanned the room but couldn't even see her. He was usually pretty good at hitting targets but the Glennisters turning up and his mother having her head publicly shaved had definitely made him take his eyes from the prize.

At least Ruby and Tyrone had caused no issues. Tyrone had limited himself to a few beers and Ruby had behaved like the nice person he knew lay underneath the overdrawn WAG exterior.

Maybe she'd allowed her head to be not so much turned as swivelled by the lifestyle that came with Tyrone's rise to the premier league but the real and warm Ruby was re-emerging from the ashes of her humiliation-by-media. As she appeared to have had no motive in turning up tonight other than to hang out with Chilly and possibly do something for the causes, Sam's confidence had increased that Jermyn's would be able to show the world that she was more than a pair of surgically enhanced breasts and a celebrity-by-marriage. She'd been kind and caring during the head shaving and Wendy, beaming self-consciously from under her newly visible scalp, had confided to Sam, 'Ruby's really nice. Just like a proper person. She was ever so sweet on stage.'

His mother was a hell of a lady – even if she'd put his heart through the mangle this evening – so if Ruby was OK with Wendy then she was more than OK with him.

Wendy was finally sitting down, periodically lifting a hand to stroke her scalp as she talked quietly with Vanessa, Neale and their friends. Sam could see that if she was scheduled to begin losing her hair during chemo then a public buzzing wasn't an unreasonable way to raise money for causes, but he hoped that in future her work for No Blame or Shame would entail speaking on local radio or at women's groups. The way she'd laid herself and her situation bare in front of two hundred people had rendered him a mess of admiration and anguish.

'Don't think that having your guts publicly wrenched out excuses you from those dances you promised me.' Ava had come up behind him.

He swung around, heart lifting. 'And don't think that acting like an emotional moron means I've forgotten.' He offered her his arm so that they could thread their way in amongst the dancers. In moments, Ava's hands were resting lightly on Sam's shoulders and her body drifting against his for the end-of-evening smooches.

Like most men, Sam didn't mind shuffling around a dance floor if it meant that he got this close to someone he wanted to get this close to. He'd had so much opportunity to watch her tonight that he felt pretty certain he'd be able to pick out her shape from a line up of silhouettes, and undo the black ribbon that criss-crossed her back with his eyes shut. He focused in on Ava, the smell of her hair, the movement of her hips, until he began to feel as if they were the only three-dimensional people in the room. Everyone and everything else seemed merely sketched in, like a backdrop.

He cleared his throat. 'I hardly ever cry on dates, by the way.'

Her eyes danced but she kept her tone grave. 'I'm sure most girls would forgive you, under the circumstances.'

He noted that she hadn't trotted out her usual 'But this isn't a date'.

'Your mum was very brave,' she went on.

He blew out a breath. 'I'm so proud of her. She apologised for keeping me in the dark but when she first decided on the stunt she didn't expect me to be here and she didn't want me to try to stop her.'

'You had to be brave, too.'

'It was certainly an intense way of facing the facts about my mother's cancer.'

'When I last saw the collection buckets they looked pretty healthy. Chilly and Ruby were fantastic.'

'Even Tyrone behaved himself,' he observed, drily. He drew Ava a little closer.

She tipped her head back and wound her arms around his neck. Her eyelids were heavy. She looked tired. But still mega hot. 'I was surprised how much you didn't want to see the Glennisters.' A song ended on a long drawn-out Christmassy mix of violins and sleigh bells and the DJ announced the very last dance of the night.

'I minded having to switch from leisure mode to business mode, assessing the situation, looking for pitfalls and worrying about Tyrone getting laddish.'

152

'But now they've disappeard and you can take your Sam the Big Important Man hat off.' A dimple appeared in her cheek. 'I used to get sick of hearing about you from Tod and Izz, you know. Then when we met you seemed so suave and kind of smug—'

'Smug?' he protested.

'—but actually I'm beginning to see what the others see in you. You're quite sweet; thinking of a great – not to mention expensive – Christmas present for your mum, showing everyone here tonight how much you love her with that big hug.'

'I'm not *sweet*,' he protested again. Sweet? Therein lay only a pat on the head and Ava treating him as she treated Tod – like a friend: safe, fuzzy, and definitely not to be slept with. There was nothing sweet about the way he wanted her.

He'd normally have shrugged off anyone who blew so hot and cold by now, but she was proving hard to give up on. If she was playing some game, no one had sent him a copy of the rules, but at least tonight she'd unbent enough to take his hand, hug him, and had even been vaguely complimentary. Now she was grinning up at him, loosened tendrils of her hair tumbling down to brush his hands, obviously waiting for him to come back at her over that 'sweet' remark.

The thought floated into his mind that maybe he could make something happen tonight.

The music tailed away for the last time and he dropped his voice. 'Why don't you let me show you whether I'm "sweet"?' The dance floor began to clear as people dispersed, yawning and chattering their way to collect purses and coats.

Ava's eyes blazed as she silently returned gaze for gaze.

153

He waited for a smile to curl her lips, waited for her to agree.

But, instead, she turned to look over at where his mother sat with his aunt. 'We're being watched,' she said, softly.

'Does it matter?'

The lights came up and her pupils shrank, making her look suddenly distant.

Then she answered his question in totally the wrong way. 'I think it matters. We can't faux date to please your mum forever. When are you thinking of ending the pretence?'

He let his hold on her slacken. If she'd been teetering on the brink of showing interest, the moment had passed. She'd flung up a wall with no warning or regard for how snubbed it made him feel. Disappointment washed through him and made his response blunter than good manners dictated. 'Either when she's so ill from the chemo that she won't care or when she's better and will accept that we've each moved on. If you have a preference, state it now.' He let his arms fall away completely, breaking contact to let her see that she'd trespassed too far. 'Or if you want it over I'll manufacture a row right here, as you seem to be trying to provoke one. I'm not sure what's best and definitely not sure I should have ever suggested "the pretence" because Mum has enough going on without being lied to. But at least it was a desire to make her happier that made me reluctant to correct her misapprehension about us.'

Frustrated irritation made him add, 'And if you didn't understand why I told you earlier that you can be annoying, rerun the past few minutes in your head.'

An answering anger flared in her eyes as her chin came up. '"Fucking annoying", I think.'

They were now alone on the dance floor and, stinging

from this new rejection, he barely lowered his voice. 'However annoying you are, when I think of fucking, I do think of you.'

Her eyes glittered but she didn't drop her gaze. 'You were right. You're not sweet.' She moved back a step.

Disappointment and irritation escalating at the realisation of how badly things had just gone off track, he stepped back, too. The way he felt right now, a bit of space between them was probably a good thing. 'Let's get your stuff together and get out of here.'

Anger crackling where seconds ago there had been excitement, they marched over to the hat display. Shocked at how quickly the atmosphere had changed, Sam yanked hatboxes from under the table, flipping off the lids so that Ava could nest the hats in her preferred order while he gathered up the hat stands. They worked in taut silence, Ava yawning behind her hand.

Wendy and Vanessa bustled up onto the stage with Ruby Glennister a step behind. 'Guess *what*?' burst out Wendy, who looked tired but elated. 'Ruby's offered to be our special guest at the village Christmas Fayre tomorrow!' She grabbed Ava's arm. 'Oh, Ava, you are staying with us, aren't you? Middledip's only a ten-minute drive from here but it would be about half-three before you got home to London – and even later for Sam.'

Anger taking second place to amusement, Sam hid a smile at the cornered look in Ava's eyes.

But then her expression gradually turned to one of resignation as she glanced at her watch and saw the truth of Wendy's assertion. 'If you're sure it's not putting you out, it would be a lot fairer on Sam.' She shot him a look as if to say that such consideration was more than he deserved.

Vanessa nudged her sister meaningfully. 'Perhaps they want to go home to *their own* bed.' Ava blushed and fumbled over closing one of the hatboxes.

Although she giggled, Wendy brushed Vanessa's remark aside. 'If you're staying, can I coax you to do another hat show at the Fayre tomorrow afternoon?' She drew in a long breath to add impressively, 'Ruby says she'll come too and be your model if you do! It will be so fab, Ava. Please say yes!'

Sam glanced at Ruby, who was grinning, her eyes as clear and bright as if this were the middle of the day rather than what it was fast becoming – the middle of the night. 'What d'you think, babes?' she demanded of Ava. 'I used to be a model. It was perfume ads in magazines, not catwalk, but I think I can swan up and down while you tell people about your fab hats. Then maybe Wendy can add a bit more to her charity fund.'

Wendy chimed back in. 'We thought we could charge people two pounds to take a selfie with Ruby in one of your hats. And even Carola won't have organised anything so good as a real live WAG and a hat show.'

As Ava was looking bewildered at this last comment, Sam enlightened her. 'Carola's the formidable woman who organises everything at the village hall. It's a bit of a sport in the village to one-up her but don't let yourself be cajoled into anything if it's interfering with your Sunday plans. I'll survive driving home to London tonight.'

For several seconds Ava's gaze locked with his, her eyes huge. He caught a tiny sigh, then she fixed a smile in place and turned back to the waiting women. 'How can I resist the opportunity to have Ruby Glennister modelling for me?'

By reflex, Sam found himself switching to work mode.

'You're right, it's an opportunity. It's a shame that it gives us no time to get the word out though.'

'Who to?' Ava looked from him to Ruby.

'The world, the press. I can use this to raise Ruby's profile as well as raise money. The fact that the event's so small could be a hook in itself. I'll take a video and photos, and it can be "leaked" on Monday that Ruby did all this for a woman she'd only just met, just because she admired the causes. It's a chance to present a client in a positive light.'

Ruby clapped her hands. 'Blimey, you never miss a trick, do you, Sam Jermyn? I can see what we're paying you for.' With an enthusiastic hug for Sam, then no-less-enthusiastic hugs all round, Ruby tottered off to where Tyrone and Chilly were waiting pointedly by the door.

Ava nodded slowly. 'I can see what she and Tyrone pay you for, too.'

'That's our boy. Always switched on.' Wendy patted Sam's cheek then, wreathed in triumphant smiles, she and Vanessa scurried off to collect their coats.

Sam couldn't resist a last tease. 'Does it matter that they only have one spare bed and their fat silly Labradors sleep on the couch?' Then, hastily, as Ava dropped a hatbox on her foot, 'I'm joking! You'll have my old room and I'll sleep on the sofabed. And I'll make sure Mum and Aunt Van know that our sleeping arrangements are our business, OK?'

Instantly, her expression lightened. 'Thanks.'

'You don't have to look so pleased about it.' He deliberately put himself in her path as she stooped to retrieve the fallen hatbox. 'Don't you even admit to a frisson of excitement when they mentioned us sleeping together?'

Her answer was a frown. 'Like I'd do that to poor Izz.' She made to push her way around him.

He side-stepped, deliberately misunderstanding her. 'It wouldn't have to be at your place. I live alone.'

She glared at him from under her brows. 'I can see why.'

He laughed and let her past. He wasn't sure why he was baiting her. Yet he was. It was because she wasn't following where he wanted to lead. Unslaked desire was a bitch.

The night was starry. Sam had spent ten minutes de-icing the car and his hands hurt. When he was finally able to drive to the steps of the hotel he found Ava shivering beside a tower of hatboxes, huddled into her multi-coloured coat and her breath white on the air, only a few lights left on in the hall behind her. She shoved her phone away as he drew up.

He hopped out of the car. 'Sorry that took so long. The windscreen was frozen.'

Ava tried to pick up a hatbox. 'It's OK.' Her voice shook with cold.

He took the box from her hands. 'Get in the car and I'll load up.'

For once she didn't argue, but trailed down the stone steps and around to the passenger door. He packed the boot quickly and they were soon purring down the steeply sloping drive.

Ava yawned.

'It's only a ten-minute drive so you don't have to stay awake long.'

Obviously unwilling to accept his remark as the olive branch he'd intended, she sniffed ungraciously. 'If I nodded off you might tell everyone you'd slept with me.'

Snapping down the indicator and spinning the wheel

to turn right out of the black metal gates and onto the lane to Middledip, he shot her a look. 'I don't pull those macho bullshit tricks! It makes the woman uncomfortable and makes me look like a prick. I think all I've ever indicated is that we ought to give each other a try. But you've conveyed your lack of interest so, fine. End of.'

Silence.

But slow realisation made his fingers begin to tighten on the steering wheel. 'Shit,' he swore softly. 'I did act like a prick tonight. I let my frustration get the better of me.' Remorse settled in his guts. 'Really, I'm sorry.'

'Sure.'

What did that mean? He drove through the darkness and glittering frost, kicking himself. Why had he said the stuff he had? It was so against his personal code. He wasn't that guy. Usually. He'd been disappointed but that was no excuse to be a creep. 'That reminds me. I've received a Facebook friend request from a Harvey Snaith. Looks like your ex.'

Ava turned sharply in her seat. 'Why would he do that? Did you accept him?'

'I haven't accepted him but I haven't deleted the request, either. What would you like me to do?'

'Delete.' Ava groaned. 'I'm sorry. I think I told him that you and Tod worked together.'

Sam shrugged. 'Then all he had to do was look on the agency website and match my picture to my name. Don't worry about it. I'm fussy about who I accept on social media.'

He tried to turn the conversation towards a happier path. 'Tonight should help improve your finances.'

'Yes.' Then, as if realising that he was making an effort, 'Thanks for the help you've given me in the shape of

159

chauffeur/business guru. I appreciate it.' Yet she sounded flat and dismal.

He gave her a minute. Then tried again. 'Are you OK, Ava?'

To his horror, her voice began to tremble. 'Oh no, don't start being nice. Don't make me remember how decent you are. Please. Don't come on to me like you did tonight because I have too much stuff going on in my life to get involved with anyone. Harvey's still being a problem and I don't want to get anybody else mixed up in that nightmare.' She clapped her hand over her mouth as if to stop the flow of words.

Alarmed, knowing he was almost within sight of the village, he pulled onto the verge and killed the engine. 'Hey,' he said softly, trying to see her face in the dashboard lights. 'How's he being a nightmare? Just trying to make a connection with me on Facebook because he saw us together is no big deal.'

In the near darkness he saw her fumble in her bag and snatch out a tissue. 'You're right. I'm overthinking it. Can we go?'

After a moment more of staring at her he restarted the car. What was he missing? What could Harvey the Ex be doing?

Sam drove slowly on, passing the first of the village street lamps then the familiar houses of Port Road, hating that the urge to take an uncharacteristic excursion into stupid macho posturing had hit him tonight. Ava seemed as if she needed someone she could trust and instead he'd given her yet another man to treat with suspicion.

Ava watched the road unwind like a moonlit ribbon in front of the car, as cold and grey as her feelings. She was desperate to get to bed yet wished she could somehow magic herself into her own room in Camden, instead of facing the prospect of tomorrow, an entire day of faux dating Sam under the delighted eyes of his mum and aunt.

She'd let her anxiety betray her over Harvey reaching out to Sam but she'd checked her phone to pass the time while she waited on the steps and her stomach had plummeted at finding a notification: *Harvey Snaith tagged you in a photo on Facebook.*

Her breath had frozen in her lungs.

It had seemed to take an age for her to tap *See photo* with stupidly sweaty fingers, hardly daring to look yet desperate to see. A weak signal had made loading slow. Dancing on the blades of a thousand knives of panic, she'd gone through torture until the picture loaded – Ava vamping it up for the camera . . . but fully clothed. No mutual friends had 'liked' it, probably confused as to why Harvey should be posting pictures of her now that they were no longer together. She wished that amongst all the permutations of the *like* button there could be one for *loser.*

Ava was still shaking, not just at the sly games Harvey was playing but at the knowledge that he and his threats hadn't gone away. He was messing with her.

In her peripheral vision she could see Sam casting her curious glances. Apart from the occasional blip when he was being an arse he was so solid and reassuring that a compulsion to tell him about her private shame swooped down on her. But she controlled it, in the same way that she'd controlled the compulsion to respond to him this evening as they'd danced, the heat of him filtering through their clothes. Why had Harvey tried to 'friend' Sam?

It couldn't be for a good reason.

She didn't even want to be social media friends with Sam herself. What if Harvey began sending explicit images of her around? Instead of gazing around at the pretty moonlit village they'd entered, she screwed her eyes shut in mortification.

She couldn't see Sam again after this ever-extending weekend.

Apart from at Wendy's second hat fitting, anyway. Even if Sam was truly over what happened between his ex-girlfriend and his best mate—

Best mate. Izz. Ava's conscience gave a fresh, savage twinge as she was assailed by a vision of the wistful, isolated figure of her friend on the pavement earlier this evening. Ava had no business enjoying being with Sam, weekending with his family or wrapping herself around him for the slow dances. How would Izz feel if she'd witnessed that – or one of the occasional kisses that seemed to somehow have become the norm? They were hot kisses, too, not casual kisses; kisses that burst inside Ava like pleasure-filled fireworks . . . yet she'd set her mind against letting them carry her away to dates with Sam, bed with Sam. And especially not a relationship with Sam.

Izz would probably love the opportunity to take any or all of those options. Sam and Ava had been thrown together by events recently but she made a silent vow to make that stop. Ava wasn't the kind of person to jump all over the feelings of her friends; she found ways to help them and make them happy. Neither did she string men along when she had no intention of letting anything happen, occasionally blowing on the spark between them just to see how hot it glowed. Here was where she called a halt.

She took a deep breath. 'Would you go out on a date with Izz?'

The car jinked threateningly towards a pick-up parked at the side of the road as Sam's head whipped around. 'What? Why?' He sounded dumbfounded. 'I've told you that there's no prospect of that, even if we didn't work together. And don't tell me it would only be a faux date because it can't be right to faux date two women at once.' He returned his attention to the lane that was carrying them between ironstone cottages and brick-built Victorian terraces, a few with lights showing at their windows, but most in darkness.

Her toes curled inside her party shoes. 'I wasn't thinking that the date should be faux. I just feel so bad that I've been dancing with you and everything when she has such a crush. And now, regardless of the sleeping arrangements, I'm going to be staying out overnight with you. She's one of my best friends.'

For a minute he drove in silence, taking a right turn into a charming cul-de-sac, its sign proclaiming it to be Church Close. He brought the car into a drive beside an overgrown hedge in front of a long, low house. 'I see your side of things but it's not right for me to patronise her or raise her hopes. And I'd never date someone who worked for me.' He shoved his hair back from his eyes. 'I'm sorry if the faux dating is an issue between you and Izz. She wasn't in my mind when I suggested it.'

Ava gazed at the wedges that the headlights cut from the darkness, illuminating mellow brickwork laced with patches of stone. Light streaming from small windows confirmed Wendy and Vanessa had beaten them home. 'No, nor mine. I'm afraid that sooner or later it will upset her and I was thinking of ways to make her feel better. But I can see that it's a stupid idea. She might just crush on you harder and I can completely see why you'd be uncomfortable with the work thing.'

His voice became soft. 'You're a good friend to worry about her feelings when you obviously have worries of your own.'

'Am I really?' A sigh escaped her. 'Not only is she one of my best friends, she's my oldest. I live in her house, I work in her house, she's the person I spend Christmas Day with, yet I keep finding myself in your company and leaving her out. She hasn't even been snarky about me seeing so much of you when I'm clear that we're not actually dating.'

'We're all pretty clear on that point,' he returned, drily, before adding more gently, 'I do think I see why Izz is on your conscience, though. Maybe it's because I've just come back to Middledip where I'll know just about everyone I meet . . . but I get the best friend thing.'

The front door to the cottage flew open and Wendy stood shielding her eyes against the headlights' glare and holding a finger to her lips, simultaneously blocking the path of two excited dogs with an outstretched leg.

Sam snorted a laugh as he switched off his engine. 'I'm being reminded that this isn't London and it's inconsiderate to leave the car running this late at night. I'll get the bags and we can go in.'

Indoors, Ava stepped over Wendy and Vanessa's shoes abandoned in the hall and was introduced to the two over-excited, over-friendly and overweight chocolate Labradors. 'This is Snickers and this is Mars. Ouch,' said Wendy, getting a slap from an enthusiastically wagging tail. 'Say hello to them so they can begin to calm down. Sam, are you and Ava going to sleep—'

Sam put both overnight bags in one hand to give Wendy a squeeze. 'You can leave me to look after Ava. I did used to live here, and you look shattered.'

'Good,' Vanessa answered before Wendy could, slipping an arm around her sister to usher her away. 'My bed's been calling me for hours.'

Wendy allowed herself to be shepherded up the stairs and Sam led Ava down a hallway. He pushed open a door to display a simple white suite with a knitted green octopus perched jauntily on the cistern. 'Shower room.' A few more steps and he reached into another room to flick the light on. 'You're in here. Still a bit reminiscent of teenage boy, I'm afraid, but Mum has at least got rid of the posters of metal bands and Lara Croft. This part of the house used to be a stone pigsty but there's been no oinking for years.'

Ava glanced around the room, seeing blue walls, plain carpet. And a double bed. She cleared her throat, suddenly seeing two people sleeping there, limbs entwined, waking in the morning to stretch and yawn and cuddle up.

As if seeing her vision, his voice dropped to a deep drawl. 'I won't be sleeping alone, by the way.'

Ava turned to him, her heart pressing hard against her chest wall.

Then he grinned and winked. 'It will be me and the fat silly Labradors. Goodnight.' He brushed a kiss on her forehead and left her alone but his return to teasing ways was somehow reassuring. Or, at least, it was simpler to deal with than being in his arms while he stared down at her with unconcealed heat and told her that he wanted her.

Chapter Seventeen

Village affairs

Sunday 16 December, daytime
If Ava had gone to bed a reluctant guest in Middledip, at least she'd slept like a log in the centre of the big bed, if only after a few disturbing minutes of picturing Sam's long frame in exactly the same spot.

She awoke to a dazzling morning of winter sunlight, throwing back the curtains to gaze at a garden of bird feeders and wind chimes and brown ploughed fields over a shaggy hedge. Frost outlined every leaf with delicate precision. She imagined waking every day to such prettiness, wondering whether Sam's younger self had noticed the greens of spring and golds of summer, or simply taken them for granted.

Turning eventually from the landscape, she examined the pictures on the wall – a couple of cars, a pencil drawing of a dangerous-looking bear and a cityscape of neon signs and traffic, then gathered her things and slipped across the hall for a brisk shower.

After dressing, she followed the sound of voices and the smell of bacon until she found a long rustic kitchen

166

and Wendy, Vanessa and Sam chatting around the stripped wooden table. The dogs skidded up to greet Ava as if propelled by their whirring tails and she made a fuss of them to hide her self-consciousness at intruding into a very family scene.

Wendy obviously had no intention of treating her as an intruder, though. 'You're up!' she cried, climbing to her feet. 'We've been waiting to take the dogs out and show you the village.'

'I think Mum's pleased to have you here.' Sam's hair was unusually tumbled and he hadn't shaved, the very picture of a man relaxing on a Sunday morning. He got up and gave Ava a warm hug and a quick kiss, the way he might if he and Ava were an item even if not yet sharing a bed. It occurred to Ava that the sleeping arrangements had probably made Wendy and Vanessa think Ava was unusually proper, which was very nice, if not very accurate.

Flushing because Sam's arm was still warm around her, Ava smiled at Wendy. 'I'd love to see the village.'

'Bacon sandwich first?' Sam suggested.

'Oh yes, of course.' Wendy lit the grill, beaming, without waiting for Ava's answer. 'And tea. Or coffee? Sam, get Ava the juice. Ava, bacon soft or crispy?' Gently, Sam sat Wendy down while he took over the grill.

After eating thick bacon between slabs of white bread into which the butter melted mouthwateringly, Wendy found Ava boots, gloves, scarf and a wadded waxed jacket suitable for the country while the dogs whirled in circles, as if tripping everyone up was the best way to ensure they weren't forgotten.

Soon the little party was leaving Church Close, Wendy wearing a thick blue knitted hat, Vanessa towed by two Labradors but trying to hold them back to Wendy's gentle pace. Bringing up the rear, Sam took Ava's hand. She gave him a startled look but then realising that it was all part of the faux dating, grinned. 'I'm going to pretend to twist my ankle so Wendy and Vanessa will expect you to carry me all the way back.'

He raised a lazy brow. 'Happy to.' And he swooped her up and over his shoulder in a fireman's lift, his hands somehow ending up on her buttocks.

'No!' she yelped, half-blinded by her hair tumbling over her face and totally discomposed by the view of his buttocks inches from her face. Laughing, he swept her back down and onto her feet.

Breathless but giggling back at him, Ava was aware of Wendy and Vanessa glancing around and exchanging smiles. Reminding herself that the larking around was as faux as the dating, she gave him a friendly shove in the middle of his solid chest before she let him take her hand again.

Middledip village was an interesting mix of rust-coloured cottages huddled in groups and tall brick houses with pointed gables. Sometimes stone and brick met in one house, as Ava had already seen at Wendy and Vanessa's. At the centre of the village the lanes joined to form a three-legged cross where a corner shop did brisk business in Sunday papers and a garage stood with its doors firmly folded shut.

Wendy called back, 'We'll have lunch in the Three Fishes because they'll let us take the dogs in if we eat in the bar.'

Ava put a hand to her stomach. 'That bacon sandwich was so filling I don't think I could manage a thing.'

'You will. We're going on a good long walk so that Carola can't find us and make us put up stalls.' Then Wendy and Vanessa recounted, with great glee, how they'd phoned village-organiser Carola as soon as they'd got up that morning to demand a rearrangement to the Christmas Fayre to accommodate the real live celebrity they'd managed to snare.

'It was the nearest I've ever known Carola to being speechless.' Vanessa sighed in satisfaction as they crossed the village on a circuitous route that would keep them out of sight of the village hall and down a bridleway so that the dogs could bound off, breathing clouds into the crisp air.

The sun rose high enough to melt the frost from the hedgerows and Wendy spread her arms and twirled, gazing up at the clear blue sky. 'What a glorious day. It makes you feel good to be alive, doesn't it?'

Ava had to swallow the most enormous lump in her throat before answering. 'I felt the same when I opened the curtains this morning.'

Vanessa's smile wavered as Wendy suddenly had to bump down onto a log to catch her breath, saying, 'Every day's a good day.'

Sam said nothing at all, but his hand became tense in Ava's.

Stepping inside Middledip Village Hall in the wake of his mum and aunt, Sam felt a tug of nostalgia at the sight of villagers dressing stalls in red and green crepe paper and suspending decorations from the beams on loops of tinsel. He must have been to a hundred fetes, fayres, parties and receptions. Wendy and Vanessa had dragged him into fund-raising when it was necessary to buy new curtains for the long run of windows and doors and then teenage parties had found him exchanging kisses with flirty girls behind those very same curtains. At various ages he'd

169

skateboarded in the car park, swung on the swings outside and played football on the grass.

What was new was the presence of Ava, her hair brushed and put up since the morning's walk, smiling and chatting with his mum, attracting a lot of beady gazes as people he'd known all his life mentally calculated what it meant that Sam Jermyn had 'brought a girl home'. He gave an inner sigh. The more Ava Blissham tried not to be woven into the tapestry of his life, the more it seemed to come about.

'Jermyn! Still feeding bullshit to journalists?' A man with dark curls and glittering black eyes tied off a string of silver tinsel and jumped lithely down from a stepladder to greet him.

Sam grinned, extending his hand and bracing himself for a manly shoulder slap. 'Pretty much, Ratty. You still selling heaps of rust and calling them classic cars?'

'As long as people will pay for them.' Ratty greeted Vanessa and Wendy before they plunged into the ant-like gathering of people then turned to regard Ava with one raised brow.

Sam was obliged to make introductions. 'Ava, this is an old buddy, Ratty – Miles Arnott-Rattenbury. He owns the garage at The Cross. Ratty, Ava's a milliner and Mum's talked her into doing a hat show at the Christmas Fayre.'

Ratty was polite and smooth. 'I've been hearing about this. Hasn't your mum secured a real-life WAG to model the hats? That's impressive.' But his eyes said to Sam, *She's gorgeous. Well done, mate,* making Sam feel as uncomfortable as Ava looked.

Then other old friends bustled up, Pete and Angel with hugs, Jos introducing his wife, Miranda. Ava managed to smile under the onslaught of names and faces, then they were both distracted as they caught sight of Wendy removing her hat to reveal her naked head, her friends gathering to offer hugs or stroke her scalp, their eyes shining with tears. Such compassion stole over Ava's face that a lump jumped into Sam's throat.

Ratty bumped his shoulder. 'Seriously shitty about your mum, man. How's she doing?'

Pete and Jos looked gravely sympathetic and while Sam was clearing his throat to mutter, 'She's amazing,' blonde Carola popped up and grabbed Ava by the arm.

The look Ava sent back to Sam as she was dragged away was beseeching. 'Hats!' she mouthed.

'I'll get them from the car.'

Ratty laughed. 'Oops. You've let the wolf get her. Bad boyfriend.'

Sam thought about protesting that Ava wasn't his girl-friend but glancing back to his beaming mum, who'd plunged into a spirited discussion with Carola while Ava looked on, he gave up. The main thing was that, for now, Wendy was happy. 'I'll make it up to her by carrying her hatboxes.'

No sooner had he ferried in the last box than Ruby arrived and he stepped automatically into the role of making sure she had what she wanted and that Ava and Ruby held sway over anything Carola might take it into her head to demand. As a stream of villagers paid their fifty pences at the door and crowded into the hall exclaiming that the WAG rumours had been true, he took photos on his phone of Ruby in front of the hat display, holding hats, modelling hats, chatting to milling villagers and even giving a brief, bright speech about how touched she'd been by Wendy's buzzing the night before.

When her spot was finally over, Ruby sat down with

Ava at one of the little tables that formed 'The Crimbo Café', i.e. the usual serving hatch surrounded with red streamers and silver tinsel, to eat mince pies and drink coffee from proper cups. Ruby continued to generously allow anyone to take her photo, 'As long as you put two quid in this dish for Wendy's charity collection and if you put the pic on social media you include the hashtag #RubyGlennister.'

It was an hour later, when Sam had rescued Ava's samples before they were destroyed by overeager tryings-on that Ruby sought him out. 'Gotta go, Sam.' She hauled him into her usual exuberant hug. 'Let me know where the pics appear tomorrow, yeah? I'll do all the sharing on Twitter and that.' She embraced Wendy and Vanessa, then turned to Ava. 'Honest, babes, I don't know why you're being so coy. Get a bit of free promo, that's what it's all about.'

Ava went scarlet. 'You're a client, Ruby. It's different.'

Ruby tutted. 'Sam, you'll make sure the journos get that the hats were made by Ava Bliss, won't you? Don't take no notice of Ms Conscience, here.'

Sam was glad to comply. 'Your conscience can be quiet,' he told Ava, who looked as if she wished the floor would open up. 'You're the creator of the hats, the hats will be featured in the shots so you automatically get a credit in any coverage. Besides, my client has requested it.'

'But—' Ava protested.

Then they were drawn apart by requests to buy raffle tickets and guess the weight of a Christmas cake while 'Jingle Bells' followed by 'I Wish It Could Be Christmas Everyday' burbled over the PA. The next time Sam looked at his watch it was nearly five, already dark, and time to think about heading home.

He found Ava once again at The Crimbo Café, this time devouring stollen with Wendy and Vanessa. 'We ought to think about making tracks.' He tried not to let his heart lurch when his mum's face fell. He dropped into the chair beside her and gave her a quick hug. 'We'll be seeing each other really soon, though, won't we? Soon be Christmas.'

Wendy managed a grin. 'Of course. It's going to be lovely. A really special Christmas, eh, Ava?'

Ava only looked as if the stollen had stuck in her throat, so it was left to Sam to reply. 'You bet.' But his voice sounded hollow in his own ears.

Although Sam had begun making noises about leaving hours ago, Ava didn't complain when he let Wendy prevail upon them to go home for cheese on toast and mugs of coffee before setting off for London. Her heart had felt so full today, watching Wendy with her friends and neighbours and the affection and worry that had clouded their eyes. Carola had even declared that she was going to propose to the Village Hall Committee that a donation be made to No Blame or Shame from today's event, as it was the news crackling around the villages that Booby Ruby was going to be at the fayre that had made the coffers so healthy.

Vanessa had already said her farewells and driven off to meet Neale and now Wendy stood grating a heap of cheese as the grill heated. 'Carola has a heart of gold, even if she goes through life convinced that nobody but her can organise themselves to walk and talk at the same time. You were great, Ava, so just sit down with Sam and rest before your journey.'

'But you must be tired,' Ava protested.

'Not really.' But Wendy's eyes looked bruised with

fatigue so Sam and Ava took over the making of supper, then, while Wendy grabbed forty winks in the kitchen rocker, washed up.

'It's a shame to wake her,' Ava whispered, when the kitchen was restored to order and Wendy snoozed on.

'She'd hate not saying goodbye, though. Let's give her ten more minutes – we'll load the car.' Sam's voice was hoarse and Ava's heart ached when she saw the naked grief in his eyes, so they awarded Wendy an entire half hour while they not only loaded the car but Sam took Ava on a belated tour of the house, Wendy's room filled with homemade rugs and curtains, Vanessa's bedroom and study plain but comfortable.

'It's lovely that they can live together so harmoniously,' Ava said.

Sam's expression darkened. 'Especially as when my grandparents died they left everything to Vanessa.'

Ava felt her breath catch in her throat. 'You're kidding?'

'Nope. Vanessa used the inheritance to buy the house and simply put it in joint names. She was furious at the way Mum was treated.' He glanced at his watch and sighed. 'If either of us are to be any use at work tomorrow, we really ought to go.'

'Of course.' Ava ignored a curl of dismay. She should be glad to be heading back to Camden, shouldn't she?

Wendy blinked sleepily when Sam woke her but got up to hug them both goodbye. 'See you soon. Can't wait for Christmas!'

'See you soon,' Ava echoed.

She climbed into Sam's BMW still waving. They drove out of the village and traversed country roads and Peterborough's parkway system in silence until they joined

174

the motorway, the tarmac glittering with frost between the tyre tracks.

'Thanks for staying over,' he said, eventually. 'It meant a lot to Mum. I know I keep saying that about various things, but it keeps on being true.'

'I know.' Her sigh was so deep it actually hurt her chest. 'And she's so lovely that I honestly don't begrudge the time. I'm only worried about the overnight stay because of Izz.'

His sigh was almost as loud as hers had been. 'I'm sorry. You're getting drawn deeper and deeper into the faux dating because of Mum.' They lapsed back into silence.

By the time they reached School Road, Ava's eyes were gritty with the need for sleep but she was reluctant to leave the warmth of the car.

Sam killed the engine and turned in his seat. 'OK, I have a plan but it's probably manipulative and you may not like it.'

'You're not selling it so far.'

His smile was pensive. 'I'll agree to an accidentally-on-purpose date.'

'I have no idea what you're talking about.'

'With Izz. Surely you used to do accidentally-on-purpose dating when you were a teenager? You'd find out someone you liked was going somewhere and arrange to be there, too?'

'Oh. Right. Yes. I suppose everyone does. It's not a statement of intent like when you ask someone out, so there's less to lose.'

'Exactly, particularly the statement of intent part, in this case. Arrange to meet Izz somewhere near the agency and I'll come in and just happen to be in the same place.'

A strange feeling sank through Ava's insides, surprising in its intensity. 'It sounds juvenile.'

175

He laughed shortly. 'Some people would say a crush is juvenile, too. But you asked me to go on a date with Izz and though a proper date's obviously not appropriate, I'll do this if your conscience will be assuaged by me spending time with her to balance our faux dating.'

Ava turned the idea around in her mind. Now she was being given what she'd asked for, a date for Izz, she didn't feel she could complain that it was the wrong kind. 'You won't ignore her? Or make I-don't-want-to-be-in-this-conversation conversation?'

'I'll make certain to interact properly with her.'

'OK,' Ava agreed slowly, trying not to examine too closely why his abrupt compromise on something he'd seemed *un*compromising about should make her feel so empty. She deflected a stab of disappointment, not sure if it were disappointment in herself, or in him, and focused on the fact that at least he seemed motivated by trying to make people feel better, even if his approach was unorthodox. His plan didn't seem very honest but it might go some way towards consoling Izz.

Ava refused to examine how she felt about the idea of Sam and Izz together.

They agreed on Thursday as accidentally-on-purpose-date night and he carried her paraphernalia into the house as quietly as possible.

It wasn't until he'd kissed her gently but chastely on the lips and driven off that she realised that what she'd agreed to would mean she'd be seeing Sam yet again – but surely that was OK when she was doing it for Izz?

Chapter Eighteen

Putting the 'trick' in Patrick

Wednesday 19 December

On Wednesday, Ava fulfilled three orders for gift certificates, typing names and amounts into the template Tod had made for her then giving each a reference number.

Her heart gave a little hop and skip to see the income in her bank account, and, later, another email enquiry resulting from the Rotary Ball lit a warm glow of satisfaction within her. Someone else had already made an appointment in early January for a hat for her daughter's wedding.

Then Sam texted her to arrange Wendy's second fitting on Friday week.

Ava replied, confirming also Izz's accidentally-on-purpose date with Sam the next evening. She wondered if it would be possible to leave them to it if Izz and Sam showed any signs of conversing easily. Izz might get on much better without Ava there. And Ava wouldn't have to watch it happening.

She got out her sewing machine to make the lining to Wendy's hat, using the same block as before for the sizing, then trimmed it neatly and stitched it in place with painstaking little stab stitches that wouldn't show, before making the head fitting. The hat itself then complete, she planned the embellishment ready for after the second fitting and began cutting the peacock feather eyes to fabulous points with a sharp craft knife. Laying them out on her work surface she looped the gold ribbon over and around them experimentally to admire the effect.

For the first time in ages she had a fully productive day. At the end of it, she changed and set out to the gym. The year's subscription she'd paid in more lucrative times would run out at the end of December so she might as well enjoy her six o'clock booiaka class while she still could.

The class was fast and noisy. Some of the girls wore tinsel to tie up their hair and one had a flashing reindeer nose pinned to her singlet. Ava enjoyed the fun and was even prepared not to hate Christmas too much in her current buoyant mood.

After a fast shower, she clunked through the turnstile at reception ready to scramble into her coat for the chilly walk home.

'Ava!'

Ava halted in surprise in the middle of the foyer. 'Patrick? What are you doing here?'

Patrick looked to be dressed for work rather than a workout. 'I'm thinking of joining. Are you a member?'

'For now. Why would you join a gym in Camden? It's not exactly convenient for Balham, is it?'

He grinned boyishly. 'I like to go to the gym straight after work and it's cheaper here than around Brick Lane. I'm spending time in this area with a client so I thought it was worth checking out. Anyway,' he rushed on, before she got a chance to query whether he seriously visited one client enough to warrant gym membership nearby, 'it's handy that you know the place already because you can give me the insider view. Over a cup of coffee?'

Switching her bag from one shoulder to another, Ava remembered Izz saying that Patrick kept asking about her and debated the wisdom of providing even slight encouragement to him, but an Americano sounded irresistible. 'OK. There's a bar upstairs.'

With a wide grin, Patrick followed Ava up to where the landing broadened out into a carpeted area with a bar at one side and a balcony looking out over the gym rats on their treadmills on the other. The air was warm and the noise level set to gentle hum. Ava grabbed a table while Patrick ordered the coffee.

He returned with two large Americanos and the snacks menu. 'I'm famished. These clients are really buzzy but proper slave drivers. I haven't had a chance to eat.'

Ava had eaten no more than a banana since lunchtime herself and she found her stomach rumbling as Patrick decided aloud from a tempting range of wraps and baguettes. 'I think I'll have the prawn. How about you?' He turned the menu around so that she could read it.

Ava had intended to eat at home but she was starving, and she had actually earned some money today. 'The roast chicken sounds good.' She stooped for her gym bag. As she never brought her purse to the gym, in view of the flimsy nature of the lockers, she kept a tenner tucked in an inside pocket for just such eventualities. But Patrick had jumped to his feet and was at the bar before she'd straightened up.

He waved away her attempt to pay him when he returned. 'We pay when the food's ready. So what do you like about this gym? They seem to have a good range of equipment. Do you use their personal trainers?'

'It's pretty much like any other gym. Machines, trainers, classes in the studio, changing rooms.'

The subject was exhausted by the time their order was called and Patrick sprinted off to collect it. When he returned, there were two glasses of rosé on the tray along with the baguettes.

'Patrick!' Ava protested. 'I didn't ask for wine.' Her tenner wouldn't cover it. But it did look mouth-watering with its delicate little jacket of condensation forming on the glass.

He grinned boyishly. 'I've got almost no cash with me and they won't accept a card for transactions amounting to less than £15, so I had to pay. Anyway, as I've steam-rollered you up here, it's the least I can do.'

In view of her own limited cash situation, Ava couldn't really argue further and prepared to make conversation while they ate. 'I met Ruby Glennister and she told me you're working on a campaign for her. Is that interesting?'

Patrick's grin flashed again. 'Very. Where did you meet her?'

Instantly, Ava found that she didn't want to tell him any more than she had to. 'I'm making a hat for Sam's mum and Ruby got involved in a charity thing with her,' she babbled. 'Tell me about the campaign.'

But Patrick's eyes had narrowed. 'Apparently Ruby got involved with two charity shindigs for Wendy, last Saturday evening and Sunday afternoon. Which were you at? Or perhaps you were at both? Perhaps you and Sam over-nighted somewhere?'

Ava cursed herself for a blabber-mouthed moron as she felt her cheeks scald. How could she have forgotten Sam saying he'd be utilising the images from the Middledip Christmas Fayre to add positivity to Ruby's profile with the media? Hadn't she begun this conversation with a remark about Patrick working on that very campaign? 'Um,' she said, feebly.

Throwing back his head, Patrick let out a delighted laugh. 'Don't look so guilty! Don't you think I know they were your hats Ruby was modelling? Wendy was crusading on behalf of her women's group and you and Ruby were big-hearted enough to help out and, in Ruby's case, Sam saw how the situation could be exploited in our client's favour. My role means I was thoroughly briefed! You did me, Manda Jane and Emily a favour because we're trying everything we know to get Ruby into the public eye over Christmas when people have a lot of time to browse news sites and may be feeling benevolent. Manda Jane has clout with some online magazines and we're targeting them at the same time as trying to get in the print media for January. The celeb mags keep their front pages open until the last minute but you've got to be really sensational and topical to hit them and we're still looking for ways to make it a big enough human-interest story.'

Smarting at his evident delight in so thoroughly winding her up, Ava ripped her baguette in half, spraying crumbs over the table, grateful that at least she'd chatted to Izz about the recent weekend over breakfast, careful to make it sound more about business than pleasure. Although Izz had worn the kind of blank expression that usually disguised deeper emotions, hopefully Sam turning up at work with a phone full of pictures to be 'leaked' would have helped support the impression Ava had taken pains to create. 'Not a campaign that will bring you to Camden, then,' she said, shortly. 'Do you really think you'll join this gym?'

Patrick turned to his own food. 'It's not impossible.'

181

'But not probable.'

He brushed past the point with a wink. 'How about coming out to dinner with me sometime soon?'

She smiled neutrally. 'Thanks, but I'm not dating at the moment.'

His face fell. 'Any particular reason?'

'I need to concentrate on my career.'

'Right.'

They ate in silence for a while. Then Patrick wiped his hands on his paper napkin. 'I know you stayed with his family at the weekend but if you're waiting around for Sam you're probably wasting your time. He's avoided relationships recently. He's focused on the agency.' Patrick warmed to his subject as he swigged his wine. 'I wouldn't choose work over women myself.' He waggled his eyebrows.

Ava was half-surprised that Patrick didn't trot out the Mariah-breaking-Sam's-heart situation. She opened her mouth to say, 'But Sam asked me out,' then closed it again. Why make it obvious that she had turned Sam down? There was something about Patrick's heavy-handed attempt to put her off Sam that didn't sit well with her. He seemed not much better than Sam's old best friend, the unknown Elliot.

Sam was leaving the agency on time, for once. Opportunity was running out for him to finalise his online shopping order and generally get organised ready to host Christmas for his mother and aunt and it was on his evening's 'to do' list.

'Sam?' Just as he thought he was making a successful escape, Barb called after him from the front desk, telephone in hand. 'Bloke requesting your mobile number. I asked his name and he said Harvey.'

Sam considered this surprising information. He didn't ask 'Harvey who?' as he was pretty sure he knew the answer. His first reaction was to keep Ava's ex at the greatest distance possible, but if Harvey wanted Sam's number he wanted it for a reason, and he didn't mind Sam knowing that Harvey wanted it. Interesting approach.

Sam pondered. Ava might not want Harvey to have Sam's number. That would be for a reason, too.

But Sam *was* on Ava's side, he argued with himself.

The desire to make Ava's world better rose up in him. He'd never experienced the urge so acutely and it wasn't particularly comfortable that he was feeling it for a faux girlfriend, but . . . 'Let him have it,' he said as he turned towards the door.

Later, lounging on his sofa with his iPad and his online Christmas grocery shopping list, Sam's phone gave the polite hiccup that meant it had a message waiting for him, and the screen told him that came from an unknown number.

Congrats on snaring the lovely Ava.

Sam sent back: *??? Sorry, your number's not coming up in my contacts.*

Another minute before the phone hiccuped again. *She's quite a girl.*

He stared down at the screen. It was too much of a coincidence for it not to be Harvey. Was he basing his assumption that Sam was seeing Ava on the fleeting scene in Blaggard's – when Ava had been not only with him, but with a group of people?

Or had he seen them together since? Uneasiness prickled across Sam's shoulders. How would Harvey have seen them? By hanging around and seeing Sam bring Ava home . . . ?

He returned to his iPad and opened a new browser window to remind himself of what it said on the No Blame or Shame website about escalation of behaviour.

Nothing good, he decided ten minutes later. He frowned as he stared out at the nightscape of the Olympic Stadium and the wild and wonderful sculpture of the ArcelorMittal orbit.

He should tell Ava about the text. It was the right thing to do. But should he tell her about his disquiet?

Good question.

Chapter Nineteen

The gallery of shame

Thursday 20 December

Sam was at the coffee machine when Patrick wandered in. 'Hi, boss.' He threw his man-bag onto his workstation and joined Sam to wait his turn for morning caffeine.

'You look happy.' Sam watched steaming water and milky froth fill his cup in twin jets then stepped back to give Patrick access to the machine, enjoying the mellow coffee fragrance on the air.

Patrick pressed a couple of buttons as he sent Sam a big wink. 'Great evening.'

Sam sipped at his froth. 'Anyone I know?' The machine began to gurgle.

'Ava. Supper and drinks.'

Sam's coffee suddenly tasted odd. 'Like a date?'

Patrick patted his jacket pocket where, presumably, his wallet resided. 'Worth every penny. Taking it slowly because she's a bit wary, you know, with the ex and everything. But I asked to see her again.' He gave Sam a 'you know the score' grin, swooped on his drink and sauntered off towards his desk, whistling.

Sam made for his office fighting an urge to snap, 'What the hell?' at Patrick, even though he knew that Patrick never got on board with the guy code thing of not girl-poaching if a friend had already shown interest. Patrick was more into the every-man-for-himself code.

He closed his office door with a snap, fighting bubbles of anger. He had no rights in this. He was faux dating Ava but there was no reason why she couldn't genuinely date Patrick. Even if she'd refused to genuinely date Sam for no-men-all-career reasons that seemed not to apply to Patrick.

It was time to accept that even if Ava made him ache to take her to bed she wasn't going to let it happen.

But . . . bollocks. Just superbollocks.

The bar was the nearest to the agency, an ex-industrial venue with huge windows once designed to save on the lighting bills of a factory owner. Inside, festoons of red tinsel and oversized frosted baubles in blue hung incongruously on its bare brick walls.

Because it was early when they arrived, Ava and Izz were able to grab comfortable squashy leather seating in a corner rather than having to stand up in the vast seatless desert that made up the majority of the space. Ava manoeuvred so that Izz faced the door.

Ava wasn't feeling as cheerful as she had yesterday, though yet another Rotarian had bought a gift voucher and at a nice value, too. Maybe it was the approach of Christmas that was getting her down. Not the accidentally-on-purpose Sam and Izz date, she assured herself.

She ordered a large glass of wine and listened to Izz talk about Sam who had, apparently, been shut in his office almost all day. 'Everyone noticed, because he usually spends a lot of time around the agency talking to everyone about their projects.'

'What does he say about yours?'

Izz did a sudden meerkat impression, bolting upright and staring fixedly across the venue. 'There he is!'

'Who?' Ava sipped her wine without looking round.

'Sam!'

This time Ava feigned mild interest. 'Really?'

'He's gone to the bar.'

'I expect he wants a drink.'

Izz craned. 'He's drinking Cobra. He's looking at his phone. Now he's looking around the bar. He's seen us!' Then, incredulously, 'He's coming over.'

In a few moments Sam loomed over them looking amazing in a dark suit and a darker expression. 'Are you waiting for someone or can a tired and frazzled bloke join you?'

'Join us,' invited Ava, as Izz had turned as red as the tinsel above her and seemed temporarily struck dumb. 'Tell us about your frazzles.'

Sam plumped down into a seat. 'The press haven't been particularly interested in the charity angle and so we're chasing our tails – as I'm sure you've been hearing, Izz – over the Ruby Glennister campaign. Trouble is Ruby's fixated on us working some magic over Christmas and it doesn't give us much time to plan.' Sam dragged off his tie and rolled it up into his pocket.

He spent the next hour talking about work. To Izz.

Izz, as stunned as if Hugo Boss Christmas Man himself had walked into the bar and begun chatting her up, didn't contribute hugely to the conversation.

As Sam was labouring to achieve more than one-word answers, Ava realised she'd have to give the conversational ball a nudge. 'I meant to look to see what bands are playing over Christmas, now I've got a few quid to spend. Have you checked it out, Izz? Vibe's just up the road from here, isn't it?' *Anyone* could talk about music with Izz. She was a contemporary music encyclopaedia.

Sure enough, once Izz's favourite social common ground had been broached she launched into the list of bands and venues she carried in her head – she was incredible at retaining that information. All Ava had to do was sit back and smile and nod as Izz and Sam chatted about The Libertines, After Alice and other bands on Izz's playlists.

They were halfway down their second drink when Sam broached a new subject. 'Are either of you going to Comic Con or True Believers next year?'

Ava glanced at Sam in surprise.

Izz frowned. 'Tod goes, but with his housemates.'

Sam looked interested. 'I've never been. I wonder if Tod would mind me tagging along?'

'Are you into comics?' asked Ava, disbelievingly. The bar was filling up and she had to raise her voice to be heard over the noise level in the high-ceilinged space.

Sam switched his gaze to her. 'I've got a collection. Old-school stuff, you know – *Justice League of America*, and League members like Superman and Green Lantern.' He turned back to Izz. 'What about you?'

Izz was staring at him as if he'd just transformed from Hugo Boss Christmas Man into The Riddler. 'We're not into comics.'

Sam's eyebrows flipped up. 'But you were at Tod's BalCom event.'

'Only because Tod likes us to go to his Christmas do, not because we like superheroes in tights.' Izz looked mildly insulted.

The corners of Sam's mouth turned down. 'Shame. A graphic novel can be really engrossing escapism.'

Izz continued to stare at him. 'Tod will be here any minute so you can talk to him about "sequential art narrative".'

'Will he?' Ava looked at her friend in fresh surprise.

Izz nodded. 'I told him at work today you and me were meeting and he said he'd join us.'

Sam's smile faltered. 'I expect he knows a lot more about comics than I do.'

His gaze caught Ava's and she read the alarm there. The penny dropped. 'Tod's an aficionado,' she agreed sweetly. 'Don't worry if you don't feel your knowledge matches his. He'll be happy to educate you.'

'What am I an aficionado about?' Tod came up behind Ava, Louise in tow, literally, as she had the kind of grasp on Tod's arm that said 'he's mine and where he goes I go'.

Izz frowned. 'You didn't tell us that Sam's into comics, like you.'

Beaming, Tod swung on Sam. 'Seriously? I honestly didn't know that. What are you into?'

Then Sam had to struggle to keep his end up in the conversation as Tod kindly filled in all kinds of gaps in Sam's knowledge about comics in general and the Justice League in particular.

They were interrupted in his discourse about *Justice League International* and *The New 52* by Izz's phone ringing. She answered as if glad of something to do other than listen to comic talk, jamming the handset against one ear and her hand over the other. 'Mum? Sorry, say that again. What about Christmas?'

While Izz screwed up her face in an effort to hear and said, 'Oh?' a lot, Louise instigated a change of subject.

'Speaking of Christmas, what's everybody doing? We have plans with my family. We're wrapping presents at the weekend, aren't we, Tod?'

Looking as if it were a lot less inspiring a prospect than talking about Comic Con, Tod agreed.

'As you know, I'm not a big fan of Christmas,' Ava contributed. 'As Tod's busy, it'll be just Izz and me this year. We'll stick dinner on, watch TV and drink fizz.'

Izz finished her call, dismay all over her face. 'Oh Ava! I've got to go to my parents' for Christmas. That was Mum. My sister Danielle's being sick constantly now she's having a baby and Mum says she and Dad can't manage the grandparents on their own. Grampie keeps falling over and Nana can't cut up her own food.'

Ava gazed at Izz, cold tentacles of disappointment creeping around her. 'We're not spending Christmas Day together?'

'I couldn't really say I wouldn't go.' Izz's eyes filled with tears. 'You can come, too, but you know how they do Christmas. Kind of . . .'

'Full on,' Ava finished for her, knowing all about the hours spent slaving in the kitchen, Christmas hats all through dinner, flaming pudding, extravagant presents and family carols after the Queen's speech. 'I wouldn't impose, Izz.'

Louise broke the awkward silence, for once sounding sympathetic. 'You could visit your parents, Ava. A French Christmas would be fun.'

Ava nodded but she knew that if she could get flights at this late stage the cost would be prohibitive, especially as she had Wendy's hat to finish so wouldn't be able to fly until Christmas Eve. She blinked and tried not to look at Izz, not wanting to read guilt in her face for something she couldn't help, or Tod, who could convey more sympathy in a look than most people could in an essay. She needed a moment to absorb the fact that she'd wake up on Christmas morning alone. Spend the day alone.

That was a lower-key Christmas than even she wanted. Lower even than the years after Gran died, when her parents tried their best to get the whole nuisance festive season out of the way as briskly as possible.

Christmas truly sucked.

Sam nudged her. 'I don't suppose you'd come and help me create Christmas for my mother and aunt, would you? As you know, it's the first time I've had to do it and I'm floundering.'

Ava managed a wobbly smile. 'That's kind of you but I'll be OK. I've always said that I'd like to pretend Christmas doesn't exist. Now I can.'

He sighed, propping on his palm a jaw shadowed with end-of-day stubble. 'If that seems more attractive than helping me out then I completely understand. Aunt Van will pitch in but she only gets a couple of days off work for the festivities and so I really wanted to give her a break. Also, I want her to stop Mum from doing anything.' His voice dropped. 'You know why this Christmas is . . . special.'

Her smile remained pinned in place. 'I still think—'

'You'd be doing me the most enormous favour. It would help stop Mum brooding and leave Van free to spend Christmas evening with Neale. I've been hoping Mary Berry or Nigella would pop round, but they seem to be busy. Will you come?' He picked up his drink and held it poised to clink it to Ava's glass as a seal to the deal.

Ava tried to read the lights in his eyes. She wanted to question the wisdom of deepening the faux-dating pretence, what with Wendy already seeming uncomfortably invested in what she thought was their relationship, but Tod and Izz were looking so relieved that Ava heard herself saying, weakly, 'Well . . . OK. Thank you.'

Izz finished her drink and sighed. 'I'll get myself over to Piccadilly. Now I'm going home, Mum wants me to get all kinds of stuff from Fortnum's.'

Ava suspected the urge to shop was more an urge to hide away, feeling that she'd let Ava down. She tried to catch Izz's eye so that she could send her a reassuring grin but soon Izz was calling her goodbyes over her shoulder as she made her way through the noisy throng between the bar and the door.

Then Ava's phone buzzed and she saw, with plunging heart, that Harvey had sent her a message.

Just been looking at those pics. Fancy a little fuck at Christmas?

Her heart leaped up to her throat. The *bastard*. He was just not going to go away!

All the emotions of the past weeks, the money troubles, the Harvey worries, set the blood boiling in Ava's brain. In fury, her fingers flew over the keypad: *Not if you're the little fuck on offer.*

She hit send.

She slapped her phone back into her bag.

Then cold horror flooded in to quench all anger.

What had she *done?*

Even now, Harvey would be opening the message. Reading it. Reacting. There was no way of reversing its route through cyber space.

She began to shake. She must have lost her mind! Harvey was rancid when he was drunk. All that time she'd kept it together, kept her cool, made sure not to antagonise him while she waited for him to move on – all compromised by a moment's unthinking rage.

Her phone buzzed again. *You wait, bitch!!!!! Remember that I have the gallery of shame.*

Another buzz. This time an image . . . Trembling, Ava opened it. A picture of herself, laughing at the camera. The fascinator of flamboyant cerise feathers that was her only adornment made her look like a tawdry 1940s porn star. The message beneath read: *And remember this isn't the worst of them. I have hot action shots . . .*

Hands sweating with shame, she fumbled through the process of closing the message down, feeling sick at the thought of how it would feel to know that images were circulating of her 'in action'.

'Are you OK?'

Ava started. It seemed that while she'd been occupied with Harvey's shitty antics, Louise had commandeered Tod's attention. Sam was now staring at Ava and frowning. 'Yes.' She put her phone away and wiped her damp palms on her dress.

Sam's gaze didn't waver. 'Sure?'

She tried to smile but her lips took on a piteous wobble. 'Positive.' *Don't ask me any more. I'm so close to tears you wouldn't believe it.* She grabbed her bag with shaking hands. 'Back in a minute.'

Taking refuge in the ladies, she shut herself in a cubicle, sat down on the loo and slapped her head into her hands. She felt very strange. Shaky. Sick. Her lungs seemed to have forgotten how to suck air in past the sobs crowding her throat. Her hands and feet fizzed as if their veins were filled with prosecco and there seemed to be moths fluttering in her ears.

Familiar flashes of white light appeared at the periphery

of her vision. A band formed around the left side of her head. Barely able to make her hands work, she scrambled in her bag for her migraine medication, gulping down the smooth white pill.

Vaguely, she was aware of people coming and going outside the stall, banging the doors of the other stalls, flushing, washing. Asking each other if her cubicle was broken. Giggling that someone might be in there and would hear them. Whispers that someone might be ill.

Eventually, she heard the outer door open again. 'Ava? Are you in here? Are you OK?'

Louise's voice surprised Ava into drawing a proper breath. Then another. The prosecco and the moths began to recede. The white flashes started to fade. She licked her lips. 'Yes. I'll be out in a minute.' Her voice seemed to come from a distance.

'Oh. OK.' Louise hesitated. 'I'll go back to the others, then.' The door squeaked as it opened and closed.

Ava rose on unsteady legs, sucking in several more deep breaths. She looked in wonder at her hands. Trembling. Sweating. Dimly, she recognised that as well as an incipient migraine she had probably just suffered a panic attack.

She tried to take stock. Her phone was quiet. No Facebook email notifications that Harvey Snaith had tagged her in a picture. None of her friends sending her *WTF????* or *OMG!!!!* texts. Maybe the world wasn't going to end after all? Maybe Harvey had harmlessly passed out and would awake in the morning with a slamming hangover and a blank in his memory.

She continued to breathe, letting her brain enjoy the oxygen. Letting the fizzing and the fluttering fade to nothing.

Finally feeling strong enough to leave the sanctuary of

the cubicle, she washed her hands and wrists in cold water, patted her hair and ventured back into the racket and red tinsel of the bar.

Tod, Sam and even Louise broke off their conversation to regard her with varying degrees of curiosity and concern. She'd no idea how long she'd been but as Louise had been despatched to check on her it had obviously been longer than was necessary for a quick pee. 'Have I been ages? Sorry. I thought I felt a migraine coming on so I took my Immigran and sat quietly for a minute.'

'Do you want me to get you home?' Tod looked concerned.

'No, I'll be fine soon, thanks. The medication stopped it really happening.' She sank down into her seat. Panic attack or migraine, what had happened in the ladies had turned her muscles to mush.

Tod and Louise returned to their conversation. Incredibly conscious that Sam was staring at her as if he could read everything she tried to conceal, she cast around for something to divert him.

'I'm not sure of the ethics of accepting an accidentally-on-purpose date for the specific purpose of deliberately putting the date off you,' she said, reprovingly. 'You remembered me telling you that she'd gone off Frankie for getting into comics.'

His mouth quirked up at one side. 'Guilty.'

'I bet you don't have a single *Justice League* comic.'

'I have hundreds . . . in Mum's loft. I haven't looked at them since I was fifteen. One day I'll get them out and have a charity auction. Perhaps give the money to No Blame or Shame.'

'Poor Izz.'

The face Sam pulled wasn't unsympathetic. 'I can't fall

in love with someone because she's your friend and your heart's touched by her, Ava. What I did might be juvenile but it allows her crush to fade, leaving her free to carry on working at Jermyn's without either of us feeling uncomfortable. An inelegant but functional solution.'

'I suppose so,' she admitted reluctantly.

'Thanks for agreeing to join us for Christmas.'

Another pre-panic subject to address. 'It was kind of you to offer but—'

'You're not going to go back on it, are you?' He shrugged out of his jacket and laid it on the seat beside him, making Ava realise that it must be hot in the bar now it was filled to capacity. Funny. She was cold. She glanced around. All she could see were people standing, except for a few who'd squashed into the other half of the corner seating.

He leaned in, his voice low. 'Are you sure you're OK? You're very white.'

'Are *you* sure you want me crashing your family Christmas? I'm not very good at Christmas, you know.'

'Positive. I meant it when I said you'll be doing me a favour.' He cracked a pained smile. 'You can only imagine how much Mum will love it.'

Ava struggled with her conscience. 'The deeper we get into faux dating the more Wendy will be upset at the end.'

'But we want her to have a happy Christmas and she'll be no more upset at the end of a faux relationship than she would have been if it were real dating.' His voice was sombre.

She heaved a sigh. 'OK. I'm in.'

Then Tod began to recount a story about Frankie being pursued by a conquest who'd proved reluctant to limit the fun to just one weekend and Ava joined in the laughter as Tod described Frankie's hunted look. She began to feel more normal.

Turning to Sam to make a joke about him giving Frankie lessons on how to put a girl off him, she halted.

Sam was gaping at his phone.

And then at Ava.

Unease bit at her guts. She couldn't make her lips move to ask Sam if he was OK or what was making him look as if he'd just discovered someone had wiped his bank account. The moths fluttered up into her ears again.

Tod's voice slid into her consciousness. 'We're going off to Louise's, if you're certain you'll be OK getting back?'

''Course.' The moths fluttered so loudly she could barely hear her own reply.

'Right, see you whenever. See you tomorrow, Sam.' Louise latched herself on to Tod's arm and they began to edge into the crowd.

'Yes.' Sam sounded as if he were rousing from a dream. He stared at Ava again, his emotions all over his face. Astonishment. Horror. Compassion.

Sick dread took hold of her. She felt as if she was in one of those dreams when a huge juggernaut was bearing down on her and she was glued to a spot in its path. To avoid Sam's gaze she stared into her wine. It really was the most perfect delicate pink imaginable. One day she was going to make a hat that was exactly the colour of Zinfandel rosé. Maybe she'd have shoes dyed to match.

'Ava?'

Her lungs flattened into useless empty sacks. She couldn't make them work. Sweat began to prickle down her spine.

He leaned in close. 'We need to talk.' He was trying to get her attention, frowning, squeezing her hand.

The moths fluttered as if they knew she didn't want to hear. If she'd thought her limbs would carry her she would have leaped up and sprinted out of the bar rather than hear what he was about to say.

He put his mouth close to her ear. 'Your horrible ex has just sent me picture messages.'

The moths fluttered harder and harder. A sweating, cringing mass of humiliation, Ava clamped her eyes shut.

'This is what you've been frightened of, isn't it?' His warm hand closed more tightly over hers. 'That shit has these images of you and he's been tormenting and threatening you with them.'

Chapter Twenty

The zombie formerly known as Ava

Sam's mouth was completely dry. It had taken him several seconds to process the fact that the giggling naked woman who'd appeared on his phone screen, her hair spilling across her breasts, was Ava, presently decorously dressed and sitting right in front of him. His heart had given a gigantic thump of dismay that instead of learning what lay beneath her clothes in a joyous and sensual sharing of bodies, it had been shown to him by that little shit Harvey out of a spiteful wish to humiliate her.

But now the shock was beginning to recede and his brain began to do the job he usually expected of it, everything resolving into pin-sharp focus. This wasn't about him. This was all about Ava. And so much was now making sense.

The way she'd changed colour over the seemingly commonplace action of texting this evening.

Her overlong absence in the ladies.

Her occasionally distant or erratic behaviour.

White-hot fury coursed through him and he knew a compulsion to grab Harvey Snaith by the throat. Tightly.

But right now his concern was whether Ava was going to make it through the next few minutes. Her hand was sweating in his but her skin was icy cold. Her breathing was in rags and he tried to remember what to do when someone hyperventilated. Or even suffered cardiac arrest.

Reassurance seemed a good first measure. 'It's going to be OK.' He had no real idea whether OK was even attainable. He was still firmly rooted in 'unholy mess' but nothing good would come of him sharing that perspective. 'Don't worry.' Of course she was worried. She was terrified. 'I'm going to help you.' That much he could guarantee. 'But we need to talk and I don't think this is the best place, do you?'

He reached for her coat. 'I'll see you home.' Damn. Izz would probably turn up before too much longer and while he suspected that Ava would have confided in Izz, he stood a better chance of unravelling this mess without her. 'We'll go to my place,' he amended, 'where we can sort this out. OK? Come on.' He knew he was talking to her as if she were a child, but it allowed him to coax her rigidly to her feet and into her coat. He wound her scarf gently around her neck then took her freezing hand to lead her through what had become a raucous crowd.

Out in the street the wind rushed up to greet them, spitting chill raindrops into their faces as people milled in and out of the nearby Bangladeshi-Indian restaurants under red and green neon signs. At least the crowds attracted taxis and it wasn't long before Sam spotted one with its yellow light aglow. Outmanoeuvring four girls waving foil balloons, he clamped his hand onto the door handle. 'Sorry, my friend's not well.' He ignored their tutting and muttering and bundled Ava into the back seat.

'We're going to sort this out,' he repeated when he'd climbed in beside her.

Ava sat perfectly still and gazed ahead all the way to Stratford. She didn't argue when he paid the cab fare. He curled an arm around the zombie formerly known as Ava Blissham and guided her through the lobby and into the lift. In his flat he sat her down on the sofa. 'I'll make coffee.'

When he looked at her again he saw that she'd dropped her face into her palms, like a picture titled 'Despair'. His heart twanged with her pain.

He wished for his mum. She knew what to say to women that had been through the same kind of ordeal as Ava. But he'd have to draw on whatever knowledge he'd absorbed from his mother, throw in sympathy and good sense and wing it.

He deposited the steaming coffee mugs on the table. 'He's been holding these pictures over your head,' he suggested, gently.

From behind her hands, she nodded.

He settled on the sofa, his shoulder brushing hers so that she knew he was there but only on the edge of her personal space. 'Has he been blackmailing you for money? Is that why you've been so broke?'

She shook her head.

'You can trust me, Ava. Tell me what happened so that I can help.'

The silence seemed endless. Then she gulped, 'I'm ashamed.'

Rage rushed back, but he held it off. He'd find a way to channel his revulsion for Harvey-shitty-Snaith later. Now was the time for Ava, for sympathy and compassion. 'Don't be. Honestly. I don't think you've done anything wrong.'

With gentle fingers he guided first one hand and then

the other away from her face and pressed one of the coffee mugs upon her. 'Come on. Drink.'

Eyes averted, she began listlessly to sip.

'If you had a bit of fun with your boyfriend and a digital camera, a lot of people have done the same.'

No reply.

'Harvey's the one who's in the wrong. What we need to do is look at your options and see what can be done to stop him hurting you any more.'

No reply.

'I think that you need to talk to someone and get help. If you don't want to talk to me then Mum will put you in touch with someone. Or you could ring a helpline. What about the police?'

A single, vehement shake of her head.

'They're the ones with clout. You could request a female police officer.'

She grimaced, then took two gulps of her coffee. Huskily, her voice returned. 'Until tonight, he's only threatened to spread the images around and the police need something more to go on than threats nobody else heard being made. If you were to offer whatever he's sent you as evidence those images would have to be seen not only by every police officer and police civilian involved, but also lawyers and everything. My dad was a senior police officer in the Met. I know all about the strict confidentiality but . . . I also know how whispers can spread within the force. He'd die of mortification if one of his old mates told him. Harvey—' Her voice wavered. 'Also, Harvey says if I go to the police he'll send the images to Dad. Can you imagine?' She clamped one hand to her eyes again.

Under his breath, Sam swore comprehensively.

Despair rang in her voice. 'Digital images can spread

like the plague. YouTube. Red Tube. Twitter. Facebook. Sites for pathetic creeps to perv over.'

It was hard to argue with her. In his job he'd seen the results of whispers, hacking, 'accidental' forwarding of data. He'd been involved in trying to retrieve the victim's image or create a tide of counteracting positivity so that the public found it hard to credit the negative stuff.

He left that question for the moment. 'If he hasn't asked you for money . . . is it sex?' His guts pulled tight. If Snaith had forced Ava, Sam thought he might have to go into the bathroom and throw up.

'No!' She emerged from behind her hand with wide, horrified eyes. 'Well, he suggested it tonight, in a text, when he was drunk, but I was obviously never going to agree! I think it was my insulting reaction to his suggestion that hacked him off enough to send the pictures to you.' She shuddered. 'I deleted the original images from his phone myself. If automatic backup even entered my head I'd *never* have thought Harvey would be such a bastard.'

The sentences flowed like waves of helplessness. How Harvey seemed to feel humiliated at the acrimonious death of the relationship. How he alternated between trying to resume the relationship and threats of revenge. How she knew it was all her own fault—

'It's not your fault.'

Her gaze was filled with pain. 'The photos were consensual.'

He took her hand. 'You were having fun and you were OK with your boyfriend taking intimate photos. You trusted him. It's Harvey who's to blame. He's acted reprehensibly.'

'But if I hadn't let him take the photos he couldn't threaten me with them.'

'You couldn't know what was going to happen.' He stroked her fingers. 'Is he stupid enough to make his threat real by sending the images to your dad? An ex-cop? It would be an offence, wouldn't it?'

'Yes! But would he do it when he was drunk? Yes! The idea of Dad opening a text message and seeing . . . !' Her voice broke on a sob, mouth squaring off in her anguish. 'I couldn't *bear* it.'

Ava struggled to get her breathing under control as Sam gazed at her, saying, slowly, 'If that's your major fear, I think you should ring your dad. Tell him the situation. Call Harvey's bluff.'

Consternation twisted her stomach. 'I couldn't,' she whispered.

Sam actually laughed, albeit grimly. 'But think about it. The diamond-edged point to Harvey's weapon is the shock value of your dad opening a message, all unsuspecting. But if you warn your dad, he'll have the option of deleting the messages unread. Or blocking Harvey's number.'

Ava weighed the idea for several seconds, her mental scales tipping wildly between hope and hopelessness. 'But that won't stop Harvey putting those images on Facebook or sending them to other friends.'

Sam frowned in thought. 'The images probably wouldn't be up on Facebook for long. There are pretty tough policies on nudity and harassment. Have you ever read their community standards page?'

Hope crashed. 'But a photo like that only needs to be up a few seconds and people will copy it! Then it could appear anywhere. And Twitter would be worse. Tweets are retweeted in seconds!' She realised she was gripping

Sam's hand, and that her voice was rising but she didn't seem capable of bringing it down. 'And if Harvey's threat is empty then I'll have upset my parents for nothing.'

In contrast, his voice was slow and reassuring. 'And if he does carry out his threat? How will that be for your dad? Whether Harvey sends the images to your parents is outside of your control. But how they find out about the existence of those images is within it.'

They sat in silence, hands clasped. Ava felt as if sadness and fear were pressing down on her with suffocating weight. Graeme and Katherine were living their dream in leafy Alsace. That could be shattered by being confronted with such an ugly truth in the worst possible way.

Slowly, sadly, she freed her hand, took out her phone and went to her contacts list.

'Do you want privacy?' Sam's voice was soft.

'No, I need you to stay here in case I chicken out, please.' She knew that she sounded pathetic but she felt that he was all that was keeping her from descending once again into panic.

Rrriiing. 'Oh shit,' she groaned, clenching her free hand into a fist.

Rrriiing. She whimpered.

Rrrii—'This is a nice surprise.' Her father's voice travelled the hundreds of miles from the outskirts of Strasbourg and straight to Ava's heart. 'We have neighbours here. Just hang on while I go into another room so I can hear you.' Background voices receded, a door opened and shut. 'That's better,' said Graeme. 'How's everything?'

Ava swallowed, heart racing. She inhaled, as if she could breathe in all Sam's support and positivity. 'Dad, I've got to tell you something. It's not very nice and you're not going to like it but it's better if you hear it from me.' She screwed up her eyes and screwed up her courage and poured out the whole horrible, disgusting story.

Graeme remained quiet during the miserable confession, only indicating with the occasional grunt that he was listening. It was once Ava finally tailed away, her voice tiny with tears, that he really spoke. 'This kind of thing makes me so angry.' Fury vibrated in every word.

Ava gulped. 'I'm sorry! You don't have to tell me how stupid I've been.'

'I'm not angry at you!' Graeme snapped. 'It's that little turd Snaith. I'd like to stuff his phone up his idiotic arse.' He breathed like a bull while Ava sniffed and tried to absorb the fact that she wasn't listening to a hail of recriminations.

When Graeme spoke again he was still gruff but he'd obviously got himself together. 'I can't help but feel that some of this is my fault.'

'Yours?'

Graeme swore. 'I never liked that man when you were going out with him. I had a mate who worked on his patch and I put out a few feelers. Snaith's known to him.'

'Harvey's known to the police?' repeated Ava blankly. She actually took the phone from her ear to stare at it incredulously.

'Not for anything serious or I would have had no choice but to talk to you. It was all alcohol-related stuff – he's one of the local Hoorays that have been picked up for drunk and disorderly and getting into fights. Spent a couple of nights in the cells, got two warnings and a reprimand.'

Ava felt like pinching herself. 'He never got in trouble with the police when he was with me.'

'Common behaviour pattern.' Graeme snorted. 'It's a form of pack instinct. Young men out with their mates, acting like idiots, all bravado and aggression, letting their testosterone talk for them. Completely different with their girlfriends.' His voice softened and he sighed. 'I had quite a debate with myself about whether or not to tell you but you were being very independent, leaving your job with Ceri and striking out alone. I felt as if you were pushing us away and I wasn't sure you'd welcome my interference.'

'Wow,' breathed Ava, hardly able to credit this version of history. 'I didn't know I was pushing you away. It's just that you were retiring to France and I wanted you to feel free to go. You were always so keen on me standing on my own two feet.'

'Well, perhaps. But if you'd have known the truth you might have dumped Harvey earlier and have been saved all this stress. Anyway,' he went on, suddenly businesslike, 'the important thing now is to look at our options for giving young Snaith a wake-up call. I'll update myself on the relevant laws, for a start.'

When Ava eventually ended the call her head was spinning. Sam waited patiently beside her. She summarised her father's side of the conversation. 'He said to leave it with him for a day or so and he'd think about what can be done.'

Sam's expression relaxed into a smile. 'He sounds like a great bloke.'

'Yes.' Ava rubbed the sweat from her palms 'He's always hated injustice, of course, which is what made him a career police officer. If there was a duty to be volunteered for, Dad was usually the one with his hand in the air. He worked hard to be the kind of policeman that everybody wants to believe in, and to help people in trouble. I've never been the one that needed his help so I wasn't really aware . . . well, how great he can be.'

'That's fantastic,' Sam returned absently.

When Ava turned to glance at him he wasn't even looking in her direction. He was frowning at the lights studding the dark cityscape outside his window.

Ava's momentary euphoria gurgled swiftly away. Sam's scowl reminded her that this thing was a long way from over. She let her head fall back against the squashy sofa. 'How many photos did Harvey send you?' She had to take a new breath before she could force out, 'Were they very . . . bad?'

'What? Oh. Yes. No.' He shook his head and turned a smile on her. 'Sorry. I was thinking. He sent two photos. One was explicit but the other was kind of cute.'

She groaned, boiling with fresh mortification. 'Cute?'

'Really.' His frown returned as he retook her hand, lacing their fingers together. 'Listen, I've got an idea. Or the beginnings of one. I need time to work on it but have you ever heard that saying "success is the best revenge"? It's based on that.' He breathed in slowly. 'It's going to need a lot of trust on your part though. Because my idea's based on one of those pictures.'

Chapter Twenty-One

A pretty cheeky idea

Ava's eyes were bigger than Sam had ever seen them as she treated him to a silent stare.

'Also,' he continued, because she might as well have all the bad news at once, 'it's going to mean me giving at least a superficial version of events to other people. And one of them is Patrick.'

She frowned. 'Why Patrick?'

He glanced down at their entwined fingers. Crap. He supposed he ought not to have been holding hands with Ava because his guy code was better than that. His heart shifted in his chest as he studied the way that her fingers curled neatly around his. 'Because he'd be involved in my idea as the writer on the Ruby Glennister campaign. I can see that when you're first dating someone you probably don't relish the idea of having to tell them about bedroom photos taken by your ex but he would have to be involved for my idea to work out.'

'Dating *Patrick*?'

His gaze flew to hers. 'Aren't you?'

'No.' She shook her head. Then she laughed disbelievingly and repeated, 'No!'

'Ah.' He took a moment to reorganise his thoughts. 'He mentioned that you'd been out together last night.'

'I had breakfast with you at Gaz's Caff, but it wasn't a date.'

'So I recall,' he agreed drily. 'So I'm not sure why I made such an assumption about Patrick.' He tried to rerun the morning's conversation in his head. Had Patrick actually said it was a date? He seized on a detail he had definitely taken on board. 'It sounded as if he'd bought you dinner, so—'

'Hadn't we agreed that deciding it's a date if the man pays is old fashioned?' But a small smile softened the reproof in her voice. 'He turned up at my gym last night and said he was thinking of joining, asked for my views on the place over a cup of coffee and somehow baguettes and wine got included. I only had a tenner with me so he paid and I returned my share via Izz today. To be honest . . .' Ava rolled her eyes. 'I think he pumped Izz about my interests and contrived to turn up just as my class ended.'

'Right.' So Patrick probably had made it sound like a date deliberately.

She coughed delicately. 'I don't want to seem self-absorbed or anything but could we get back to what the hell you want to use one of those images for, and why other people have to know?'

Sam jumped his mind back into the moment, conscious of Ava waiting with thumb-twiddling impatience. 'I don't want to get your hopes up but if my glimmer of an idea were to work it'd kill more than one bird with one stone.' He turned to gaze out at the night again as he returned to rounding up the thoughts that had come galloping into his brain a few minutes ago.

A slow smile began to take charge of his face. 'It could work. But we're going to have to work like crazy and Mum and Aunt Van arrive tomorrow so I'd have to get them to take a cab from Euston. Ruby Glennister would have to give her OK, but once the premise is agreed it's the others who will pick the idea up and run with it.' He fell to watching the flickering of Christmas lights in emergency-service blue. There was something about watching the nightscape, the white lights, the coloured lights, the still and the moving lights, that freed his imagination to flip around.

'But what?' demanded Ava, shaking his hand as if to jerk him awake. 'What idea? And what's it got to do with Ruby?'

He blinked. 'For you, I see two major issues. One is Harvey's threats; the other's lack of income. I think I can use one to generate the other. So far as Ruby's concerned I see her as a huge opportunity for reciprocity. Huge. It'll work for her, too, but we need her fully engaged because it's a pretty cheeky idea. Hopefully she'll love it and the others won't mind me charging into their campaign. It's not as if they've come up with anything smoking so far.'

He threw up a hand to ward off her next question, hovering so obviously on her parted lips. 'But I need space to do some ideas storming. Can you get a cab home? I'll call you tomorrow. Will you keep yourself free? You're going to need to be involved. But I can't tell you any more yet because I need to grab the idea while it's hot and if I explain it to you too soon I'm frightened it'll fade away.'

She hesitated. 'OK but . . . well, which photo do you need to use?'

He read the fear in her face and renewed compassion reared up in him. 'The *cute* one! *Obviously* the cute one.' He fumbled his phone out of his pocket in his haste to prove to her that she had nothing to fear from him. 'Here. They'll be the last two images in my photos so you can delete the other one yourself. The cute one will have to be recreated anyway for quality and copyright reasons but leave it there for now as a reference.'

Ava slowly picked up his phone. He watched her as she located the images. Her bottom lip quivered for an instant before she deleted the offending image with a savage little stab.

'Check my settings and make sure my photos aren't automatically set to sync to another device. I'm pretty sure they're not because I like to keep different folders in different places and move stuff manually when it's needed.'

'I don't need to.' She made to return the handset.

Gently, he blocked her. 'Check it out. Then you'll know you can trust me. Because I'm going to need you to.'

He watched as she did it, her movements calmer now. Then she returned to the image, the one she hadn't deleted. He watched her examine it. 'This is what you call cute?'

'I think it qualifies.' He gazed out of the window again so that she'd know he wasn't ogling. The image was branded into his memory, anyway – Ava from the waist up, a tall black-feathered fascinator in her hair, holding hats over each breast; red on one and blue on the other. Fun and mischief glowed out of her.

He wished he'd seen that Ava more. The happy one.

Chapter Twenty-Two

Hats off to Ava Bliss

Friday 21 December

At nine-thirty on Friday morning, Ava received a brief call from Sam. 'Can you come in at about one? Working lunch and think tank.'

'I can,' she agreed cautiously. She mentally reviewed what she knew about a working lunch in a comms agency. Zippo. Izz had already left for work, so she couldn't consult her. 'Will I have much to offer?'

He sounded surprised. 'We can't do much without you agreeing stuff – or not – can we? See you later.' Then he was gone.

Do much? Ava tried to keep herself occupied and tried not to think about Sam seeing those images while the morning crawled by in the quiet house. At least Harvey had stopped short of sending one of the 'action shots'. The thought of Sam seeing her engaged in a sex act was a universe beyond any level of mortification she'd felt so far.

This evening would see Wendy's second fitting and the unembellished hat was waiting on the stand but, as she was in completely the wrong state of mind to do any useful work, she tidied her studio and cleaned the sitting room, arranging recently arrived Christmas cards in a row.

She put up her hair in a subdued knot and was almost ready to leave, anxiety making her clumsy to the point of violently swearing at uncooperative coat buttons, when somebody clattered the knocker on the front door.

Impatiently, she threw it open. And stared. 'Dad?'

The grooves either side of Graeme's mouth moved as he smiled at her. 'Do I get invited in?'

'Oh *Dad*!' Ava threw herself into the safety and warmth of her father's arms. 'I have missed you! I'm sorry I've been so stupid. But how fantastic that you're here.'

Graeme hugged her tightly. 'We miss you, too, sweet-heart. We both thought I should pop over and help you out, so I got the first plane out of Strasbourg.'

Hot tears leaked from under Ava's eyelids onto the wool of her father's coat. 'That's amazing. Oh—' She pulled away. 'I've got to get over to Brick Lane.' Quickly, she explained as much as she understood – which didn't seem that much when she was running it in front of her father's perceptive gaze – about her summons from Sam.

Graeme nodded briskly. 'Good, especially the lunch part. I've come straight from Gatwick and haven't eaten since croissants in the airport. I'll come with you.'

During the walk to Camden Town tube station under a hurrying grey sky, then riding the underground trains, they talked about France, Christmas, hats and everything but Harvey and explicit photos. It wasn't until after they'd arrived at Aldgate station and emerged into misty daylight that Graeme took out his phone. 'Just give me Snaith's phone number and email address, will you?'

Ava took out her own phone and opened her contacts.

'What are you going to do with them?' She located Harvey's details and tapped 'share'.

'Got a little idea.'

Hunching her shoulders against the drizzle, Ava shoved her hands into her pockets. 'I hope it's an idea that will make him go away. I feel sick every time I get a message in case it's him. The texts are so nasty, Dad. You don't want to see them, believe me.'

Graeme halted suddenly. 'The texts themselves are threatening or abusive? Show me immediately!'

Her stomach dropped to the pavement. 'You'll have to see the pictures!'

He paused. 'I understand. But if the messages themselves are threatening, you need to read me some.' He pulled her over into an alcove between two shops while Ava mumbled her way through a few texts, cringing with mortification.

'Gold dust!' Graeme grinned in triumph. 'Don't delete those, whatever you do. That prat has never heard of the Communications Act, and malicious communications offences, obviously. I thought he'd had the good sense to keep his threats verbal, when he thought no one was listening. You do know that you could go to the police with this evidence, don't you? It's real and tangible.'

In alarm, Ava thrust her phone deep in her pocket. 'What, make a complaint? Go through the interview process and make a statement?'

Graeme's eyes softened. 'I could help you through it. But I understand if you really would prefer to find other ways to make it all go away.'

'Without question,' said Ava, fervently.

When they finally arrived at Jermyn's, Ava came out in an anxious sweat again. With no idea what was about to happen she was beginning to have nightmare visions of everyone at the agency sitting around and dissecting her stupidity. But it warred with a spark of hope that Sam could actually come up with something to make things better, so she pressed the intercom button and made her voice steady. 'Ava Blissham for Sam Jermyn.'

Crackle. 'Please come up to the first floor.' *Crackle.* The door clicked as the lock was released.

Graeme clapped her reassuringly on the shoulder. 'Let's go see what it's all about, shall we?'

His warmth and solidarity made Ava feel a tiny bit better.

Upstairs, Barb hugged Ava as if they were old friends. 'Hello, darling! They're in the big meeting room. I'll show you.' She segued effortlessly into flirtatiousness. 'Who's this? Your father? Blimey, what a good-looking dad!'

Up a short corridor, lush green plants spilling from white planters, they followed Barb into a square room containing a round table. People were grouped haphazardly around it, some sitting and some standing, their chairs shoved out untidily. Huge whiteboards clothed two walls. Izz wasn't there but Ava knew she would be glued to a computer somewhere, grappling with the database.

Tod's head popped up from the melee. 'Graeme! Didn't expect to see you.' He crossed to shake Graeme's hand and then to hug Ava hard, whispering, 'Sam's briefed us. Don't let that bastard Harvey get to you.'

Emerging from his embrace Ava found Sam already introducing himself to her dad. 'We've got a lot to accomplish, so shall we sit straight down?' He kissed Ava's cheek. 'Would you sit with Ruby?'

Ava noticed Ruby for the first time, twinkling her fingers in a little wave and looking almost as nervous as Ava felt. Ava's sensation of unreality increased as she took the empty chair beside the WAG that all of tabloid-land and social media now knew as Booby Ruby.

'Right,' began Sam, which had the effect of making anybody still standing instantly find a seat. 'For the benefit of our guests let me make round-table introductions. Ruby Glennister, client; Ava of Ava Bliss Millinery; Tod, graphic design; Jake, photographer; Manda Jane, media buyer; Emily, social-media manager; Patrick, writer; Graeme, Ava's dad.'

Ava tried to smile at everyone, but Sam, obviously a very direct creative director, was already moving on. 'The agency's aim is to promote a better relationship between Ruby and the tabloids because they've been giving her a rough ride. It's hard to change how people feel about someone but it can be done. My idea is for a campaign to involve both Ruby and Ava in these last few days before Christmas. It's a cheeky and unsophisticated idea that relies heavily on Ruby sending herself up and dependent partly on the willingness of people to swap nonsense at Christmas when servers everywhere process more e-cards and jokes than work-related emails.'

He paused as Barb bowled into the room with a trolley loaded with steaming jugs of coffee and tea, a platter of triangular sandwiches, and a dish of green salad that she passed straight to Ruby.

The sandwiches circulated as Sam continued. 'Ruby, something that happened to Ava has sparked this idea and my plan depends upon her willingness to be a vehicle. She'll gain exposure along the way but I hope you'll be happy with the mutual gain.'

Ruby shrugged and nodded. She looked as clueless as Ava felt.

Not really wanting food but dimly aware of not having

eaten since yesterday, Ava took a sandwich to nibble. It also prevented her from seizing Sam by the lapels and shouting, 'BUT WHAT IS THE *IDEA*?' She accepted a white porcelain mug of coffee from Tod and forced herself to be patient.

Beside her, Graeme beetled his brows and tapped something into his phone.

Smoothly, Sam moved on. 'As a platform for the viral part of the campaign, I propose a fairly standard feature in an online magazine. This will take the form of Ava making – or pretending to make – hats for Ruby. You have enough samples for the purpose of the feature, Ava.'

'How's that going to do anything?' put in Ruby, looking disappointed.

Sam silenced her with a movement of one finger. 'It's just a platform. As we've got no lead-in for the print media, Manda Jane's called in a favour from online magazine *Alive Today*, which gets a huge hit rate on its celebrity gossip pages. The feature will go in tomorrow, so this afternoon I'd like Jake and Patrick to go with Ava and Ruby to Ava's studio to do the words and pics.'

Patrick snorted. 'With a deadline of this evening?'

'Six o'clock.' Sam confirmed. 'Ruby, the slant on the feature will be that you found this fantastic young milliner and fell in love with her product and it helped you through a bad patch.'

Ruby shrugged again, looking no more enthusiastic than before. 'Doesn't seem particularly original, but OK.'

'The interviewer,' he pointed his pen at Patrick as he consulted his notes on his tablet, 'will tease out of you that you realise you've been unwise in your recent responses to the press. Patrick, your angle will be "defensive response" and "understandable lapse", right? You're brilliant with persuasive language – steer clear of brutal words like "lies". As an attention grabber, use a subheading or a box-out with a joke about making a clean breast of things. Then, in the final line, Ruby must say, "Hats off to Ava Bliss." *Alive Today*'s content often gets into BuzzFeed and the like. That's what you're aiming for.'

Patrick looked interested. 'Got it.' He began tapping notes into his laptop.

'The interview will have to be done while Ava's trying hats on Ruby as if she's there for a fitting. OK, Ava?' Sam glanced her way.

'Easy enough so far.'

Beside her, her father took up his phone again, tapped the screen and exclaimed, 'Ha!'

Ava glanced over but Sam had already moved his pointing pen to Jake. 'While this is going on, take loads of pics of Ruby looking fantastic and WAG-ish in Ava's hats. I asked Ruby to bring several tops, jewellery etc.' He glanced questioningly at Ruby.

She lifted up a mock-croc bag and pointed to it in confirmation.

Sam opened his laptop beside his tablet. 'Those shots will take the minor places in the feature. You're all aware how image heavy *Alive Today* is. The two major pics will be Ava and Ruby, each based on this.' He picked up a small remote and pointed it. A screen slid almost noiselessly down one wall.

A few keystrokes on Sam's laptop then Harvey's 'cute' picture of Ava sprang to life on the screen, three feet high. Ruby laughed delightedly. 'That's awesome! Ava, you look gorgeous, babes.'

Patrick whistled under his breath.

Ava felt heat boil up from her neck to her hairline. She couldn't look at her dad.

Graeme cleared his throat and frowned blackly at Sam. 'I trust that this is necessary.'

Sam met his stare evenly. 'I believe so.'

'Really?' Ava blurted. 'Are you serious that that picture of *me* is going in *Alive Today*? Why me?'

''Cos you look gorgeous, babes,' Ruby repeated, still grinning at the picture. 'Can't you see us both wearing nothing but your hats over our boobies? We'll look amazin'. Sam, you're such a cheeky sod – what a sly dig at my boob job.'

When Sam smiled, every line of his face softened. 'You have to be seen to send yourself up. And you'll look every bit as good as Ava, won't she, Jake?'

Jake was still studying the image of Ava. 'No prob. You'll both be on fire. That's an amazing picture, Ava.'

Ava didn't think she could go any redder but at least nobody was looking at her in horror and disdain.

In fact, Patrick was looking at her in all-too-frank admiration. 'Incredibly hot,' he agreed.

Sam cut him off. 'Jake, it's imperative that you don't use the same two hats for Ava's new photo. We want the taker of this particular image not to be able to claim that we stole his copyright as he's Ava's ex-boyfriend and he and she are . . . not currently on good terms.'

'Oh!' squeaked Ava, disregarding this masterly under-statement as she got a glimmer of what Sam had meant when he'd talked about revenge and success. 'But if he sees the image, he'll know he sparked the idea.'

A satisfied light flitted through Sam's eyes. 'Exactly.' He paused to pour himself black coffee. 'And he will see the image, don't you worry.' Fatigue lurked in the lines of his face but his voice was energetic and enthusiastic. 'The viral part of the campaign is trickier and it's going to involve

220

Tod doing absolute shitloads of work, at furious speed. To give up his evening, and probably work into the weekend.'

Tod nodded philosophically. 'I knew I was here for something.'

Sam flicked to another slide. 'What we need, Tod, is an animated Christmas card along the lines of this one – one of those where people can upload their own headshots to become part of the animation.' He clicked on the triangle in the centre of the image and it turned into a band of cartoon bodies with photograph faces singing 'Jingle Bells' and dancing.

'Oh, I know, a sort of "star in your own cartoon" thing.' Tod grinned when he saw that each band member wore the face of a Jermyn associate, the chins bobbing up and down to create rudimentary working mouths.

'You've got it. I want singing and dancing. The punters won't be able to mess with two of the characters – those will have Ruby's and Ava's heads and wear the same hats as in Jake's photos on their chests. The three supporting cast members will be the ones that people can use to become part of the cartoon themselves, by uploading their images.'

'This could be awesome!' Emily was almost dancing in her seat. 'If this is clever and funny enough we ought to be able to make it fly round social media. We can link it to the platform feature in *Alive Today* and everyone will get the joke. The feature and the card should be everywhere!' She wriggled with excitement.

'Amazin',' breathed Ruby.

Sam turned to Ruby with a wink. 'There's going to be a punchline.'

'Oh yeah?' She quirked a quizzical brow. 'This is where good old Ruby gets sent up, is it?'

The grin broadened. 'You remember the final line of the article? "Hats off to Ava Bliss?" Your character will say that – we'll use you to voice it – and fling off the hats. Ava's avatar will blush and look aghast. The supporting cast of animations will burst into applause.'

Ruby stared at him for a full five seconds. Then burst into delighted laughter. 'Sam Jermyn! My cartoon's really going to flash her boobs?'

'Really,' he confirmed. His grin was wicked.

Ruby threw back her head as her laughter peeled out. 'You're a cheeky sod, Sam Jermyn. Yeah, go on then, if you think it'll get on the right side of the press jackals. Anythin'. Ava, babes, we're going to go viral. We're going to look hot!'

'Mm,' Ava said uncertainly. It was confusing, but exciting. She had trouble keeping up as Sam tried to iron out more details with people starting up side conversations in furious whispers, stabbing at their tablets, interrupting Sam for information.

Ava, a creative person herself, worked alone. Never had she been in a small room with several other people literally jumping out of their seats with ideas. She began to feel as if someone had plugged her into the mains.

They were doing it all for her and Ruby. She even felt tears begin to prickle as she listened to Emily instructing Ruby to comb her Twitter followers for WAG and footballer mates who would agree to send out Tweets – carefully constructed by Emily – and also those who'd agree to be featured in the card as supporting cast then post it to their Facebook pages.

'I almost believe in Christmas.' Ava sniffed. 'All you little elves working furiously to make things happen.'

Even Ruby, who would be more used to having a team

222

of people doing stuff for her, had a beaming smile all over her face. 'Awesome! Awe*some*. You guys rock.'

Sam didn't pause in firing out instructions. 'Ava and Ruby, a car's waiting for you downstairs to take you to Ava's studio. Get your make-up on when you arrive. Patrick and Jake, car for you in thirty minutes, so get your shit together. Jake, I've emailed you the original image for reference. I want fun to shine out of these lovely ladies. Take plain backdrops.'

'Black,' put in Ruby. 'White makes me look ten years older.' She didn't look as if she intended to let that happen.

Sam rose. 'Tod, do you need me to ideas-storm the animation with you?'

'You've given me plenty to work with. Leave it with me for now.' Tod grabbed his tablet and almost ran from the room.

Ruby linked arms with Ava. 'Come on, Ava, babes. When we're in the car I'll ring my beauticians and see if they can send someone to your place. We'll get our nails done as well as our faces, yeah? 'Cos our hands will be on show. French, probably, so our nails don't clash with your hats.'

Ava glanced at her hands. 'I don't have nails. I have working hands, always in steam and stiffener.'

Ruby shoved her way flamboyantly through the agency door. 'She'll give you fake ones for the day. Easy.'

Chapter Twenty-Three
The collateral consequences of criminal convictions

What had been a hive of activity became a quiet room containing only Sam and Graeme Blissham. Sam sank back in his chair, the fatigue of a two-hour night washing over him as the energy of the meeting ebbed. But satisfaction at the way his ideas had been seized upon shimmered through him. That was his job. To excite the others.

For the moment, it didn't matter that his schedule for today and the weekend had gone to hell. Everyone had been enthused, Ruby had been pleased. Ava . . . Ava's big eyes had been fixed on him as if he were the guy who had all the answers.

Graeme reached over to pour more coffee into Sam's cup. 'If you can bring this off, I think we'll all be tipping our hats to you.' He sent him a contemplative glance. 'You look knackered, but do you have an hour to spare? I'd quite like you to come with me to Harvey Snaith's place of work.'

Picking up the coffee and inhaling the steam, Sam's tired brain tried to unscramble Graeme's words. 'Where does he work? Why do you want me there?'

Graeme sat back comfortably. 'He's an accountant in Hoxton. I want to mark his card for him and I want a witness. The kind that will only remember the bits I want him to. It seems to me that you might be that man.'

'OK,' Sam heard himself saying, curiosity beginning to charge his batteries anew. Being that man might work for him, too.

Ava was getting tired of placing hats on Ruby's glossy dark hair and taking them off again, tired of being careful of her unaccustomed manicure. Tired of Jake saying, 'Once more, Ava. Glance up at me as you do it,' at the same time as Patrick was 'interviewing' Ruby into the voice recorder on his phone, which seemed a giant waste of time as they both knew what he was supposed to be asking and what Ruby's replies should be.

Patrick was good at returning to a subject in a different way until he got answers he could use, Ava acknowledged, as she tilted a canary yellow straw hat over one of Ruby's eyes. Just like the day he'd turned up at the gym, really. Approaching his goal indirectly, hoping to get under someone's defences.

'Doesn't that yellow make me look sallow?' demanded Ruby.

Jake tipped his head, considering. 'I think it's just the autumn colour of your top. Try it with the white one.'

Patrick waggled his phone under Ava's nose. 'Where would she wear this hat?'

Ava resisted the urge to swat him away like a fly. 'Ascot or a posh garden party. Or a wedding.'

They all waited while Ruby shrugged out of a bronze-striped blouse and stood unselfconsciously in her bra and camisole while she searched out a layered floaty white top

225

and changed her earrings to white stars dangling from gold chains.

Watching her check herself out in the mirror and make miniscule adjustments, Ava was reminded of being at Ceri's, where monied clients had often relieved their own tedium by adding greatly to Ava's, primping and preening long after there had been anything left to achieve.

But, this time, Ava didn't mind. Anything to put off the evil hour when Harvey's 'cute' picture was to be replicated in what Jake referred to as the 'boobs-in-hats shots'. Jake had already selected four cocktail hats, black and puce for Ruby, sky blue and gold for Ava. For now, she was secure in a plain black stretchy dress that wouldn't compete with what Ruby wore.

'Ava?'

She blinked. 'Sorry?'

Jake waved an impatient hand. 'Hat? On Ruby's head?'

'Oh! Sorry.' Ava stepped forward with the canary yellow again.

Ruby turned her head, studying her reflection. 'Thanks, babes. Can we do the white one with black feathers next? Can you twist my hair up high for that? I've brought a black flowered silk dress that will go amazin'.'

'OK, Ruby, smile up at Ava from under the brim, Ava tilt your head as if you've just applied the finishing touches . . . now, Ava glance at me and smile, Ruby gaze at your reflection.'

The canary yellow straw done with, Jake and Patrick turned their backs while Ruby changed into the black and white dress that was *amazin'*.

Ava watched enviously. Ruby having so much made Ava realise how used she was becoming to having so little.

But finally they finished with the Ruby-supposedly-

226

shopping-for-hats shoot. 'Time for boobs in hats,' announced Jake. 'Patrick's going to help me with the backdrop while you girls change.'

Ava's heart tripped. But she had no choice except to lead Ruby to her bedroom so that they could remove most of their clothing.

Ava's hands shook as she pulled off her dress and unhooked her bra.

'Gawd, you're gorgeous.' Ruby had already wriggled out of her own things. 'Good job we've got big knickers, innit, with Jake saying no tights in case they come up too high and into shot.'

Ava nodded. Usually a thong girl, she was glad she also had some more modest black bandeau shorts in her collection. 'Do you think Patrick's staying?' Now the time had come to almost bare all, she felt sick.

Ruby had brought a silky pink wrap and now she swept it around herself with a cheerful grin. 'Got eyes everywhere, that one, ain't he? Let's get rid.'

'Yes, let's,' Ava agreed with feeling.

Not having a silky pink wrap, Ava settled for her thick white towelling bathrobe and tightly tied the belt as she trudged back to the studio in Ruby's wake.

Sweeping in, Ruby gave Patrick a quick kiss on the cheek and a twiddly little wave of her fingers. 'See you, then, babes. You've got lots to write, eh?'

Patrick already had his slim laptop open. 'I'll write here, time being of the essence.'

Ruby waved at the studio door. 'Fab! You go down in the kitchen, then. Me and Ava don't want you tippity-tip-tapping in the corner while we're having our picture took. Do we, Ava?'

Clutching her bathrobe, Ava shook her head. Her throat

227

was so dry that she was sure words would stick to the sides.

Patrick's dark gaze rested on her for a second. 'Right.' He left the room and Ruby closed the door behind him.

Jake was studying his iPad. 'This original image really captures something, Ava.'

She gave a tiny whimper of dismay.

He lifted his gaze. 'Are you uncomfortable about this shot?'

Her dry throat managed a hoarse, 'A bit.'

The situation was obviously not a new one to Jake. 'Don't worry. You probably show more in your bikini than you will in the finished shot and I'll turn my back while you arrange yourselves,' he said, easily. He went back to his iPad. 'I think you're standing up in the original shot? We'll do the same because it will be better for posture. Can I pull the blind over the skylight? I don't want the backdrop bleaching out at the top.'

He wound the blind into place then turned to face the wall. 'Right, ladies, grab your hats. Tell me when I can turn round.'

'Here we go, babes.' Ruby shrugged off her wrap and reached unabashedly for her designated hats.

Trembling and reluctant, Ava followed suit, the cool air touching her skin making her tinglingly aware of her naked top half. This shoot was evoking bad memories.

'Graeme Blissham for Harvey Snaith.' Graeme smiled genially at the waif-thin girl on the front desk of a reception area notable mainly for spiky sculptures on shining white plinths. 'He said he'd be in this afternoon if I wanted to drop in,' he glanced at her name badge, 'Jyoti.'

Dark brown eyes, kohl-enhanced, and thick black hair

shining under the fluorescent lighting, Jyoti nodded and smiled, picking up a desk phone.

'I don't suppose he actually said that?' Sam murmured.

'Of course not,' Graeme muttered back. 'It would probably have made her tell me if he wasn't in, though. Front desk's goal is always to get rid of you.'

Jyoti removed the phone from her ear with an expression of professional regret. 'I'm so sorry, I'm afraid you've caught Harvey on the hop. He says can you leave a number where he can contact you?'

Graeme smiled even more genially and raised his voice to a level that end-of-the-phone Harvey couldn't help but hear. 'If Harvey's not available I don't mind speaking to one of the senior partners.'

Jyoti looked appalled at this intrepid bandying of senior partners but a buzzing from the telephone saved her from having to find a graceful way to protect the upper echelon from the hoi polloi. 'Oh . . . OK. Thanks,' she said into the phone, obviously relieved, before clicking it back into its rest. 'Harvey says he'll make five minutes for you. I'll show you into Meeting Room Two.'

'Wonderful.' Graeme's smile was as wide as a crocodile's.

Meeting Room 2 held a desk and five navy leather chairs and looked out onto a side street. As they waited for Harvey, Sam's phone vibrated with a text from Jake. *Sent low-res files to server for you to check out. Also sent to Tod for his reference.* Clicking the link, Sam entered his password quickly. Soon he was flicking through the sample images from Jake's shoot.

Oh.

The camera loved a pouting, smouldering Ruby. But Ava looked like a wooden carving of a beautiful rabbit caught in the headlights.

Quickly, he texted back to Jake. *I'm looking for warmth and twinkle from Ava.*

Jake responded in seconds. *So am I!!! She's trying, but she's hating the whole thing with the hats, though she was OK earlier, when she was fully dressed.*

Sam glanced at his watch. *I'll try and get over there. Take a coffee break and chat about other stuff. Maybe she'll slide into an easier frame of mind. Ruby's pics are coming along.*

OK. Yeah, Ruby's fantastic.

It hadn't occurred to Sam that recreating the original image would throw up this problem. Frowning, he stowed his phone as Harvey Snaith sidled into the room, opening and closing the door quickly as if he was afraid something in the room might bound out into the wider workplace. The back of Sam's neck prickled and he fondly revisited his fantasy of shaking Harvey un-gently by the throat. The look Harvey shot Sam was so full of dislike that it somehow made Sam feel better. If such a disgusting weasel had liked him it would have felt like an insult.

Wearing a dark blue business suit and white shirt that was boringly immaculate, his dark hair looking as if he'd just arrived from an expensive hair salon, Harvey cleared his throat and extended his hand. 'Graeme.'

Graeme kept his own hands in his pockets. 'Sit down.'

Silently, Harvey sat, looking even more uncomfortable than Ava had in the images Sam had just viewed. He clasped his hands tightly on the desk.

Graeme fixed Harvey with a gaze that glinted with malice. 'Harvey Snaith, you've been causing my daughter a lot of worry.'

'I don't know what you're—'

'You know exactly what I'm referring to so don't dick

me about.' Graeme's calm delivery was somehow scarier than bellowing rage. 'Get your phone out.'

Harvey hesitated.

Mistake, Sam told him, silently.

Graeme's voice dropped an entire octave. 'Get your phone out. Or I'll have to turn your life into very deep shit, and damn me if I'll care about your suffering.'

Reluctantly, Harvey dipped into his inside jacket pocket and produced an iPhone. He made as if to offer it to Graeme.

Graeme shook his head. 'Find me those intimate shots of Ava.'

Fumbling, Harvey tried. He tried for over a minute. Then his gaze lifted slowly.

Spreading his hands in mock astonishment, Graeme grinned. 'Oh dear. Have they gone?' He leaned forward. 'I think you'll find that they've gone off your tablet, your laptop and the Cloud. That's strange, isn't it?'

Although he hid his surprise, Sam wanted to burst into applause.

Harvey's near-black eyes were wary and confused, fixed silently on Graeme.

'What hasn't disappeared is the stream of threatening and abusive texts you've sent to my daughter.' Gently Graeme shook his head. 'Silly boy. Stupid boy to provide an ex-police officer with clear evidence. As the sentences for malicious communication offences have just been beefed up, now seems a good time to tell you a couple of things.' He sat back, steepling his fingers. 'The collateral consequences of criminal convictions are a nuisance. Criminal convictions have to be declared on job applications, they stop you entering certain countries, they even affect your insurability and your creditworthiness.

Wouldn't it be dreadful if you got one? Some people convicted of malicious communication offences even go to prison. And now you've sent some to my friend here,' he indicated Sam, 'we have to consider the new law on disclosing private sexual images to cause distress, which also carries a prison sentence. It deals nicely with scum like you.'

Horror burst across Harvey's face, *kapow*, as if dealt by a giant fist.

Graeme rose easily to his feet and planted his hands on the desk, getting right in Harvey's face, voice dropping to a smoothly dangerous whisper, every day of his life as a cop etched on his features. 'In case you've squirrelled those pictures somewhere we don't know about, *we'll keep your texts nice and safe*, and trust the images never find their way out into the public domain.'

Minutely, Harvey shook his head. Sweat shone on his pale forehead.

Sam's heart thudded with satisfaction. It would do Harvey good to be scared. It would give him a taste of how he'd made Ava feel. Sam rose, too. 'If you have a spare moment, look up a support group called No Blame or Shame. Read their website. Pick up a few tips on the acceptable way to treat women.'

Harvey's gaze cut to Sam. Slowly, he nodded.

'Right, bye then.' Graeme sounded almost jovial. 'I hope I won't have to bother you again.'

Harvey shook his head.

Once on the pavement outside Harvey's building, Sam and Graeme didn't even discuss their next move. Graeme hailed a taxi and gave Ava's address and Sam followed him into the back seat.

'That was awesome,' said Sam, sincerely. An ex-police

officer issuing promises of retribution had probably been more effective than dragging Harvey across the desk by his bright white shirt and throttling him, as Sam had felt the urge to do, and carried far less risk.

Graeme seemed gently pleased with himself. 'I'm glad that Ava asked me to help with this. I admire her trying to handle it alone, of course. We brought our girl up to be self-sufficient. It meant throwing her in at the deep end sometimes but Ava's a swimmer, not a drowner.'

Despite the obvious pride in Graeme's voice Sam halted in the act of buckling his seat belt, blinded by this spotlight-bright insight into Ava. Her prickliness over money. The way she'd tried to hide her desperation until it had nearly destroyed her. The thought made his guts ache. 'Are you sure that was what she wanted?' The cab jerked in a sudden change of direction as the driver took advantage of a gap in the inside lane. Sam caught Graeme's gaze and held it. 'One man's self-sufficiency is another woman's being left to cope alone.'

Graeme's smile of satisfaction slid from his face. Slowly, frowning, he looked away, to gaze out through the cab window.

When they'd completed what proved to be a mainly silent journey, they found Ava, Ruby, Jake and Patrick on coffee break in Ava's studio, Ruby swathed glamorously in silk, Ava huddled miserably in towelling.

Sam wanted to wrap comforting arms around her and tell her that everything was going to be all right. But today that wasn't his job.

'I'm sorry,' she blurted as soon as she saw him. 'Jake's being fantastic but I'm like a sour-faced shop window dummy.'

He didn't bother to pretend that he thought otherwise. 'It's OK. Your dad's about to cheer you up.'

Her eyes swivelled to her father. 'How?'

Graeme pulled her up off her stool and scooped her into a big fatherly hug. Some of his earlier bounce might have vanished, but his smile oozed confidence. 'Your old man is a magician, sweetheart. I waved a magic wand – well, actually a contact in a civilian high-tech surveillance agency I used to use – and it all went away.'

Ava pulled back to gaze into his face. 'Went away? What?'

'Every image on every device, Cloud or other online storage associated with Harvey Snaith's email or accessed from any of his devices. Harvey's been hacked. Poor lad. The only record of the images he held are probably on your phone – and we're going to keep them and his texts very safe indeed, aren't we? In the event we need them?' His grin would have done justice to any wolf.

'Dad,' breathed Ava, her eyes beginning to dance. 'You're not supposed to do that sort of thing.'

'What?' He shrugged, pulling off his coat. 'I didn't do anything. Someone I used to encounter in the course of my employment was annoyed that we were being caused anxiety, that's all. Abracadabra.' But then his voice became husky. 'I'd do anything to help you, sweetheart. I hope you know that.'

Joy blazed across Ava's face. She gave a tiny scream. 'Dad! I love you!' Flinging herself onto her father, she danced him round in an excited circle, then swept on to treat Sam to the same triumphant jig.

It felt amazing, even bundled up in that shapeless bathrobe, to have her body pressed against his. Like Christmas had come early. He probably held on to her longer than

234

he should have done, momentarily frozen by the assault on his senses; the scent of her hair, the sound of her laughter.

'What about hugs for the rest of us?' demanded Patrick.

From within the circle of Sam's arms, Ava grinned. 'Dad? Patrick needs a hug.'

Everyone roared with laughter at Patrick's expression of alarm. Then he looked from Sam to Ava with a half-smile and a small nod, as if acknowledging that he wasn't to be the provider of hugs for Ava.

When they finally disentangled themselves, Sam had to swallow before he could grin at her. 'Now would be a good time to try those shots again, Jake. I think Ava's going to be OK.'

Chapter Twenty-Four

Bubbling under

Still Friday 21 December

Ava hummed as she waited for seven o'clock to roll round, the time of Wendy's next fitting.

There wasn't much to do apart from a bit of tidying up after the shoot. She'd showered and popped her black dress back on but was too antsy with relief and not quite believing that Harvey was beaten to collapse into a chair with the TV remote.

Instead, she sat cross legged on Izz's bed and helped her wrap parcels ready for her Hampshire family Christmas, gleefully reporting Harvey's downfall and that incredible melting moment of relief when she discovered what her dad had achieved.

'The photo shoot became fun, in the end. Ruby was so outraged when she found out the full extent of Harvey's behaviour that she kept dreaming up worse and worse punishments for him, which made me laugh. A testicle abscess was the least of the horrors she suggested.'

Izz giggled. 'Let him put *that* on Facebook.'

'In the end, I was sorry to see everyone rush off to

meet their deadlines.' Ava picked up a crackly sheet of bright red paper sprigged with holly. 'Dad's gone to stay with an old police buddy who has a guest room, as we can only offer him the sofa. I'll see him again before his return flight on Sunday. He's really insistent that I hang on to the threatening texts from Harvey, just in case. Do you know if there's some way to backup message threads?' Ava's crippling fear of exposure had vanished but she wasn't quite so giddy with joy as to throw caution to the wind.

Izz readily held out her hand. 'If you give me your phone I can back them up to iTunes.'

'Seriously? That would be fantastic. You're magic at this stuff.' Ava gladly passed the phone over. It seemed that everything was going her way, today. 'I'm really sorry you won't be here for Christmas. I'll miss you, Izz.'

'You'll be with Sam.' Izz kept her head bent over the phone as her fingers and thumbs got busy on the screen.

'Only because you made other plans.' Ava hesitated, feeling a wriggle of worry. There hadn't been much indication as to whether Sam's comic-geek efforts had killed Izz's crush. The thought caused a tiny wrinkle in Ava's euphoria. 'Do you still like Sam?' she asked, tentatively.

Izz shrugged. Then she peeped up at Ava from behind her hair, cheeks colouring. 'Actually . . . I'm going out tonight. With Patrick. He turned up at work as I was leaving and he told me what was happening with the Ruby Glennister campaign and why the agency had more-or-less emptied this afternoon. We got talking. Then he looked up some gigs and said there's an indie band on tonight at Koko, did I fancy it.'

'Wow,' said Ava. Then, aware she'd sounded astonished rather than pleased, 'That's great, but you took me by surprise! You've been working together for months but I didn't know you liked him.'

She passed back Ava's phone. 'There, all backed up. We don't seem each other's type, do we? I suppose I thought . . . Well, I've never gone out with such a jack-the-lad before. Cocky, confident men don't usually hit on me so I decided, hey, give it a try. He didn't say it was a *date* date.'

'It sounds like a date to me.' Ava beamed, glad that Patrick was sufficiently attuned to Izz to take her to a Camden music venue. 'Have a fantastic time.' Ava gave Izz an enthusiastic hug. 'What are you going to wear?'

'Flat shoes,' said Izz, pragmatically. 'And a grateful expression.'

'*Izz!*' protested Ava.

Izz laughed, eyes dancing. 'OK. That dark purply top with my sparkly jeans.'

'You look great in that top,' Ava assured her. 'And I won't even tell you not to keep Patrick out too late because those involved in Ruby's campaign, including me, are going to turn ourselves into a bit of a social-media hub at the agency tomorrow, even though it's Saturday. In fact, I hope that your evening goes on until breakfast.' She wouldn't have picked Patrick as a likely date for Izz but, you never knew, he might bring her out of her shell a bit. In turn, Izz might encourage him to be a bit less . . . Patrick-ish.

Then the doorbell shrilled and Ava swung her legs off the bed. 'That will be Sam bringing Wendy for her hat fitting. Want to come up? It won't take long this time so we can ask them to stay for wine. I bought mince pies, too.'

Izz checked the time self-consciously. 'I need to get ready.'

'OK. Offer's open if you change your mind.' A last hug and Ava flew down the stairs.

When she answered the door, she found Wendy was already wearing a hat, in the form of a knitted Christmas pudding complete with sprig of holly. She beamed from beneath it. 'Ava! I'm all excited but I don't want to spoil the Christmas Day surprise. Can I have my fitting with my eyes closed?'

'No reason why not,' Ava laughed, standing back to let her guests in. Wendy promptly rushed over the threshold, dragging Vanessa with her.

Sam, hands in pockets, brought up the rear. He kissed Ava's temple. 'I'm knackered to the point of ruin but everything's coming together really well. We all love the images and the files have been sent to *Alive Today*. I'll show you later.' He smothered a yawn.

'Your team has worked so hard.' Ava gave him a grateful hug. 'Let's all go up to the studio, shall we? This won't take long and then you can get off home if you want.' With a tiny sink of disappointment she shelved her plan to break open the wine. It looked as if she'd have to find a way to settle down and enjoy her own company this Friday evening.

As Wendy was serious about having her fitting without seeing the hat, Ava ran ahead and hid it. Then Wendy bowled happily into the studio, plopped down onto the stool and screwed her eyes tight shut. 'Ready when you are!' She whipped off the Christmas pudding hat. Her smile never faltered but everyone in the room gazed at the way her scalp shone white. Her hair had just begun to emerge in a hint of suede-like fuzz.

Ava swallowed. 'Here we go, then.' With a glance at Sam, who was regarding his mother with what looked suspiciously like pain, she shifted the box she'd dropped over the jade felt and positioned herself behind Wendy.

'This is such a lovely Christmas,' Wendy confided. 'Sam sent a car to pick us up from Euston this afternoon. Not an ordinary taxi but a lovely long white car. I felt like the queen. They didn't even mind that we had the dogs.'

Ava turned the hat in her hands, finding the front. 'I didn't know Mars and Snickers were invited, too.'

Wendy giggled. 'We couldn't leave them with friends over Christmas.'

In the mirror Ava could see Wendy's screwed-up eyes and expectant smile. The hat slid on smoothly, perfectly framing Wendy's small features. Behind her, she heard Vanessa draw in a sudden breath.

'How does it look?' Wendy's smile widened expectantly.

'Gorgeous.' Ava shifted the hat experimentally, studying the effect on Wendy's reflection. 'How does it feel? Is it soft?'

'Oh yes. I barely know I'm wearing it.'

'Not too tight?'

'Not at all.'

'Give your head a little shake to see if you can feel it moving. No? I guess we're done, then. Hang on a second while I'll cover it up again . . . OK, you can open your eyes.'

Blinking in the light, Wendy beamed. 'I can't wait to see the finished thing. And Sam says you're coming on Christmas Day! That's so, so lovely. Isn't it, Van?'

Vanessa gave her sister a fond smile. 'Fabulous.'

Wendy picked up her pudding hat and crammed it back on her head. 'We're off to see *War Horse*, now.'

Sam, who had been leaning against the wall by the door, straightened. 'We are?'

'*We* are.' Vanessa patted his shoulder. 'We knew it wouldn't be your thing. There should be a taxi coming for us soon. You can stay with Ava.'

Sam frowned. 'Are you sure? I could drop you off and pick you up. It's a bit sad, that show.'

Stubbornly, Wendy shook her head. 'Spend some time with your girlfr— with Ava. Vanessa and I will have a lovely little cry over the poor horsie, then a glass of wine in the bar and get a taxi back to your place. Vanessa says she'll take Snickers and Mars for their last walk. I can sleep in tomorrow morning if I'm tired, can't I?' Wendy bestowed a smacking kiss and a quick hard hug on Ava. 'See you on Christmas Day, if not before. Won't it be wonderful? Christmas together?'

'Wonderful,' Ava echoed, dizzy at the speed with which the hat fitting was being wrapped up.

'Vanessa's looking at her watch – it's time for us to leave!' In a very few minutes, Wendy and Vanessa were gone.

Sam turned away from the front door after seeing them safely into the taxi and passed a tired hand over his face. 'Sorry about them being so obvious. They've clearly cooked this up to leave us alone together.'

'It's very sweet of them.' Ava hesitated, feeling a bit like a teenager whose mates had fixed her up. 'We could open a bottle of wine, or there's coffee to keep you awake. But I won't be offended if you'd rather go straight home.'

Sam was already heading for the sitting room, throwing his jacket on a chair and falling backwards onto the sofa as if the muscles in his legs had given up. 'Both, please. Then, if you get me your laptop, I'll access the agency server and show you which images we've chosen.'

Butterflies fluttered at this reminder of the saucy image

241

that was about to go viral, if the agency could make it happen. Had the Calendar Girls ever felt this nervous? Ava busied herself opening the wine and filling the kettle. Then she fetched the computer from her room and sank into the place Sam indicated beside him on the sofa.

He called up the image with a few seconds of tapping, and then turned the screen so that she could see it. 'You look fantastic.'

A large and bracing gulp of wine, then she sneaked a peek. 'Ohhhhh . . . !' An oddly unfamiliar Ava glittered out at her, eyes shining with laughter and what looked suspiciously like triumph. Shocked at the way Jake had captured her carnality, Ava gazed at her body rising above the shielding hats. Who knew shoulders could be that sexy? The black background had worked beautifully and her skin looked luminous, her hair caught up on one side in a turquoise fascinator and streaming like liquid gold over a shoulder. The image depicted an assured, sensual woman that Ava had trouble associating with herself.

She was very conscious that Sam was beside her, studying the same image.

'That's the one we're going with. And this one of Ruby.' He clicked over to another image and Ruby laughed into the camera lens.

'She's amazing,' Ava said involuntarily. 'So at ease with the camera.'

Examining the image critically, Sam nodded. 'She has that aura that says "pro model", though. You're less contrived and, therefore, more interesting.' He flipped back to her image. 'You look as complicated and enigmatic as the *Mona Lisa* – but as though you know a naughty secret. There's a real feel of you bubbling under. I'll send you a copy but keep it under wraps for now. Emily will give you some help tomorrow on how to get the best out of it.' He closed the image files down while Ava wondered what 'bubbling under' could mean.

He clicked on another folder. 'Patrick's article's good, too. *Alive Today*'s production team will lay out the copy with the shots of Ruby wearing your hats in the more conventional manner.'

Ava was relieved to move on to images in which everybody was fully dressed. 'I'm in those more than I expected.' She studied the pictures of herself positioning the yellow hat, expression serious as she studied the effect, then glancing into the camera as she took away the white looped one and, lastly, just beginning to smile as she looked into Ruby's face. 'Ruby's make-up lady did a good job.'

Sam moved the computer onto her lap so that she could continue to flick through the folder, and reached for his wine. 'If she can't make you two look good she needs a new career.' He closed his eyes and leaned his head back against the sofa.

Ava began to read Patrick's article. Ruby's voice came through clearly: chatty, joking, but shadowed with something more pensive as she talked about bad patches and silly mistakes. *My life recently has been like a 'how NOT to' manual. It only took one thing, just one thing I handled badly, and I was in the middle of an epic shit storm.*

Somehow, Ruby's supposed interest in hats was made to feel completely natural, as if a milliner was the obvious person to look to for solace. *'And Ava's become a friend, as well as someone who helps me look my best, haven't you, Ava?' says Ruby, taking a critical look at herself in the jaunty hat she's had made for a spring wedding. 'Suppose it's the model in me that makes me ornament myself if I need cheering up.'*

243

As directed, Patrick had concluded with: *Ruby says, 'Hats off to Ava Bliss.'* Ruby was depicted tipping the looped hat to the camera.

Thoughtfully, Ava put the laptop down, hit by exactly what Sam Jermyn and his associates had made happen. 'Thank you,' she said quietly. 'Ruby mentions turning her life around but you and Dad turned mine around between you. Dad I can understand but you could easily have done all this without me. As it is, there's potential for a lot of people to see that article, and my name. I might get loads of new clients.'

Sam's shoulders heaved on a silent laugh, eyes remaining closed. 'If you don't get loads of new clients I might as well join the make-up artist in finding a new career.'

Gravely, she regarded him: the lashes fanned on his cheeks, the laughter lines crinkling. 'I hardly dare let myself believe that. Why are you helping me?'

Blinking his eyes open, he pulled himself up, putting down his wine glass and picking up his coffee. His smile was crooked. 'It's what any faux boyfriend would do for a faux girlfriend.' Then, when she arched her eyebrows sceptically, 'Harvey made me angry,' he admitted. 'I liked the idea of helping you get one over on him. You've been great with Mum during a particularly shitty time and if she'd been aware of what you were going through she would have wanted me to help. The image of you with the two hats sparked off ideas I could use for Ruby. Why shouldn't you profit, too?'

A bubble of emotion rose unexpectedly in Ava's throat. 'Thank you.'

'You're welcome.' His gaze locked with hers for an instant. Then he reached for the laptop again. 'Now I'll show you what Tod's come up with. Social media's going to go mad for this in the pre-Christmas lunacy.' His fingers raced over the keyboard. 'He's set up a page on our website for people to upload their own images to the e-card. They can send it to everybody in their address book if they want, and we hope they will. These things cost a quid or so on other sites so hopefully ours being free will encourage participation.'

Soon Ava was watching five stiff little animations doing a chorus line dance to 'Jingle Bells', vaguely burlesque cartoon bodies with photograph heads – Ava and Ruby with Tod, Louise and Patrick.

Ava's animation and Ruby's were hampered in their dancing by the need to keep their hats clamped over their breasts. As others in the chorus line tried to link arms Ava and Ruby had to manage the hats, clutching and swapping hand-to-hand to keep themselves decent.

Ava giggled, blushing on behalf of her 'mini me'.

Then came the final moment when 'mini Ruby's' chin moved to mimic the act of speaking and Ruby's merry voice cried 'Hats off to Ava Bliss!' Then she whisked off her hats. Beneath her naked boobs could be seen tiny stitches.

Animation-Ava's jaw dropped and the cartoon ended on applause.

'Wow!' gasped Ava. 'Has Ruby seen this? Will she mind?'

'She gave me a four-lettered earful,' he admitted. 'But then she roared with laughter and upgraded me from cheeky sod to bleedin' piss-taker.'

He touched the screen to rerun the video. 'Lucky that Tod has mates in animation that have the software to produce something like this in such short order. Because, hopefully, tomorrow this goes viral.'

Chapter Twenty-Five

Bubbling over

Sam had yawned for about the twentieth time when Ava took his empty coffee mug from his hand. 'Why don't you drive home while you still can?'

'Maybe I should.' But before Sam could finish his next gigantic yawn Tod and Louise rang the front door bell.

'Sorry we're so late.' Tod's glasses steamed up as he bounded in from the cold. 'That bloody Glennister/Blissham campaign kept me at my machine.' He put down the bags he carried in each hand to give Ava a big hug.

The hug she returned was even bigger. 'I've just seen your star-in-your-own-cartoon e-card. It's amazing. You're a genius.'

'It's shit-hot, isn't it?' Tod grinned immodestly.

Behind him, Louise hurried to get far enough into the hall to close the door behind her, huddled in a Puffa coat that made her look like a chrysalis. 'As Tod was held up at work I got all the wrapping done this evening. On my *own*.'

Suspecting that she was expected to apologise, Ava offered drinks instead, and Sam sat back down and accepted another cup of coffee.

Tod unwound himself from a long black scarf. 'We've come to put your gift under your Christmas tree.' Clutching a gift wrapped in cutesy little bear paper, he glanced around the room as if a tree might sidle out from behind a curtain.

'I haven't got a tree but I have a parcel for you.' Ava reached down beside the sofa where her tiny stash of gifts-to-give were stored. 'It's kind of a joint one,' she said hastily, because it hadn't occurred to her to get a separate present for Louise. The gift was a Lego Arkham Asylum because you couldn't go wrong giving Tod anything to do with Batman, and he could always let Louise help him build it. Maybe she should have gone for Ironman Mr Potato Head, so Louise and Tod could play it with Louise's family.

Tod accepted his parcel and shook it, eyes gleaming. 'Sounds like fun.'

Louise sent Ava a pained look but fought her way out of her chrysalis coat and sat down to accept a glass of wine. 'I had a wish list for Tod. You could have bought from that.'

'But Ava knows what I like,' Tod responded firmly. 'We've managed to buy each other gifts without wish lists till now.'

Ava stifled an urge to ask for the wish list anyway, just to see what horrors Louise had included. Probably matching tableware or gift vouchers for a cosplay website.

'Hi, Izz.' Tod looked past Ava towards the doorway. 'Going out? I've got a pressie for you.'

Ava turned to see Izz standing in the doorway, her big black coat over her arm and a gift bag in her hand. Gently flushed, she looked striking in skinny jeans and kitten heels. 'Got to rush, but Merry Christmas. I don't know if I'll see you before I leave for Hampshire.' She and Tod exchanged gifts and hugs.

'Where are you going?' demanded Louise.

Izz exchanged glances with Ava. 'Just out with a friend.'

'What friend?' Louise looked interested.

Izz flushed, but Tod was obviously in a masterful mood. 'It's not really our business, Louise. See you, Izz. Have a fantastic time.'

Louise looked put out at Tod setting her right for the second time in as many minutes so Ava jumped up and went with Izz to the front door. 'You and Patrick enjoy yourselves,' she whispered, as Izz hauled on her coat. 'You look great.'

Izz fidgeted, anxious and excited both at once. 'Better not to tell Sam who . . .'

Ava was already nodding. 'It's OK, I understand. Keep it out of the office.' She stood for a second at the door after Izz hurried away, marvelling that somehow Izz and *Patrick* had ended up going to a gig together.

She returned to the sitting room to find Tod and Louise thrusting their arms back into their coats. 'Are you going already?' she cried, dismayed. 'I thought you'd stay for a while.'

'I'm walking Louise back to the tube station. She's going home.' Tod's words were clipped.

'Oh. OK.' Ava elected not to wish them Merry Christmas, as merry was the last thing either of them looked as they tersely took their leave.

After seeing them out, Ava rejoined Sam with her eyebrows raised. 'Did they have a row?'

A smile lurked at the corners of Sam's mouth. 'They're probably having one by now. Louise told Tod not to talk to *her* like *that* and he replied that it was about time she learned to take it as well as dish it out. Hence her sudden determination to go home.' He yawned. 'Probably they're

248

having a conversation that's past due and either they redraw the lines in their relationship or Tod will be around for Christmas after all.'

'You're shattered,' said Ava, seeing the yawn. 'You should go home, too.'

He stretched. 'I should. But what about you? I can hang around if you'd rather. Or did you want to catch up with Izz and her friend?'

'Oh no,' Ava denied, hastily. Then, as she'd only agreed not to share the identity of Izz's companion with Sam, not the nature of her evening, confided with a waggle of her eyebrows, 'She's meeting a man. I'll be OK. You're exhausted with the campaign. I'll have another glass of wine and think about how amazing it is that everything's coming out so well after what I did. Thanks to all you guys at Jermyn's.'

He groaned and let his eyes shut again. 'You didn't "do" anything. It *wasn't you*. You were let down by someone you trusted. If you carry on feeling shame, Ava, he'll have won. He'll have harmed you. Don't let him win!'

As he hadn't got up to leave, she settled back beside him. 'But think how people would have felt about me if those photos had got out.' Her stomach gave a twirl at the mere idea.

'I'm not underestimating the horror and humiliation if that had happened. But your friends and family would have been outraged on your behalf. They wouldn't have blamed you.'

She wasn't convinced. 'But they would have lost respect.'

'No.' He felt for her hand and gave it a comforting squeeze. 'They wouldn't. They would have felt for you. It would have been about sympathy, not condemnation.'

His eyes remaining shut as he talked, she let her gaze

low the way his hair curled behind his ears and the
nd-of-a-long-day stubble made his cheeks look hollow.
His deep blue shirt clung across his chest, tightening on
the rhythms of his breathing. She wondered how many
times he'd held her hand when she needed comfort over
the short time she'd known him.

He'd been more supportive of her while they'd been
faux dating than most real boyfriends ever managed.

A thought hit her like a blast of cold water.

Izz being out on a date indicated that she'd got over
Sam.

Surely that freed Ava from the restrictions of the best
friends' code?

She poured herself another glass of Zinfandel and took
three big, strengthening gulps. Then let her thoughts drop
uncensored from her lips. 'Do you still want to sleep with
me?' At hearing the words out loud, her heartbeat took
on a different rhythm.

Slowly, Sam's eyes opened. Something hard blazed from
his no-longer-sleepy gaze. 'Hell's bells. Having had it
pointed out to me in the bluntest terms on so many occasions that you don't have time for a man in your life blah
blah blah blah *blah*, I can only presume this to be a
rhetorical question. So you're using the fact that I have
the hots for you to reassure yourself? Fantastic. Thanks
a bunch. Well you can find someone else to provide vali-
dation. I don't appreciate it.' He dropped her hand and
rolled quickly to his feet. 'I'll see you tomorrow at the
agency.'

Ava gazed at him in dismay. 'That wasn't what I was
asking. I wouldn't play you like that.' After the wracking
emotions of the day, her voice actually trembled.

Comprehension stole into Sam's expression. Slowly, he

sank back down, rubbing a sheepish hand over his face. 'Oh shit, I'm sorry. I completely misinterpreted and over-reacted. Put it down to overwhelming and undermining fatigue affecting my usual functions.' His eyes shone with remorse. 'If you're asking whether my having seen a couple of those images has stopped me wanting to sleep with you, the answer is no, they have not. You keep calling them "horrible images" but believe me neither of those images were horrible to me. Or most straight men, I'd imagine.'

His foot-in-mouth embarrassment was so comical that Ava's dismay flipped into an urge to giggle. 'Right.' She struggled to keep the grin off her suddenly heated face. 'I didn't mean that either, but thanks for the reassurance.'

That got his attention.

Complete, unwavering, intense attention. His gaze burned into her as, slowly, an eyebrow lifted. 'OK, this is getting interesting. Spell out for me what you do mean.' His voice was low and soft.

She peeped at him. 'There's a good chance I can relax about my career now the financial heat shows signs of abating – thanks to you. You know about Harvey and don't judge me for it. Izz seems kind of sorted . . . so I was reconsidering your suggestion that we should give each other a try.'

He didn't return an answer. But his smile said a lot.

'But I'd obviously underestimated the degree to which you're shattered, overwhelmed and not functioning,' she added, kindly.

If anything, his expression shifted up the intensity scale a notch or two.

She studied her nails with an elaborate air of unconcern. 'Don't you worry. You get off home to sleep.'

He lifted her hand, brushing her fingertips across his lips, sending desire flittering through her. 'Suddenly I'm not tired. I can show you how much I still want to sleep with you. I'm all about measurable data.'

She teased him for another few seconds. 'Sure you're not too tired?'

He grinned. 'Quite sure.' Pulling gently on her hand, he reeled her in until she was brushing up against him. 'But I do want to go to bed . . . if it's yours.' His lips touched hers, soft and hot, sending her into a gentle simmer.

She let her head tip back as his lips moved on to her throat. 'It could be mine.' With no Izz here to worry about. 'I think I'd like a hot man in my stockings for Christmas.'

His hand began to travel south. 'You're wearing stockings with a dress this short?'

Her voice was beginning to clog her throat at the feel of his hand passing over her. 'I ripped my tights earlier so I had to make do.'

'Don't apologise for stockings.' He stroked her thigh, first over the fabric of her dress then under, breath catching audibly in his throat as he encountered bare flesh.

Although the heat from his hand was spreading through her in waves, part of her mind stayed on track. 'Upstairs. I know Izz left but I'd hate her to come back—'

'Definitely upstairs.' He jumped up, pulling Ava with him.

It took time to feel their way up two staircases, especially as Sam, teasing up the fabric of her dress, found bare buttock with his palm. He groaned, 'You're wearing a thong,' like an accusation. He braced against the wall of the narrow staircase to investigate further, yanking her against him, curling around her, biting her neck, cupping her buttocks. When his fingertips began to follow the line of her thong all the breath whooshed out of her lungs. Her attempt to say, 'Really, let's get to my room,' emerged as 'Reeeee . . . gnhnnumph.'

He laughed against the crook of her neck. His grip tightened, his knees straightened and she was off the ground as he carried her up the rest of the flight onto the top landing.

Her lungs suddenly didn't fit inside her rib cage. 'My bedroom's through that door—'

'Do you think I hadn't worked that out? Every time I was in your studio I thought about this room and hoped I'd get to see it.' His breathing was fast but his movements were slow as he closed the door with his back, shutting them into the room, the only light coming from the distant glow of streetlights filtering through the skylight. He let her slide down his body and onto her feet. Kissing her. Taking his time. Stroking. Finding the small buttons at the back of her dress, unpopping them, one . . . two . . . three – pausing to trace the top of her spine – four. Touching her as if everything in his life had led to this moment of having her under his hands.

Ava gave herself up to the pleasure of being slowly undressed while her fingers wandered up under his shirt, skimming his ribs, his back, his abs. Learning him; his shape, his smell. Following his happy trail down into the waistband of his jeans.

She shivered as her dress began to slide from her shoulders, his hands nudging it down her body, exploring as he went, flipping open the catch of her bra, pulling that slowly from her, too. The cooler air hit her skin, goosebumps tingling over her.

His searching hands halted at the small of her back. 'What's this?'

She put her own hand back to touch the little circlet of metal. 'Thong ornament. Where the pieces meet.'

'Lights,' he said, hoarsely. 'I need to see "thong ornament".'

She giggled. 'By the bed.'

In the near-darkness, he steered her to where a small lamp stood on her bedside table. She blinked as it spread a pool of light.

But his gaze was steady, hungry, burning down her body as he turned her around. 'That's hot,' he said hoarsely, flicking his thumbnail across the spiral design of the circlet in a way that vibrated through her. His hands drifted up her back and down over her collarbones, down the front of her, cupping her breasts in the warmth of his hands. 'You're amazing.' He pressed himself against her, letting her feel how much he wanted her.

Groaning, she rotated her hips against him.

In slow motion he wrapped himself around her, turning her so that the front of her was crushed against his chest. On tiptoe she wound her arms around his neck and pressed her mouth against his throat.

It was a perfect moment. The air around them seemed thick and soft.

Then suddenly the feelings were bubbling over. 'Need you.' He dragged his shirt over his head, crushed a kiss onto her mouth, attempting to maintain that contact as he yanked at his belt and the fastening of his jeans. She tried to help him but it was all she could do to stay on her feet in the flurry of him abandoning his clothes.

It didn't take him long to get naked. Then he swept her backwards and onto the bed. She landed with the coolness of the duvet against her back and the heat of a large excited man on her front.

'Yep, lots of need,' she gasped, arching against him as his mouth left a trail of kisses down to her breasts, each one cooling on her skin as he dragged the thong down her legs then swore a lot as he realised his wallet was in his jeans and his jeans were somewhere over near the door. And his condoms were in his wallet.

She didn't have time to mention that, as a modern woman, she did actually have condoms in the bedside drawer. He was off her, leaving the space where he'd been shiveringly empty, as he wrangled his wallet out of a reluctant pocket and fought the condom wrapper. Then he was back, he was on her. Burning, pushing, sliding.

She stopped having coherent thoughts.

Her voice still worked, though. It didn't make much sense but it was satisfactorily loud, making Sam laugh and groan as he went harder and faster.

He didn't seem tired at all.

Chapter Twenty-Six

Going viral

Saturday 22 December

Sam woke with the realisation that he wasn't in his own bed. It was smooth and comfortable, but it wasn't his.

He forced his brain to move a level closer to the surface. Not only was it not his bed, a woman was lying against him, soft and warm, her hair spilling over his shoulder.

Ava.

Stray filaments of her hair had caught on his stubble. Usually he hated that but this time it didn't tickle. It was Ava.

Ava. Excitement flashed through him as the past hours burst back into his memory. The first time, fast and furious. The next, he'd managed to keep some control. Just.

Ava. The happy mischievous Ava that he'd known existed somewhere, Ava, laughing, rolling over him, taking him in as if he was her new favourite thing, exploring him with hands and mouth. Exhausting him to the point that he didn't actually remember sliding into sleep. Ava.

How long ago had that been? Beside the bed an electric clock read 05:33. Damn it. He needed to leave.

Edging onto his side he slid an arm around Ava's curves until his hand was resting on her behind. A hell of a behind. That little spiral thong ornament nestled between the dimples low on her back had really done it for him.

Regretfully, he slid his hand up her back, before he forgot all about leaving. He nuzzled her hair. 'Hey,' he murmured. 'I need to get home to shower and change. We have a full-on day.'

She protested sleepily, snuggling up to him. 'Right now?'

'About five minutes ago.' His hand slid back to the luscious twin mounds of her buttocks.

'Mmm.' She nibbled his neck. 'I suppose I can't complain. I'll see you there about ten.'

'About nine,' he corrected. 'Or even eight-thirty. Ruby said she'd get there by eight-thirty.' Her breasts nudged against him and what he wanted most in all the world was to get his face down there with them. 'We've got a lot of social media networking to do.'

'Slave driver.'

'Yep. Bring your laptop.' He sucked in his breath as her fingers trailed up over his stomach. And down again. 'Ava! I'm trying to be strong here.'

Her laugh was sleepy and sexy. 'OK. Go get 'em. See you in Brick Lane.'

After one long last kiss, resolving to get himself back into her bed at the first possible opportunity, he left, cursing the campaign that was dragging him into the agency on a Saturday even though Ava was an integral part of it. It was torture to peel himself off her curvy soft warmth to meet the cold, dark, wet December morning outside.

This campaign had better be worth it.

*

257

Ava did manage to get to Jermyn's on time, if you allowed for the fact that she'd never actually agreed to eight-thirty so could legitimately claim nine as 'on time'. After Sam had left she'd crashed back into sleep and only woke at seven because he rang her and whispered, 'Are you still in bed?'

Starting guiltily, she'd slipped out from under the duvet and onto the carpet so that she could answer truthfully. 'No.'

His chuckle had told her he didn't believe her. 'But you're getting up now?'

She'd grinned inanely down the phone. 'Promise.' But then she'd slithered back under the duvet for a delicious last few minutes, her thoughts floating like the dust motes in the early morning light breaking through the skylight as she revelled in the memory of him reducing her to jelly one lick at a time.

Eventually, reluctantly, she'd yawned her way to the bathroom. There had been no sound from Izz's room as she paused on the landing before pulling on her coat and skipping off in the direction of the station.

When she reached the agency nearly an hour later, she was buzzed up by Tod.

'Are you OK?' she whispered, as she met him in the foyer. 'You and Louise . . . ?'

'. . . are fine,' he finished, 'now we've had a little talk about things.' He nodded once, firmly.

'Good.' Ava gave him a quick hug, then he found somewhere for her coat and umbrella while she checked her hair and her mascara. A quiver in her stomach reminded her that any moment she was going to see Sam again, and the knowledge of what had happened last night would be between them. An exciting, golden secret.

Tod took her into the same meeting room as before. Ruby hailed her loudly, a tablet in one hand and a big mug of coffee in the other. 'Mornin', Ava, babes!' Her make-up was perfect and her hair brushed smoothly into a doughnut. 'Have you seen what these cheeky sods have done with this e-card? It's awesome, ain't it? It's going out to all the tabloid journos with Tyrone's and Chilly's faces on alongside ours. The article in *Alive Today*'s amazing. We look soooooooooo hot.'

Emily, Tod, Manda Jane, Patrick and Sam were all in the room, the atmosphere set to subdued buzz as fingers tapped busily at laptops or tablets.

Sam looked up and his eyes gave her a long burning smile, sending her internal quivering into overdrive. But he kept things professional. 'Glad you could get here. Got your laptop? Great. Open all your social media accounts and then Emily will set you going.' He pulled out the empty seat between his place and Emily's invitingly.

Though she tried to act as if nothing had happened between yesterday and today, Ava knew she'd turned pink. Sam's eyes glittered with amusement, then he turned away to Tod on his other side and left Emily to update Ava with everything she needed to know.

Emily looked very off-duty in jeans and a knitted top with Aztec designs, her hair in a ponytail. 'All very straight-forward,' she breezed. 'First, send the Christmas card. Have you got pics of some friends on your laptop? You just crop their heads and upload them to a character . . . look, I'll show you.' Her hands got busy, tapping keys of her funky purple laptop. 'I've hooked you up to our wifi. Remember to put the link to the article in every card and include a personal message so it doesn't look spammy. Or I've got a few pre-written sentences for you to use if you want to.

'Every card will have another link for if recipients want to make their own version and send it out themselves, so hopefully they'll all begin to flock to the page. I'm monitoring the hits. People can put your card or their version on Facebook or Twitter etc. After you've sent the card to everyone you can think of – it doesn't matter how tenuous the connection or whether you've already sent them a card, send it anyway – we'll start on your social media. I'll go and fetch another jug of coffee. It should have dripped by now.'

She bustled off, leaving Ava to begin at the top of her list of contacts and work down. Once or twice she glanced across at Patrick, wondering how his date with Izz had gone and wishing Izz had been up this morning so Ava could have checked all was OK. Izz wasn't a big dater and Patrick was so laddish. Patrick looked a bit pale and hungover. He didn't look up from his task much.

'Fun, ain't it?' called Ruby from the other side of the round table, her head bent over her tablet. 'I'm sending the card to everyone I can think of, all the players and their wives and girlfriends, everyone I've met on the TV and radio and at parties.'

Then Manda Jane gave a crow of satisfaction 'Twitter's waking up to the *Alive Today* article. You'll probably have to start doing interviews, Ruby.' She turned to Sam. 'Who have you got lined up to do the "tell all" article?'

He dragged himself from his laptop screen. 'Wait for offers. It would be good if it was a tabloid. Monitor the inbox, please, and everyone keep checking all direct messages and mentions in your social media accounts.'

'What's the "tell all" article?' demanded Ava.

Ruby tapped away at her tablet. 'A platform for me to confess that I fibbed.'

Manda Jane nodded along. 'It's a step-further piece, filling in the blanks left by *Alive Today*. We're hoping that, as they don't do exposés themselves, the hints in the *Alive Today* piece will prompt such a storm of attention that journos will gather around, hungry for the bigger story. We made sure they published a footer to the article to say Jermyn's is working with Ruby. We'll keep linking back to the original article so it won't get lost in the scrum, don't worry.'

It took a few moments for it to sink in that Manda Jane was telling her that they were trying to keep Ava's millinery business in the public eye, too. She felt almost afraid to believe that anything wondrous might come of it.

'Erm, thank you.' Ava went back to her laptop. Uploading faces to each card was time consuming but fun. Posting it on Twitter, Facebook and LinkedIn brought a satisfying wave of smileys and intrigued comments. Pausing to respond expanded her task to Forth Bridge proportions.

At one point Sam leaned behind her to chat something over with Emily and his hand coasted casually over the small of Ava's back. Ava reddened to the tips of her ears, knowing he was checking her out for hidden thong ornaments. But this time she was wearing cage-back panties. Maybe he'd find out later . . .

'You know what,' pronounced Ruby. 'I really enjoyed the shoot yesterday. I reckon I'm going to take another pot at modelling and this campaign could really help.' She paused to fold her hands under her chin and tilt her head prettily as if to prove her credentials. 'Ava, what do you think of me wearing Ava Bliss hats at Ascot and Cannes? I could be kind of "the face of Ava Bliss".'

'Um . . .' Ava felt almost faint at such extraordinary largesse.

'Take it,' advised Sam, without looking up from his conversation. 'We can worry what to do with it later.'

'Yes, of course. That would be fantastic, Ruby.' Ava hoped that she didn't sound naively shell shocked. But she was so firmly in wildest-dreams territory that she could scarcely take in everything that was going on. Then there was that *we* from Sam to think about, too. There was a *we*?

Lunchtime arrived and a delivery person from a local café buzzed from street level with a platter of salads and sandwiches.

While Patrick set the platter in the centre of the table, Emily gave out white paper plates and napkins from a cupboard in the corner and brought fresh coffee. The agency was all set up for working lunches, even when Barb wasn't around to facilitate. People began to stretch and take a break from their machines as they reached for sustenance.

Only Tod was left frowning at his laptop. 'Why would data be uploaded to our server in the early hours of this morning?' He tapped and clicked. Then his jaw dropped. 'Wow! Oh fuck.' He tapped and clicked again.

'What?' Sam looked up.

Tod cleared his throat and his gaze shifted reluctantly to Ava. 'It's a file containing about six pictures. Of you.' He looked hugely uncomfortable. 'They're . . . they're *those* pictures.'

If Tod had jumped up and punched Ava in the belly she couldn't have felt more winded or sick. Her mood flipped. One moment, floating happiness. The next, panic and scalding fear.

She clamped a hand over her mouth, her stomach contents threatening to rise up. 'No,' she moaned. Her blood pounded in her ears. 'Dad said it had all gone away. How could Harvey send them here?' And now Tod had seen them? No! It wasn't fair! It had *gone away*!

She wanted to curl into a tight little ball of humiliation. A pain grew behind her eye, flashes erupted in the periphery of her vision.

Sam was staring at Tod with a frown like a gryphon. '*What?*' he snapped.

Tod was gazing at Ava miserably. 'I don't see how it can be him, unless he's developed hacking abilities. How would he access our server?' He took to his keyboard again. His eyebrows shot up, then crashed down. 'The file appears to have come from *your phone*, Ava. 02.06 today.'

Shock shimmered through her. At 02.06 she'd been in bed . . .

Fury boiled up in her, hot and destructive, a lava flow that blackened and destroyed everything in its path.

Someone else had been near her phone at 02.06 this morning.

Chapter Twenty-Seven

Ava's hotspot goes bad

As if in a nightmare, she swivelled slowly to face Sam, in the grip of an emotion so powerful that she almost couldn't speak. 'How could you? *Why* would you? All this time you've been making out that you thought Harvey was such a shit. Then you go and save the images to your own server? What's wrong with you?'

'*Me*?' Sam thundered, shock blazing across his face. 'You can't seriously think—' He leaped to his feet, banging his legs on the table so hard that it shifted a couple of inches.

Ava, shaking with horror, was unable to tear her gaze from his. 'How can I think it's anybody but you? Unless you're suggesting that I did it in my sleep?' Her throat was closing with grief. 'How could you?' she repeated.

'How could I? How could *you* think I'd do that?' he hissed. 'What do you think—?' Then he hauled himself back under control, glaring around at the others in the room until they closed their open mouths and directed their gazes to their work. Contenting himself with sending Ava a filthy look, he resumed his seat, swiping away the plate Emily had set in front of him.

In the stoniest of silences he turned his attention to his screen.

Moments ticked by. He didn't move a muscle.

'Gawd,' breathed Ruby.

'Sam wouldn't . . .' Manda Jane murmured tentatively.

'Not a chance,' agreed Emily.

Patrick said nothing, but he looked horrified, his gaze flicking from Ava to Sam and back.

Ava couldn't stop looking at Sam. Her blood pounded until she couldn't think straight, physically unable to differentiate between possibility and probability. She had to fight to achieve some semblance of joined-up thinking.

Last night had been so fantastic. She'd been stupid enough to think that it might even be the start of something. That those horrible images were safely corralled on her phone and she could leave them in the past.

Sam had made love to her as if he'd been waiting all his life to do it. He'd stroked and kissed every inch of her; murmured, whispered and even shouted her name. In her turn, she'd been uninhibited and adventurous, thinking she was falling in love with somebody she could trust.

Her brain pulsed with questions. *How could he do this to her?*

The only sound to break the silence was the tapping of keys, seeming to Ava as if they echoed the rhythm. *How could he?*

Heart breaking, she stared at Sam as Sam stared at his screen, as still as a statue.

How could—

'Erm, hang on.' Tod was still frowning at his computer, his glasses glinting in the lights set into the ceiling. 'You've still got an iPhone 4, Ava, haven't you?'

Ava had to concentrate hard not to scream, 'Yes! I

couldn't afford anything more recent!' But it wasn't Tod's fault that her heart was being slowly ripped in two by the knowledge that Sam, *Sam*, however much he had tried to pretend otherwise, was no better than Harvey Snaith. 'Yes,' she muttered.

'But the screen-res is too high for a 4. It's 414 x 736. That's a much more recent phone. More like a 6 or 6+.'

Sam looked up sharply. 'What explanation can you suggest for that anomaly? Tethering?'

Slowly, Tod nodded. 'Could be.'

Ava looked between the two men. Her fury seemed suspended in mid-air, poised right above her like a demon who'd paused part way through savaging his prey.

Sam was looked as if he might be in the grip of a demon of his own. His fists clenched on the table top. 'Whoever it was must have had access to the pictures,' he growled.

'Yes.' Tod heaved a huge sigh.

'And be able to get into the house. And have an iPhone 6 or 6+.'

Bleakly, Tod nodded.

Sam gave Ava a pointed look, a look that said he expected her to join the dots.

But it was taking Ava's brain longer than that to abandon the explanation it had seized upon and admit new information. 'What?' she demanded of Tod. 'What are you saying?'

He took his gaze off his computer screen. 'The res is wrong for your phone, which suggests that your mobile signal was utilised by someone else. Tethering.'

With a titanic sinking feeling, Ava clasped her hand to her forehead. 'That hotspot thing?'

Tod nodded. 'I presume that Sam was with you at the time of the upload.' He didn't look shocked by this knowledge. 'But his phone's a Sony – a different screen res again.'

With a slow shake of her head, Ava became hotly aware that everyone in the room was staring at her apart from Sam. Unease began to prickle over her like a rash. 'What does all this mean? For non-techie types?'

Sympathy burning in his kind eyes, Tod spelled it out. 'It looks to me as if someone knew that the Internet Protocol address would give them away so they used your mobile phone signal to make the download. Can I see your phone? Pop in your passcode, so I can get into it.'

Heart suddenly banging, Ava fumbled it out of her bag and did as Tod asked. Belatedly, she realised that, last night, Sam, who was still pointedly not looking at her, would have had no way of knowing her passcode.

Tod was soon burrowing into the parts of her phone that Ava never bothered to try and understand. He grunted. 'Yep. There's an isolated upload. Have you tethered your laptop to it lately?'

Painfully, Ava shook her head.

'Would Izz know your hotspot password?'

Her voice emerged as a croak. 'She knows I use the same password for most things. But it couldn't be Izz!'

Misery was written across Tod's face. 'It's someone who could get into the house,' he said carefully. 'If you were in your bedroom that person could use your mobile phone signal from, say, the landing, and probably wouldn't think about the different screen resolution being a telltale. But that's only a hypothesis. I can tell you for definite that the facts don't fit with it being Sam, but I can't tell you how whoever it was could have got the pics. Were they only on your phone?'

Ava's voice emerged as a croak. 'Dad was so insistent

that I didn't lose them that Izz backed them up to my iTunes account for me yesterday.'

'Shit,' Tod muttered.

In the following silence, Ava's brain tried to supply her with an image of Izz lurking on the landing. Ava and Sam hadn't exactly been quiet, thinking themselves alone in the house, but surely *Izz* wouldn't . . . ? Hardly able to process the horrors that this scenario suggested, Ava turned slowly to face the man on her right. The man who was gazing fixedly at his computer screen. The man who, last night, had made love to her with heat and intensity. Who had woken her with soft kisses this morning. Who had been concerned for her ever since he'd walked into her life. Her heartbeat threatened to deafen her. 'Sam, I'm so sorry. I jumped to conclusions. I should never have accused you.' The words seemed shamefully inadequate.

He didn't remove his attention from his computer. 'True. I suggest you turn off your hotspot and change all your passwords. Manda Jane, any journos trying to make contact regarding other interviews?'

'The *Sun* and the *Daily Mail*.' Manda Jane spoke in a death-like whisper.

'Good. Look into both. Let me have your recommendation. I'd rather have coverage than exclusives.'

Then Sam stood up, and walked steadily from the room.

Only the tapping of keys and the occasional rattle of a coffee cup broke the silence he left in his wake. Ava could feel condemnation and outrage zinging through the air from all directions. All the associates at Jermyn's loved Sam and Ava had insulted and humiliated him in the worst possible way.

She couldn't make her fingers function to retweet Ruby's tweets and link to the *Alive Today* article, as she was supposed to be doing. She could hardly make her lungs work to draw in air as the enormity of what had just happened filtered through her. She gathered her strength and followed Sam.

She found him in his office, walled in by a smoothly contemporary charcoal grey desk, expression bleak. Her voice trembled over the space between them. 'I'm so sorry. I jumped to the worst conclusions. I had no right.'

'Yup,' he agreed coldly. He kept his gaze on his desktop computer as it fired up.

'To accuse you in front of everybody—'

'Unbelievable.' He didn't even sound like himself.

'I'm sorry! I panicked—'

He still avoided her gaze. 'I accept your apology and, believe it or not, I can understand why you made the assumptions you did. Harvey's destroyed your faith in men and so it was natural for you to take the facts at face value and not believe in me. But I didn't see it coming and I need you to go away while I calm down. I have to withdraw Izz's remote privileges and change passwords and entry keycodes. Then I have to email her and ask her to be in my office at nine on Monday so I can find out if Tod's hypothesis is true.' He glanced meaningfully towards the door.

'But—'

'Lots to do. The client paying us is sitting right out there. I've got to get back to it as soon as I sort this out.'

Ava felt sick with remorse. *The client paying us . . .*

Ruby was paying; Ava was freeloading. She wished she hadn't charged Sam for Wendy's hat now, but no doubt even if she'd had a crystal ball and been able to foresee today's events Sam would have insisted on paying. Being in Ava's debt in any way would not suit his present mood.

Furious.

This time he actually pointed at the door. 'Please, Ava.' He waited, almost quivering with every word he was biting back.

Wretchedly, she mumbled, 'Sorry,' again and turned and left.

The email he'd sent to Izz before returning to the meeting room had been steely and polite. He could have simply told her that her services were no longer required and monies owing to her would be paid promptly upon receipt of the proper invoice but doing that without a hearing wasn't Sam's way. Even though Sam felt like roaring his wrath, he had to clamp down on his feelings for the rest of the afternoon as the campaign he'd been so pleased with proceeded to surpass all reasonable expectations.

Downloads of the card were in the hundreds of thousands, he anticipated a massive hit rate for the *Alive Today* article, journos were queuing up for Ruby to explain that she'd been feeling vulnerable after surgery when she'd first denied her boob job. Now she wanted to 'clear the air with all the lovely journalists. We had such a great relationship before.'

#RubyGlennister was trending on Twitter and being picked up by news sites.

Since he'd all but kicked Ava out of his office, her fingers had moved mechanically over the keys of her laptop but she'd been awfully and perfectly silent unless someone spoke to her directly. He was half-surprised that, however white-faced, she was sticking out the day, picking up and sharing whatever Emily or Manda Jane asked her to.

Last night had been so intense. But that was then. Before

Ava had entertained the thought, even for a minute, that he was capable of stealing those images from her phone, of being exactly the kind of man he wasn't. Then his control and professionalism had clicked briefly to 'off'.

Sam had never been so disappointed. It was a bitter taste, a sinking sensation.

To add to everything, he received a cheerful text from his mother. *Will we be seeing Ava tonight? Vanessa's cooking.*

He swore under his breath. Soon he'd be obliged to go home and be a good Christmas host. His guests were already putting up with him working for the first day of what he'd promised would be their Christmas break together in the frightening hinterland between his mum's surgery and chemo.

He tried to sound normal in his return text: *Ava has plans. Why is Van cooking? She's supposed to be on holiday and I've booked a restaurant in the Olympic district.* He'd been going to take them to Searcy's Champagne Bar first but now he wasn't feeling very celebratory.

It's very busy out there. We thought a nice meal in. Ava could bring her dad if that's who she has plans with. Love to meet him.

He ignored the question of Ava's dad. He didn't need his mum meeting Graeme and the relationship horror show that it implied. *Are you tired?*

No! I'm enjoying Christmas. Is Ava coming with us to the Leicester Square Christmas fair?

Sam stared at his phone. *Don't think so.* He'd had hopes. When he'd been driving home through early morning London he'd felt optimistic that Ava could be involved in his family plans for the last weekend before Christmas and Christmas Eve, as well as Christmas Day.

He'd hoped to give her a taste of what a good Christmas was about. Hope was a cruel bastard.

He cut his eyes her way as she went on typing like a robot. He couldn't even shut the door behind her at the end of this afternoon and make himself forget that she ever came into his life with her jaunty little hats and her rounded body. Her wounded eyes. Her secrets. Her laugh, her smile, her humour, her candour, her concern for others.

He gave an inner groan at the thought of Ava spending Christmas Day with his family.

How was he going to cope with that hideous nightmare?

OK, Ava didn't deserve what life had handed her this Christmas.

But neither did he.

The hands of the clock eventually crawled around towards six, the agreed time to break up the Glennister Festival of Social Media and Press Manipulation. Ava knew some of the associates would be in on Monday, which was Christmas Eve, and the rest would continue to log in from home. They'd explained that there was still a lot of valuable work to be done in keeping the Christmas card going tomorrow and Monday. These would be the golden days. After that they'd let the Christmas holiday hold sway and then take stock of what they'd achieved when they returned to work, most of them not until the new year.

Ava had felt queasy all afternoon as she sent out cheerful messages that didn't reflect the realities of this particularly gritty, shitty Christmas. Why could she not have talked to Sam instead of blurting out foul accusations? *What the hell was she going to say to Izz?*

But at least Ava could leave Jermyn's soon. Escape the squirmingly cool courtesy of the others, if not the consequences of her impulsive accusation. This evening, as well as somehow finding a way to confront her best friend with a horrible suspicion, she would have to do more sharing on social media and cook dinner ready for when her father arrived. Maybe they could Skype her mum. Ava felt a sudden wave of yearning to see her mother in reality rather than cyberspace. To be held and hugged, even if it meant a dose of maternal exasperation at the way Ava had messed up.

'Ava?' Sam's voice was cold and impersonal but Ava's head jerked up. He didn't remove his focus from his screen. 'Can you check the email account associated with your website, please? We're all about measurable results.'

Not really knowing what he meant, she did as he asked. To her surprise there were eight enquiries about hats. Astounded, she saw that two were from people she'd heard of – a singer with a rock band and an actress – or, at least, their 'people'.

'Wow.' Feeling unequal to formulating an explanation she turned the laptop so that he could see the screen.

With a tiny lift to his eyebrows he nodded. 'Good start. It would be great if you could keep Emily updated. I expect there to be more.'

Manda Jane chimed in. 'I've got an enquiry for you from a women's mag, Ava. They want to do a thing about whether hats are coming into fashion. Obviously, we want to suggest that they are.'

'Amongst some groups they're already big news,' Ava began automatically. 'The steampunkers have taken to hats in a massive way.'

'Fab.' Manda Jane turned back to her keyboard as if glad not to have to look at Ava for too long. 'I'll send her some copy about hats moving from exciting niche groups into the mainstream and how a hat's a must-have. I'll give her your contacts and ask her to approach you for quotes.'

Sam moved things on. 'Manda Jane, what do we have for Ruby?' He smothered a yawn.

Ava yanked her attention back to her computer. Before her mega-gaffe she would have sent him a tiny conspiratorial smile: *and we both know why you're so tired . . .*

He would have smiled back: *And I'm up for more, believe me.* But now she just felt sick with guilt.

Maybe if some of these email enquiries paid off she'd go and see her parents in the spring. Get away from London for a while. Away from men. Away from her mistakes.

The last few minutes ground by. As others were beginning to close laptops and pick up their bags, Ava began to do the same. 'Ava?' Once again, she jumped when Sam said her name. Now he was standing by the door with Patrick. 'Can you give us a moment, please?'

She felt as if every gaze in the room was upon her as she rose and followed the men back into Sam's office. She was sickeningly certain that they were going to tell her that they were going to drop her from the remainder of the campaign. She'd accepted their huge favour and then acted like an irrational bitch.

Her legs trembled as Sam reached around and closed the door behind her.

Patrick spoke almost before the latch had clicked. 'It was me,' he said.

Chapter Twenty-Eight

Stuck between Christmas and a hard place

Sam stared at Patrick. 'You?' he repeated, stupidly.

For once, Patrick's smile was absent. He began to speak in jerky sentences. 'We had a lot to drink. I couldn't leave Izz to stagger home alone.' He paused and swallowed. 'We got back to her house and I helped her upstairs.'

His eyes flickered to Ava, who was standing statue-still. 'I'm incredibly sorry,' he said. 'But we could hear you. I wasn't sure if Izz was going to get upset so I made a few jokes, saying I hoped Harvey wasn't up there with his camera phone. Then Izz told me she'd been backing up messages and images so that Ava had evidence about her ex's threats if needed. I said . . .' He closed his eyes and took a big breath. 'I was drunk. I said the pictures would be really safe on the server at the agency and maybe we ought to send them? I was laughing, it was an outrageous idea, never meant to be taken seriously. Izz started spouting off tech-talk about being able to identify where they'd come from by the IP address, then she got the giggles and said the most confusing scenario would be if the images appeared to come from Ava's phone. She told me how it would work. I asked her to show me. And . . . we did it. It seemed quite funny.'

Ava's eyes dilated fearfully. 'You mean you've *seen the images*?'

'No!' Patrick assured her hastily. 'I promise I never saw the actual images. It was just a file.'

'Then why would it seem funny?' Ava whispered.

Patrick winced. 'Because we were drunk. I could hear Sam's voice and knew who was up there with you and, in that state of inebriation, it felt as if a practical joke was justified in a stupid, juvenile getting-my-own-back way because he'd scored . . . I mean, was successful with you when I wasn't. Ava, I am most terribly sorry. Sam, you must hate me.'

'Right now?' Sam croaked. 'I hardly trust myself to speak to you. You know I could terminate my agency agreement with you over uploading these images onto the company server, don't you? Hell, I could probably get you arrested.'

Panic flitted over Patrick's face. 'I thought I could put it right. I was trying all morning to get onto the server and delete the files but the way we were working today I couldn't get the privacy I needed for long enough. I kept texting Izz but she didn't wake up until mid-afternoon, and then she couldn't get into the system.'

'Because I've revoked her remote access privileges.' If Sam had felt anger towards Ava earlier, it was nothing compared to this. He seriously thought he was in danger of getting a nosebleed.

'She texted me in a panic but it was too late – I had to tell her that Tod had already found the file.'

Desolation made Ava's eyes blank. 'Is this why you and Izz joined forces? To find a way of doing something

276

like this? Was Izz really that angry to know I was with Sam?'

Patrick dropped his head in his hands. 'No! We hardly even mentioned you. We— we just had a good night out. There were three bands on and she knew someone at Koko and we got backstage. When you can get past Izz's barriers, she's good company.'

'Fine time for you to finally work that out,' snapped Ava, bitterly.

When Ava got home, Izz was in the sitting room in the dark, crying in the kind of gulping sobs that were painful to listen to, a mountain of damp tissues on the floor around her feet.

Ava switched on a lamp and dropped down in the red chair, shattered in every sense of the word. 'There's no point crying,' she said, flatly. 'I know what happened. I know you were drunk. I know you probably didn't intend the harm you caused. Patrick has explained and taken all the blame.'

'I'm so sorry!' Izz wailed. 'I showed him how to do it.'

'I know. You were drunk. It seemed like a prank. Alcohol's got a lot to answer for in my life.'

Izz cried harder. 'Don't be . . . nice to me! Do-on't forgive me!' she sobbed. 'Patrick phoned and said you and Sam have had a massive row and are hardly speaking.'

'That's right.' Ava felt numb. 'I guess it's over before it began.'

'Oh no! I didn't mean that to happen. Honestly, Ava, I did get over my stupid crush on Sam.'

Ava shrugged. 'I think it probably was an infantile prank rather than malice, but the damage is done. In the same way that Sam feels hurt and betrayed by me I feel hurt and betrayed by you, but both of us can understand how it happened.' She dragged herself to her feet. 'My dad's coming round. Can you do me a favour and get lost? I don't want to have to make awkward explanations.' She turned towards the stairs.

Izz sobbed. 'Sam's told me to stay away from the agency until he contacts me in the new year while he decides what to do.'

'I know.' Ava kept on walking. 'He said the same to Patrick.'

As she was preparing the meal, Ava snatched moments on her laptop to play her agreed part in the campaign, picking up links to retweet and share as more websites, blogs and paper.lis picked up the story; going through the motions with none of the earlier part of the day's excitement. The links came from Emily, from Manda Jane and from Sam. The girls were coolly polite but Sam was terse and remote. She didn't blame him for only accepting her apology superficially.

She knew the passion and vulnerability that simmered beneath Sam's surface. The pride and integrity. And now she knew the rage. Ava had accused Sam without evidence and without hesitation.

When her phone rang she read *Tod* on the screen, and answered.

'Are you OK?' His voice was soaked in sympathy.

Ava had to blink back tears. 'I will be.'

'Look . . .' He let a pause draw out. 'About Christmas. I don't *have* to go to Louise's family. You and I could do Christmas together.'

Ava was incredibly touched that he was prepared to

risk incurring the wrath of Louise, just for her. 'I couldn't let you do that. But you're a lovely friend, Tod.'

When they'd ended the call the house was quiet. No music blasted from Izz's room, because Izz had packed and gone off to Hampshire, miserably contrite. Flowers had arrived from Patrick, probably costing a fortune at such a busy time of year and at such short notice. She'd taken the bouquet to a nearby community centre. The manager had accepted them gladly, saying they had a 'do' that evening where she'd raffle them off in aid of the Christmas dinner for the homeless.

Graeme turned up about half an hour late. 'I've been having a drink with a mate,' he explained, dropping a kiss on her forehead. 'Mmm, something smells good.'

'Bolognese. Very unChristmassy.' Ava hugged him hard, comforted to see him, however tardily. Glad to see anyone whose expression wasn't full of either accusation or guilt. 'Was it the mate in high-tech surveillance who can make things disappear?'

Graeme tapped the side of his nose. 'Make things disappear? Can't think what you're talking about.' He grinned, hotching himself inelegantly onto a stool, the one that was usually Izz's. 'What exciting thing was it you were up to today?'

Ava explained about the Glennister campaign and trying to drive it viral as she warmed the garlic bread and set the plates on the breakfast bar. She didn't mention accusing Sam of stealing the intimate photos from her phone.

Or his pain, which she'd recognised eventually, when her own pain and panic had subsided sufficiently. No question about how to bitterly insult Sam Jermyn: publicly accuse him of having no integrity. For added power, do it fresh on the heels of a shared sweaty night of sex.

Papering over the cracks of her despair with a smile, she presented the meal and sat down.

'You're quiet,' Graeme said, when he'd talked about Le Café Littéraire Anglais for about half an hour and Ava had cleared less than half her plate.

She manufactured a smile. 'I was just interested in what you were saying. I miss you, you know.' She blinked prickling eyes. 'I thought we might Skype Mum after dinner.'

'Good idea.' He tore off a double chunk of garlic bread. His gaze had sharpened. 'But before that, why don't you tell me what's gone wrong in your life since yesterday? I left you euphoric over defeating the dreadful Snaith and come back to find you looking as if your puppy has just died.'

Ava swallowed a sob.

Graeme's voice softened. 'Whatever it is, sweetheart, you can tell me. Hasn't the crap over Harvey convinced you of that?' He paused to clear his throat. 'I will always be on your side, you know.'

The muscles in Ava's face were seized by an involuntary spasm.

'Hey, hey,' Graeme rumbled. He scrambled off his stool and Ava found herself in her dad's arms with tears pouring down her face as she burbled and blubbed out the whole sorry story.

Graeme held her until the sobs finally subsided and his cashmere jumper was soaked at the shoulder.

Not sure if she felt better or worse, Ava reached for the kitchen roll and trumpeted her nose dolefully. 'I feel a complete worm and Sam hates me.'

Graeme's arms remained solidly around her. 'He might think he does, for now. Give him time. You hit him where it hurts but you've apologised and that's all you can do. Let him cool down.'

Ava gave a strangled laugh. 'No magic mate to sort this one out for me, Dad? To make it disappear?'

'Afraid not,' he said ruefully, stroking her hair. 'The only ones who can sort this out are you and Sam.'

Laying her cheek against her father's comforting strength, Ava closed her sore eyes to ease her aching head. 'Thanks for coming to England to help me with Harvey. You were fantastic and it must have been expensive to fly out last minute right before Christmas. I love you.'

He held her closer. 'I love you, too. Are you going to be all right if I go home tomorrow, sweetheart? I could try and change my flight to Monday.'

She pulled away a fraction to blow her nose again. 'Christmas Eve? I doubt it would be possible. Anyway, I'll be fine. I can stand on my own two feet.'

He smiled sadly. 'That's what we brought you up to do, wasn't it? It's what you said when we talked to you about us going to live in France. "I think thirty is old enough for me to stand on my own two feet." Was it true?'

A shaky laugh. 'It was a bit tougher financially than I thought it would be but things are looking much better.' *Sam helped a lot. Too much to bear thinking about right now.* 'I was even thinking today I'd be able to afford to visit you and Mum in the spring.'

'Why not come back with me for Christmas? We've got things planned. Le Café Littéraire Anglais has provided all kinds of goodies for the children's Christingle and I've been dressing up as Papa Noël . . .'

'Why now?' Ava asked, carefully.

Graeme hesitated.

Maybe it was the catastrophe her year was turning out

to be, but his answer assumed huge importance, as if in it lay the key to the part of Ava's relationship with her parents that she'd never understood. 'Why are you suddenly doing Christmas now that your only child is grown up? Why are you dressing up as Papa Noël for other children?' Ava could hear injury in her voice but couldn't seem to stop. 'When I was a kid, Christmas was just a nuisance to you. A time of extra shifts and extra pressure, "stupid commercialism" and "convenient religion" and "utter hypocrisy". You and Mum used to try and make it home for Christmas dinner between fighting crime or saving lives. You *volunteered* for it.' Fresh tears began to skate hopelessly down her cheeks. 'You made me hate Christmas, too.'

'Oh shit,' breathed Graeme. His arms tightened around Ava until she could hardly breathe. 'Sweetheart, I'm so sorry. We thought that we were getting the best of both worlds. We were ambitious and career orientated and then you came along—'

'And spoiled it all.'

'No.' He swallowed noisily. 'You were a bit of a surprise but we adored you from the moment we knew you were on the way. I was going to say that you came along and we thought we could just absorb you into our world. We had certain ideals and we held fast to them.' Remorse thickened his voice. 'We thought we could bring you up as a kind of mini-adult, to care for others and be on the side of good. We didn't really realise that sometimes children need to be children and they have a right to enjoy Christmas.'

A sigh shook him. 'I can't say you're wrong about how we used to feel about Christmas. It can be a time of commercialism and religious convenience and hypocrisy.

But what we've discovered in our new, more relaxed life, is that it's other things. It's a time for family, for love, for community. For fun for the sake of it. For giving and receiving, sharing and laughing.'

Ava swiped at her tears with the sodden piece of kitchen roll and looked outside of her own desolation long enough to see that Graeme's face was drawn in lines of grief. 'It sounds lovely,' she said, with compunction. She inhaled a long wavering breath and tried a laugh that didn't quite come off. 'I'm sorry I cried, Dad. It's really my day for upsetting people. I didn't mean to be so "poor little me". I'm glad that you're loving your new life, truly.'

Graeme didn't let her step away when she made to, but captured her hands. The tiny lines beside his eyes glistened with moisture. 'I meant it when I asked you to share this Christmas with us. It's not too late. I'll get on the internet and find flights, or a Eurostar seat. Worst-case scenario, I'll find a car to hire and we'll drive. You can learn carols in French and come with us to Midnight Mass. Mum would adore it.'

For about half a second, Ava was tempted to let her dad make everything better for her once more. He'd been so successful in making those images go away. She could let her parents give her the kind of Christmas she'd always wanted. She could be cosseted and loved.

But that wasn't the person she was. Eager hope had barely formed on Graeme's face before Ava was shaking her head. 'I'd love to next year, Dad. It sounds great, but I have plans for Christmas Day, and work to finish before then.'

It might be a giant leap of faith on her part but she was going to try and repay Sam for everything he'd done by staying in England to be available to help give Wendy her pre-chemo Christmas.

Graeme hesitated delicately. 'Are you certain that your plans will come off?'

Ava found a new piece of kitchen roll and blew her nose defiantly. 'Nobody's told me that they won't.'

If Sam did un-invite her she'd just be alone and ignore Christmas. She didn't like it, anyway.

Wendy's face was a mask of fatigue. She ate little of the meal Vanessa had prepared though it was exactly the light and tasty dinner she'd usually have chosen. Sam was glad he hadn't insisted they go out. By nine o'clock his mother was finding it hard to bear her part of the conversation and Snickers and Mars were lying at her feet, watching her anxiously.

'If you need an early night, Mum, just go ahead.' Sam watched her discard her after-dinner coffee, half-drunk.

'It seems wrong when we're your guests.'

He gave her a careful hug. She'd always been slight but now it felt as if he could snap her. 'You're my mother. You don't have to feel like a guest. Go to bed, stay up, go out, stay in, nobody minds. Make yourself at home.'

'Are we seeing Ava tomorrow? Or Christmas Eve?'

He made his voice casual. 'She's getting a lot of sales enquires so I wouldn't count on it.'

Wendy's eyes were trusting, without guile. 'What time's she coming on Christmas Day?'

'On the "to be decided" list. It's been a bit hectic.'

Yawning, Wendy untangled herself from his hug. 'Of course. It's not as if she's likely to forget the date, is it?'

'Doubt it.' It came out hoarsely and he had to manufacture a wide smile as his mother went off to her room.

Vanessa, curled up in a chair, waited until her sister was out of earshot. 'I think Wendy overdid things today. She's so excited to be here and she wanted to go to a matinee of *White Christmas* and for lunch and everything. The spirit was willing but the body was weak.'

'Yeah.' Tiredly, Sam rubbed his eyes. He felt as if he was seeing through grit.

'But I think she'll come through.' Vanessa moved over to the sofa and gave his arm a comforting pat. 'She's been so excited that she probably didn't sleep well for the last night or two. If you and I are slow to get moving tomorrow morning and claim that we need a lie in, she'll rest more.'

He nodded. 'A lie in sounds fantastic.'

'If you're going to be here in the morning? Not going to Ava's tonight?' A glint of mischief lit her eyes.

He shook his head and changed the subject. 'How about you? Would you like to go out for a drink or to catch a late show at the cinema?'

She smiled, tidying his hair in a way that only a woman who had built her life around Sam and his mother could get away with. 'You don't have to entertain your aged auntie, Sam. Get off over to Ava's house, if you want.'

'I'm not seeing her tonight,' he insisted truthfully, slamming a door shut in his mind against a wish to drive to Camden and see what could be retrieved.

'OK, but I want to go to my room and Facetime Neale, so you feel free to do your own thing.'

Wondering how old you had to get before an aunt would have to stop bossing you about, he yawned. 'I'll take the dogs out, then get an early night.'

'Get off then.' She made a shooing motion. 'I'm going to talk to my lovely Neale.'

In defiance of being shooed, Sam got himself a healthy slug of Jack Daniel's with a chunk of ice and stared into space for a while, feeling like crap and not knowing what to do about it. He sipped the cool liquid that turned to fire as it hit the back of this throat, as if it could take away the taste of Ava. One night and he missed her.

His phone vibrated with a message.

Sorry not to have the chance to say bye but was good to meet you. Have tried to persuade Ava to experience Noël en France but she says she has plans so I'm returning home tomorrow. FYI, you were right that I should ask Ava about her self-sufficiency. I discovered that she sometimes needs help, just like anyone else. And makes mistakes, as we all do. Graeme Blissham.

Ava's latest 'mistake' was too raw for Sam to do more than politely acknowledge the text. He put on his earphones and listened to Radiohead so that he didn't have to re-hear Ava's accusation in his ears. He played a mindless brightly coloured game on his phone so that he didn't have to re-see her horrified expression as she realised her mistake.

But he couldn't prevent himself uncomfortably reviewing what he'd said in the heat of the moment . . . *it was natural for you to take the facts at face value and not believe in me . . . I need you to go away while I calm down . . . Lots to do. The client paying us is sitting right out there. I've got to get back to it as soon as I sort this out.*

Words could be weapons. It was analysed on the No Blame or Shame site. His words had shown her that sorting out the agency's end of things was much more important to him than sorting out the Sam and Ava angle – which he hadn't made the slightest attempt to address. Instead, he'd retreated behind a wall of cold, self-righteous anger to hurt her as much as she'd hurt him.

When the glass of JD was gone he took the dogs out, taking comfort from their doggy grins as they wagged and sniffed in the cold night air. Getting them home and settled in their beds, he took himself off to his bedroom to watch a film. It failed to hold his attention and he took out his phone and glanced through his contacts, wondering what Patrick and Jake were doing. Until Patrick's confession, their brand of entertainment had always suited his off-duty mood, and the worst he'd have had to put up with would have been incessant talk about the ski trip he wouldn't be going on over New Year. But because of Patrick's confession – damn his drunken sense of humour – there was no question of him firing off a *What you up to?* text, then jumping up to shower and change, making it to central London within the hour. He could only lie here stewing in a welter of betrayal and anger and brooding on where he'd really thought he'd be tonight – with Ava.

Tonight could have been about celebration and triumph. An expensive meal and superior wine – a proper date, how was that for an idea? – buzzing with the success of the campaign. Even if they'd only curled up here on his sofa with a takeaway and their respective laptops as they stoked the buzz on social media, they would have been curled up together.

Not furiously apart with miles between them as well as angry words, lies, pretence and a massive question mark over what happened next because they had too many tiny threads tying them together to make a clean break. And a lot of those threads were also connected to other people.

With a huge sigh he realised he couldn't put it off any longer, and rang Ava's phone.

She picked up just as he thought she wasn't going to. Her voice sounded small and flat. 'Hey.'

'It's probably too late to ring you.'

'I'm awake.'

'Right.' He rolled down on his pillows, wondering if she was in bed. Picturing her as he'd last seen her there, her golden hair tumbling across her naked body. 'My mother's asking whether you'll be joining us on Sunday or Monday.' He sounded ridiculously formal, as if he had no interest in her answer himself.

'I'm afraid not. Sweet of her to think of me, though.' She met his neutrality with her own.

The awkwardness increased. He cursed Patrick and Izz. If not for those pictures appearing on Jermyn's server this morning he could be not just with Ava, but in bed with her. The thought tightened his groin. Instead there was a yawning gulf of anger between them that made this conversation feel like chewing ground glass.

'As you're obviously having trouble saying it,' she interrupted his thoughts, making him realise that he'd been silent for an uncomfortable length of time, 'I understand if you don't want me with your family on Christmas Day. I'll get Wendy's hat to you on Christmas Eve. You might have to pick it up, as I expect the couriers are booked. But, anyway, it can be done.'

Dismayed at the flip in his stomach her words prompted, he answered cautiously. 'To be honest, I was hoping for the opposite. You know my reasons for wanting to make this Christmas special. For Mum.' He winced at the way that rider had sounded, as if Ava didn't matter. 'She's looking forward to you being there.'

'I don't want you to be uncomfortable.'

'I can work around it.' He was fairly forced by good manners to add, 'What about you? Can you manage it?'

Her laugh was no more than a breath. 'I don't have high expectations of Christmas. I expect I can faux date one more time.'

He wrestled with himself. Half of him was still processing his anger. The other half wanted to go to her. Letting those two halves meet was probably a bad idea.

But, shit. Her father was going back to France, her best friends were spending Christmas elsewhere. What would Ava be doing with herself? 'Mum would love it if you could join us for something over the next two days,' he pressed, experimentally. *I want it too. But I can't make myself say it.*

'Two of Vanessa's Rotarian mates are coming tomorrow to buy from my samples. Now that they've seen the *Alive Today* article they want something with an Ava Bliss label before I "put my prices up".'

This was an easier subject to deal with. 'They must think they're being astute if they're prepared to make the trip this close to Christmas. Good for your bank account. If they try and buy any of those hats Ruby wore in the feature, charge them double.'

'Is that how big business works? No wonder I've been crap at it.' She didn't sound as if she cared much.

The silences punctuating their sentences were becoming painful. He didn't try again to change her mind about pre-Christmas. She rang off with an abrupt, 'Well, if that's it, bye.'

He got himself another glass of Jack Daniel's. The idea of her spending Christmas Eve by herself wouldn't quite leave him, no matter how many times he told himself that she must have friends to hang with and Camden High Street and the markets would be buzzing.

Another JD and he was falling over from fatigue, but his mind was too active for sleep. He opened his laptop and went on Twitter. Masochistically, he went onto Ava's page. She was busy retweeting tweets from Ruby, Emily and Manda Jane. They were popping up at the top of her timeline as he watched so she was online right now.

He retweeted one of her retweets.

Her tweets halted.

Feeling like a stalker, he went off her page and began experimenting with hashtags, the Twitter device designed to help people identify trends and join conversations. #RubyGlennister, #BoobyRuby and #RubyGlennister-Christmas were all part of active conversations. Searching further he discovered #AvaBliss, too. It looked as if Ruby herself was using it, chatting to her WAG and footie mates. Whether it was a wish to help Ava or to grow a buzz about the brand preparatory to resurrecting her modelling career wasn't clear. But, good.

Ava ought to get something out of this ferocious mess. A line of WAGs, cash in hand, would set her up.

Sunday 23 December
It was Sunday morning, the day before Christmas Eve, and the house seemed eerily quiet. If ever Ava had disliked a Christmas, it was this one.

Even though she was appearing in an article and a Christmas e-card with a celebrity who was trending on Twitter, and her Ava Bliss email inbox was filling up with enquiries and people were even pressing her for bank account details so that they could send deposits to secure a place in her schedule, her best friends were somewhere else and she didn't know how things would go with Izz in the future – she could hardly bear to think of that. And for the sake of his fragile mother she was going to spend Christmas Day with a man who probably didn't want to spend Christmas with her.

The two ladies from Rotary, wearing waxed jackets and

scarves with little round bells on the ends, arrived on her doorstep at ten, when Ava was barely ready to receive visitors. The taller of the two stepped forward. 'I'm Rayne and this is Vicky. Hope you don't mind us being early but we thought we'd get off into town and see the lights, after.' They stepped into the hallway without waiting to be invited.

'Of course I don't mind. Would you like coffee?' Ava went automatically into looking-after-clients mode.

'Lovely,' said Rayne, glancing around as Ava led them upstairs. 'I didn't realise that your business premises would be an ordinary house. But I expect all that will change soon, won't it? What's Ruby Glennister like? Booby Ruby! Not that I usually take much notice of what the celebs are up to.' She laughed heartily. 'The photos of you both with the hats instead of bras was funny. Eh, Vicky?'

Vicky sniggered, eyes shining.

'Ruby's lovely.' Ava showed them into the studio, wondering with neck-prickling irritation why they'd viewed the article in *Alive Today* if they didn't care what the celebs were up to. 'She's been kind to me.' Then, accidentally-on-purpose forgetting the offer of coffee, 'What sort of thing are you looking for?'

Rayne darted across the studio to where the samples waited. 'Was this the yellow hat that Ruby wore in *Alive Today*? Isn't it beautiful?' She snatched up the stylish straw and plopped it on her head like a child playing dress-up, her curls bursting out beneath the brim.

Smile glued firmly in place, Ava gently removed the hat and took charge, guiding Rayne towards the stool before the mirror. 'Shall I take your coat and scarf? Would you like to comb your hair or anything?'

Rayne giggled, looking abashed. 'Oh, of course. I'm getting carried away.'

When she'd tidied herself, Ava set the hat well back on Rayne's head. 'If you'd like your curls to frame your face—'

'But that's not how Ruby wore it.' Rayne looked childishly disappointed.

Rayne was never going to look like Ruby Glennister, but Ava repositioned the hat so that it tilted coquettishly over Rayne's eye. 'More like this?'

'Ooh, Rayne,' whispered Vicky. 'That's so you.'

Ava smiled neutrally. There were better colours than yellow for Rayne's silver hair and light skin. 'Would you like to try something else? This pale blue—'

'I want this one.' Rayne preened. 'I loved it as soon as I saw it on Ruby.'

'If it's a touch tight—'

'This one.' Rayne removed the hat and clutched it to her for emphasis.

Vicky simpered at Ava. 'I want the black and white one. I think it's ever so stylish.'

The looped cocktail hat suited Vicky marginally better than the yellow picture hat had suited Rayne. 'How does that feel?'

'It's gorgeous.' Vicky beamed at her reflection. 'Rayne, isn't it gorgeous?'

'Gorgeous,' repeated Rayne, still clutching the yellow straw.

'So you wouldn't want to try—'

'It's not as if we take much notice of what the celebs are doing but we know what we like.' Rayne beamed approvingly at Vicky.

Ava, giving up, priced the hats at double what they'd been, exactly as Sam had suggested.

Rayne and Vicky went into immediate giggles, fingers over mouths, eyes wide with delicious horror.

Ava waited, curious to see whether Sam would be proved right. Three weeks ago she would have been offering them discounts.

'Well, it *is* Christmas,' breathed Rayne, taking a break from round-eyed mock-consternation.

'It *is* Christmas,' echoed Vicky. 'And Ruby wore these actual hats. They *are* the actual hats?' she snapped acquisitively at Ava.

'The very same. I can box them up for you if you want to pay now and take them today or you could pay directly into my bank account and I'll send them to you. P&P is £30, though.'

A whispered consultation, as Ava brought out flat-packed hatboxes and flipped them into their three-dimensional forms, resulted in the decision that if Rayne and Vicky went to the nearest ATM they could pull together enough cash to take their hats that day.

'They won't be too much trouble when you go into town to see the lights?' Ava nestled the canary yellow straw in black tissue.

'We'll manage.' Rayne beamed. 'I don't know what my hubs is going to say, though.'

Ava lowered the black-and-white hat into a box lined with royal blue. 'Hopefully, he'll say you look fantastic.' No harm hoping. 'Got a special occasion coming up?'

'Not really.' Rayne looked struck. 'I could wear it on Christmas Day!'

Ava ran a mental image of Rayne wrestling the turkey into the oven with her Ruby Glennister hat tilted over one eye, and managed a genuine smile. 'Fabulous!'

'So where's the nearest ATM?' Vicky was already

halfway out of the door. Ava gave them directions and then was left in the silence of her studio, checking that each hat was secure within its tissue-paper bed before popping the hatbox lids in place. As it seemed the hats were to be dragged around London all day, she tied the lids in place with lengths of ribbon, twisting it through the cheap silver bells that had decorated her studio, glad to have an excuse to get even these meagre Christmas decorations out of her sight.

When Rayne and Vicky returned they had to exclaim 'How *pretty*!' and take photos on their phones before they finally handed over the money and marched off along School Road with their hatboxes borne proudly before them.

Heaving a sigh of relief, Ava went back to her laptop. Emily had sent her links to Sunday tabloids running sympathetic stories about Ruby 'coming out about her boob job' or 'ending the lies at last'.

Bizarrely, people she knew were sending her the animated Christmas card with their own faces featuring on the bodies of the supporting cast and messages like *Couldn't believe this! This is so cool! Wow, how did you get in THIS?* It made Ava feel odd all over again, as if Ava Bliss were someone else, not her at all.

Then she found Ruby had sent her a direct message via Twitter: *Hope yr home cos I'm on my way to yours. Rubes xxx* ☺

Half an hour later Ruby breezed in, scattering hugs and kisses along with raindrops from her coat. 'I ain't got your phone number. Pop it in there for me.' She dropped her phone into Ava's hand. 'I brought us some champagne, Ava, babes. Ain't it been brilliant?'

Bemused, Ava realised that Ruby had a cylindrical carrier

dangling from her shoulder by green and gold cord. Inside was an ice pack and a bottle of Cristal.

'Clever, ain't it?' Ruby slid the carrier off her shoulder. 'Nothing worse than warm bubbles.' Then she hesitated, her beautifully manicured hand on Ava's. 'Is it OK to invite meself? Tell me if I'm stopping you doing something.'

'Not a damned thing,' Ava replied frankly. 'But I don't have champagne flutes.'

'Got them!' Ruby shifted the ice pack to show two glasses nestling below, then picked the foil from the Cristal and popped the cork with an expert twist, pouring the foam into the flutes as Ava held them. 'Here's to us, babes. Do you think it's a good idea for me to wear your hats?'

Ava dropped down on a chair and took her first sip of chilled champagne, shivering in appreciation. 'Fantastic. But you know I can't pay your fees.'

The point was waved away with a twiddle of the manicure. 'I want you to pay me in hats. They're going to be part of my signature look. You make me a hat, I blether about Ava Bliss. No money changes hands.' She wrinkled her brow. 'Except if we decide to run ads. Then we'll have to talk.'

Ads sounded unlikely, but as Ava had an inbox full of enquiries to deal with as a direct result of her serendipitous association with Ruby, she could certainly afford to make a few hats for free.

Abruptly, Ruby changed tack, her eyes glowing with sympathy. 'Terrible foul up between you and Sam, yesterday. My heart did bleed for you, babes. I just couldn't think of nothing to say to help.'

Ava coughed as champagne bubbles collided with a

sharp intake of breath. Any residual positivity from selling Rayne and Vicky ex-Ruby hats at a stupid price evaporated.

'I know.' Ruby looked sympathetic as Ava dropped her gaze. 'Sam's lovely but he likes to be on top, don't he? Figuratively, I mean. I ain't been under him in reality.' She paused as if considering the prospect and not finding it unpleasant. 'What I mean is it would have been better if you'd had a quiet word with him rather than blurting out an accusation. And yellin'.'

Ave slid a hand over her face. 'Don't you think I know? In the shock of the moment I couldn't see any other explanation for what happened. It was incredibly stupid of me.'

'Yeah.' Ruby tapped a fingernail on her teeth. Then she brightened. 'At least you got all this lovely publicity before you pissed him off. You were dead crafty, there.'

Ava regarded her with horror. 'I wasn't! He helped me out because I – unknowingly and unintentionally – gave him the idea for your campaign.'

Ruby's eyes rounded between the sweeps of liquid liner that coated her lids. 'You pulled off getting Jermyn's working for you for nothing and don't even know how you did it? That's impressive, babes. Well agile.'

Gulping the champagne, feeling worse and worse, Ava gazed at Ruby pleadingly. 'I didn't! Sam just involved me. I wouldn't have known where to start.'

'Seriously?' Ruby did the eye thing again. 'I wish he'd "just involve" me instead of sending me a big hairy invoice.'

When Ruby had left, cheered by half a bottle of Cristal, Ava curled up miserably in the green chair, her conscience twanging like a cheap guitar.

Finally, she snatched up her laptop and sent an email to Sam, Manda Jane, Emily, Patrick, Tod, Jake and Ruby.

Subject: Campaign
Dear Everybody,

   I owe you all a million thanks for involving me so kindly in Ruby's campaign. I truly appreciate the creative genius and hard work that made it happen, and Sam's and Ruby's generosity. It will make a huge difference to Ava Bliss Millinery.

   Ava x

Then she trailed off down to Camden High Street because if she was going to Sam's for Christmas Day then she couldn't go empty handed, even if the thought of Christmas shopping made her feel like running laps of the house and wailing like a siren.

Late that evening, when the presents were wrapped, and Ava had Skyped her parents and steadily made her way through a bottle of Zinfandel that was her Christmas present to herself, she received a reply to her earlier email from Sam.

   Glad it worked for you.
   Intend to pick you up 10 a.m. on Christmas Day. Let me know if this isn't OK.

Well, it wasn't really. But it would have to be.

Christmas Eve

Ava made a bit of a slow start on Christmas Eve, owing to the Zinfandel of the evening before.

Having deliberately left completing Wendy's hat until today to keep her occupied, she played loud music so that she wouldn't realise how quiet the house was while she fanned the peacock feathers and stitched them and the gold ribbon in place.

She placed the finished article on a stand and took a couple of photos for her website gallery, boxed it, and fixed more gold ribbon on the outside.

Then, having bought some glowing scarlet jersey silk yesterday, she set about making a soft and silky hat, pleated and draped coyly to one side and studded with a spray of tiny black felt flowers. It was the sort of hair-loss hat that Wendy could wear anywhere from bed to a restaurant, warm, soft and sweet. Much like Wendy herself.

That was the last present to wrap.

There. All she had left to do was live through Christmas Day, the culmination of all the faux dating.

Then it would be over.

Chapter Twenty-Nine

The final faux date

Christmas Day

Even for someone who wasn't a big Christmas fan, waking up entirely alone on Christmas Day was strange.

Ava Skyped her parents, catching them drinking Buck's Fizz with the ex-pats and neighbours for whom they'd apparently opened the café side of Le Café Littéraire Anglais. Graeme turned the laptop around so that Ava could see the guests in their Christmas finery around a tree laden with silver and red baubles. 'Wish everybody Merry Christmas!'

'Merry Christmas!' called Ava, obligingly. Being a virtual presence felt like the cyber equivalent of being in a bubble, able to see and speak and hear but not to exchange hugs, taste the wine or breathe in the spices on the air.

A forest of glasses waved in front of beaming smiles. 'Merry Christmas! *Joyeux Noël*!'

Graham and Katherine turned the laptop back to face them and enquired anxiously about her plans for the day. 'We really want you out here next year, sweetheart.'

'Put it in your diary now!' Katherine urged.

Ava tried her best to make 'everything's fine, my Christmas is sorted' noises. She could tell by her parents' expressions that they weren't convinced, but she was glad that they didn't press her. She was so on edge that she felt she could wobble off and not know where she'd find herself.

After the conversation ended on another chorus of '*Joyeux Noël*!' Ava breakfasted with CapitalFM. Then she opened her present from Tod and Louise. Usually Tod's gifts were jokey or more about what he would have wanted than what Ava might like. But this year Ava assumed Louise had advised his present buying – an oatmeal cardigan guaranteed to appeal to the over sixties.

Izz's gift was much more 'her' – a silver cat that presented its tail for her to store her rings on.

Ava shoved the cardigan in a drawer, sat the cat on her dressing table and, after she'd showered, dried her hair and plaited a section across the top of her head. She slipped into a bright red jumper dress and was ready for when Sam arrived. Carefully, she put the presents she was going to give with Wendy's hatbox in the hall.

By the time Sam turned up Ava was feeling jittery, hoping that Wendy and Vanessa would be in the car so that Ava wouldn't be alone with Sam. Or, alone with Sam plus a horrible atmosphere.

Wendy and Vanessa were not in the car.

The atmosphere was.

Ava and Sam exchanged polite Merry Christmases and Ava watched Sam stow the hatbox in the boot then she slid into the passenger side of the car. Today was going to be a nightmare, the gulf between them dark and deep.

They travelled through the oddly empty streets for several minutes. Ava felt the need to break the silence. 'How's your mother?'

300

'Tired, but determined to enjoy Christmas. I left Aunt Van with strict instructions to restrain Mum from doing anything in the kitchen while I fetched you.'

'I hope that she enjoys the day.'

'So do I. It's all about her.'

'Of course.'

Ava watched out of the window as the buildings slid past. She didn't think that she'd been driven through London on Christmas Day before and the lack of traffic was almost eerie. Soon the garish decorations and coloured lights would be gone and the streets would turn to grey January normality.

There ought to be a colour named January Grey, she thought, maybe for top hats for winter weddings. The wedding flowers could be white and lavender; the brides-maids' dresses navy watered silk. A winter's day palette.

She tried to think about wedding hats because if half of the emails in her inbox came to anything she'd soon be flat-out working on hats and fascinators. That ought to fill her with joy. She expected it would, soon. When she'd got over Christmas. Over Sam.

She suddenly realised that they'd turned into a side road. 'Where are we?' She peered through the windscreen at a splash of green ahead.

'Highbury Fields.' Sam found a place to park and switched off the ignition.

'Why have we stopped here?' She was pretty sure they were only about half way between Camden Town and Stratford.

His expression was guarded. 'Elephants in the car. I think it would be best if we at least gave them a chance to disembark before we get to my place.'

'Yes.' She didn't pretend not to understand. 'I've been

worrying about it all morning. What if we can't pretend we like each other? Then there's no point in this whole dating and Christmas charade. We're only doing it because of Wendy.' Unshed tears made her throat ache. 'I know it could have been different.'

'But now's not the time to get into that. Not today.'

'I understand. Your mum told me about Mariah. It must make it worse that it's Christmas again.'

His face stilled. 'What about Mariah?'

Ava scrabbled in her handbag for a tissue, more to give herself something to do than because she thought she'd need it. She'd tamped down hard on the urge to cry and even his apprehensive expression when she mentioned Mariah wasn't going to unblock it if she could help it. 'Wendy said it was Christmas when you found out about her and your best friend and that you haven't dated since. Christmas must be a rubbish time for you.'

He stared for several seconds, then snorted a half-laugh, his face softening. 'Does Mum think I've been nursing a broken heart?'

Ava halted in her tissue search. 'Well . . . yes, I think so. She said that you were in love with Mariah and was gutted when she . . . when your friend . . . when you found out—'

He shook his head, still smiling, but reminiscently. 'It wasn't quite as you make it sound. I was never in love with Mariah. I was in lust with her. Most red-blooded males would be.' Rubbing his jaw ruefully, he laughed again. 'The truth is that it was never serious. She began seeing my mate, Elliot, too. I was uncomfortable with that and backed off but wasn't prepared for how I'd feel when she told me that she and Elliot were committing. I was a sore loser and said it wouldn't last, which alienated both

302

of them. Elliot said my behaviour was about me seeing Mariah as a trophy. I didn't take well to that hypothesis.' Sighing, he shifted in his seat. 'But they're still together and they've bought a house and an engagement ring, which leaves me with egg on my face and having lost a good friend for a bad reason.'

He blew out a breath. 'I hadn't realised that Mum had filled in the blanks for herself and decided I was heart-broken. But it makes sense of her anxiety to—'

'See you in a relationship with me?' she ended for him. She made her voice bright and positive. 'Well, now you can explain how things really were with Mariah, and Wendy will accept the end to the faux dating without being upset.' She pulled her coat around herself. The interior of the car was cooling down, hastened by the icy reminder that after today the faux dating would end.

'I think Mum's emotional attachment to the idea of "us" goes a little deeper than merely wanting me to be happy. She thinks a lot of you.' She felt his gaze on her for several seconds while she struggled to maintain a neutral expression. Then he leaned in close and brushed a kiss on her cheek. 'Merry Christmas, Ava. You're a good person and I appreciate you spending the day with us for Mum's sake.'

She bared her teeth in a smile, not remotely warmed by such an impersonal, you're-just-an-acquaintance kiss. 'It's not as if I was inundated with options.'

His frown fleeted back across his brows. But he just said, 'Let's go, then.'

Sam's flat had received the Christmas treatment since Ava had seen it last. She detected the hands of Wendy and Vanessa in the wreath on the door and the tree in the corner of the lounge area, hung with baubles and crowned by a little white ragdoll fairy with silver tinsel hair and suggestively puckered lips.

Wendy shoved aside a table decoration of berried holly as soon as Ava stepped into the room. 'We thought you'd got lost!' She beamed, pulling Ava into a warm hug. 'I'm sorry that your family are abroad so you can't be with them but it's so lovely for us to have you here.'

Ava's last doubts about the wisdom of joining the Jermyn Christmas were vanquished by the pleasure on Wendy's face.

While Ava reacquainted herself with Snickers and Mars, who muscled their way into the gathering with windmill tails and Labrador laughing faces, Vanessa waited patiently in the hug queue. 'If a couple loses half an hour on a comparatively short journey, Wendy, it's discreet not to mention it.'

Wendy giggled while Ava made a fuss of Snickers and Mars so that she didn't have to look at Sam at the word 'couple'. Sam hung up the coats and turned to the business of the day. 'Right, you lot, out of the kitchen, especially you, dogs. I've got stuff to do.'

'I can help,' volunteered all three women simultaneously.

Sam gave his mother a stern look. 'You? No. You're absolutely not going to help. The most you're going to do is sit down and watch. You,' he said to his aunt, 'are supposed to be on holiday.' He moved his gaze to Ava. 'I might let you help, working on the basis that you're the only one who doesn't try to boss me about.'

'Big of you.' Ava felt her tension ratchet down a notch or two. Sam teasing she could cope with. It produced a more natural result than the stilted politeness with which they had begun the day. She sniffed appreciatively. 'Something already smells good.'

'Duck cooking slowly in foil with truffles and baby onions. Potatoes go in now, then roasting veg, homemade bread sauce and stuffing, then steamed veg.' He slipped a magazine out of a drawer and waved it – 'Christmas cooking for idiots – can't go wrong'– then he frowned at the page. 'How are you with gravy? Because I bet I can go wrong with that.'

Ava grinned. 'I can manage gravy if you put a glass of wine in my hand.'

'Drinks! You can help with those as well because I need my attention for the potatoes.'

'But what about presents?' Wendy pretended to pout.

'After dinner.'

'Noooooooooo!' Wendy clutched her scalp, shining through its suede covering. 'You promised me a hat. I *need* a hat. Look at my head.'

Pain lanced across Sam's face and his smile wavered.

Wendy's laughter halted mid-peal.

Ava felt her breath catch at the raw emotion arcing between mother and son. She moved briskly around the dining island. 'I'll get those drinks. What have you got, Sam?'

'Champagne in the fridge,' Vanessa answered for him, busying herself with reaching for champagne flutes from a glass-fronted unit. Her eyes were shining suspiciously but her usual easygoing smile remained in place. 'Do we wrestle with the bottle ourselves or fail our sex miserably by asking Sam to open it?'

Ava found several misty cold bottles of Bollinger lying in the bottom of the fridge. 'My dad taught me how to open champagne. I haven't exactly had the money to drink it recently but this will be twice in a couple of days.' She began to pick at the foil covering the wire cage around the cork.

Sam looked up from studying the Christmas cooking for idiots instructions. 'Did your dad bring some with him from France?'

Ava shook her head as she flicked off the wire, grasped the cork and began to turn the bottle against her hip. 'Ruby Glennister brought "bubbles" round, to celebrate the success of her campaign.' Bottle and cork began to part company and she let them ease free instead of popping the cork across the room. When she'd poured the sparkling foam into the champagne flutes, she passed Sam a glass. 'Cheers.'

'To the campaign.' He touched his glass to hers.

'To the campaign.' A nice safe topic.

As Sam clung tenaciously to the task of cooking, Ava and Vanessa tried to keep Wendy entertained and prevent her from rolling up her sleeves and joining Sam in the kitchen. Although she protested loudly that she felt *fine*, Wendy's face was without colour. Sam tried gently to get her to sit in an armchair until the meal was ready but she clung obstinately to her perch on a bar stool.

Ava was impressed at Sam's kitchen philosophy of everything planned, nothing rushed. He basted the potatoes and, under his direction, she readied the steamer for the baby carrots, fine beans and asparagus – which, very sensibly, he'd bought ready prepared.

'I'll chop a few button mushrooms and half an onion for the gravy. Can you take over from there?' Sam reached a long arm around Ava to grab the chopping board.

'As soon as you've finished in front of the hob,' she agreed, brightly, pretending she hadn't even *noticed* how close he was to her.

In between shifting carefully around one another so as not to touch, Ava and Sam chatted and laughed with

Wendy and Vanessa, sent Snickers and Mars out of the kitchen with boring regularity, and sipped champagne.

Finally, even the port gravy was declared done and Sam and Ava carried the dishes over. Snickers and Mars took up station nearby, noses woffling at the delicious smells on the air.

Wendy raised her champagne glass. She'd only had half a glass to begin with but there was still some left. 'To Sam, for being the best son ever, and Vanessa, for being the best sister. And to lovely Ava, for sharing her Christmas with us.'

A clinking of glasses. Ava raised her champagne flute to Wendy, unable to find any words to express her hopes for the valiant little figure, and Vanessa and Sam made the same silent toast.

'Right!' beamed Wendy, using a jolly red napkin to wipe the corner of her eye. 'Let's eat this fantastic dinner. Then, don't think you're going to make me wait until we've washed up for my presents, because you're not.'

Which made everyone begin their meal with laughter but also with brimming eyes. Then Vanessa began asking about the campaign for Ruby and Ava and the atmosphere lightened.

After the succulent duck and crispy potatoes had proved such a success that everybody ate twice as much as they needed, they voted to eat dessert later, as it was a cold Christmas Bombe that Sam, knowing his limitations, had bought. Vanessa gave Snickers and Mars their own Christmas dinner topped with scraps of duck and the remains of the port gravy while Ava and Sam cleared the plates and shoved everything out of sight in the sink and the dishwasher.

Ava discovered that the Jermyn family made a little

ceremony of present giving. There was no free-for-all or even everybody having one present to open all at once. Instead, each person gave their presents out one by one so that everybody else could observe and enjoy. Also necessary was more champagne and open access to a huge box of chocolate Christmas trees. Snickers and Mars, who'd scoffed their Christmas dinner, came to gaze hopefully at the Cadbury's.

Vanessa gave her gifts first: two shirts for Sam, perfume for Ava, light-up collars for the dogs and turquoise cowboy boots for Wendy.

Wendy stroked the violently coloured tooled leather in awe. 'Vanessa, these must have cost you a month's salary.'

Vanessa smiled. 'Quite cheap in Kansas, actually. My Neale has just been there on business. He sent me photos until he found a pair I liked.'

Wendy went next, with a dress for Vanessa, rope toys for the dogs, who immediately began nudging her for a game of tug o' war, and a beautiful floaty panelled skirt for Ava. 'I got your size from Sam,' she smiled.

Ava wondered when he could have peeped in her clothes for that information.

For Sam, Wendy had bought a leather jacket, dully beautiful and smelling expensive. Sam put it on and then picked Wendy right up out of her chair and hugged her. 'It's awesome. But you shouldn't have.'

Wendy laid her face against his shoulder. 'I wanted to.'

Ava gave out her presents shyly. 'I haven't bought anything for the dogs, I'm afraid.' For Vanessa, Wellington boots with London street signs all over them, perfect for dog walking.

The red hair-loss hat for Wendy, who yelped with joy. 'It's so soft and gorgeous!' She pulled it on and Sam took photos on his phone. She looked like a pixie.

Because of the froideur of the past couple of days, Ava hadn't conferred with Sam on the subject of gifts for one another. Obviously, Wendy and Vanessa would expect her to have bought Sam an array of presents, in time-honoured girlfriend fashion, but common sense told her that the most likely post-Christmas scenario would be that they return their 'gifts' for refunds pending the faux break-up. She'd bought him a wallet of the kind that was supposed to stop your credit cards being read by scanning scammers, pocket headphones with a retractable cord, a nice bottle of red wine and the *Top Gear* quiz book.

What she hadn't expected was that when he smiled and thanked her, Wendy and Vanessa would call loudly, 'What about a thank-you kiss? Anyone would think you were strangers.'

Ava felt her eyes widen. Then Sam tilted up her chin and kissed her softly on the lips. She blushed. The embarrassment wasn't because of the kiss being public but because even such a barely-there kiss shot straight through her, ricocheted off her groin and blanked her brain. Obviously her body hadn't got the memo that Sam's kiss was faux. He hesitated, as if perceiving her reaction.

Then he began to hand out his own gifts. First, a Guess watch for Vanessa, and then dog shampoo for Snickers and Mars.

'I hope you're not suggesting my dogs smell!' protested Wendy in pretended outrage.

'Who, me?' Then, his face changing, Sam presented his mother with the hat.

Wendy stroked the hatbox. 'It's almost too nice to open.' She paused to take off the red hat, then tugged gently at the hatbox's ribbons, lifted the lid, parted the white tissue and lifted out the dashing cloche that was Sam's Christmas gift to her.

The jade glowed in the lights from the tree, the jaunty peacock feathers a geometric fan, the looped golden ribbons adding exactly the right degree of bling.

'Gorgeous,' murmured Vanessa.

Sam's lips were pressed tightly together.

Wendy glanced at Ava and made a tiny motion with the hat. Understanding, Ava took it from her hands and settled it gently on her head. The perfect angle.

Wendy's smile was beatific, though a tear detached itself slowly from her lashes.

Sam held out his hand, helped Wendy up and led her to a mirror in the small hallway.

From the lounge, Ava could hear whispers from Wendy and murmurs from Sam. She had an uninterrupted view when Wendy turned slowly from the mirror, dropped her face against her son's chest and began to sob. As Sam's head was bent his face was hidden but grief was in the line of his shoulders.

Vanessa clamped her hand to her mouth, tears raining down her face, and made a dash for her room.

Quietly – or as quietly as it was possible to move with two pantingly enthusiastic Labradors trying to guess where you intended to go and get there first – Ava took herself to the kitchen to improve upon the earlier cursory clear up, binning the duck bones, to the obvious disappointment of Snickers and Mars. The tableau of unbearable sorrow in the hall hung before her eyes as she set the dishwasher going and washed the glassware by hand, listening to shuffles and murmurs disappearing down the hallway. She even dealt with the hideous roasting tins and crusty sauce-pans without really noticing.

310

Finally, she wiped and polished dry the luxurious granite and steel surfaces.

Wondering what to do next in the silent apartment, she turned to find Sam watching her, his eyes dark with pain.

She twisted the tea towel between her hands.

'It's the not knowing that's hard,' he explained gruffly. 'We know the odds are with her but she's got a lot of treatment ahead.'

Ava nodded, not trusting her voice.

'She does actually love the hat. She just can't tell you right now.'

Ava tried to telegraph 'absolutely fine' with her smile.

Slowly, Sam approached, slid his arms around her and pulled her against him for several seconds. 'Thank you. The hat has made her Christmas.' He put her from him and headed back towards the hall without letting her see his face.

Chapter Thirty

Not on the Christmas agenda

A half hour later, Wendy declared herself ready for a Christmas walk with the dogs. She'd redone her make-up and popped on the jaunty scarlet hat, flowers bobbing. The jade green one was displayed in its splendour atop its hatbox, which Sam had lifted up onto the dining island in case the dogs saw the feathers and confused the hat with food.

Sam gazed at Wendy with misgiving. 'You're pretty pale, Mum.'

She rubbed her cheeks vigorously to bring colour into them. 'No, I'm not. Come on, we always walk our Christmas dinner down and Snickers and Mars need a run. It's a beautiful crisp day and we shouldn't waste it.'

As every day of comparative health had to be valued when human and cancer were joined in battle, he instantly gave in. 'OK. We'll go to Stratford Park because I can't get four people and two stupid dogs into the car to get us to Olympic Park.'

'Don't you listen to him, darlings,' Wendy cooed as the dogs milled about her feet. 'You're very clever.'

Sam was trying not to fuss around his mum but it was hard when she looked almost transparent and had to keep pausing to cough. He was hoping that it had just been the champagne that had made her feel so scalding hot as they'd shared a hug during her storm of tears.

But this was her Christmas. If all it took was Snickers and Mars lolloping around, their leads jingling, to set Wendy beaming as if this was the very best Christmas anybody had ever had, *ever* . . . they'd take a Christmas walk.

Ava was quiet as she slid into her patchwork coat. His conscience pinged. For someone who didn't like Christmas he'd sure as hell landed her in a strange one. Uncomplaining, she'd joined in where she was expected to join in and hovered on the sidelines when the emotions had careered out of control. Stoical. Pragmatic. Understanding.

Most of him wanted to find an opportunity to make it up to her for dragging her into his family's happy/unhappy Christmas. In fact, if he was honest with himself, it had crossed his mind to use Christmas harmony as an opportunity to thaw towards her.

But part of him wouldn't co-operate. His head was being obstinate about leaving himself vulnerable to a woman who could, even briefly, believe him capable of such hypocritical creepiness. He'd been brought up despising it so thoroughly. It was almost shocking how savagely self-preservation had kicked in.

At the park, Vanessa strode ahead, throwing a ball for the dogs to pant after. Wendy and Ava walked together with Sam following.

It was hard not to watch Ava as she strolled towards the lake along the path fringed with the dank brown leaves that were all that was left of autumn's glory. Her hair glowing in the winter sun, her head was turned towards Wendy, and Sam could see that she was smiling. He liked her smile. Her mouth.

Sam's attention switched to Wendy, who had hooked her arm through Ava's. A companionable act or a need for support? Was Wendy dragging her feet? Slowing?

Ava's smile was turning into a worried frown. As if in slow motion, Sam watched Wendy begin to sway. Ava reached out to her, lips moving on words he couldn't hear as she struggled to keep her clear of the cold ground, clasping the slight figure, staggering and slipping amongst the wet leaves.

He was only yards behind but his legs felt as if they were taking hours to respond as he ordered them to carry him to where his mother's knees were buckling, her head tipping back helplessly on her neck.

Then he snapped back to reality and in three strides had taken Wendy's weight. 'I've got her.'

Ava was white with shock but she kept her composure, not releasing Wendy until Sam had her secure. 'She seemed OK then she said she felt swimmy and suddenly she was crumpling.'

'I saw it. Well done for catching her.' Breathing hard, he adjusted his hold on Wendy, light and fragile in his arms, seeing, with a wave of relief, her eyelids fluttering.

'I'm all right,' murmured Wendy, dazedly. 'I didn't faint. I just came over peculiar.'

Vanessa came running up, the dogs gambolling joyfully beside her. Snickers had the ball in his mouth and Mars was wagging all over as he tried to snatch it. Then he paused and his ears went up. He approached Sam at an anxious trot, gazing up at Wendy. He even stood on his hind legs to see better, brown eyes questioning.

'We've got to get her home.' Sam spoke to the dog to avoid seeing his own fear reflected in Vanessa's face. He turned around and began the short march back to his flat with his precious burden. Vanessa hurried at his elbow. Dimly, he was aware of Ava taking the leads from Vanessa's hands and clipping them to the dogs' collars.

'I think we should call a doctor.' Sam studied Wendy, small and vulnerable on the sofa.

Wendy smiled wanly. 'There's no need.'

'You fainted and you were sick when we got home. It's not that long since you had an operation and you're waiting for chemo. You have a temperature.'

'I feel lots better now.' She'd slept for an hour, a clammy feverish sleep that had had Sam pacing with anxiety and on the verge of phoning for an ambulance, but the creamy pallor had disappeared when she woke up.

'We should at least phone the National Health helpline.'

Wendy was already shaking her head obstinately. 'I feel *better*. I don't want to spoil anybody's Christmas. May I have a cup of tea? And less fuss?'

Ava started towards the kitchen, but Sam stopped her. 'I'll do it.' It occupied him so that he didn't gather his mum up and beg her not to get ill when it wasn't supposed to be on the agenda. Mind whirring, he put the kettle on to boil. Should he ring the helpline despite Wendy's wishes? Another fit of coughing had seized her and he could really use someone telling him either to take action or not to worry.

Vanessa hovered over her sister. 'Maybe Sam's right and we ought to check.'

Wendy blew her nose. 'Please don't.' She was beginning to sound irritable. 'Poor old Snickers and Mars hardly got a walk at all. Why don't you take them again before it gets properly dark? Get some of the fidgets out of them. And you.' But she smiled at her sister.

As Snickers and Mars were milling annoyingly at Sam's feet, he could see the sense of Wendy's suggestion. 'That might be a good idea, Aunt Van.'

So Vanessa got the dogs' leads again and Snickers and Mars whooshed across to the front door, ears up, tails whirring.

Absently, as he slopped milk into the tea mugs, his mind still occupied by what would be the best thing to do, he heard Ava's phone chirp.

Then, 'Oh no . . .'

And then Wendy enquiring sympathetically, 'What's the matter, Ava? Bad news?'

'I hope not.' Ava sounded flat and dreary as she tucked her phone away.

Grabbing up all three mugs, Sam crossed to her. 'What's up?' He'd seen that look of trouble on her face after text messages before.

She sighed. 'Harvey.'

Chapter Thirty-One

Trust issues

Sam clattered the mugs down onto the coffee table with more than the necessary force. 'You've got to be *kidding*.'

'It wasn't a dodgy message,' she put in hastily. 'It just gave me an odd feeling.'

'May I know what he said?'

With indications of reluctance, Ava read it out. 'Merry Christmas, Ava! Ironic after your dad's unpleasant little visit that I'm now seeing you half-naked all over the internet. Congratulations on your exposure. I hope to see more of you again soon. xxx'

'Creep. I don't doubt he meant to give you an odd feeling.' Grimly, Sam watched as she tucked her phone away.

'It's not a threat but it makes me feel slightly threatened.' Ava laughed unconvincingly.

Wendy was listening with a frown, lying back on the cushions. Her eyes were bright as she followed the conversation. 'I don't know the entire history of what happened to you, Ava, but any time someone's making you feel threatened you have every right to take action. I'm not a legal expert or a counsellor but I've been involved with No Blame or Shame for long enough to know you need only concern yourself with how you're made to feel.'

Ava heaved a broken sigh. 'I honestly thought he'd been forced to go away.' Her eyes were big with tears as she looked at Wendy. Then the entire story came spilling out, what she called her 'stupidity' in letting her boyfriend take intimate pictures of her and how she'd thought Graeme had made everything come right.

Wendy coughed occasionally and sipped her tea as she listened.

Sam found himself clenching his fists, newly angry, despite knowing it all already. But he let Ava, voice wavering, unravel the story without interruption.

She wound to a close before the episode of the pictures ending up on Jermyn's server, the part Izz and Patrick had played and the part that Sam hadn't. She shot him a look, as if uncertain whether he'd approve of the omission.

Wendy nodded compassionately. 'He *could* be clumsily trying to put the tension between you in the past . . . or he might still be looking for revenge – revenge being amongst the most common reasons for harassment from an ex. My advice would be to hope for the best but prepare for the worst.'

'How?' Ava looked wary.

'There are all kinds of things you can do to protect yourself. You can block his number from your phone and unfriend and block him on Facebook and any other social media where you're connected. You can get phone software that will create "white lists" for you, so that only accepted numbers can contact you, so he can't change his number and reopen communication.'

But Ava was already shaking her head. 'At least while

we're Facebook friends I can see what he's posting about me. And if he sends more threatening texts I'll have them as evidence.'

Wendy nodded, huddling into her cardigan. 'I can see that reasoning, but you should still understand your options. One of those is that you can try to get a court order to keep him from contacting you. No Blame or Shame has a fact sheet on its website, explaining how to get financial support for the costs or how to do a DIY injunction. I'd say that resorting to such an action is a way down the road, though. Legal remedies could have a significant effect on his life, especially if papers are served on him at work.' She thought for several moments, her shaven head tilted thoughtfully. 'I think your first step is to tell him you want him to stop texting, stop tagging, stop all forms of contact.'

Sam watched as Ava absorbed this with a tiny frown of disbelief. 'It can't be that simple. Can it?'

'It can, though it isn't always,' Wendy admitted. 'But if his behaviour escalates and you have to involve the law, you have evidence that you asked him to stop and he disregarded your wishes. So long as you're interacting with him he can excuse himself that the channels of communication were open. He can legitimately say that you never objected to text conversations or communications on Facebook.' She coughed again. 'Did you ever untag yourself from the Facebook photos he posted of you?'

'No,' Ava admitted, wonderingly. 'It didn't occur to me. But it should have.'

'You can review any posts you're tagged in, and choose to hide them from your own timeline, but that doesn't exclude it from newsfeeds, so it can give a false sense of security. You might want to put him on your restricted list to stop him reading your posts, though. To him, it will just look as if you haven't posted in a while.'

'Wow,' Ava breathed. 'You really know this stuff.'

Sam didn't want to interrupt the conversation but having noticed Wendy pulling her cardigan closer he rose and padded out to the hall cupboard where junk usually ended up. With some burrowing he found a fluffy blue throw an old girlfriend had given him in the assumption that the lack of throws on his furniture must mean that he was in want of some. Back in the lounge, he dropped it casually over Wendy's legs.

With a quick smile, Wendy dragged the fluffy monstrosity further across herself. 'It's best to use direct language. "Please stop" rather than "I'd be grateful if you'd stop". Use words like "immediately". Be clear about what you're asking and if he asks why or otherwise tries to engage you in conversation, just repeat the same text. Don't be drawn into discussion.'

Looking intrigued, Ava took up her phone again. 'It's worth a go.'

While she frowned over her screen, alternately tapping and deleting, Sam smiled at Wendy. Though obviously fatigued, she smiled in return. 'Need anything?' he murmured.

'Not a single thing. Thank you for giving me a lovely Christmas.'

Sam's eyes burned that, despite everything, she still thought today 'lovely'. 'Sure about the doctor?'

'Positive. I'm just tired.'

Ava cleared her throat. 'What do you think about this? "Harvey, please stop contacting me by phone, email or any other method, immediately. Do not tag me in Facebook or other social media posts and do not post pictures of me. Do not try to see me."' She glanced up at Wendy enquiringly.

Wendy nodded. 'Sounds good.'

After some lip gnawing Ava added 'thank you', in the interests of not provoking unnecessary antagonism. With the fingers of one hand crossed, she pressed send with the thumb of the other.

'If that doesn't do the trick, you don't have to cope with it by yourself.' Wendy yawned and settled deeper into the sofa. 'There are people who won't require any convincing that you need support – including me. It's OK to acknowledge that you're being targeted and take action. You've done nothing wrong and you don't have to put up with your ex being obnoxious.' Her smile was regretful. 'It's the powerlessness, isn't it? That's what people like him play on. They like the feeling it gives them to toy with you. Whether they understand the lasting nature of the damage they do . . .' She shrugged.

Ava kicked off her shoes and curled her legs up, almost swallowed by Sam's big armchair. 'Like what?'

'The victims of harassment are frequently left with trust issues – they might find that occasionally they're too quick to treat even those closest to them with unwarranted suspicion.'

Ava looked struck. 'I suppose so.' Her eyes flickered guiltily to Sam and away.

Sam froze in his seat.

'Definitely.' Wendy yawned behind her hand. 'Trust issues affect future relationships. The new boyfriend suffers for the sins of the old boyfriend when the woman's quick to imagine him capable of unacceptable behaviour. You need the new boyfriend to be a special man.' She sent Sam a fond smile. 'A man who can empathise and make allowances, who won't be the fall guy but will be able to point out, without drama or confrontation, when you're making him one.'

Dismay ran its cold finger down his spine.

Ava's cheeks were glowing pink as she gazed at Wendy. 'Thanks for all your advice. I'm so glad you like both of your hats.'

Wendy looked surprised. 'You're welcome. About the advice, I mean. I probably shouldn't say this but I'm hoping that you've found that special man already.' This time she winked at Sam. 'The one who knows what you've been through and doesn't underestimate it.'

Ava examined her hands. 'If you like the scarlet hat, I could make another for you in another colour.'

'I love it, but I thought you were going to be very busy?' Wendy glanced between Ava and Sam with a tiny frown.

'But not too busy for that.'

Sweat broke out on Sam's forehead. The cold finger of dismay jabbed him in the heart. Ava was protecting him. Her weak changes of subject were prompted by her not wanting Wendy to know that Sam hadn't performed in the special department.

The first time she'd had a trust issue he'd flung her away from him.

What had happened to his protective instinct? His empathy? He'd talked the talk so far as understanding women in jeopardy was concerned – until it had actually affected him. Then he'd made his hurt more important than her hurt.

He'd failed to acknowledge the effect that panic was having on her actions and, although he'd appeared to be the only suspect, had expected blind trust from her without ever earning it. He hadn't thought what it must feel like to be her. Worse, he'd let everybody in the meeting room at Jermyn's see how pissed he was with her and watched her withdraw into miserable despondency. Then Sam had done what her parents had done. Left her to sort things out for herself while he attended to his own self-important life.

Suddenly, he didn't want her to tell his mother either. Wendy had brought him up to be aware that situations like Ava's were prevalent and abhorrent but, as he had with Mariah, he'd let his ego get in the way of what was right.

Ava's phone chirped again and she made a face as she picked it up. 'Harvey says: "I'm really hurt that you feel like that. Wasn't setting your dad on me at work enough? What's up with you, Ava?"' She grimaced. 'I'll send the first text again.'

In fact, she had to send it twice more before Harvey's texts paused.

And all the time, Sam didn't think he could feel any worse.

Vanessa returned with Snickers and Mars galumphing around and greeting everybody with pinned-back ears and madly wagging tails, bringing with them the scent of frost. Shucking off her coat, Vanessa looked at Wendy keenly and was obviously reassured. 'Neale's just rung and we wondered—' She gave a comical double take, her attention on the foot of the Christmas tree. 'Sam! You haven't given Ava her presents.'

Sam swung to look at the parcels still on the floor where he'd left them when Wendy had broken down.

'Oh, *Sam*,' reproached Wendy.

'Doesn't matter.' Ava's voice was light.

And Sam discovered it *was* possible to feel worse.

Chapter Thirty-Two

Christmas spirit and black roses

Ava wished that she didn't blush so easily. Now her face and neck were on fire and it was probably making her seem unconvincing when she protested that it didn't matter that Sam hadn't given her a Christmas gift. But it honestly couldn't matter less. They were faux gifts for a faux date and she expected to discreetly return them when Wendy was back in Cambridgeshire.

It was the fact that the gifts drew attention to the Sam and Ava Christmas Lie that was making her colour up.

That, and Sam looking remorseful and guilty as he gathered up several parcels, prettily wrapped, and presented them to her with an awkward kiss.

Both Wendy and Vanessa clucked about Sam's outrageous memory lapse but that didn't stop them craning to watch as Ava unwrapped the first gift, a Molton Brown hair care set. 'Lovely!' She smiled brightly. It would have been a fantastic present if it had actually been for her, she thought with a pang. She'd never had hair care that ritzy.

Next came a hangover remedy, which defused the tension by making everybody laugh, and the cutest possible phone case made of interlocked silver daisies. 'That's incredibly cool,' she marvelled, taking her phone out to try the lovely bit of bling. If it wasn't too expensive, she'd give him the money for the phone case rather than let him arrange for a refund.

'One more parcel,' Wendy pointed out.

The wrapping came off to reveal a small jeweller's box. Flipping it open, Ava couldn't restrain a 'Wow!' of admiration. Gold earrings with black jade roses nestled in white silk, crying out to her, 'Wear us! We're gorgeous and you'll look stunning.' But while her heart was falling in love with those sultry blooms her head was pointing out that earrings were the wrong present. No shop would take earrings back unless they were faulty. What was Sam thinking? Maybe he could keep them for Ms Girlfriend Future. She stifled the urge to sigh.

Of course she had to thank Sam, following his earlier lead and kissing him briefly on the lips. 'They're amazing. I love them, thank you.'

'Go on, then,' urged Wendy. 'Put them on.'

'Oh but—' Ava sent Sam a wild look. If she put them on then he couldn't even give them to Ms Girlfriend Future.

Sam just smiled easily. 'They're meant to be worn.'

So Ava had little choice but to go to the hall mirror with the tiny box in her hand, remove the plain hoops she'd been wearing, take out the black roses, shining dully in the light, and hook the earrings through her ears. They looked expensive and maybe a little gothic. She adored them.

'Show us! Show us!' cried Wendy and she and Vanessa cooed over the earrings for so long that Ava felt she'd been ungracious in her level of thanks and gave Sam a hug and said, 'Thank you, again.' For a few seconds he held the embrace. His body seemed to flow around hers in the same way the gold of her earrings held itself around the black jade to keep it secure.

A flash went off as Wendy took a phone photo. 'Christmas kisses!'

They jumped apart, and that marked the end of the Christmas business.

Wendy wanted to watch some Christmas television and Vanessa spent half an hour prettying herself then slipped off to meet Neale, a bag of presents on her arm and what Sam described as a dopey smile on her face. She winked at Sam. 'I'll be back in an hour to be with your mum so you won't have to hurry back when you take Ava home.'

'Thanks,' he said neutrally.

Ava just smiled politely. Sam had gone the traditional peace and goodwill route for Christmas Day but she didn't kid herself that they were living a Christmas fairytale. Or, if they were, it was the one where Prince Charming had quickly got over his enchantment.

In Vanessa's absence, Wendy divided her time between napping and declaring herself to have had the best Christmas ever. Ava kept catching Sam frowning over at the sofa as Wendy nodded off.

At nine o'clock, when Vanessa reappeared with Neale, Wendy waited only until Christmas greetings had been exchanged and then gave in to her yawns. 'I'm going to bed. But it's been a fantastic Christmas Day.' Wrapping herself up in the blue throw like a toga, she shuffled over to kiss Ava. 'Are we seeing you tomorrow? Boxing Day?'

'I've got work piling up,' temporised Ava, feeling slightly sick that all she ever gave this warm and genuine woman were half-truths and lies and that even those were coming to an end. She might never see Wendy again, The thought made her give Wendy an extra tight hug.

'Oh.' Wendy looked disappointed. 'Let's hope that Sam can change your mind.'

While Sam was seeing that Wendy had everything she needed, and Vanessa and Neale were staking their claim on the sofa with the TV remote, Ava gathered up her possessions. Her heart gave a peculiar skip as she realised that it wasn't only Wendy and Vanessa that Ava might not see after tonight. There would no longer be a real reason for her to see Sam. She could return his gifts via Tod. Ava picked up her coat and waited, gazing absently around the lovely apartment with its living art of the east London nightscape through the glass wall. Her mind wandered to the idea of making a hat in the same colours. Black, embroidered with shiny beads in silver and gold and the occasional red or green. Velvet would work.

'You're ready to go?' Sam was standing in the doorway, expression inscrutable.

Ava turned. There didn't seem much to say but 'Yes' as she was standing there with her things. Wendy had gone to bed. The charade was over, wasn't it? Except for this last thing – her faux boyfriend seeing his faux girlfriend safely home.

Slowly, he nodded. 'OK. I'll get my keys.'

Soon they were cruising along in the comfort of his BMW, frost sparkling on the pavements and people hurrying in hats and scarves. There were a few more cars on the road than this morning.

Sam was silent as he drove.

Ava glanced at the set lines of his profile. 'I'm sorry about the earrings.'

His frown deepened as he changed down for some traffic lights. 'Sorry?'

'I mean me putting them on. But earrings for pierced ears are usually not returnable, anyway, and it would have seemed odd if I'd insisted on leaving them in the box.'

The car idled and he glanced at her, one side of his face red from the traffic signal. 'Did you want to return them?'

'I thought you would.'

The lights turned green but he didn't drive off. 'Why would I want to do that?' His frown deepened. A car hooted from behind and he turned his attention back to the road, accelerating quickly as if to make up for having dallied.

'I sort of assumed we'd return the stuff we bought each other.' She began to stumble over her words. 'Because of the charade. Because we're not really . . . Well, I can see that it would have looked strange not to buy me s-something substantial but it doesn't seem fair . . .' She tailed off uncertainly.

'I'll return to you what you bought for me, if you wish,' he said, with icy politeness. 'But I'll be offended if you try and refuse what I gave you.'

'Oh. I'd never actually thought of it that way round . . . I suppose . . . It's just that those earrings must have carried a huge price tag—' Her voice strangled as she felt a monumental herd of the stupids lumbering into the conversation. In a second she was going to say, 'You can keep your gifts, too, then,' like some bumbling child needing to make sure that the scales of giving and receiving were balanced.

He gave a single sharp shake of his head. 'You really don't have the Christmas spirit thing, do you?'

'Probably not,' she admitted, sadly. 'But perhaps at least

I recognise it when I see it. Your family are loving and giving and want nothing more than to share the day with each other, even when they have to adapt because things aren't going well. Christmas is a time you use to express your family affection and celebrate the fact that you have each other. Have I adequately understood?' She kept her gaze fixed to the passing buildings that were lit from the inside like huge lanterns.

After several moments he spoke again. 'Sorry. I'm angry but I shouldn't have said that. It was aggressive and stupid. I understand what you were saying about the presents and I appreciate the thought behind it. You weren't being ungracious, you were trying to do the right thing.'

'No problem.' Ava so wished the journey over. The first stabs of a headache began and she closed her eyes against the strings of shimmering Christmas lights. Once home she could change into her oldest jeans, surround herself with wine and chocolate and switch on the TV. Maybe Dolce & Gabbana Christmas Man would come on.

There would be no Izz there to share him with. Which gave her heartache to go with the headache.

But not as much as the bleak realisation that all day Sam must have been acting his big heart out, maintaining a thin veneer of teasing affection between them for the benefit of Wendy and Vanessa. The black jade roses were probably meant to symbolise the death of what had been between them. He was still so furious with her that now they were alone he couldn't even be bothered to hide it.

That sucked.

That seriously sucked.

When they finally drew up in School Street the atmosphere in the car was as frosty as the trees that lined the street.

Ava had her bags ready in one hand and the door handle in the other. 'Thank you for the lift and for the gifts. Sorry that you've had to come out to bring me home. Enjoy the rest of Christmas.'

He didn't reply.

She couldn't even give him one last kiss, however chaste, unless she wanted to begin to blub like a baby. She shoved open the door and swung her feet onto the kerb, shivering as the crackling evening air swept in to cling meanly to her skin. Closing the car door, she halted as the sound was echoed. She blinked. Sam was out of the car and stalking around the back of it to join her on the pavement.

'Can I come in for a minute?'

His expression didn't tell her much. She fished for her door key. 'Do you need the loo or something?'

'Um . . . no.' He sounded bemused. Waiting for her to unlock the house, he followed her into the hall. 'I want to say something to you.'

Oh great. More remonstrations. She heaved a dramatic sigh. 'Fine.'

She sent him into the sitting room while she dawdled over hanging up her coat, dumping her bags on the stairs and reading a note from a neighbour apologising in advance for the party they were throwing on Boxing Day. Marvellous.

Finally, she followed Sam into the sitting room, unplaiting her hair in the hopes that it would ease the tension in her scalp. She decided not to offer him a drink. No point drawing out the conversation.

She found him standing in the centre of the room. He'd hung his jacket over the door and it reminded her of that first evening, when he'd followed her home in the rain in case Harvey was lurking around to cause trouble.

His eyes were very dark. 'You could have gone to France for Christmas.'

She halted, wrong footed by this opening gambit. 'What makes you think that?'

'Your dad told me he'd tried to persuade you to go with him but you'd refused.'

'Oh.' She eased off her shoes, not caring that it made her shrink several inches. 'But you said yourself that I don't understand the Christmas spirit. And Wendy . . . well, you know.' Poor Wendy. She couldn't have had the nicest of Christmases, regardless of her protestations to the contrary. She manufactured a smile.

'You turned down Christmas with your parents for the sake of my mum? That demonstrates a lot of Christmas spirit – and we've already established that it was stupid of me to say that.'

'Well . . . other reasons. Work, money, plans. You know.' Her face began to heat up. She was so not going to admit to him that in some dark and shameful place in her mind a teeny tiny hope had lingered that he would calm down. That he would realise she was sorry for her accusations and somehow everything would come right again.

'That was nice of you.'

'I can be nice, occasionally.'

'More than occasionally.' His smile was twisted. 'You've spent all today being nice to me, even though I proved not to deserve it.' His eyes were sombre. 'I wasn't the special man Mum talked about. I let you down.'

She stared at him. '*You* let *me* down?' she repeated, idiotically.

Slowly closing the distance between them, he lifted his hand and took over her abandoned mission to smooth out her hair, unravelling the plait, making her scalp tingle.

'I really did. I reacted badly. All I saw was my own hurt that you could say those things. After the night we'd spent in your bed.'

She was heating up again, but it wasn't out of embarrassment. It was the memory of his nakedness against her, the down of his body hair electrifying her nerve endings. Everything seemed to speed up, her breathing, her pulse, her heartbeat.

'It was me who reacted badly,' she croaked. A hot tear escaped the corner of her eye. 'I can't even promise that it wouldn't happen again. If Harvey hasn't really gone away I've got to learn to cope—'

He stilled her words by tracing her lower lip with the pad of his thumb. Reflexively, her tongue tip came out to taste the salt of his skin. He expelled a sharp breath. 'If Harvey tries to give you grief in the future, we'll sort him out together. Even if the Man in the Moon comes down to watch us through your skylight, his camera phone at the ready, we'll get whatever help's needed from a victim support group or the law or our families. I'll try and remember the trust issues and you'll try and trust me enough to remind me if I don't quite make it. In the end, the trust issues will go away. We'll make them disappear, together.'

Blood flushed into her brain in a dizzying rush. *Together* was suddenly her favourite word in the English language. *Closer together* would be even better. The distance between them was no longer a desert of hurt and misunderstandings but only two inches of carpet. Ava made it no inches in a split second, reaching out her arms, lifting her face. Closing her eyes as his lips came down hard and slow on hers and his arms folded her against his body.

Ava felt safe just feeling the thud of his heart echo through her.

But then need flickered into a flame and she made a slow movement of her hips.

He groaned his appreciation, shifting his hands down to cup her buttocks. 'I'm not a fan of thick tights.'

She moved against him again, feeling his hardness. 'I could take them off.'

'Allow me.' His hand slid up her thigh and under her dress.

She let her head tilt back as he began to pull the fabric from her, cursing gently as the elasticity worked against him and he had to use both hands.

He paused to nuzzle her neck. 'Is there a way of securing the external doors from the inside?'

It was a breath of negativity to jar her from the moment but Ava could appreciate his thinking. Izz had come back before and would, at some time, come back again. Ava had no real suspicion that Izz would ever again do anything to hurt them but barring the doors, with Ava and Sam on one side and the world on the other, was symbolic. 'Let's do it.' Leading him by the hand, she pulled the chains into place across first the back door and then the front, which left them nicely positioned to move on up the stairs and into her room.

Sam moving in to peel Ava's clothes from her focused her. His hands, his mouth, his skin, his voice. As he slid inside her it was as if the past few days had never happened. All that mattered was now and their bodies moving against one another, slow and smooth, hard and deep.

Together.

Sam could indeed see the moon through Ava's bedroom skylight. Ava was snuggled up to his side, her leg riding

333

high over his, her hand on his chest. She was motionless but he knew she wasn't sleeping.

He stroked the side of her face. 'I've got something to ask you.'

'Mmm?' She turned her head so that she could press a tiny kiss on his hand.

He assumed a mock solemn voice. 'Are we going to start dating properly? Before you answer, note that if you say "no" I'm going to be so pissed with you that I may have to get up and go home.'

Laughter shook through her. 'Dating properly would be fabulous.'

'Join us for Boxing Day tomorrow? I know you've got loads of work but—'

She gave a little wriggle. 'Work can wait. Your mum would probably like it.'

He stroked her hair. 'I'd definitely like it.'

'I'd like it, too.'

From somewhere in the darkness a phone began to ring.

'Damn, that's mine.' He kissed her forehead and extricated the top half of himself from her warmth so that he could hang over the side of the bed and feel around for his jeans on the floor. When he saw the name on the screen he answered quickly. 'Van? Is everything OK?'

Vanessa sounded breathless. 'I'm not sure, Sam. Wendy's throwing up.'

He swore. 'I'll come straight home.'

Ava sat up beside him, naked breasts catching the moonlight. 'What?'

'Mum.' He felt for the switch to the bedside light, fumbling through lack of familiarity. He slid out of her bed. 'I've got to go.'

'Of course.' She watched him hop into his jeans.

He zipped himself up then halted. 'Will you come, too?'

'OK.' She didn't waste time in protesting or checking that he really, really wanted her there. She just wriggled into jeans and a top.

He kissed her hard then took her hand and rushed her downstairs and out to the car.

On the drive she seemed quite comfortable that he didn't want to talk. She sat beside him, giving his thigh the occasional comforting pat and letting him get the excruciating eight miles to Stratford over with as quickly as possible.

Vanessa was visibly relieved when they burst into the flat. 'She keeps throwing up and she's got a fierce temperature.'

Sam's hand shook as he dialled 999.

Chapter Thirty-Three
The best Christmas ever!

Boxing Day (early hours)

Ava woke with a start, confused by the overhead lights and the cramp in her back. She lifted her head slowly, wincing at the stiffness.

She'd fallen asleep against Sam's shoulder. She gazed at him blearily.

He smiled and kissed her nose. 'Do you want to go home? Neale will come for Aunt Van if she rings him so I'm sure he'd take you, too.' Vanessa was curled awkwardly in a red vinyl chair on the opposite side of the wide corridor, her folded coat pillowed under her head.

Ava sat up properly, senses returning. The hospital smell, the night-time hush punctuated by occasional footsteps and trolley wheels. Wendy, somewhere behind one of those doors. 'I'll stay with you.'

Sam obviously hadn't been to sleep. His face was lined with fatigue. 'I don't know how long it'll be until we hear something. Even for you, this Christmas must be the worst.'

Slipping her hand into his she leaned in to press her

lips against his cheek, just above where stubble shaded his jaw. 'No. The best.'

'We've really got to work on your Christmases.' His eyes smiled. Then he looked at his watch and yawned behind his hand.

Ava didn't remember falling back to sleep but she was suddenly jolted awake by hissing trolley wheels, hurrying attendants holding bags of fluid over the prone passenger. 'Wendy?' She tried to shake herself awake. 'Where's Vanessa?' Vanessa was no longer sleeping in the red chair.

A reassuring arm slid around her. 'Mum's safely on a ward and they're sending someone to talk to me soon. Vanessa's gone home to bed.' Sam's voice was gravelly.

Relaxing, sorry for the person on the trolley but selfishly glad it wasn't Wendy, Ava yawned. 'I'll go and find us some coffee.'

'That would be fantastic.' His hand glided familiarly down the back of her leg as she rose stiffly to her feet. 'This isn't the way I'd have chosen for us to spend the night together.'

She winked. 'You definitely need to make it up to me.'

Heat flared in his eyes. 'That's a promise.'

It took a while for Ava to find a coffee machine that felt co-operative enough to dispense hot liquid. When she returned, Sam's seat was empty, but she could see his head and shoulders through a circular glass aperture in a door at the end of the corridor, nodding and frowning along to a conversation. She sat down to wait.

Finally, he pushed back through the door, many of his frown lines smoothed away. 'Infection,' he reported. 'Always a risk with cancer patients. But she's responding to antibiotics and her temperature's dropping already.' He sipped from the plastic cup Ava handed him and then looked down at the muddy liquid as if wondering what it was meant to be. 'They want her to see her oncologist but the thinking is that her chemo will have to be delayed by a couple of weeks. Her oncologist's great and she's going to make time to see her tomorrow.'

He lifted a hand to follow Ava's cheekbone with his thumb. 'I'm going to come back to take her home this afternoon when she's had some rest and a couple more doses of antibiotics. Her home, I mean. Then I'll go with her to her oncologist in Cambridge tomorrow and return to London when she's well enough.'

'So you can go home and sleep now?'

He nodded. 'Let's go.' They navigated the corridors and stairs until they found the big glass sliding doors at the front of the hospital. It was already light. 'Happy Boxing Day.' He yawned. 'This doesn't count as our first date, by the way.'

Ava laughed, linking her arm through his and squeezing it. 'It'll be worth waiting for.'

Epilogue

First date

Sunday 30 December
I'll pick you up at 8, OK? xx
 ☺ Very OK. Where are we going? Xx
 For a meal. xx
 Gaz's Caff? xx
 Not this time. I'm saving Gaz's up for a special anniversary. Please prepare to turn off your phone and leave at home any other device that might make you contactable by the outside world. Tonight's our first date. xxx

Sam was almost ready to set out for Camden. He'd allowed plenty of time because, on the 30th of December, London was busy enough to indicate that it was forgetting Christmas for another year. The lights were still up but lots of people had returned to work today and were no doubt already talking about New Year.

His phone vibrated with a text message. *Ava*. He clicked it open immediately, heart hopping in case something had happened to spoil his plans.

Phone me when you're outside and I'll come out.

He frowned. *Why?*

Izz's back. She's anxious about seeing you again. She and I have more or less kissed and made up but it might be awkward for you.

He paused for thought, rereading the conversation. Why couldn't Izz have stayed away for one more hour? He'd wanted his and Ava's first proper date to take place in a sort of magic bubble, separate from all the things that had haunted them for the past weeks. Harvey had remained blessedly silent since Christmas Day, although both Sam and Ava understood that that didn't mean he'd gone away forever. Wendy was in as good a place as she could be.

But now part of Ava's mind would be preoccupied by Izz-related anxieties instead of all of her mind being occupied by Sam.

See you soon xxx

He slid his phone back into his pocket.

Sam rang the doorbell fifteen minutes before he was due, willing to exasperate Ava for not skulking outside in the dark as requested.

And, bingo. The door was opened by the tall figure of Izz, surprise, dismay and discomfort chasing one another across her face when she saw who was waiting on her doorstep. Ignoring the social convention of waiting to be invited in, Sam brushed past her and into the lit hallway. 'I've come to pick Ava up, but I thought you and I had better clear the air first.'

From above, he heard the sound of running feet. A breathless Ava rounded the turn of the stairs. Her dress was twilight blue, picking up the colour of her alarmed eyes. Her hair streamed loose over her shoulders.

Slowly, he smiled. 'You look amazing.'

'You look early,' she returned. Her gaze jumped to Izz.

340

'Sorry. You can never tell what the traffic's going to do.'

Her expression suggested that she had a pithy comment or two about that, and about him coming to the door instead of waiting outside. But she glanced again at Izz and said nothing.

'It looks as if you're almost ready. Although shoes and a coat might be an idea.'

Her lips set. 'I haven't put my hair up.'

His gaze travelled over the mass of hair shining in the overhead light. 'It looks great as it is.'

Ava didn't move back up the stairs.

'I'll have a word with Izz about her contract while you get your things,' he encouraged, knowing she could hardly insist on being present during that conversation.

'Right.' Slowly, she turned and disappeared back around the turn of the staircase. Sam waited until he'd heard her move onto the flight above. Only then did he turn to Izz.

Her gaze was fixed on the hall wall. 'I'm sorry,' she mumbled. 'I was completely out of order. Are you . . .' She swallowed noisily. 'Are you cutting my contract short?'

'You were worse than out of order. What you did was gross misconduct and there are no excuses.' He let her stew for ten seconds. He even waited while one big tear oozed out of the corner of her eye. 'So I've changed your access privileges to reflect my altered faith in you.'

Her gaze flipped up to meet his. 'I'm *staying*?'

'If you want to. Mainly, if I'm honest, because it will make my life easier.'

Her shoulders sagged. 'With Ava.'

'Because you're good at the job,' he corrected. Then he added, honestly, 'And with Ava. But,' he made his voice soft, 'now that we've sorted Harvey out you're the only way that those images can get loose.'

She pulled herself up to her full height, eyes flashing. 'I was drunk when I did that stuff. I'd never hurt Ava on purpose!'

'Then you'd better hope that you don't drunkenly hurt her again. You only get this one chance.'

She swallowed audibly. 'Thank you. I appreciate you letting me see out my contract. What about Patrick?'

'When he returns from his skiing trip Patrick will be looking for another opportunity. We agree it's for the best. His position at Jermyn's is not that of a short-contract employee, like you. He's an associate and I can't half-trust him. His actions have to be above reproach.'

'I understand.' Izz nodded dolefully.

Having been the stern boss, Sam allowed his voice to soften. 'Izz, just because he's parting ways with Jermyn's doesn't mean you can't see him again. I expect his phone's switched on.'

Izz gave him an uncertain smile. 'You mean I should . . . ?'

He shrugged. 'Your call.'

'Yes. Literally.' She looked struck. Then smiled, tentatively. 'Thanks. Regarding Jermyn's, I mean. Most people wouldn't have given me another chance. I won't let you down.' She melted away towards the sitting room, repeating, 'Thanks,' over her shoulder.

Sam heard Ava's footsteps on the stairs again and waited in silence. When she arrived, her hair loose down her back, he pulled her close enough to kiss. Then opened the door and led her out into the night.

They chatted in the car: idle, catching-up talk. Tod was home but Louise had stayed with her family for another couple of days. Graeme and Katherine had declared themselves in love with Christmas, which was a bit rich, considering, and were already pestering Ava to say she'd join them in Alsace next year for at least a week. They were adamant that she'd adore the town of Muntsheim and were already making plans to take her to see the Christmas lights of Kleber Place in nearby Strasbourg. Harvey was still keeping a low profile but Ava had talked next steps through with a counsellor from No Blame or Shame ready for if he popped up again, which gave her a feeling of having at least some control over the situation.

Wendy was home and resting. Her chemo had been delayed for two weeks while she regained her strength. Sam recounted his conversation with Izz.

Ava turned to him with her eyes shining. '*Really*? Oh, Sam, I'm so glad! I was going to ask you—'

'I guessed, which is why I got it out of the way this evening. Now you don't have to spend any of our first date coaxing me to give her another chance. Deal?'

'Deal.' She beamed. Ava hadn't really been paying much attention to their route, but when Sam drove into the garage under his building she woke up to her surroundings. 'Your place?'

His grin gleamed in the low lighting. 'Do you mind? I've held a booking for a restaurant if you'd rather, but dinner's in the oven upstairs, and,' he flipped open his seatbelt and hers, then leaned across to scoop her up, his voice not much more than a whisper, 'I want to be alone with you.'

Suddenly she was breathless. 'Cancel the restaurant.'

He laughed and kissed her, taking his time, her lips, her face, moving on down to her throat.

When they eventually got up to his flat she found he'd set up a bistro table near the glass wall, flickering candle flames reflecting in the glass and silverware, delicious smells wafting from the big black oven. She threw off her coat, switched her phone to 'do not disturb', dropped it into her bag and dumped her bag on a chair. 'The world is shut out.'

'Finally.' Sam's shirt was crisp and white, he was freshly shaven, his hair falling over his forehead and curling behind his ears. She wasn't sure who moved first but suddenly she was in his arms and he was almost lifting her out of her shoes to hold her against him as if he were inside her already.

Her brain turned to fuzz as his hands curved around her buttocks and his mouth whispered over hers. She nibbled gently at his lips, making him groan.

'Dinner could wait,' he murmured.

'But you've gone to so much effort,' she teased.

'Don't mind me.' He hoisted her up onto the dining island, shoving aside a barstool so that he could place himself between her knees, his hands moving surely to her breasts.

She let her head fall back, absorbing the feel of him, tracing his shoulders through his shirt as his hands passed over the skirt of her dress and up under the hem. Licking flames of desire burned in every place he touched her.

Then he stopped, lifted her down from the surface and smoothed her clothes back into place.

She opened her eyes and looked at him enquiringly.

'No. We're going to have a date.'

'Seriously?' His hardness against her told her that it had cost him something to halt where they'd been going. But then she looked around at the beautifully laid table, catching a waft of whatever was cooking, and she under-stood that he was drawing a line. 'I suppose it would be a shame to waste all this.'

'And I have plenty of Christmas champagne left.' He

reached over and dragged a cooler near, pulled out a misty-cold bottle, popped the cork and poured, the hiss of the froth loud in the otherwise silent room.

Ava pressed the glass against her cheek. 'I need to cool down.'

He laughed. 'Just until after dinner. Come and help me with the food.'

Apart from a short interval where he became distracted by a need to discover whether he could drink champagne from the hollow of her collarbone, he kept his attention on preparing the meal until it was time to extract the coq au vin and rosemary roast potatoes from the oven.

Then they sat down together at the window looking out over the lights of the Olympic Stadium.

He lifted his glass. 'To our first date.' The gold in his eyes was bright in the candlelight.

Ava touched his glass with hers. 'Our first date.' Her heart quivered. Then, as he went to speak again, 'But, as this seems like a beginning, you should know a couple of things about me.'

Wariness stole over his face. 'Go on.'

She took her time, sipping champagne and letting the deliciously cold liquid tingle on her tongue. 'You don't have to slay dragons for me. You've been totally supportive about Harvey and really understanding about Izz, but my life isn't usually this chaotic. I'm not a damsel in distress who wants, needs or expects a knight in shining armour to fix my life. This isn't negotiable.'

His eyes crinkled. 'Dragons to be jointly face. Noted. Accepted. Respected.'

'Even when the shining knight happens to be protective by nature?'

He leaned over to touch his lips to hers. 'Especially

345

then, because the shining knight occasionally needs to remember that he's not the only capable one around here. What's the other thing I need to know?'

She leaned in to return his kiss, tasting champagne on his lips. 'I never sleep with a man on a first date.'

He laughed against her mouth, reaching out to tangle his free hand softly in her hair. 'That one I would normally completely respect. But, on this occasion . . . I'm going to negotiate hard.'

Author's Note

In case you're wondering how things worked out for Wendy, she stuck around to wear her fabulous hat – to Sam and Ava's wedding two years later – tilted neatly over her short hair, grown back quite satisfactorily after her chemo. She looked fantastic and beamed all day long.

She made certain that every guest knew (just in case anybody had somehow missed it) that her new daughter-in-law was *the* Ava Bliss who made those fantastic hats for footballers' wives and girlfriends and was in all the magazines. 'In fact,' she ended happily, 'my own hat's a creation by Ava Bliss Millinery. A Christmas present from my son.' She smiled mistily at where Ava was laughing up into Sam's face, her wedding dress streaming out behind her as they danced, her veil flowing from a tiny pillbox the delicate pink of Zinfandel rosé.

Wendy sighed happily. 'I thought that it was my best Christmas present ever. Until now, of course – a Christmas wedding! The first time I saw him with Ava I knew that he'd met The One. You can't pretend about things like that, can you?'

Alive Today lifestyle magazine fashion pages

~ inspirational, aspirational and ahead

This season's top accessory? A hat! Queen WAG Ruby Glennister's setting the trend in chic and sexy headpieces as she rocks from 'sleb party to top nightclub. Ruby's grabbed herself the title of 'the face of Ava Bliss Millinery' and she's threatening to become every bit as starry in the modelling field as her old man Tyrone Glennister is on the footie field. And, exclusively, *Alive Today* can bring you the skinny on hats and how to wear them – from Ruby's very own hatmaker!

What do fashionistas need to know about buying the perfect hat?

Should it be bespoke? (What is 'bespoke', anyway?)

Over to Ava for—

Top Tips from Ava Bliss!

A good first step to searching out the perfect hat is to understand the basics. Here's your Hats 101:

Brimless hat styles include the chic pillbox and the easy-to-wear beret. Small or medium brimmed hats come in the shape of bowlers, top hats, cloches or boaters and large brimmed hats encompass picture hats, fedoras and cartwheels.

The thing of beauty and elaborate decoration that is a cocktail hat is, as its name suggests, perfect for evening. A cocktail hat's based on a definite three-dimensional shape, which is where it differs from a fascinator, also highly decorative but fixed directly to your hair with a comb or hair band.

As well as a world of shapes, colours and sizes, hats come in a fabulous array of materials. Choose from the softness of wool felt, the light crispness of straw, the versatility of sinamay or the sexiness of satin. Ornament with feathers, net, sequins, beads, ribbon, buttons and bows.

Whether your taste's for a hat in one simple cone or bell, a definite brim and crown or a more whimsical abstract form, you'll never rue the price if you find the perfect hat.

The perfect hat

... for your face

If you have an oval face, then lucky you. The classic oval looks great with most hat shapes. Try them *all*.

Celeb oval face: Kate Middleton

A heart-shaped face looks fantastic with a small or medium brim. Avoid large brims that might exaggerate the breadth of your brow.

Celeb heart-shaped face: Reece Witherspoon

Do you have a long face? Choose a wide brim with a deep crown but avoid the small-brim-deep-crown combination of, say, a top hat. That will only emphasise length.

Celeb long face: Sarah Jessica Parker

Square jaw lines work well with rounder softer hat shapes. Or try something asymmetrical for a funky look. I recommend avoiding down-brims unless you can get the slant just right.

Celeb square jaw line: Emily Deschanel

A round face is pretty with a hat of sharp lines and straight shapes. And place that hat at a jaunty angle.

Celeb round face: Beyoncé

The perfect hat

... for the perfect you

- Be mindful of balance and proportion. Your hat brim should never be wider than your shoulders.
- If you wear glasses, be careful about down brims. They can overshadow and clutter your face.
- A little height can be elegant on a short woman but be careful not to go for oversized hats that might swamp you.
- Be sure your hairstyle will work with your hat style.

The right hat

... for your occasion

- You may need to transport your hat to, say, a wedding venue. Does the appropriate size of hatbox fit into your travel plans? If not, is it feasible to parcel it up and send it ahead?
- Perhaps you want the option of not wearing your hat for part of the event. Where will you stow it? Will you be left with 'hat hair'?
- Be mindful of season and time of day when making your choice. A buttery yellow straw with a sinamay bow will look sensational at a day at the races in spring; your sequinned black cocktail vamp number will wow at a nightclub.
- You'll feel fantastic when you're wearing your hat but be considerate – don't ruin someone else's event by blocking their view.
- Outdoor venue? Secure the hat in case of a breeze or you'll be seen clamping it to your head in every photo.

The perfect hat – what's next?

You've carried home your flattering fedora or perfect pillbox. It's worth getting to know yourself in your hat, especially if you're new to the hat-wearing craze. You might want to:

- Try different hair styles with your hat
- Place the hat at a variety of angles while a friend takes your picture so you can view yourself at a

remove. Do you look as good as you did in the mirror? How about in profile? And from the back?

- When you're happy, try on the outfit you intend to wear with the hat and check out the combination.
- Wear your hat around the house for an hour (not while you're cleaning out the grate!). Make sure the fit's comfortable rather than precarious.
- Have you planned your make-up? Don't fall victim to a last minute clash between orange lipstick and a purple hat.

Can the perfect hat be ready to wear?
Or does it have to be bespoke?

A lot depends upon your budget. 'Bespoke' means 'made to order' and any handmade item catering to your precise requirement is normally going to cost more than something mass-produced.

To help you make up your mind, let me run through a few of the benefits of a bespoke hat:

- A woman's mass-produced hat is made to fit the average female head circumference of 22.5" (56.5cm). But not everybody has an average head. A tight hat is a headache; a loose hat can slide over your eyes.
- Your bespoke hat will be unique.
- You won't have to search for a hat to complement your outfit. It will be made that way.
- Colour matches can be precise and decorative elements dyed exactly.

- You can choose the materials that feel best against your scalp.
- Old items can be repurposed – your grandmother's vintage veil bleached and incorporated into a wedding headpiece that's just your style gives what Gran wore on her wedding day a touching role in yours.

A hat made specifically for your head in the colours and materials you choose can be a luxury but it will also be a treasure.

But whether bought in a department store, from a market stall or from the swankiest couture milliner, what's important is that you wear your hat with style and pleasure! And have a great time.

Hats off to Ava Bliss!

Media for Ava Bliss Millinery and Ruby Glennister handled by Jermyn Associates

Q&A with Sue Moorcroft

What's your writing routine? Are you a plotter/planner or do you see where the story and characters take you? Lucy Catten

'Routine' sometimes goes out of the window, I visit my editor to discuss plans for a book, go to publishing parties and writing conferences, teach a fiction course abroad or whizz off on a research trip. Otherwise, I reach my trusty iMac at about 07.20, dealing with email over my first cuppa and Twitter and Facebook along with my porridge. Then I begin on writing, planning, editing or promo. I'm a plotter, but a messy one. I call mine 'the compost heap method' because I pile together a morass of information on character biographies, dynamics between characters, research, answers to questions about conflicts, goals and quests, what keeps characters together and what keeps them apart. I plan by hand but write on my computer, keeping my mind open to new and better ideas. I usually take a break for a piano lesson, Zumba, FitStep or yoga and finish work around 6.00pm. I email or go on social media in the evening too, from the comfort of my armchair. I love being my own boss and the necessary discipline comes easily.

What led you towards the story you tell in The Christmas Promise? And why write about revenge porn? *Mark West*

I meant to write a novella. I began thinking the story might deserve a bigger stage and my agent was enthusiastic, liking the idea of giving Sam and Ava serious issues to deal with during a period mainly associated with joy and sparkly things.

Ava needed a conflict, bigger than being skint and not liking Christmas; a contemporary issue that I felt strongly about, something that could pose a serious threat to Ava's happiness and what might develop with Sam. I turned to the kind of responsibly handled human-interest features that make me think about the real lives of real people. There were several about revenge porn. I became furious on behalf of the victims and wanted to shine a light on the subject. During the writing of *The Christmas Promise* the authorities went this way and that on whether our existing laws were sufficiently far reaching and so I had to keep updating my storyline. I was quite relieved when, in early 2015, a specific law was introduced to make it an offence to share sexually explicit images without the subject's consent.

Did you write as a child? And if so, what did you write? *Ann Cooper*

Because of slightly interrupted education I was late grasping the mechanics of literacy but once I 'got it' I escaped to the world of fiction. Not knowing any better, I pretty much copied *The Famous Five* books because I wanted to be in them. I used to send my characters off on adventures but had no real understanding of over-arcing storyline and so my tale always petered out. At that point I turned to drawing the cover for the book instead.

What was the best Christmas present you ever received? *Joanne Baird*

As a child I was given a candy pink space hopper. We were living in Malta and I used to boing about our army barracks. Because it could be deflated, it was easy to take with us when Dad was posted back to the UK.

What was your inspiration for the Christmas theme in this book and are you all Christmassed out now? *Louise Styles*

Christmas stories are perennially popular and it seemed time I wrote one. I wasn't sure I could spend all year being Christmassy, so I made Ava dislike it. Then a magazine asked me for a three-part Christmas serial – and, yes, I did feel Christmassed out for a bit.

What is the one Christmas tradition or food that's a 'must' have? *Manda Jane Ward*

On Christmas day a roast dinner with everything the family likes even if it doesn't really go together, such as lamb with bread sauce.

Do you have a favourite place to go and think and find inspiration and ideas? *Louise Spence*

I like my study, where everything's to hand and I can have peace and quiet. It would be lovely to say I had a leafy bower where music played and inspiration was always waiting for me but, sadly, it's not true.

What do you read to inspire you, to inform you and to relax? *Carmen Walton*

I read mainly the genre I write in – stories that grab me by the heart and carry me off to a happy ending. I like the occasional biography, too, and love the Formula One news websites (I'm an avid fan).

Your top five tips for aspiring writers? *Leanne Francis*

- Take classes, courses and workshops, read writing manuals, magazines and newsletters. Learn about publishing and marketing as well as writing.
- Create vivid characters with conflicts, goals and quests.
- Persist. Giving up is not a good way to achieve your aim.
- Be professional towards industry members, readers and other writers.
- Don't make enemies.

What do readers have to look forward to next, be that another book or adventure? *Louise Styles*

My next book is due out with Avon Books UK in summer

357

2017. Its working title is *Just for the Holidays* and it's about Leah, who's determinedly single and child free, spending the summer in France looking after her sister's husband and children. But it's just for the holidays. And the 'flingette' she embarks upon with Ronan, the grounded helicopter pilot next door? That's just for the holidays, too. Except that too many people have Leah by the heart for her to simply reclaim her old life when the time comes.

These questions were kindly (and enthusiastically) posed by members of Sue's street Team, **Team Sue Moorcroft**. *You can learn more about Team Sue Moorcroft at www. suemoorcroft.com/street-team. If you like the idea of being part of the Team, spreading the word about Sue's work and chatting to her on Team Sue Moorcroft's private Facebook group click the 'Street Team' button and sign up! #TeamSueMoorcroft*

If you'd prefer simply to get news of Sue, go to www. suemoorcroft.com to click the 'Newsletter' button and sign up for her free newsletter instead.